Cry of Silence

a novel

by Catherine Gigante-Brown

Cover and interior design by Vinnie Corbo
Author photo by Anne Coleman

Volossal
Publishing

Published by Volossal Publishing
www.volossal.com

Copyright © 2023
ISBN 979-8-9886107-8-6

Publisher's Note

Cry of Silence is a work of fiction. Names of characters, places, and incidents are products of the author's imagination or are used fictitiously. Any resemblance to actual events, locales, or persons, living or dead, is entirely coincidental.

For Paul Siederman

"I am Alpha and Omega, the first and the last: and, what thou seest, write in a book…"

Revelations 1:11

Table of Contents

Dedication 5
Epigraph 7
Prologue 11
One - In the Beginning 17
Two - The Big Hole 25
Three - Emergency 31
Four - The Road 43
Five - Second Start 55
Six - Food for Thought 65
Seven - Take Me to the River 75
Eight - Onward and Upward 83
Nine - Nik and Jenn 89
Ten - Nik and Jenn and God 93
Epilogue 101
Midlogue 105
Eleven - Starry Nights 111
Twelve - Starry Days 125
Thirteen - Sunset 133
Fourteen - Cliffhanger 139
Fifteen - If I Were a Carpenter 145
Sixteen - New Beginning 153
Seventeen - Swing Low 163
Eighteen - Almost There 171
Nineteen - On the Morro 183
Twenty - Prince of Irony 189
Twenty-One - Duckling 201
Twenty-Two - Dick of Life 213
Twenty-Three - Dinner and a Show 219
Twenty-Four - Photographs and Memories 231
Twenty-Five - Yeorpi Skies and Sea Lions 237
Twenty-Six - New Dawn 247
Twenty-Seven - Tough Choice 259
Twenty-Eight - Slim Pickings 269
Twenty-Nine - Walk across the Water 279
Thirty - Take Off 285
Fine 297
Acknowledgements 301
About the Author 303

Prologue

The moons of Alpha 49C shone brightly through the hatch. All seven of them were in slightly different phases. Jenn thought this was perhaps the most beautiful thing she had ever seen. The past few months had brought so much ugliness, so much pain, so much that she wanted to forget. Yet, here Jenn was, trying to remember. And halfheartedly at that. There was nothing else she really had to do. Nothing but this: to remember.

Jenn rolled the slip of FleuroPaper out of the antiquated machine. The sheet was light, almost weightless in her hands. Her broken skin had long healed. Her fingernails were strong, unblemished and clipped to a short, manageable length. No chewed cuticles. No sign of stress or worry. Yet still, a heaviness took residence in Jenn's chest. The heaviness of recollection.

On the desk beside her, several other pages were scattered. She brushed them into a small stack and flipped to the first one. Then Jenn read what she had written. She immediately hated it.

Noah thought I should write this down. All of it. He said my story needed to be told. I'm not sure if it will do much good in the Aftermath but I am writing it anyway. Just to please him, if nothing else. To earn my keep, so to speak. After all, he is my savior, my...Noah. Thanks to him, I have lived to see the dove return with the olive branch in her mouth. On Earth, that used to be a sign of peace. A sign that the suffering was over. But here on Alpha 49C, who knows? It's too soon to tell. The wounds are still as raw as newly-skinned knees.

You will soon discover that I am not a real writer. At the very least, I am a fake one. But I did write a poem once, in the eleventh grade. It was called "Before the Gold Rush." It was a response, of sorts, to Neil Young's "After the Gold Rush." (Do you know who Neil Young is? Was? In what seems like a hundred and forty-three years ago, my poem represented New Utrecht High School in a citywide contest. Do you even know what cities were?)

Well, in the hope that you do, the city I lived in was called New York City. In it, was in a borough called Brooklyn. And that's where I was born. New York was very big as metropolises go. When I was coming up, there were more than ten million people squished into it. Most of them ill-tempered.

New York was a very famous city. Many songs were written about it and sung about it, mostly by Italian Americans, for some reason. (Italy was a country about five thousand miles away from the United States, the country where New York City had been located. On Planet Earth, where I'm from, countries were similar to PlotDivs here.) People like Frank Sinatra, Liza Minelli and Tony Bennett sang these New York City songs that basically said New York was the best city in the world. Maybe it was.

I'm an Italian-American too. Or at least I was. I'm not sure what I am now. But anyhow…

After I won the high school poetry competition, there were small articles written about me in small hometown newspapers with names like The Spectator *and* The Courier. *But those papers are gone now, just like the big city is gone. In* The Spectator, *there was even a fuzzy photograph with Principal Gearhart's hairy arm wrapped around my shoulder. At the time, I was embarrassed, although I should have been proud. Everything embarrassed me when I was seventeen. I wasted so much time feeling embarrassed when I was a teenager. Even as an adult. But no more.*

As it turned out, my family was very proud of the article, even though they misspelled my father's name in both newspapers. They spelled "Francis" with an "e," making my dad a woman with the careless stroke of a key. But never mind, my parents were still proud. Even though "Before the Gold Rush" was about greed and oblivion.

Even though the poem ended up coming in thirty-seventh out of forty poems in the citywide contest.

But the judges gave me a five-dollar prize, nonetheless. (Dollars were what we bought things with on Earth, mostly things we didn't need.) So, that technically made me a professional writer. Although I never wrote anything of worth since. Until now. Maybe. I suppose you will be the judge of that. Of this tome's worth, if any. I only ask that you don't judge me too harshly. I don't think I could bear it. Not with all I've been through.

I'm afraid that my writing is as unpolished as my Grandma Rachel's old silver. Slightly tarnished. But please try to understand that there is a shine somewhere underneath. There is always a shine underneath everything, Noah says. Sometimes you can't see it but you can feel it if you try hard enough. So bear with me. I'm doing the best I can. And that's the most any of us can do. That's what Noah tells me, at least.

Ω

I will try not to dwell on the worst of it. On the running sores, the perfect ponytails coming out in clumps, on the stark agony or the gut-churning screams. But some of this cannot be avoided, so I apologize in advance. Ugliness is necessary to properly paint the picture. Bottomless blacks, bland grays and sad purples are as vital to the portrait as smiling pinks and sunny yellows. You see, unpleasantness is as much a part of the story as I am. As hope is. Or Nik. Or Philip. Or the squirrels. Or Carpinteria.

I promise to be truthful and to tell things just as I remember them. Sometimes, I will have no choice but to upset you. For this, I am sorry. I still can't decide whether it's a gift or a curse: remembering everything. Having total recall. I remember every tear. Every sour breath. Every snaggle-toothed smile. From the tiniest details to the largest. Like how many pillows were on Linda's bed. To bigger things. Like the hull of the Queen Mary. Or the clams on Pismo Beach.

I remember it all; I just don't want to write it down. To write it down is concrete. Undeniable. To write it down makes it real, gives it substance.

I'm sorry if my memory fails me in certain places or if I mangle the names of highways, motels and truck stops. But I guess it doesn't really matter because those places no longer exist. And who would really know if I made a mistake? Right?

Again, my apologies for upsetting you before I actually do. But whether you're someone who's survived the Aftermath like me or whether you watched it from a VeloScreen in Clocania, you know that in life, there is always sadness woven into happiness. It's there somewhere, even in the joy. If you know where to look.

At any rate, I pray you will decide to suffer through this with me. And suffer you might, from a literary standpoint. Noah refuses to change a single word of my pitiful scribble. Or to read it before it is set into LaserType and shot into cyberspace. He doesn't want to disturb its "stark authenticity," he said.

"This is your story," Noah told me. "No one saw it the way you did. No one lived it but you. Who has the right to alter even a comma? Or unsplit an infinitive?" It was a rhetorical question, I guess, but a good one.

Ω

The only parts of this reflection that aren't mine are the interpretations of well-known Alpharian artists who have become my friends. BK. Margaret. Claudio. Jo-Ann. My flimsy words don't do their intaglio pencil markings justice. My paltry paragraphs don't hold a candle to their three-dimensional brushstrokes.

Through some miracle, these artists have recreated the scenes and emotions I described with eerie exactness. Even though they have never seen or experienced what I have. But perhaps they've felt these things through my earnest but inadequate words. Yes, I think maybe they have.

I am told that accompanying the electronic version of this book will be holograms. So that when people read it in the virtual sphere, they will also see the images somewhere in the back of their minds. Somehow. Noah explained how but I didn't quite grasp it. I just kept nodding and pretending. But I don't think I fooled Noah, though. No one can fool Noah.

In the HoloBook, there will also be pop-up definitions for terms unfamiliar to Alpharians. Place names like Costa Mesa, concepts like vacations and items like water wings and nose clips will be explained and, if necessary, illustrated.

Of course, there will be no holograms or pop-ups in the print version of this book, however, there will be drawings. But no one reads book-books anymore, do they? Only oldsters. So, there will be a small number of FleuroBooks published for the Dearmars and Pop-Pops. For those who like the weight of a hardcopy in their hands, for those who crave the scent and texture of a tome. Although books aren't made of real paper here. Because there are no trees on Planet Alpha 49C. Never were, I'm told.

Noah has great plans for my humble memoir. He intends to beam it to all fourteen planets in this vast galaxy as well as the three adjoining ones. (They each have unpronounceable names, so I won't even try to spell them here.) Noah is in the process of finalizing intergalactic media coverage and promises to get me onto all the pre-eclipse talk shows. And so on. Not for the money, you understand. Or for the AlphaBucks, as Alpharians call them. But to save what is left of the universe. Imagine that.

In the short while I've been here, four planets, two satellites and one space station have been blown into memories. And that worries me. Noah, too. His ectoplasm is working at warp speed to devise other ways to get this book "out there."

"Out where?" I asked him.

"Everywhere," he said. "Even places you can't even fathom."

Ω

Perhaps you are reading this in a new age. In a peaceful age after many effinities have passed. In a different place than I am now. But then again, maybe this is too much to ask for: that green bits have sprouted on Earth again and that life there has started anew on some tiny fragment that was left of it. Perhaps even flowers like peonies have begun to grow, which were my favorite. Maybe that capsule we launched on Mursday actually reached some survivors before Earth self-destructed. But honestly, I don't think anyone could have survived for this long. I wasn't exactly thriving when I was found. Far from it. I don't think anyone could still be there. Alive.

Who exactly am I talking to? Who is my audience? A mutant in Big Sur? Or a Cygnian, a Vegalian? A chartreuse-skinned, suction-cupped, six-fingered hermaphrodite from Outer Andromeda? Maybe you are an Alpharian who wishes to learn something about a place that no longer exists, about a race of people you have studied extensively but still don't understand. (Believe me, I don't understand humans either. Or cats.)

But at the very least, I know you want to learn how not *to destroy your own planet. Why else would you be reading this? Why else would you be subjecting yourself to these horrors?*

So, I ask myself, do you care where I came from? Does it matter? Noah says that everything matters if it teaches someone something, anything. Then it matters a lot.

In any case, I hope you are not disappointed—but I have no answers for you. No solutions. Only my story. The answer isn't in me; it's in each of you.

There's a line in a song that the band Aviation once sang. It went, "The key is me…" And it is.

Instead of crumpling the pages in her hand, Jenn shuffled them back into a neat pile and set them face down on the desk. She cranked another sheet of FleuroPaper into the outmoded, putty-colored machine and continued her story.

One

In the Beginning

It was the first vacation Jennifer and Nikolai Taverna had taken in five years. Soon after they landed at Sky Harbor International Airport in Phoenix, they noticed the frightened headlines. The hysterical, red Times New Roman font silently screamed out from several newsstands. It seemed that the United States was on the verge of war. A nuclear war. Again.

Nik and Jenn had heard it so many times before that they ignored the Henny Penny "the sky is falling" headlines as they made their way to Baggage Claim. At first.

There had been threats of annihilation during the Albanian Missile Crisis when they were just toddlers. There had been fears of a Third World War hatching during the Ghana Hostage Crisis when there were teenagers. There had been dirty-bomb threats after the USS Warner incident when they were newly married. Nik and Jenn had heard apocalyptic portends so often that they were growing tired of hearing them. But still, what if this time, it was true?

"What if this is it?" Jenn echoed to Nik as he pulled her beat-up, blue rolling Samsonite from the thumping baggage carousel.

"It's never *it*," Nik insisted. "People aren't that stupid."

"They're not?" she gasped. Nik shook his head, convinced, confident. But Jenn wasn't so sure. "People are idiots," she tacked on in afterthought. He agreed; they were. But he didn't think they were *that* idiotic.

To Nik, this was the war that cried wolf. To Jenn, it was a death knell. A sense of dread stalked her as she and her husband made their way to Car Rentals, dragging their suitcases behind them.

As they zig-zagged through the corridors toward the Avis counter, Jenn recalled the sketchy details of the oxymoronic World "Peace" Summit that staggered forward amid Switzerland's jagged but placid peaks. Since Day One, the press had made unfounded claims about punches that had almost been thrown and arms agreements that had been torn to shreds and flung into the tense air. "Do you think we should still go away?" Jenn had asked Nik as they finished packing back home on Day Two of the violent "Peace" Summit.

"Of course," Nik had said. "Our tickets are nonrefundable."

"But what if..." Jenn countered. She lived a life governed by "what ifs;" Nik was more an "if not now, when?" sort of fellow.

At a Sky Harbor kiosk, he attempted to overlook the fiery headlines that mocked them at yet another newsstand and bought Jenn a box of Raisinets. Nik held firm to the belief that sugar could mend anything, even impending doom. Chocolate-covered fruit had a magical way of making everything better, for his wife, anyway. *We're on vacation,* Nik tried to convince himself. *We're supposed to have fun. We're not supposed to think about war.*

Instead of war, around the next corner, Nik and Jenn found Avis. It was still "Number Two" among car rental companies, meaning it still tried harder, like a second-best friend. Jenn and Nik liked the very idea of Avis. They admired its sense of honesty and its nonapologetic way of admitting that the company was second-rate but didn't give a damn. They appreciated Avis's sense of longing, its striving attitude. Besides, Avis had a special that week: no drop-off charge. Jenn and Nik could drive from Arizona to the coast of California without penalty. Or so they thought.

Ω

Along the flat, dusty road to the Grand Canyon, the couple encountered many things that were starkly different than what they saw in Brooklyn. For example, the tall, cloudless sky that seemed to yawn into forever and cactus like big, twisted, arthritic, old men. Jenn told

Nik that the lazy, rolling tumbleweeds reminded her of a "Twilight Zone" episode.

"I think it was 'The Outer Limits,'" he corrected in that gentle way he had. Nik possessed the knack of telling someone they were wrong without making them feel dumb. This was one of the many things Jenn loved about him. "I think it was called 'Cry of Silence,' wasn't it?" Nik added.

"You're right," Jenn admitted. She Googled it. Sure enough, "Cry of Silence" was Episode 6 of Season 2. In that "Outer Limits" segment, a husband and wife became stranded on a road not unlike the road Nik and Jenn traveled. The tumbleweeds ended up engulfing the couple, who were named Karen and Andy. At some point, an alien being without a body made an appearance. "I can't remember how it ended," Jenn told him.

"Me neither," Nik said. "But I remember that it scared the tuna salad out of me when I was a kid. I could never sleep after I saw the reruns on WPIX."

"Same here," Jenn shivered. "But I couldn't *not* watch it either."

Ω

Besides tumbleweeds and sky, also on the gray strip of Interstate 17 was a scattering of Native Americans. They sat very still under umbrellas in the unforgiving sun, selling their crafts. Some didn't even have tables, they just spread their wares on blankets in the parched dirt along the highway.

Nik insisted on stopping. Jenn didn't want to; she hated acting like a tourist even when she was one. But they stopped anyway. "Just for a minute," Nik promised.

Jenn immediately pitied the ancient, terracotta-skinned woman sitting cross-legged on the ground. Hand on the Cavalier's door handle, she told Nik how she felt. "That woman doesn't need your pity," Nik told Jenn. "Pick out something nice. It will help feed her family."

It was true. By selling pretty things she made with her parchment-paper fingers, the old woman managed to make a living. Probably a meagre one. "Okay," Jenn agreed. She and Nik climbed out of the car.

The heat hit them like a concrete wall the minute they stepped out of the air-conditioned Chevy. Nik and Jenn treaded past a pink

El Dorado with New Mexico vanity plates that read, "YEE-HAW." They went to the other end of the old woman's domain, as far away from the Yee-Haw couple as they could get.

The Native American lady nodded a wordless welcome to Jenn and Nik as they stood at the edge of her intricately-tattooed red, white and black blanket. She'd probably woven it herself, Jenn guessed. "Is it me or does that look like a swastika?" she whispered to Nik.

"It's you," he told her.

The indigenous woman continued patiently beading as the cowboy-hatted Yee-Haw Man drawled at her. He had the irritating sort of high-pitched voice that suggested undescended testicles. The old lady's hands were the same color as the red-brown baked earth beneath their feet, Jenn noticed. Although the craftswoman's fingers were long and graceful, they were no stranger to hard work. They didn't look soft and cuddly, but instead, seemed purposeful. The woman's bare toes fiddled with the dust as her elegant, nimble fingers guided tiny beads onto a length of fishing line.

In contrast, the white woman's fingers were short, stubby and manicured, tipped with fuchsia daggers. They were weighed down with diamonds, gold and turquoise. "Look," Yee-Haw Lady huffed impatiently. "For the last time, I'll take twenty of these little thangs." For emphasis, she dangled a necklace with a pair of miniature suede moccasins worked into it. The white woman swung it back and forth like a pendulum, as if trying to hypnotize the brown lady into agreement. "Ten of these and ten with those little Injun kids on them."

Jenn winced at the word "Injun" and felt Nik stiffen beside her. The white woman's husband corrected her. "Honey, I think they're called papooses."

"Whatever," the pale lady snorted. "Just pay the gal."

Yee-Haw Man snapped a crisp bill out of a gleaming money clip that was thick with cash. He put the Franklin on the old woman's blanket and secured it under a terracotta ash tray so the money wouldn't blow away in the arid breeze. For a brief moment, Jenn pictured someone in the earthen woman's family fashioning and firing that ash tray in a kiln behind their falling-down shack on a nearby reservation.

Money in place before her, the old woman still did not take it. She continued to bead, slowly and steadily, without looking up. "The price is ten dollars each," she told the cowboy couple. "So that comes to two-hundred dollars."

The other woman teetered in her impractical heels. They carved indentations into the earth like miniature post-holers. "The squaw down the road sells them for five bucks a piece," Yee-Haw Lady snapped.

"Then I suggest you go to the squaw down the road," the old woman suggested flatly without a shimmer of emotion or annoyance in her voice.

"We're taking twenty pieces. Two-zero," the white witch said, a bit more strident now. Her voice had elevated several octaves in a handful of breaths.

"I can't afford a volume discount," the Native woman told her. She lifted her eyes slightly to glance at the cowboy's shiny snakeskin boots. Then she looked back at her work. "Besides, Laughing Dawn makes hers on a machine. I make my necklaces by hand." The old woman's hands, Jenn noticed, were ashy and cracked in places but still graceful.

El Dorado Lady was unmoved. She stood her ground, her thin heels engraving even deeper into the dust. The Native American elder continued explaining in an even tone. "Each one takes me an hour to make, sometimes more. I am old. My fingers don't work as quickly as they used to." She flashed a small smile and met Jenn's gaze, not daring to look at the other white woman.

Jenn looked down, embarrassed at this whole exchange. Embarrassed at being white, mostly. She brushed her hand against Nik's. He curled his pinkie around hers. To Nik, this was even better than an "Outer Limits" episode. This was real life. Neither Nik nor Jenn were exactly sure how it would turn out but they both knew that it would not end well.

Cadillac Woman waved her purple fingertips in the air. "We're out in the middle of nowhere, miles away from civilization," she pointed out. "What's to stop us from taking all of your damn fool necklaces and driving off without paying you a red cent?"

Then, from the corner of her excessively-lacquered eyelids, she noticed Jenn and Nik at the other end of the blanket, looking at the bowls and vases. Undaunted, the white demon continued her rant like a human steamroller. "Huh? What's to stop me?"

Nik caught El Dorado Lady's eye. "Me," he told her.

"And me," Jenn added.

Suddenly, the woman snatched up the hundred-dollar bill her husband had left. The ash tray that held it captive rolled into the dust but did not break. "They're all the same! Greedy, ingrateful bastards..." Yee-Haw Woman spat.

Jenn wasn't sure if the aging cowgirl was talking about Native people in general or her and Nik. But it didn't matter because it wasn't true.

Pink Caddy Lady stumbled through the desert on her treacherously-high spiked heels. The cowboy trailed her like a well-trained puppy. When she twisted her ankle just before she reached the car's pink door, all three spectators smirked slightly.

Nik brushed off the ashtray and put it back on the blanket. The old woman dipped her head in thanks.

Jenn wanted to tell the Native woman that she and Nik were from New York and that they weren't raised to feel the way cowboys did about Indians. But she couldn't find words that wouldn't sound trite and foolish in the broiling, dry, quiet air. So, instead, Jenn told the woman, "You do beautiful work."

The elder nodded, a faint smile on her lips.

Now that the Cadillac couple were gone, Jenn stepped closer to where the necklaces and bracelets were carefully laid out. She didn't want a leather papoose hanging from a beaded chain. Or the head of a smiling Indian maiden strung through a leather strap. Jenn left that kind of kitsch to those with fuchsia dagger fingernails to wear from their flabby necks like badges of dishonor.

To the right, Jenn noticed a handful of necklaces that were simpler than the others. They were fashioned from glass beads that alternated with shriveled brown seeds. "What are these?" Jenn asked.

"My people call them ghost berry beads," the old woman said.

"Your people?"

"The Navajo," she explained. "They're dried juniper berries."

"They're nice," Jenn told her.

"I think so too," the woman agreed. She held out her right wrist and her left ankle. Both were ringed with rows and rows of ghost berry beads. "Some think they're too plain," she said. "They're not shiny. They don't sparkle."

"Some things don't need to sparkle," Jenn told her.

The woman bobbed her head. "Some things sparkle on their own. From within." This embarrassed Jenn because she though the woman might be referring to her.

"We'll take this one," Nik said, gesturing to a necklace lined with ghost berries and explosive blues. He knew turquoise was Jenn's favorite shade of blue, though his tongue often stumbled across the word "turquoise." "How much?" he asked the Native elder.

"For you, one dollar," she said, and broke into a wide grin. She wouldn't give the Cadillac couple that price but these two were different. These two appreciated her work. And each other, she guessed.

The three of them laughed together. The sound was empty and small in the wide desert. Louder than the cry of silence, but still, a quiet sound.

Jenn bowed her head as the woman slipped the necklace over it. The lady noticed the softness of Jenn's hair, so like the lambswool she sometimes wove into her blankets. "Ghost berry beads bring peace, harmony and safety," she explained to Jenn. "This necklace will protect you."

"From what?" Jenn wondered.

"From everything," the elder said. Briefly, the newspaper headlines flashed through Jenn's mind but she blinked away those thoughts.

Nik slipped twenty dollars into the woman's hand. When she saw how much it was, she protested, but he gently closed her fist around the money. Squeezed it. Light brown skin against red-brown.

The woman patted Jenn's cheek and said something in her native tongue. *"Nizhónígo ch'aanidíínaał,"* she sang in Navajo.

"What does that mean?" Jenn asked.

"It means, 'have a pleasant journey,'" the old woman told her.

"Thank you," Jenn said before she and Nik turned to head back to the air-conditioned comfort of their rented Chevy.

Two

The Big Hole

Nik and Jenn stood gape-mouthed at the lip of the Grand Canyon's South Rim. It was more vast than either of them had imagined and the photographs they'd seen didn't do it justice. Pallid strips of blue and red and ivory and yellow ribboned the rock walls in layers. The chasm seemed to go on forever.

The couple leaned into each other's bodies and looked in silence, trawling for adequate words to describe how seeing this place made them feel. Diminutive. Insignificant. Like maybe there was a God.

Someone approached the canyon's edge beside them, peered into the limitlessness and twanged, "Now, that's a mighty big hole," then walked away.

"I guess it is," Nik said.

"But it's also an indescribably beautiful hole," Jenn pointed out. They stood hand in hand, watching how the face of the ravine's walls changed as daylight shifted. Sometimes the shelves were splashed with Jackson Pollock smears of color. Others, the tone was fuzzy, soft and muted.

The Colorado River was a dribble of muddy blue that meandered along the canyon floor. It seemed impossible that this very same body of water had been responsible for carving out the gorge over the span of five or six million years. But it had, it did. Yet Nik and Jenn still couldn't comprehend it. To them this phenomenon was equally as confounding as how Airbuses managed to fly or how babies managed to materialize from goo and an egg smaller than a sesame seed.

$$\Omega$$

At the gift shop, Nik pulled out his US National Parks Passport and stamped it with the date. It was as if this gesture made his visit to the Grand Canyon official. Jenn laughed. "What?" Nik asked, incredulous. He thought it was perfectly normal to collect inkpad impressions of national parks and national historic sites; Jenn begged to differ.

She gestured toward her husband's well-worn, pocket-sized, blue-covered, gold-embossed US National Parks Passport. "Your nerd book," she called it.

He visibly bristled. "There's a reason they're national parks," Nik said. "You've got to admit, it's brought us to some very cool places."

"And some not-so-cool places," she countered.

"Name one."

"Wind Cave," Jenn snapped back, without missing a beat.

At the time of their visit, there were four hundred and twenty-three National Parks in all and the pair had barely made a dent. Nik's "nerd book" took them to far-flung destinations in forgotten corners of South Dakota as well as here, to the Grand Canyon, which was usually in the top ten of the most-visited national parks each year. On this trip, Nik and Jenn also hoped to visit Organ Pipe Cactus National Monument near Ajo, Arizona. Or at least Nik did.

Despite his wife's snarky comment about her husband's National Parks book, Nik bought her a pair of agate earrings at the gift shop. The gray and white striped rocks felt firm and cool against her neck until they grew warm from her skin. Like the way Nik's flesh grew warm against hers when he slipped into the cool sheets at night.

Nik also bought himself a National Parks stickers set which included the Grand Canyon and another pack that had Organ Pipe Cactus in it. "I'd say we're even," Jenn told him, touching her earrings and gesturing to his pack of stickers. "Thank you," she added. "They're very pretty."

Near the gift shop's exit, Jenn and Nik passed a busload of Methodists. They knew they were Methodists because the creaky blue school bus in the parking lot said "Mount Calvary United Methodist

Church" in chipped black letters. The Methodists wore nametags cut from green construction paper that were shaped like fish, as though they were grown-up Sunday schoolers or kindergarteners. Mary. Jeannie. Ever lovin' Adelaide. Sweet Adeline.

"All of the women have the names of old songs," Nik noted.

"And nerd books," Jenn said. "They all have nerd books they need to get stamped." This wasn't true, of course. But several of them did clutch ornate sterling silver and turquoise "squash" necklaces against their freckled, wrinkled chests. The clerk fawned over them, telling each how wonderful they looked. This wasn't true either. "It's like putting diamonds on a pig," Nik whispered to Jenn, closing his National Passport with a thump. This part was true.

As they had been doing since they touched down at Sky Harbor International, Jenn and Nik tried to ignore the newspaper headlines in the gift shop newsstand. But somehow, the dailies pushed themselves into the couple's faces. "War imminent!" the *Arizona Republic* silently cried from the pile of periodicals near the cash register. When Jenn gestured to it, Nik reminded her. "War is always imminent, isn't it?"

Ω

The Canyon Café was crowded. It brimmed with various American and foreign accents jockeying for position. The sounds mingled peacefully at first then blurred into a confused jumble, not one voice among them discernable, not one making sense. It reminded Jenn of what happened when you mixed ten vibrant colors together on a palette—the result was a lovely, dull shade of mud.

The noise and the crush of the café made Jenn want to flee for the quiet of Parking Lot # 4. "We have PB&J back in the Chevy," Jenn reminded Nik.

"I don't feel like eating in the car," he told her. After much deliberation, overpriced egg salad sandwiches wrapped in cardboard and cellophane seemed to be the least offensive cafeteria option.

"I owe you one," Nik told Jenn after he took a bite and peeled the gummy white bread from the roof of his mouth.

They had managed to find two empty seats at a table with a man who, remarkably, wasn't with the Methodists. Jenn and Nik learned that Marvin was from Missouri and that he liked jazz. Straightaway, they started discussing Billie Holiday, her distinctive phrasing and unique singing style.

When Nik asked Marvin to pass the salt, Jenn noticed that their tablemate quickly felt for the six tiny holes in the dispenser's shaker top (as opposed to the three in the pepper's lid). This is when she realized that Marvin was blind.

Placing the white plastic shaker firmly in Nik's hand, Marvin said, "Billie always said that she tried to sing the way a horn sounded."

"And that she did," Nik smiled, though Marvin couldn't see it. Jenn figured Marvin could hear Nik's smile in the warmth of his voice. Her husband's smile could light a dark, lonely room, she often thought.

Marvin, as it turned out, had a doctorate in American Music History and taught at Lindenwood University back in Saint Charles. Over the summer, he was compiling material for a seminar on Lady Day and Gloria Lynne. "The one who sang about the folks who live on the hill'?" Jenn asked.

"The very same," Marvin told her, raising his eyebrows slightly. "I'm impressed," he admitted. "Most people don't know who Gloria Lynne is."

"I'm not most people," Jenn told him, laughing.

"Indeed, you aren't," Marvin conceded. "Gloria lived in Harlem most of her life. She was a New Yorker, like you two."

"What else do you know about her?" Nik asked.

"Well, Gloria Lynne was among the hundreds of artists whose work was destroyed in the Universal fire," Marvin told them, his eyes filling with tears.

"That's a shame," Jenn said.

"It was."

The cafeteria was beginning to empty. Perhaps Marvin sensed this change, the growing vacancy, the growing silence in the room. He felt the face of his wristwatch. "I'm afraid I have to go," Marvin said suddenly. "I have to meet my wife outside the gift shop at one."

The three parted, warmly shaking hands and exchanging telephone numbers but they would probably never call each other. Strangers who exchanged phone numbers rarely did.

Zunilda, Marvin's wife and driver, was taking pictures of the Grand Canyon, he explained. Zunilda was deaf, he said. Although Zunilda had tried to describe the brilliance of the canyon to Marvin, he'd grown frustrated because he'd forgotten what colors looked like. So, instead of feeling upset, he decided to let her revel in what he could not enjoy and go for a mediocre cup of coffee in the café. Which had sparked his fortuitous meeting with Jenn and Nick, for which he was glad.

Marvin departed with a small, ceremonious bow, leaving the couple to contemplate how a blind man and a deaf woman communicated.

"Ain't love grand?" Nik said to Jenn.

She agreed that it was. "Most of the time."

"There's a lid for every pot," Nik said. It was an old Southern adage he'd learned from Thorold, one of his coworkers. It meant that there was someone for everyone in this unhinged world. This was a thought that always gave Nik a flicker of hope.

Ω

In the parking lot's blistering sunshine, the temperature was at least one hundred and eight degrees. It batted Nik and Jenn like a sledgehammer wrapped in velvet. But the park ranger, who perspired at an astounding rate through her uniform, making it a dusky shade of green, swore that it got even hotter in August.

"Thank you, global warming," Jenn quipped.

"But it's a dry heat," the park ranger countered, sweat visibly trickling down the inside of her thighs, darkening the seams as though she'd pissed herself.

Out of earshot, Nik told Jenn, "I'm going to slug the next person who says that. About the dry heat."

"Promise?" she asked. He did.

Near the restrooms, they ran into a man who had a diaper-wearing chimpanzee on a chain. Nik and Jenn laughed at the absurdity. "I mean, why would you bring a monkey to a National Park?" Nik wondered.

"Maybe the monkey has one of those nerd books too," Jenn told him.

They walked on.

The sky was bright blue and cloudless. The gray agate chips thrummed against Jenn's face in an uneven rhythm with each step. *This is a good day,* she thought to herself. *This is the sort of day you remember on your death bed. A Top Ten day in decades of days.*

In the car, Nik smiled at Jenn for no apparent reason except that he was happy. She smiled back because she was happy too. He was thinking the same thing about the day's easy perfection. *God is good,* Jenn thought to herself behind the wheel of the airconditioned Cavalier. She wasn't a religious person but a profoundly spiritual one. *Yes, God is very good,* she told herself again and flicked on the turning signal. To Jenn, "God" was the essence responsible for all of this, the good and the bad.

Mirroring her thoughts, Nik quoted Lou Gehrig in *The Pride of the Yankees.* Or at least Gary Cooper. "Today...I consider myself... the luckiest man...on the face of the earth...the earth...the earth." Complete with pregnant pauses and echoes. Jenn immediately got the reference. She got all of Nik's references. Which is why the couple made sense to each other, why their quirky sort of love worked: they were beautiful misfits who somehow found each other in this great mess of a universe. Kind of like a blind man and a deaf woman. The same but different.

Both a bit dazed from the long car ride, the short hike and from the heat, dry or otherwise, Nik and Jenn agreed that it was worth going hundreds of miles out of the way to see something they would remember for the rest of their lives. Which would soon be very different but neither of them knew that yet.

Three

Emergency

Jenn and Nik didn't pass the Native American woman on the road again because they only drove as far south as Flagstaff. There was no sign of the pink "Yee-Haw" Cadillac either.

Predictable comfort awaited them beneath Howard Johnson's vivid orange roof. Nik and Jenn's room was on the third floor of a five-story complex. It was appointed with the usual second sink outside the bathroom—a nice touch so one person could poop while the other prepped. There was also the expected ultraviolet light in the bathroom to dry bathing suits quicker. HoJo's was the picture of certainty, coziness and affordability.

As Jenn did in every HoJo's she visited since childhood, she jumped from double bed to double bed like a hyperactive pony. But Nik wasn't inclined to join her as her brother Brian had always done. Instead, Jenn's husband just popped a Coors and watched her frolic, a slight grin skimming his lips. "Long day," he sighed.

"But a good one," she added.

"With you they're all good ones," Nik said, "even when they're bad."

"Thanks…I think," Jenn told him.

To save time and water in the perennially-parched Southwest, they took a shower together. Jenn soaped Nik into a thick, happy tree branch. They made love quickly and urgently, the water pulsing against their slick skin. Accomplishing standing-up-sex was always quite a feat because the couple was almost the same height. Jenn had to stand on her tippy-toes, which usually brought on a leg cramp. So, they were fast, passionate and efficient before charley horse attacked, each stroke deliberate and purposeful.

Despite the swiftness of their encounter, Jenn was plagued with guilt about having an aquatic meetup in drought-plagued Arizona. What first seemed like a good idea now seemed selfish. What if the entire population did this? Simultaneously? The result could be disastrous and drain Lake Powell in an instant. It could undam the Hoover Dam. It could…

Reading her hive mind, Nik nibbled on Jenn's ear and whispered, "Stop worrying about the water supply and just enjoy it." They'd had this water conservation conversation many times before—the waste, the greediness—yet still, Jenn was drawn to the allure of shower sex.

"Shush," she said, reaching between her thighs to coax them both to the finish line. Jenn watched their future babies slip down the drain as they scrubbed each other clean, trading a bar of palm-sized Sweet♥Heart hotel soap back and forth between them.

Ω

Friday happened to be Fried Clam Day at Howard Johnson's. Just their luck, this particular Friday fell in the middle of Blueberry Month (July). Nik and Jenn thought themselves extremely fortunate as they enjoyed a post-coital pig-out, gorging themselves on tender, deep-fried-to-a-delicate-golden-brown bivalve mollusks then ordered blueberry ice cream slathered with blueberry sauce for dessert. It was a cheap slice of heaven.

As Jenn and Nik strolled back to the adjoining motel after supper, a family played joyfully in HoJo's swimming pool. The girl wore water wings and the boy, a nose clip. The mother was decked out in a bathing cap topped with fake blonde hair. The father's big belly drooped over the top of his Speedos. The water was obviously ice-cube cold because the kids' lips were tinged with purple. Mom's pencil-eraser nipples poked out through her tankini top. Dad's jewels were shrunken walnuts. Nik and Jenn tried not to stare but they were drawn to the chilly nips and nuts like rubberneckers to a roadside accident.

As the couple approached, all four family members said, "Howdy" in unison. The Easterners replied, "Howdy" back because, after all, they were in "Howdy" country.

Climbing the outdoor stairs to their room, Nik laughed. "I've never said 'Howdy' in my entire life."

"Me neither," Jenn admitted. "But it felt good."

Ω

Safely sealed inside Room 313, Nik and Jenn carefully spread AAA maps of Arizona, Nevada and California across one of the full-sized mattresses. On the striped HoJo bedspread, each state bordered the other, just like they did in real life. Nik traced his finger along the blue and red veins of highways, revisiting their proposed journey over the next three weeks. Organ Pike Cactus National Monument was too far away, they decided. "Next time," Jenn promised Nik.

The following day, they planned to begin their trek by trailing along 40 West to Kingman, then take 93 North to a short stretch of Interstate 95 which led to Las Vegas. Maybe they would even stop to see Hoover Dam. "Before global warming dries it up," Nik tagged on.

After Vegas, a crooked line of highways ran like a crack in a pane of glass from Nevada to California.

Leaving no stone unturned, the Tavernas also preordered a AAA TripTik Planner for the voyage. A TripTik Planner was a personalized, wire-bound, flip-topped booklet which broke their voyage into small, digestible chunks. Each page zoomed in on about a hundred miles of their pilgrimage, the details blown up and easy to read.

"Look," Jenn gasped. Following Nik's finger, she noticed an unsettling amount of nuclear power plants, military bases and naval weapons centers both in the desert and dotting the California coast.

"Nothing of concern," he told her.

"You sure about that?" Jenn worried.

He nodded. "Look at this," Nik pointed out, circling his finger along the map's unfolded folds. "Look at all this useless beauty. Try to focus on that."

Jenn did.

Before the potential radioactive minefield and possible recipe for disaster, Nik showed Jenn that their voyage would take them to a series of scenic natural wonders. After Red Rock Canyon in Nevada, they would wind through the Mojave Desert and Joshua Tree, yet another national preserve and national park, respectively. "More nerd-book stamps," Jenn sighed, then smiled.

Entrenched in Flagstaff's HoJo, the pair indeed fancied themselves free spirits. There were no hotel reservations besides this one and they had no deadline—besides getting to San Francisco for their flight back to JFK three weeks hence. The plan was to stay in mom-and-pops along the way. But plans, like anything else, were made to be changed.

The idea was to stop wherever and whenever they liked in that lovely, almost-empty land: roadside markets, cozy diners, fruit stands, local attractions. Maybe they would even take a detour to see Meteor Crater in Winslow, Arizona. If they so desired, they might even stand on a corner, waiting for a girl (my Lord) in a flatbed Ford, slowing down to take a look at them. Just like in the Eagles song, they would take it easy.

Then Nik and Jenn would wind their way to San Diego. After a few days of basking on Mission Bay Beach and exploring the Cabrillo National Monument (for which there was also a nerd stamp), they would slowly plod up the California coast, stopping in Van Nuys to see their friends Jimmy and Alice, and eventually ending up in Berkeley, outside of San Francisco. There, they would spend a few days with their buddies Howie and Jeremy, and maybe even pop in on Ken and Susan in Sausalito before flying home. Three weeks was a good amount to spend traveling, Nik and Jenn initially thought. But time would prove to be relative and fleetingly fluid as well.

It was a lot of driving, that was true, but the California coast was stunning and therefore, drive-worthy. Jenn and Nik had saved up their measly vacation days and had amassed a small pile of cash for their current travels. With unlimited mileage from Avis and the aforementioned no drop-off charge, they were free and breezy, at least for twenty-one days.

After they folded away the brochures and maps, Jenn turned down the covers on the bed closest to the TV. Then she slipped a quarter into the Magic Fingers contraption that turned the mattress into a huge vibrator. Nik headed to the vending machines in the garishly-carpeted corridor to stock up for tomorrow's drive. He loved the way the snacks jumped down from their shelves like little kamikazes. Jenn fingered her ghost berry bead necklace and channel surfed while Nik was on his errand.

Under the stiff, white bedsheets, they ate Cheez-Its, drank Orange Crush and watched *On the Beach* on HBO. Almost halfway through, the movie was interrupted by a special bulletin. At first, Jenn and Nik thought it was a joke, like an on-air gag Svengoolie might pull. Especially since *On the Beach* was about the aftermath of World War III. But this wasn't a joke or a vintage movie starring Ava Gardner and Gregory Peck. This was real.

Ω

The Emergency Broadcast System's warning bleeped so long that it hurt their ears. Jenn covered hers with her hands. At Subaru, Nik was used to loud noises, since he worked with whirring impact wrenches and air compressors all day in the shop, so he toughed it out. Loud noises, he knew, eventually ended. Soon enough, the sound sifted into silence.

The TV screen rainbowed into a series of vertical stripes. The fuchsia was not unlike the shade of Pink Caddy Woman's fingernails, Jenn noted. Then a newscaster flashed onto the screen. Neither Jenn nor Nik recognized her because Leigh James was a local news celebrity, a household name in Flagstaff but not in Flatbush. Leigh sported a puffy, canary-yellow bouffant favored by ex-rodeo queens. Her makeup was streaked and her runny mascara looked hastily repaired. But Ms. James wasn't recovering from a bender; it was obvious she'd been crying, and crying hard.

Leigh's hands shook as she tried to tame the papers on her desk into a manageable stack. One sheet escaped and wafted lazily into the air and out of camera range. There was the melody of soft weeping in the background. Leigh began speaking in a tightly-wound drawl. "Due to a culmination of unprecedented events, the World Peace Summit in Geneva, Switzerland came to an abrupt halt today," her voice faltered. "Angered at suspected US involvement in the bloodshed at the Palestinian border last week, an unidentified Chechens warship opened fire on the USS Declaration in the Persian Gulf, killing twelve."

Leigh took a breath and continued, "In an effort to receive more aid, Contra rebels have been killing American hostages at the rate of one per hour since sundown, Iranian time. Tension continues to mount between France and the United Kingdom over the most recent Channel deaths. The People's Revolution still rages throughout Japan. The number of casualties was still unknown at press time."

Again, Leigh stopped. She shook her head, swiped her nose with the back of her hand and sighed. "Because of these instances and several others, emotions ran high at the Geneva Summit. One thing led to another." She paused, inhaled, exhaled, then held her breath.

A large tear leaked down Leigh's powdered cheek and plunked onto the desk. Another came. Then another. She didn't wipe them away. Her nose started to drip. She didn't dab it. Instead, she ahemed and went on, snot and tears and Great Lash mascara bleeding down her once-pretty, now mottled, face. "An atomic missile was fired from an undisclosed location. Its origin is unknown but weapons experts suspect it came from…"

Leigh sucked in more air and screwed up her mouth, trying not to weep. "Well, it doesn't really matter where it came from, does it, y'all? At approximately 11 pm Eastern Standard Time, that missile reached its target. I'm sorry to report, ladies and gentlemen, that New York City is virtually destroyed."

Leigh James looked directly into the camera, her expression blank, her cheeks smeared. "My brother lives…lived in New York," she said, her voice cracking. Leigh valiantly tried to seal up the fissure in her veneer, but to no avail. She rallied to snap back into character but there was no rally left in her.

As Miss Rodeo America in Prescott, Leigh had once fallen from her mount but got up and continued parading the ring on foot, bloody, dirty, her sash torn, but still waving and smiling widely. However, Leigh couldn't drill up a reassuring smile on this occasion. "Communication has been lost with all states on the Eastern Seaboard," she sighed. "But the loss is assumed to be catastrophic."

Leigh took a practiced, yogic breath, then laughed at the absurdity of it all. "But wait, there's more," she said. "The United States retaliated, striking both Grozny and an unknown target in the Middle East. A government spokesman for the billion-dollar Hades Missile Program said they were aiming for Tehran but couldn't be exactly sure where contact was made. Possibly Yemen or Greenland. 'We're keeping our fingers crossed,' a Hades spokesman said.

Ms. James shook her head. "Really, ya'll? A billion-dollar program and you 'can't be sure' and are 'keeping your fingers crossed.' Gosh-darn! Damn it to hell!" Once more, Leigh snapped back into her reporter persona. "Additional missiles were launched to return US fire. It is impossible to predict how many projectiles will be exchanged but US officials have reason to believe that an unidentified location in the Midwest or the Southwest will be the next target. Your guess is as good as mine, folks."

Leigh paused to light a cigarette. "Fudge it!" she yelled. Leigh had been fiddling with a red pack of Winstons on her lap and out of camera range and decided to just go for it. Her nerves were frazzled electrical wires and besides, what did she have to lose? Her job? The world was ending! "I just don't give a hoot anymore," Leigh said in her own defense. "Write all the dang letters you want. Cheese and rice!" A woman of principles, Leigh might smoke on the air but she refused to blaspheme the good Lord's name. Even on the eve of destruction.

When Leigh took a deep drag on the Winston, her eyes rolled back in her head in pleasure. She blew out a long stream of smoke then continued, "The government is warning citizens not to panic but there are already reports of looting and general mayhem in several states," she said, flicking ashes onto the desk. Leigh picked a shred of tobacco from her tongue. "Until roughly an hour ago, the President was unreachable for comment. But at approximately 6 pm Geneva time, the President and the First Lady were found unresponsive in their suite at the Four Seasons. At 7 pm, they were pronounced dead. Both suicide and foul play is suspected. There was a note, written Guerlain Rouge G Satin lipstick, which read, 'My fellow Americans, all hope is lost…'"

Nik and Jenn sat silent, in shock, Crazy Glued to the TV screen throughout Leigh's entire broadcast. It was Nik who finally spoke. "Is this a joke," he asked.

"I don't think so," Jenn told him.

As if in response to Nik query, the television went blank. Then the screeching sound of the Emergency Broadcast System returned, followed by a series of obnoxious bleats. Growing up, Nik and Jenn had heard these bleats often, usually between commercials when they watched *The Price is Right* or *Bugs Bunny.* A voice always come on that said, "This is only a test…If this had been a real emergency…"

But this time, the comforting yet commanding man's voice didn't come. Because this time, it wasn't a test. This time, it was real. The screen was black. Blacker than black. Jenn and Nik stared at it, expecting something to happen but nothing did. There was only the noise. The never-ending din.

Ω

When Nik stood to shut the television, the Emergency Broadcast System notification was still wailing in grief.

He joined Jenn in bed among the Cheez-Its and soda cans. The couple was shellshocked. "What the fuck just happened?" Nik asked.

Jenn shrugged and made unintelligible noises that tried to be words. Then she squeezed out, "I don't know."

They sat bolt upright on the striped "Desert Dream" bedspread, their bodies straitjacket stiff. Unsure of what to do next, they stared at the dark mirror of the TV screen much the way Illinois farmers stared up at the Empire State Building when they saw it for the first time. Except now, odds were that there *was* no Empire State Building anymore. No Manhattan. Everything and everyone in Nik and Jenn's hometown had probably ceased to exist.

Nik held Jenn suddenly, urgently. His grip was so tight she could barely breathe. Or was it the monstrous news that was making her short of breath? Jenn felt as though she were drowning, gulping in air that wasn't air at all but some thick, slimy substance. No. It was definitely the hug that took Jenn's breath away. Nik's hug was strangling her; it hurt.

But Jenn didn't complain because in an odd way, Nik's iron embrace was a comfort of sorts. At least his urgent presence made her feel something, something besides numb shock. Jenn returned Nik's sumo wrestler hug. They said nothing, just held onto each other like bobbing logs in a raging river. They'd just heard something there were no words for and needed to stay afloat.

All around them were the sounds of people giving up. Shouts. Cracks. The dull thump of a body hitting concrete from five stories. Metal hitting metal. Metal hitting brick. Gunshots, lots of gunshots. Arizona was a gun-happy, "open carry" state, meaning it was absolutely legal to have a gun without a permit just so long as you were at least twenty-one years of age. Maybe state legislators were regretting passing that law right about now. But then again, maybe not.

A tear hung onto Jenn's eyelashes. Finally, it fell. "What should we do, Niky?" she whispered. "Our family. Our friends... Is there anything left?"

Nik didn't answer. He only held Jenn closer, which she didn't think was possible. But it was and he did. Nik was always surprising Jenn with things she didn't think possible.

Jenn's right arm grew numb. She was so weary that she closed her eyes, just for a minute. Or so she thought.

Ω

When Jenn next opened her eyes, she was tucked beneath the sheets and it was morning. Only the sky wasn't bright. It was a dull, battleship gray, which was not typical for Flagstaff, where the sun was almost always shining. A thick dust seemed to coat the very air of the motel room. The space was almost foggy, like the woods in a black-and-white Wolf Man movie. The digital alarm clock on the nightstand blinked 12:00 AM PM over and over again. There must have been a power surge, an explosion somewhere close by.

Jenn's vintage Timex wind-up travel alarm clock still tisked away on the night table, though. She glanced at her cell phone's screen; it was blank. Even before this, Jenn trusted her Timex more than she trusted the clock app on her cell phone. She never left home without her palm-sized leatherette travel clock. The Timex had never let Jenn down. It took a licking and kept on ticking, even in a nuclear holocaust. This would have made a great television commercial, Jenn thought. But would there even be TV, much less commercials, anymore?

The Timex showed that the big hand was on the nine and the little hand was almost scraping the six. Yes, the alarm clock was still there beside Jenn but her husband was not. She felt a momentary clench of panic that Nik had joined the others and was a splat on the pavement. But he never was one to give up.

With a pang of relief, Jenn spotted Nik, in the green easy chair that was upholstered with an offensive cactus pattern. He was perched there like a guardian, a sentinel. Nik stared blankly through the balcony's closed sliding doors. The floor-length curtains, also cactus-patterned, were flung wide. "Thanks for tucking me in," Jenn said, trying to sound cheerful.

Nik turned toward Jenn when he heard her voice. She had never seen his eyes look so grave and hopeless before. It took her breath away for a moment. The left side of Nik's face had a horrible sunburn.

It hadn't looked like that the night before. Jenn wondered what had happened between then and now.

As if reading his wife's mind, Nik explained, "I was sitting here staring at the wall, thinking. Then there was a big flash, and the lights went out. They popped back on a few seconds later. Oh, and there were screams." His voice was expressionless.

"More screams than the first one?" Jenn asked.

He nodded. "But you slept through it. You slept like a kitten. You even purred."

"Meow," she said.

"Jenn, we have to get out of here," Nik told her.

"And go where?"

"To California," he said emphatically.

"But it could be even worse there. All of those military bases…"

"I want to see California again before I die," Nik added quite plainly.

"Niky, we're not dying," her response a kneejerk reaction. Nik only stared at her, challenging her with a hard glance.

Ω

It made no sense at all yet it made perfect sense. They had been very happy during their last trip to California so it might be nice to say goodbye one last time.

Plus, California was the Promised Land for Nik. For a car mechanic, it was Mecca. All of those classic vehicles. Lambos, Jags, Ferraris, Porsches, DeLoreans. All of those sexy convertibles. The Pacific Coast Highway hugging the rugged shoreline like an asphalt streamer. Yes, California was an auto mechanic's wet dream. Nik loved to work on vehicles like these, take them apart, see what made them tick then put them back together. It was similar to what he did with Jenn over and over again.

She could picture Nik fishing in a Salinas Valley river like a John Steinbeck character (perhaps George but not Lenny), observing the neat v's of sparrows in flight while waiting for a golden trout to bite. "People don't act like that in California," Nik was known to say when somebody cut the line in a supermarket or a driver gave him the finger on the Gowanus Expressway. Now there was no Gowanus, no finger-flashing drivers.

"They might be a little messed up in LA," Nik would add, "but at least the sun is shining most of the time and people smile when they stab you in the back."

What was the source of Nik's sunny fantasy? Maybe he and Jenn had seen too many Romcoms set on the West Coast. Maybe they had read too much Steinbeck to each other, nestled in their warm, plaid flannel sheets atop their safe, wooden Captain's bed in Sheepshead Bay.

Travels with Charley was one of their favorite books. How Jenn longed for the simple peace of drifting to sleep to the gentle racket of her husband's voice as he slowly read *Of Mice and Men* aloud to her. She would slip into dreams of plush green woods and fluffy rabbits on the weightless pillow of Nik's words.

"All right," Jenn said to her husband from their firm HoJo's bed. "We'll try to make it to California. We'll take it one day at a time, see what happens." She stood up, approached the prickly, green, cactus chair and kissed Nik's sweaty forehead on the non-sunburned side. It was hot and airless in the room. The AC seemed to have given up too. "Maybe we'll find Lenny," Jenn tagged on, trying to make her husband smile.

"Lenny is dead," Nik told her.

Four

The Road

In the stagnant air of their motel room, Nik and Jenn could pretend that none of what they'd heard on the news the night before was true. They could ignore the screams and thumps as well. But once outside, as they rolled their rolling suitcases through a nightmare, it was impossible to ignore or pretend. Dead bodies littered the ground as haphazardly as candy wrappers in a movie theater. On the pavement, skulls seemed to have crushed as easily as cantaloupes. "I can't look," Jenn gasped.

"You've got to look," Nik said. "Or you'll trip over them."

So, Jenn looked. She and Nik stepped gingerly over and around the smushed bodies.

The pools of blood had already dried to a rich shade of burgundy. All four members of the Howdy Family floated face-down in the kidney-shaped swimming pool, bloated like human marshmallows. The little girl still wore her water wings. Jenn couldn't tell if her brother's nose clip was still in place.

On the road outside HoJo's parking lot, cars were twisted into fiberglass pretzels. Some still smoldered. Jenn and Nik found their Cavalier unharmed, just where they'd left it, by a towering saguaro. The car started up on the first try, just as it had done before.

The temperature had dropped at least thirty degrees. It was so cool that the couple had to fish thick sweaters out of their suitcases. The sun was hiding but still there, glowing weakly behind a veil of clouds. "In spite of everything, the sun still shines," Nik said.

"Or at least it tries to," Jenn told him.

Once entrenched in the car, Nik blasted the air conditioner. It blocked out the aroma of death around them. The pair were the only living creatures within spitting distance.

Out of habit, Nik clicked his directional as he made a right turn, though he was signaling to no one. The sunburned half of his handsome face faced Jenn. "Here we go," he sighed.

And so, they went.

Ω

On Planet Alpha 49C, Jenn paused and looked back over what she'd written and wrote some more,

> *It astounds me that some of this is in exquisite (or horrific) detail and some of it is glossed over. Noah says not to worry about it, that this detail, or lack of it, is a protection mechanism, a survival tactic that humans often employ to help them get through an ordeal. Sometimes the details are a comfort (i.e., the Howdy Girl's water wings). But sometimes the lack of detail is a comfort too. Anyhow...*

Anyhow, Jenn kept writing. Writing in the cushion of the third person, much like the old politician Bob Dole used to speak. Imagining this was someone else's story helped soften the blow. Helped cushion the reality of what she'd survived. She persevered and typed.

Ω

Time was now divided into two neat columns: before and after.

It was tricky getting out of the parking lot, an obstacle course with humanoids as pylons. Were they all jumpers? No. Some may have taken their lives with the prescription drugs they had on hand and collapsed near their vehicles. Gabapentin for neuropathy. Adderall for ADHD. Zoloft for panic attacks. And so on.

Others may have had the bad fortune of being outside when the big blast occurred. Maybe they'd been on a Dunkin' Donuts run. Maybe they were out walking Skippy. Did they die of fright upon seeing the death flash? Or was a pre-existing condition the culprit? A heart attack from uncontrolled high blood pressure. A stroke from their body's proclivity to make blood clots. These were all questions without answers that were better not asked.

The car bottomed out when Nik scudded over the lifeless body of a small child. "Sorry," he said numbly. "I thought he was a bag of trash."

"She," Jenn told him quietly. "It was a she."

Nik kept going even though he couldn't stop crying. Under normal conditions, he felt guilty when a sparrow flew into the windshield or when a skittish squirrel scampered under the car tire. Jenn couldn't imagine how awful Nik felt running over the body of a dead girl. "Do you want me to drive?" she asked him tenderly.

"In a bit," he said. "In a bit."

Only a few cars moved along Highway 17. Many more were heaped up along the sides of the road like metal tumbleweed. Like the tumbleweed in "Cry of Silence." Some vehicles were abandoned mid-highway. This forced the driver to be alert. Both Nik and Jenn became adept at navigating the littered highway, like post-nuclear obstacle course racers in training.

Occasionally, they saw a body crawling out from a pile of wreckage. But they didn't stop. What was the use? What could be done?

$$\Omega$$

After the blasts, Nik and Jenn's cell phones stopped working; they couldn't seem to get a Wi-Fi signal. Maybe the satellites had been harmed. Maybe it was the fallout. But cell phones were useless. Which may have been a blessing because they couldn't reach their families or friends to check on the extent of damage in New York. They just assumed everyone was dead.

For a brief time, the power grid was still miraculously working thanks to solar energy backup batteries. But eventually, even solar power ended because the sun was so unpredictable. While it lasted, though, Nik and Jenn enjoyed the occasional luxury of electricity—traffic lights, refrigerators, convenience store freezers. They enjoyed it until it ended as most things they knew did.

The pair took turns behind the wheel, an hour or two at a time because the very act of driving in the end of days was tedious. They drove as fast or as slow as they wished because there were no police cars to stop them. There were no ambulances either, which was disheartening, but the whole damn thing was disheartening.

Jenn and Nik sped past the turnoffs for Phoenix, Tucson and other big cities. They sped past small towns like Gila Bend and Tacna. They drove constantly and only stopped to pee, puke or take gas from the abandoned service stations along the way. (Nik could always figure out to cajole even the most stubborn pump to work.) They also raided Chevron and Mustang's stock of Ding Dongs, PopCorners and Flamin' Hot Cheetos.

As Nik and Jenn sped west, few cars came from the east. What had happened on the coast? Was San Diego ground zero? And when the pair did pass another vehicle, they never really saw the other passengers in the car with any clarity. It was difficult to decipher the details of individual faces when you were doing eighty and they were doing at least one hundred and twenty. People were blurs to each other. But aren't they always blurred puzzles of sorts?

Often, Nik was silent. What was there to say? But when he did speak, he was as candid as a child. Nik would ask Jenn questions that needed no response. "It's so surreal, isn't it?" or "Can you believe this shit?" Life was rhetorical now; no answers required.

Jenn, on the other hand, was the opposite of taciturn. When she was terrified, she couldn't be quieted. She considered this an inherent character flaw. But for Jenn, yapping worked to calm her. Like whistling a happy tune did for Anna in *The King and I*. Although Jenn was far from being the elegant, ball-gowned Anna, somehow the quivering yammer of her own voice eased Jenn's fears.

"How could the world be destroyed for such stupid reasons?" she asked Nik as they were nearing Yuma.

"Can you think of a good reason?" he challenged. "Name one." Jenn couldn't. Nik couldn't either.

They were both tired, so very tired. And scared. This was understood. It wasn't necessary to express in words.

When they reached the California coast, then what? Somehow, they thought they'd know the answer when and if they made it there.

Ω

At a rest stop in Felicity, a floppy-eared German shepherd puppy introduced himself by bounding up to Nik and Jenn as though they were long-lost friends. His collar tag said his name was "Baron." Baron efficiently balanced on his three spindly legs, a living tripod. How he'd lost his limb, they hadn't a clue but he jumped and ran just like any other dog. Heartbreakingly skinny, Baron's ribs stood out like fence pickets. His black nose was warm and dry instead of cool and wet.

When Jenn pet him, Baron's bristly fur came off in her hand. "Can we keep him?" she asked Nik.

"Sure," he said. "He'll probably die soon anyway."

There was no witty retort from Jenn, the Queen of Witty Retorts, because Nik was probably right. But everyone, even dogs, deserved a shred of kindness and a pleasant-as-possible last few days.

At the Hypermart, Jenn managed to find a twenty-pound bag of Blue Buffalo for Baron. "He's probably eating better than we are," Nik said.

The Tavernas lived on whatever processed foods they could find. True, it wasn't a balanced diet but they figured it was safer than chancing it on fresh meat and produce that was already rotting and probably contaminated. Plus, they didn't want to take the time to cook. Finding fuel, locating utensils was another challenge. And their life was challenging enough. So, it was strictly grab-and-go.

Nik reasoned that highly-processed foods with virtually no natural ingredients were less dangerous than organics. Because of this, they favored foodstuffs with "best by" dates that were years in the future. I.e., Fritos that would possibly last longer than they would. Although everything they ate went right through them like tainted water. And given the current state of affairs, neither Jenn nor Nik had much of an appetite.

But Baron...Jenn was determined to make him live as long as possible. She'd never had a real pet as a kid. A warm-blooded pet, that is. Just carnival goldfish and turtles from Woolworths. Soon enough, Jenn would find the goldfish floating belly up in the glass tank she'd carefully arranged with Technicolor gravel and plastic palm trees. Within a week, the dime-store turtle shells would grow soft, even though Jenn gave them milk baths as though they were reptilian Cleopatras. One morning, the turtles would be lifeless and stiff, to be unceremoniously flushed down the toilet.

And Nik didn't let grown-up Jenn keep the one-eyed gray cat who had wandered into their concrete backyard one rainy night. Jenn had cried and cried nearly as much as the cat did but still, Nik held fast. "It's probably full of fleas," he explained.

However, Nik agreed to let Jenn keep Baron because the poor dog was so close to his expiration date.

Ω

At the Felicity Hypermart, they loaded the Cavalier with Utz pretzels, Cajun Spice Zapp's and Starburst. Jenn put some of the Blue Buffalo into a red plastic Solo bowl and poured Sprite into another. But Baron didn't eat or drink. His tongue lolled out of his mouth and he keeled over. "Baron!" she cried. He looked up at Jenn with his impossibly plaintive brown eyes but didn't move. Baron's skinny ribs puffed up and down in an effort to keep breathing. Then he closed his eyes.

Nik bracketed his hands around Jenn's shoulders like caring parentheses. "Come on," he said.

"But we can't leave him here like this," Jenn sobbed.

"What do you suggest we do?" Nik asked, and not unkindly. Jenn couldn't muster the words but instinctively, Nik knew what she wanted to say. He sighed. "I just don't have the strength, Jennifer," he added. "Or a shovel."

They continued west.

Ω

During a pitstop in Pine Valley, Jenn blurted out, "We're homeless." Sometimes, she was a little slow on the uptake.

"Yes, we are," Nik said.

It had suddenly dawned upon Jenn that their little perch on Batchelder Street no longer existed. And that her great-grandmother's Moss Rose china had probably been reduced to a fine powder in the blast. All of Jenn's temporal memories were erased from the surface of those plates, all fragments of the wonderful meals eaten upon them were gone. Jenn's Billie Holiday LPs had probably melted into shapeless onyx puddles. The cherrywood end tables Nik had fashioned from his own hand were probably zapped into splinters.

Except for Nik, Jenn no longer had family. He was all she had left.

Ω

Unusual things infiltrated their minds at odd moments. Perhaps this is because Jenn and Nik refused let go of their memories, even now. Especially now. They spoke of whatever popped into their heads, no matter how incongruous. "Remember those photographs from Hiroshima?" Jenn asked as she drove toward Holtville Hot Springs.

"How could I forget them?" Nik said.

The images from an exhibit at the Brooklyn Museum were etched into Jenn's memory. At the site of the first atomic bomb drop, people who had been outside during the explosion disintegrated on the spot. All that remained of them were their shadows, preserved in inky outlines and superimposed on the walls and sidewalks behind and beneath them. A Japanese photographer named Masaki had thought to photograph them and decades later, those photographs somehow made it to Brooklyn.

Several years later, on the anniversaries of the bombings of Hiroshima and Nagasaki—yes, homo sapiens were stupid enough to drop *a second* atom bomb in 1945, three days after the first one—a peace group stenciled shadows on the streets of Manhattan. This was to remind people what atomic bombs do to human beings.

Jenn never forgot these street stencils. She recalled being astonished at how rush hour crowds stepped over these outlines of bodies, these Hiroshima shadows, without much thought. But Jenn couldn't step on them; she purposefully tiptoed around them. She stopped to contemplate them, jostled by people on their way home or to an important meeting. After a few days, the rain washed away the Hiroshima shadows' ashen paint from the streets of Manhattan. And the ghosts of war were once again forgotten.

Ω

Driving down Highway 8, Jenn wondered what sort of damage nuclear missiles did to people. Had her mother been out on 86th Street with her aluminum shopping cart when the explosion came? Were people Jenn loved reduced to faint carbon impressions on the sidewalk?

Jenn wiped her tears on the sleeve of her sweatshirt. "When are we going to stop?" she asked Nik. "Stop driving, I mean."

Nik thought for a moment. "When there's no place left to go."

"But why?" she wondered like a querulous kid.

He shrugged. "What else is there?"

"What happens when the gas stations run out of gas? Or when the pumps don't work anymore?"

"Then we walk," he told her.

"Niky," Jenn sighed. "It makes no sense. There's nothing left. My body hurts. It even hurts to breathe. I'm constantly nauseous. I've had diarrhea for three days straight. And I'm so damned tired."

Jenn pressed her head into the steering wheel and settled in for a good, old-fashioned blubberfest. Nik steered with one hand and guided the car onto the shoulder. With his other hand, he rubbed Jenn's back, then pulled the emergency brake.

"I'm tired too," Nik told her. He lifted her chin with his pointer finger and looked at his wife with love in his eye. Yes, eye. Although he still had two, Nik's left eye was swollen shut. "It can't all be like this, Jenn," he insisted. "There's got to be something left. Something more. Wouldn't you feel horrible giving up if there was still hope?"

"But how would I know what I missed if I were dead?" she asked. It was a valid question but still, Nik persisted. "Things will be different once we reach San Diego. If it's bad there, then we'll head north. Carpinteria, Carmel, Santa Cruz. Morro Bay was your favorite, remember? Pleasure beyond measure in Room 9 at the Anchor Inn."

"Nine's always been my lucky number," Jenn conceded, sniffling.

"We took the same route our first trip up the coast," he recalled out loud, even though Jenn already knew this.

"And this trip might be our last," she said.

"It might," Nik agreed. "It just might. But then again, it might not."

When Jenn stopped crying, they changed places and Nik drove. The sun still hadn't burst through the smoky cloud they lived in. It seemed like the haze grew thicker the closer they drew to the coast. They needed to keep their headlights on constantly to penetrate the bleakness. "It's not so bad out here," Jenn said, surveying the empty landscape.

"Compared to what?" Nik barked.

"Not so many bodies, not so much destruction, I mean," she clarified.

"We're in the middle of nowhere," Nik reminded her as they passed Campo. "Plus, visibility isn't good," he added. Rarely could they see more than twenty feet in front of them.

But unfortunately, Nik and Jenn could still see each other. Sores had begun to spring up on their skin like wildflowers. And Nik was beginning to lose his hair in patches. When they talked (mostly about Steinbeck and old movies, for some reason), they avoided looking at each other. But once it grew dark, they did hold each other.

It was difficult to watch someone you love deteriorate. To see the skin you used to kiss and lick and savor erupt with blisters. To see the hair you used to stroke come out in handfuls. Nik even smashed the rearview and sideview mirrors so he didn't have to see his own face. When they ate, it came out almost as quickly as it had gone in, through both ends, sometimes simultaneously.

Nik and Jenn mostly slept in the car and avoided going into hotels whenever possible. The few occasions they did, what they found as they searched for an unoccupied room wasn't worth the effort. Too upsetting. Sometimes entire families had given up. This was difficult to see, even though Jenn and Nik were often on the edge of giving up themselves.

Ω

From the day they rented it at the Phoenix airport, their little red Chevy was slow on the pickup. "It has no balls," Nik had remarked the first time he sat behind the wheel. But fallout seemed to have a wonderful effect on it. Now, the Cavalier started up like a four-cylinder rocket. Without complaint, it chugged up hills and zipped through deserts. The air conditioner blasted frigid air like the frozen-food section at Waldbaum's.

Sometimes the car radio even picked up bits and pieces of broadcasts. Usually near large cities. But there was no real news because there were no real newscasters. And if any were left, why would they even bother showing up for work in the current world climate. Who could blame them? So, those who found their way onto the airwaves tended to be disgruntled receptionists, bored businessmen and defrocked priests.

More often than not, rumor masqueraded as news. Although people tried to be helpful, piecing together soundbites they'd heard, which often did more harm than good. Fake news, a disgraced former president used to call it. And fake news is worse than no news at all.

In no apparent order, these are some of the inconsistent rumors and innuendos that circulated as truth:

- That ten missiles and four atomic bombs had struck the United States;
- That three bombs, four missiles and four thousand Communist troops had made landfall in Canada;
- That the Midwest was fine;
- That the Midwest was one huge fireball;
- That four million were dead;
- That forty million were dead;
- That fourteen billion were dead.

But what did these numbers and half-truths matter? It was all guesswork. Speculation. Communication was all but broken. For some reason, the radio waves flowed longer than television or the internet did. The people who managed to get airtime tried their best to be helpful but most failed.

As Jenn and Nik drove, they listened to NPR. One resourceful software engineer offered twenty ways to dress up Spam. A well-known fashion designer named Yoko gave tips on what to wear in a nuclear holocaust. This included what was in and what was not, who wore it best, ten fetching ways to wear a head bandage and three dapper ways to masquerade a balding pate.

It made no sense but then again, it made all the sense in the world. The survivors were grappling for ways to continue to survive, attempting to keep busy doing something, anything, trying to stay sane.

At one point, Marc Ian Barasch quoted from his *Little Black Book of Atomic War.* Written back in 1983, it was freakishly relevant now. Especially useful were excerpts from the chapter entitled "Emily Postwar's Etiquette."

Near Alpine, the Chevy's radio crackled with the voice of a man who sounded remarkably like John Carradine, Nik remarked. But John Carradine had long ago died on the steps of a Milan church while filming a movie. "How I loved John Carradine," Jenn said. Nik nodded and drove. When the nameless Carradine wannabe read Puffet Morton's *The Atomic Mind Primer* in its entirety in his gravely growl, it was somehow a comfort.

As the Cavalier approached El Cajon, a woman with the vocal cords of Colleen Dewhurst recited "The Hollow Men." Nik and Jenn spoke the words along with the Colleen soundalike, her words throaty honey. It made the fine down on the back of Jenn's neck stand at attention:

> *This is the way the world ends.*
> *This is the way the world ends.*
> *This is the way the world ends.*
> *Not with a bang but a whimper.*

"It's true," Nik whimpered. "It's true."

Ω

Some of the post-nuc programming was excellent, however. Like that of a member-supported jazz radio station. "Remember WBGO Newark?" Jenn asked.

Nik remembered. "Chico Mendoza's Latin Jazz Sunday," he added.

"I loved Chico Mendoza," Jenn lamented.

"Who didn't?" Nik said.

Other makeshift DJs spun classic songs on the airwaves. Classic favorites. Timeless tunes. The Mills Brothers' "Coney Island Washboard." Oldies but goodies from different eras. Sentimental sop like The Beatles' "In My Life," which could reduce Jenn and Nik's friend Jimmy to nausea. For some reason, disco and hip-hop didn't seem to cut it when you were facing your own mortality, so none of it was played. Bob Dylan and Led Zeppelin held up, especially "Like a Rolling Stone" and "Stairway to Heaven." So did Ray Charles and Marilyn Horne. And of course, Mozart. Mozart withstood everything.

Some who managed to get on the radio just talked, and talked incessantly. About anything and everything, but mostly themselves. About their families. About their lives. Others prayed. Still others cursed God. And some just cried. Hearing the last brand of broadcast pierced Nik and Jenn to the marrow. They had to struggle not to cry themselves when these Sad Sacks commandeered the frequencies. These sobfests were even sadder than life itself, which was admittedly pretty sad.

Nik and Jen just switched off the radio when these poor souls hogged the airspace. They switched off the radio and sat in silence, for there were no words to describe what they felt.

To pass the empty hours, the young couple would sing songs to soothe their wounded, grumpy souls. Even though singing made Nik's sore gums hurt even more. The blues and Negro spirituals usually did the trick. Perhaps because they were written by people who truly understood pain and suffering. When Nik and Jenn sang "Ol' Man River," they always screamed these lines, which went something like this:

> *"I get weary, and sick of trying*
> *I'm tired of living, but feared of dying."*

But like Ol' Man River, they just kept rolling along.

Five

Second Start

In some ways, the real journey didn't truly begin until Nik and Jenn reached San Diego. Since they drove in through California's back door, passing little-known towns like Plaster City and Ocotillo, and former covered-wagon watering spots, the damage didn't seem as devastating.

On the highway, there still wasn't much sign of life. Very few moving vehicles, only a handful of moving bodies. Because these small towns weren't thickly populated to begin with, atomic disaster or not, things didn't look too bad. Selective memory? Perhaps.

However, San Diego literally took their breath away. Nik and Jenn gasped in harmony when they saw it.

Were their minds cloudy from the fallout and the trauma? Certainly. Flagstaff was a horrorshow they tried to push from memory. But they were foolish enough to think that if they made it to the ocean, things would be all right. *Might* be all right. Was it the healing, purifying power of water? The booming vigor of the waves? Senseless, yes, but at least it gave them hope because without hope there was nothing.

So, Nik and Jenn convinced themselves that they would be baptized by the sea. That they would wash their tortured skin in the warm Pacific and it would heal them. San Diego became their savior simply because they needed one. They were the Joads in a post-nuclear *The Grapes of Wrath*. But still, despite all they'd seen, Jenn and Nik weren't prepared for what they found in "America's Finest City." The "City in Motion" was motionless.

Ω

Stopping the car at the top of a hill in San Diego's outskirts, Nik and Jenn surveyed the damage, the annihilation.

The sea was a stagnant mass of black marmalade. Ships lay dormant in the harbor. Blocks and blocks of homes were leveled. Some were still smoldering. It looked as though Godzilla had tap-danced through it. Nothing moved, nothing except an occasional rodent. The only major signs of life were Nikolai and Jennifer Taverna, formerly of Sheepshead Bay, Brooklyn, New York on the planet once known as Earth.

"It looks like San Diego might have been a direct hit," Nik told Jenn.

"From the frying pan into the fire," she said. "What were we thinking?"

"We weren't," he sighed. "We're not in our right minds."

From the AAA materials, they knew San Diego had been home to a Coast Guard base plus naval and marine training centers. There was also a naval air station in the vicinity. But the possibility of "Plymouth of the West" being a target had never occurred to Nik and Jenn. They had other things to ponder. But if they *had* considered the possibility that the coast of California had been obliterated, what would they have done? Would they have joined the ranks of the hopeless and offed themselves too? No. Jenn and Nik weren't the type to surrender. Brooklyn produced a rare breed of fighters. Obstinate warriors who would just as soon battle for a parking space on the "right" side of the street during alternate side of the street parking as battle for their lives.

Ω

Perhaps San Diego might have been easier for Nik and Jenn to accept if there had been a skirmish in progress. Something dramatic. If there had been evidence that the city had put up a heroic fight. If the harbor had been decorated with little puffs of smoke, for example. If it had looked like a Turner painting or even remotely resembled a John Wayne war movie. If enemy airplanes had screeched and howled overhead then crashed into the inky water, sputtering like wet matches. But there was none of that. There was only the Aftermath.

Who was the enemy now? Who was responsible? Who could they hate? Who could they blame? This was not a war of people. This was a war of ideas, of ideals. This was a war that everyone lost.

Jenn turned from Nik as she laughed to herself. For days, they'd raced to escape the poison, the destruction, and as it turned out, they landed right in the middle of the steaming pile of shit. At ground zero. One of the many ground zeroes. It was so ironic that it was funny. 'Either you laugh or you cry,' Jenn's Uncle Ron used to say. So, Jenn laughed. She laughed maniacally.

$$\Omega$$

While Jenn laughed, then wept, Nik began driving again, his foot trembling on the gas pedal. He was so dumbfounded at the condition of San Diego Bay that he stopped the car at a green light. Then he decided that it would be more prudent to pull over to the side of the road. But Nik's foot struggled to find the brake as he slowly veered off to the right. Through her tears, Jenn watched Nik's sneaker tremble in midair. She leaned forward, pushed the pedal down manually and engaged the emergency brake. They sat there for a long while, silently staring straight ahead.

"It can't all be like this," Nik finally whispered, his voice dry as sand.

"Why not?" Jenn said, then decided this was too snarky a comment. So, she offered, "I guess we'll find out soon enough." More dead air. "I suppose a visit to the San Diego Zoo is out of the question," Jenn added for levity.

Nik laughed through one side of his mouth. The other side was crusted with a big, open canker sore that no amount of Orajel could heal. "The Cabrillo National Monument is probably off limits too," he countered.

If nothing else, Nik and Jenn still had their senses of humor, even if they'd corrupted into gallows humor.

"Let's see who else survived," Nik suggested.

"All right," Jenn agreed. "We can't be the only ones."

For days, the pair had no contact with living people, and this had been fine at the time. But suddenly, they felt the need to connect. To compare notes. To find a sign of life, of hope. The mini maps in the AAA Tourbook would help Jenn and Nik pick their way through the city.

Slowly, they drove the streets of the formerly toney Bird Rock neighborhood, maneuvering over bodies and around accordioned vehicles. They tried to find someone alive, making their way from house to house like persistent Jehovah's Witnesses. But there was no "life" to be found. For the first—and last—instance in his lackluster career, most of the population had taken the President seriously. They followed his lead and found their end just as he and the First Lady had.

Never before had Americans been so resourceful. They used ordinary household items for unintended purposes with phenomenal results. Beside bodies, Nik and Jenn discovered empty jugs of Clorox. There were Midol overdoses and hydrogen peroxide cocktails. Many of the suicide notes were peppered with optimism about the place they were going (i.e., Jannah, Shamayim or Paradise). Allah, Yahweh or God would forgive them for taking their lives in the current theological climate, some of the letters hinted.

"Do you believe in heaven?" Nik asked as they prepared to enter another home. This one, a neat ranch with yellow siding and a freshly-mown lawn that was browning.

After a pause, Jenn told him, "I'm not sure. Do you?"

Nik refused to respond. "How about God? Or the devil?" he continued.

"I don't know that I believe in either," she admitted. "Not anymore."

"But Jenn, God didn't do this to us," Nik said emphatically. "We did this to ourselves. He gave us free will and we…"

"I would believe only in a god who could dance," Jenn countered.

"Nietzsche. Very nice," he nodded then added, "Krishna dances."

"Then maybe I believe in Krishna."

Ω

It was gloomy inside the yellow-sided ranch house; no light penetrated the wide windows. "What's the name of Hindu heaven?" Jenn wondered.

"There is none," Nik told her, wiping his perpetually-running nose.
"Why not?"

"Because they believe in reincarnation. Remember?"

"Oh, great," she said. "Imagine being reincarnated into this mess."

"They say cockroaches can survive anything. Even something like this."

"Wonderful," Jenn told him. "Something to strive for."

Deeper into the living room, the light from the television set the tableau of desolation aglow. A relic of a man sat propped in his La-Z-Boy, a can of Coors in his left hand and the remote control in his right. The VCR was paused at the final scene of *A Tale of Two Cities,* the 1935 version with Ronald Coleman. Triangled onto the man's belly was a note written in a shaky hand. It read:

It is a far, far better thing that I do, than I have ever done;
It is a far, far better rest that I go to than I have ever known.

The old man reminded Jenn of her father. Except Francis had a mustache—and a mouth under it. A real cinephile, Jenn's dad would have had a shot of rye whiskey in his fist and *On the Waterfront* cued to the taxicab scene in his VCR.

This was the second-to-last suicide note Jenn read. She didn't need to be more depressed than she already was. She fingered her ghost berry beads with worry whenever they discovered a body but she refused to look too closely.

Nik, on the other hand, studied each corpse and began collecting suicide letters. He folded them neatly in half—whether they were scribbled on the back of a Ralph's supermarket receipt or on bubble-gum-scented stationery—and stashed them in his pocket, later to find a home in his Hello Kitty backpack. "They're important," Nik explained to Jenn. "Someone has to remember these people. Someone has to mourn them."

Ω

In a Pacific Beach home perched on the cliffs, Jenn and Nik found a teenage boy and girl ensconced in her fluffy, pink bedroom. The pair were lost among the fluff of the frilled bedspread and the six firm pillows in matching ruffled shams. There were perhaps fifty stuffed animals scattered throughout the room. Puffy creatures of all sizes, chipmunks that could fit into the palm of one's hand to a baby elephant one could ride.

Nik rejoiced when he found an indigo jar of Vicks VapoRub in the ensuite bathroom's medicine cabinet. When he slathered two fingers full beneath Jenn's nostrils, she winced. Her eyes watered. "I saw this on 'SVU' once," he explained. "Helps take away the stink."

"What stink?" Jenn wondered.

"You'll see," he said.

When they entered the girl's room, the uberstank struck Jenn with a left hook. The young couple lay naked on the bed, their perfect bodies curled around each other as if in sleep. Even with Vicks VapoRub, Tommy and Linda's beautiful, young corpses still reeked. Jenn and Nik knew the couple's names because Linda told them in her parting note. In curlicue script with hearts dotting the "i's," Linda explained that she didn't want to die without knowing what making love felt like. Hence, Linda and Tommy's cojoined bodies.

"I'm glad she got her wish," Nik said, nodding.

And indeed, Tommy was still nestled inside Linda for all of eternity. Or at least until his penis rotted away. Blissful smiles dabbed their faces.

"Him too," Jenn said. "Him too."

Ω

Despite the pain, despite what they inevitably found inside, Nik and Jenn kept entering houses. What were they actually looking for? Food? Drink? Supplies? Life? Whatever they were seeking, they didn't find it.

The last house they entered in San Diego was a white, shingled cape on top of a hill. They applied more Vicks then knocked on the front door as they always did before entering a home. No one answered, as was always the case.

This time, Jenn and Nik had drawn lots to see who would go in first. Nik lost so he led the way. Jenn clasped the AAA books to her chest like talismens. Inside the cape was a family of five. Two were sewn into Star Wars comforters with big, rough stitches. The three live ones were barely hanging on.

The five of them stared at each other and said nothing. What was there to talk about? The weather? It was awful. Ask how they felt?

They all felt the same—horrible. And these three looked to be in even worse shape than Nik and Jenn were.

A car engine started outside, making the quintet jump out of their silence. One woman, the mother, probably, kept nervously pushing back the hair from her forehead. Only she was bald as a newborn. The other woman did nothing but noiselessly sob. The man didn't look up. Instead, he methodically flipped through a coffee table book called *Monet: The Triumph of Impressionism.*

When Jenn caught a glimpse of Monet's "Water Lilies," her heart was glad for a moment. Seeing a speck of beauty among such ugliness was a gift. The bald woman looked at Jenn and Nik with blank eyes that had seen it all, even the death of her children. Especially that. Jenn and Nik left and closed the door without uttering a word.

Ω

Out on the pavement, they discovered that their rental car was gone. That was the starting engine they'd heard when they were in the white house. They stood at the curb, staring at the empty space where the red Cavalier had been. "Try explaining that to Avis," Nik said.

"Honey, there is no Avis anymore," Jenn reminded him.

Both women inside the white house stood at the shattered picture window watching Jenn and Nik's predicament the way they once watched reality TV shows, broken lives behind broken glass. But this was a reality show even more desperate than "Squid Game."

When Jenn started to cry, Nik steered her away from the women's prying eyes. He crooned sweet, hopeful words into his wife's ear. Jenn ignored him. "What do we do now?" she sobbed.

"We walk," Nik said.

"Toward what?"

"There has to be something left, Jennifer," he told her once more. "We just have to find it."

"Don't you know how to jumpstart a car?" she asked. Jenn knew he did. What kind of master mechanic didn't?

However, all attempts to revive the abandoned vehicles they found were fruitless. "The fallout must have messed with their electrical systems," Nik said.

Early on in this odyssey, they'd agreed that it didn't feel right taking property from the dead. Food and drink were different—they meant survival. But they didn't want to pilfer any personal belongings. As tempting as it might have been to filch a dead girl's Schwinn or zip up US 5 on a dead tween's skateboard, they refrained. They felt bad enough without piling guilt on top of their messy emotions by stealing from the dead. Somehow, a car felt less personal than a bicycle. But cars were useless now, so the point was moot.

Nik could see that Jenn was crestfallen. "What do we do now?" she sobbed again.

"Let's take it slow and make the most of it," he suggested. "Since this will probably be our last vacation."

"Vacation?!" Jenn screeched then guffawed.

Nik laughed. *When had he lost his left front tooth?* Jenn wondered. His teeth were falling out like Chiclets, while Jenn, who had been a periodontist's poster girl with her oozing gums, had never had a healthier mouth. "I knew that would get you," he admitted, still chuckling.

Sometimes Nik was so cheerful, Jenn could almost smack him. Others, he was so low, it frightened her. But that Wonder Wheel of emotion was just part of being a survivor.

Ω

San Diego was lousy with shopping malls, Jenn and Nik discovered. They went into JCPenney's through the smashed front door. Nik lobbied that it was permissible to take a pair of Reeboks and other items they needed for their journey north. Jenn still felt bad stealing from a store, although she knew Nik was right. "We need this stuff to get by," he reasoned. "It's not like taking clothes from dead bodies."

Jenn felt awkward, like Penney's chipped mannequins were watching and silently judging them as they stuffed their backpacks (also stolen) with articles of clothing: underwear, hooded sweatshirts and raingear. Jenn slipped a pair of Hokas onto her blistered feet; the engineered mesh and cushioning made the sneakers feel like leather clouds. When pilfering, why not steal top of the line goods? 'Steal big,' Uncle Ron used to say, 'Or don't steal at all.'

Ω

Nik and Jenn decided to take I-5 up north. It was formerly the scenic route that hugged the California coast. Even though they were well aware that there probably wasn't anything scenic left. Jenn was thankful she hadn't left the AAA Tourbook and TripTik on the Cavalier's dashboard. For some reason, she clutched them in her hand when they entered that last house, as if the books would bring her strength and fortify her.

Although she and Nik were still American Automobile Association members in good standing, Jenn knew they couldn't get replacement copies if the materials had been lost. Even if telephones still worked, would anyone answer AAA's Emergency Road Service number in the middle of a national emergency?

The Tourbook pinpointed places of interest along the road, so Jenn and Nik wouldn't miss a thing. The flip-up TripTix maps indicated that it was approximately 500 miles to San Francisco. To Nik and Jenn, that seemed endless. But they would stop as often as they needed. Whenever the mood struck or whenever they couldn't take another step. Whichever came first.

$$\Omega$$

On page 49 of the Tourbook was a grainy black and white photo of the beaches at La Jolla. Which either meant "the jewel" in Spanish or "land of holes" in the Kumeyaay tongue, depending on the language you favored.

Not too long ago, La Jolla was known as California's Riviera. It was dotted with large rocks, lush hillsides and shoreline caves. The latter explains its "holey" Kumeyaay nickname. But nothing was lush on Earth anymore. Holey, yes, but not lush.

Besides Nik and Jenn and a sparse handful of homo sapiens, the other life form that survived was vermin. Insects of all varieties plus mice, rats and snakes. The beach itself was crawling with them. The very sand itself seemed alive. Like the creeping flesh in monster movies which tended to star Peter Cushing.

For obvious reasons, Nik and Jenn agreed not to stray from the gray-black freeway. They passed several small signs indicating turnoffs for the Salk Institute, which they ignored. Way back when, Jonas Salk had created the polio vaccine. If he were still alive, could Salk create a vaccine to combat what people were now living through? Highly doubtful.

The AAA Tourbook said that the Salk specialized in research on cancer, diabetes and brain function. A place like this seemed ridiculous now. There was no need to research anything anymore.

Jenn and Nik also didn't veer off to visit Torrey Pines. Their friends Pat and Walter lived there. They didn't have the heart to see if this kindly older couple had survived. They didn't have the heart for a lot of things.

As they slowly pecked their way up the coast, Nik and Jenn talked and groaned and argued. Sometimes they discussed religion. Nik was Jewish—he believed that the Messiah would soon come. Jenn was brought up Catholic. She'd been taught that the Messiah had made a flashy appearance and then had been killed.

"He'll be here, you'll see," Nik told Jenn.

"He already came," Jenn insisted. "He'll come again on Judgement Day."

Nik laughed. "Look around you," he said. "What do you think this is?"

Despite their friendly bickering, Nik earnestly tried to stay hopeful. Like a cheerleader in heat, he smiled often, even through missing teeth. Jenn didn't smile much, even when Nik told her Elephant Jokes. Sometimes Jenn just didn't see the point in smiling even though her teeth were still intact. Sometimes it took an intense effort to make the corners of her mouth curl up into a halfhearted grin.

"How can you be so cheerful?" Jenn snapped as they passed the sign for the Birch Aquarium. "You make me sick!"

"You've always been sick," Nik retorted. "You married me, didn't you?"

Jenn couldn't help but laugh. He made a valid point.

Six

Food for Thought

For Jenn and Nik, sustenance was reasonably easy to come by, but good, healthy food was quite another matter. A profusion of cans and jars and packages of edibles inhabited the abandoned grocery stores. Nutritious or not, what was the difference? Without fail, they vomited and/or shat enthusiastically after every meal, whether it was Doritos or a fancy pâté on imported crackers.

Although most of the choice eats were gone, there was an abundance of items like lima beans and pickled pigs' feet. And very few cans of desirables like candied yams and cling peaches. When Nik and Jenn came across a tin of Vienna sausages, it was a *cause célèbre*. While munching on them, Nik would invariably muse, "Remember the Vienna Boys' Choir?"

Of course, Jenn did but she couldn't even begin to imagine their fate.

Spam was a rare treasure, manna from a heaven which may or may not exist. And oh, to find a jar of gefilte fish (in jelled broth, please!) with a schmear of horseradish on the side. It was like dipping a toe into a pre-fissile paradise for Nik. It literally made that Jewish boy's heart skip a beat.

And stumbling upon a shrink-wrapped package of Applegate organic turkey breast could reduce Jenn to tears. A can of black olives (colossal and pitted) made her burst into spontaneous song. Nik would slide them onto his fingertips for his wife to gently nibble off. Just like she did as a kid when her mom made *antipasto*.

At first, their preoccupation with food might be considered a bit bizarre. But what was "normal" in the midst of a radioactive limbo? And more importantly, what else was there to give Nik and Jenn pleasure? True, there was the warmth of their love for each other but even love seemed fruitless in the wake of global disaster. In their deteriorating bodily forms, corporal affection was a challenge, both physically and mentally. And consummation was improbable even if it had been of interest to them. And truly, who could fuck—or feel fuckable—when your body was riddled with sores?

Besides, there were no breathtaking landscapes to make their hearts go pitter-pat. The color was drained from everything. Shades of khaki, olive, rust, black and gray abounded. Yet, Nik and Jenn's stomachs still ached and tightened for nourishment. Their throats still became parched and longed for drink. Going in, food was the source of extreme pleasure. Even mediocre food. But coming out was another matter.

However, certain foods made them sad and simply could not be eaten no matter how hungry they were. Some nutrients even made them cry, and not with joy. Nik and Jenn did their best to avoid these victuals but sometimes they couldn't help a chance encounter. They would saunter into a minimart and there the offending edibles would be, lined up in bottles and cans like felonious troops.

Here's an incomplete list of top offenders in no apparent order:

- Cento artichoke hearts;
- Campbell's Chicken and Stars Soup;
- Mott's applesauce;
- Smucker's strawberry preserves;
- Ball Park Franks, and so on.

The long, contorted vignettes explaining the "why" is of no consequence now. But suffice to say, these foods reminded Jenn and Nik of family, family, family. Of which they had none. Not anymore. Sunday dinner, Passover seders, future barbecues, school lunches past, and simple, loving meals, all gone.

Ω

Though Nik and Jenn were ill and exhausted, still, they walked. Somehow, they always managed to walk. With wads of toilet paper stuffed into their underpants, with newspapers stuffed into their shoes. And really, what else was there to do but forge ahead? Lay down and die? They were of working-class stock, born of children of immigrants who'd left the place they were born for someplace better. They were raised to fight, and to try, always, no matter what. Even when the situation seemed hopeless.

Though they often questioned the essence of life itself, Nik and Jenn didn't want to die. They were almost killed, however, just north of Del Mar.

Hobbling along the shoulder of the road, they rested often. Moving north along Highway 5 South, they discovered, was relatively safe because they could spot the sporadic car approaching from a long way off, even though vehicular encounters were few and far between by now.

"Is that a car?" Nik wondered, cocking his ear.

"I think I hear something," Jenn agreed.

But still, they didn't see anything ahead. In the distance was the small mumble of a car engine but it seemed to come from behind. Nik and Jenn turned to discover something speeding down the wrong side of the road. But then again, was there a "wrong side" and a "right side" to anything when there were no rules?

The car drew closer, first a smear of antacid pink, then the size of a Hot Wheels toy, then a full-sized automobile. Three wide lanes of blacktop were available for the driver to use but instead, the person behind the wheel seemed to be aiming directly for Nik and Jenn. To escape, the couple dove into the dry grass beside Highway 5's gravel service lane. Jenn fell forward and badly cut her left knee. Nik was almost unscathed but shaken. A pink El Dorado with New Mexico vanity plates sped away. It must have been going at least ninety. "Was that the Yee-Haw guys?" Nik gasped.

"I don't think many cars look like that," Jenn told him.

Suddenly, the El Dorado swerved and screeched around an unexpected curve. And just like an elaborate crash in the *Fast & Furious* series, the car careened sideways over the guardrail and flipped down the hundred or so feet to the bottom of a cliff. Then came the predictable boom, followed by a flash as the pink Caddy burst into flames in pyrotechnic splendor.

"Ride 'em, cowboy," Nik said as he helped Jenn to her feet. Her palms were scratched and bloody, but they weren't as bad as her knee. Nik had twisted his ankle in his stuntman fall but was otherwise all right. At least they weren't *flambéing* like the Yee-Haw couple.

Ω

Traveling light, Jenn and Nik carried no bandages. Since there was usually an abundance of medical supplies in each town they passed, they didn't want to burden their weary bodies with unnecessary weight. In a chivalrous gesture, Nik stripped off his white Marlon Brando t-shirt and wrapped it snug around Jenn's knee. The makeshift bandage bloodied immediately. He bound it tighter and showed Jenn the map. "Think you can you make it to Encinitas?" he asked, pointing to the pale blue name.

She nodded. Even though her torn knee throbbed with each heartbeat, Jenn realized this was no time to be a baby. Encinitas was only a sixteenth of an inch away. "Sure," she said like a brave soldier, though she doubted she could make even ten steps.

In the best of days, Jenn considered herself a coward. She hated horror movies and slept with a nightlight when Nik wasn't home. But post-catastrophe, Jenn had constantly proven herself brave. However, the thought of sleeping on the side of the road with the charred New Mexicans and their vengeful wraiths was more frightening than the trek to Encinitas.

So, Jenn grimaced and began walking. Without meaning to, she dragged her left leg behind her like Boris Karloff doing the *merengue*. After a while, her knee stopped smarting because it went totally numb. Which made walking challenging in a whole different way.

Perhaps Nik saw the fear in Jenn's face because he kept talking, talking, talking, trying to distract her bleak thoughts. "Encinitas...It reminds me of Ensenada. Remember Ensenada?" he asked.

"Yes," Jenn gasped, trying to control her floppy leg.

"We took that minibus tour to Mexico from San Diego with those obnoxious people," he rallied. Jenn nodded, bit her lip. "And that little brat. What was her name? It began with an 'r.' Rina? Ruth?"

Jenn wiped a tear from the corner of her eye, hoping Nik didn't see. She didn't want to worry him any more than he was already worried. "Rivka," Jenn said through gritted teeth.

Nik laughed. "Right. How could I forget? Her parents must have said it a million times. 'Rivka, stop.' 'Rivka, come over here.' She had a scab on her upper lip that she kept picking…Are you all right, J?"

"Yes," she lied and kept walking.

It was the first time Jenn had seen Nik shirtless since their Flagstaff shower and she was taken aback. He was skin and bones. Plus, he had no hair on his chest, under his arms or anywhere. "The drive down to Ensenada was beautiful, wasn't it?" Nik continued. "Cliffs dropping fifteen hundred feet into the ocean…"

"…poor people living in tents off the highway," Jenn reminded him.

"But at least they ate well. All the fish and lobster they could catch," Nik countered. "Remember that fancy hotel in Rosarito? The one where Orson Welles and Rita Hayworth used to stay. What was the name?"

Jenn chomped down on her lip. "I don't remember."

"You're kidding," Nik said. "You remember everything."

"I know everything; I know nothing," Jenn told him.

"I know nothing," Nik countered in a cheesy German accent, sounding like a post-blast Sergeant Schultz from "Hogan's Heroes."

"And I can't remember what movie that line is from."

"I can't either," Nik admitted, then plowed headlong into his memories. "I liked Ensenada the best, though."

"The people were so destitute everywhere in Mexico. It made me feel guilty vacationing there."

"You feel guilty vacationing anywhere," Nik broke in.

"*I* feel guilty?" Jenn squealed. "The minute you stepped out of the van in Tijuana, you tried to improve the economy singlehandedly. You gave dollars to every street kid you saw. You even bought an old whore a beer."

"She looked thirsty," he said.

Despite their pain and the situation, Nik and Jenn laughed. "I think my favorite place was Tijuana," she told him.

Nik put his arm around her waist. Her hip bone felt like a dagger. "Tijuana was a hole," he said.

"True, but that's where we got these wedding bands." Jenn held up her hand. "Pure Mexican silver." The ring was so big on her now that it twirled on her finger. Nik wore his on his thumb, she noticed.

Nik and Jenn hadn't kissed since their amorous Flagstaff shower. (A lack of ChapStick and Tic Tacs can do that to a person.) But on the road to Encinitas, Nik pressed his dry, cracked lips to Jenn's.

"I missed that, Niky," she told him, digging her forehead into his.

"I know," he said. "I know."

Ω

Nik grasped Jenn's hand as they followed the exit ramp to Encinitas. They stayed at the Sanderling Place, which AAA had given three diamonds. The couple took a suite with a view even though there was nothing to see. There was no nightly turn-down service but they didn't care. It was a place to rest their shattered heads and the body stench wasn't too pronounced there.

Jenn plopped onto the king-sized bed and propped up her leg so Nik could take a closer look. As gently as he could, he peeled off the t-shirt he'd wrapped around her knee, but the blood had dried and the material stuck. The scab tore and the wound started to bleed again. "That's an infection waiting to happen," Jenn sighed.

"You always look on the sunny side of the street," he told her.

Nik had no other option but to soak a washcloth in the lukewarm greenish water that drizzled out of the tap. As he pressed the cloth to Jenn's knee, she tried not to cry but couldn't help herself. She felt so tiny and vulnerable, plus it hurt like hell. Nik sat on the edge of the bed and stroked her back while still keeping the cloth affixed to Jenn's knee. She crawled up into his arms and he held her close.

It was so quiet they could hear the bathroom faucet dripping. With her head against Nik's chest, Jenn could feel a rumble starting from deep down as he began to sing. Nik's voice was weak and wavering, but it was nice just the same. One of Jenn's favorite songs bounced off the Sanderling Place's tastefully-painted walls: Blind Faith's "Can't Find My Way Home." It was about longing, wanting and receiving. About someone special being the reason for the wait, and that person holding the key. Being near the end and not having time. Being wasted and unable to find your way home.

Basically, it was Jenn and Nik's odyssey in a nutshell; it was perfect.

Ω

When Jenn drifted off to sleep, the blurry, leaden sun was setting. And when she woke, it was already light. Or as light as it gets with fallout misting the day. Nik was sitting in the desk chair, watching Jenn sleep. He found it difficult to sleep these days, while Jenn, usually an insomniac, generally slept straight through the night. A clean bandage covered her torn knee and little green stalks peeked out from under the gauze. "What's that?" she asked.

"Aloe," he told her. "I went down to the Quail Botanical Gardens while you slept. I couldn't settle down."

"I wonder why," she yawned.

Nik ignored her. "You wouldn't believe that place. It was a jungle."

"Was everything dead?"

Nik lifted himself from the chair to the bed. "Far from it," he said. "Everything was thriving, growing wild." He rubbed his left eye, which was permanently sealed. "It makes no sense," Nik tried to explain. "Some things die immediately but others flourish. Some people get super sick while others hardly show any effects."

"What are you trying to say?"

"I don't know exactly," Nik admitted. "But you seem to be a lot less sick than I am. I'm…"

"Stop!" Jenn gasped. But Nik didn't stop; he kept right on talking.

"I think I'm dying, Jenn," Nik plodded on. "You can't ignore it. But you…you seem to be…adjusting…adapting."

"I'm not," she insisted.

"You were always better at change than I was," he told her. "At accepting things."

Jenn shook her head. "You're just more stubborn," she said. Nik was saying something she didn't want to accept but it was true. She traced the contours of her ghost berry beads as though they were rosary beads. Then she looked down at her knee and picked out a squished sprig of aloe from behind the bandage. "You just could have gotten Bactine," she said. "It helps the hurt stop hurting." *Is there anyone left besides me and Nik who remembers that old TV commercial?* she wondered.

"Aloe is better," he told Jenn. "You'll see."

Ω

Nik and Jenn stayed at the Sanderling Place for two days. During that time, he alternated between changing her bandages and warming up cans of Spaghetti O's and Dinty Moore beef stew in the microwave. They marveled that the power grid was still working in Encinitas and wondered how long this would continue. The electricity winked on and off like Christmas tree lights, taunting them.

Soon enough, Jenn was able to bend her knee and take furtive steps without cringing. When they took to the road again, Nik filled his backpack with boxes of clean bandages and tubes of aloe vera gel from Walgreens. He'd also procured a box of Fi-Bars, which he knew Jenn loved. Mandarin orange flavored, coated with chocolate yogurt.

Finding—and lugging—your partner's favorite snack was a simple gesture that said love, love, love without words. Packing your bag with items you knew gave someone pleasure wordlessly spoke volumes. And besides, if need be, Nik could use the Fi-Bars like a carrot to a reluctant horse, to make Jenn move forward.

As they ambled down Highway 101, Nik assured Jenn that there was something special in store for her a few miles ahead in Carlsbad. Sometimes that was the only thing that kept Jenn going: the thought of something better, something to take away the pain. His surprise would stop Jenn from hurting, Nik swore. "I don't think that's possible," Jenn belly-ached, her lower lip quivering. "I hurt in so many places, in so many different ways."

Nik shook his head and continued. Jenn followed. She hated secrets, hated surprises, so she tried to guess. "What is it? A bullet with my name on it?" she prodded, laughing at her own feeble joke. But Nik didn't think it was very funny. He just kept moving forward.

At times, that short trip to Carlsbad seemed like a journey to the edge of eternity. Whenever Jenn thought she couldn't take another step, the promise of Nik's surprise kept her feet moving. After the first couple of miles, Jenn's knee began to stiffen again. When Nik told her that she was limping like Grandpappy Amos from "The Real McCoys," Jenn squealed, "Luke! Luke!" just like Pappy did. Pop culture references helped pass the monotony.

On the rare occasions Jenn and Nik passed people on the road, they scarcely spoke. Maybe there was a nod, but they didn't exchange words. Each didn't want to know what the others had seen, what devastation they were escaping, and vice versa. The others did not want to know how badly the south had been hit while Jenn and Nik didn't want to know what awaited them in the north. Where else was there to go except straight ahead? What else did any of them have but hope?

Ω

Near San Elijo Beach, Jenn and Nik came upon two men fighting over a bicycle. It seems that the rightful owner had gone into the bushes to pee and came back to find the other man tiptoeing off with his Cannondale. "My wife and kids are in Hermosa Beach," the thief explained. "I was in San Diego on business when all of this happened. I just have to get north. Fast. I have to see if they're still alive. You understand, don't you?"

The other man snatched back his bike. "Do you think you're more important than me? Do you think I don't have people I need to get to?"

The Cannondale snatcher hung his head. "I don't care," he said in a hiss.

"No one's alive in those northern beach towns," the bicyclist spat cruelly.

"You're lying," the would-be thief said, his eyes cold as a python's.

The other man shook his head. "I wish I was. I just came from there. Mar Vista. My fiancée's down south. In Chula Vista."

The wanna-be thief laughed. "San Diego was a direct hit. Trust me, there is nothing 'chula' about Chula Vista anymore."

(Nik whispered to Jenn that "Chula Vista" meant "beautiful view.")

The determined bike robber continued, viciously, "And if your woman's still alive, you wouldn't even recognize her. Or want her."

With that, the rightful owner threw his bicycle to the ground. He jabbed the offender in the face. The thief, in turn, slugged him in the stomach. The fight was over fast because the thief picked up a jagged rock and smashed it into the side of Cannondale Man's head. Blood spattered out of his skull like rain. He fell to the ground and lay motionless.

Neither Jenn nor Nik had ever witnessed such stark, sudden violence before, except in movies. Neither imagined that a human skull would split so easily. Like an overripe watermelon.

Now the man from the North Country was a murderer as well as a thief but it didn't seem to bother him. "What the hell are you looking at?" he shouted at Nik and Jenn.

They didn't answer, afraid he'd bash in their heads too. The Bicycle Thief slowly rode the blue Cannondale past them. "You would have done the same fucking thing," the man yelled.

Jenn and Nik still didn't respond but somehow, the man knew their answer. No, they wouldn't have.

"Look," the man tried to explain, "I've seen so much death, this doesn't mean a damn thing to me." He paused. "I don't want to go to heaven, if there is one. I mean, what kind of God would do this to his children?"

It was a good question. What kind of God indeed?

Seven

Take Me to the River

For Nik's benefit, Jenn read aloud from the AAA Tourbook during a rest stop. "Carlsbad, California was named after the Czech spa Karlovy Vary in West Bohemia. Their magical, mystical mineral waters are very similar in chemical composition and are said to cure all ills." However, Jenn didn't think anything could cure the demise of the world. She didn't tell this to Nik, though.

When they arrived at the famed springs of Carlsbad, they only found puddles of mud. Jenn ticked it off as one more disappointment in a long string of disappointments. She could tell that Nik was crushed, however. Why? Because this was the surprise he'd pumped up since the Sanderling Place. Nik was fully convinced that bathing in Carlsbad's miracle waters would heal Jenn's knee, her broken skin and perhaps even her broken spirit.

Despite the mudpies, Nik convinced Jenn to go for a dip anyway. She hated to multiply his disappointment by refusing so she agreed. A flash from Nik's stormy brown eyes (now, eye) could convince Jenn to do almost anything.

After being lovers for the better part of a decade, Jenn was suddenly embarrassed to take off her clothes in front of Nik. But then she remembered the litany of compromising positions he'd seen her in—peeing blood with a UTI, moaning with cramps from colonoscopy prep, doubled over and passing clots in the throes of a miscarriage—yet Nik still loved her. Being a gaunt warrior princess could now be added to that list.

As the days passed, Jenn grew more and more emaciated but the hair on her head bloomed like an unkempt lawn. Back at the Sanderling, she'd examined herself in the three-way mirror one afternoon and was shocked at what she saw. She could count all two dozen ribs. The knobs of her hips jutted out at a painful angle and her pelvis curved in like a spoon. Her right knee was as swollen as a softball. The other looked like scabby chopped meat. She probably looked ten times worse now.

But despite her rough appearance, Jenn disrobed in front of Nik at the Carlsbad mudhole, and to her surprise, he didn't avert his eyes, horrified. Instead, he looked at her with love.

Jenn knelt in the goo, a broomstick version of Psyche, the White Rock Soda girl. The mud was cool and comforting against Jenn's ragged kneecap. Then came the pleasing sensation of Nik's hand on her back. His fingers ran down the knots of her spine then trailed up the tines of her chest, tracing them one by one. Jenn's muscles unfurled at his touch; she was a stray mutt rescued by a kind stranger.

"Please don't look at me," Jenn begged.

"Why?" Nik asked. "I still love you."

What could Jenn say except, "I still love you too."

Nik spread the thick, dun gunk across Jenn's shoulders. "It looks like Fox's U-Bet," he remarked.

Jenn pictured the chocolate syrup dripping down a pile of ice cream. "I miss ice cream sundaes," she said.

"Me too," he told her. "Me too."

The mud felt good, soothing. Jenn still wasn't sure it would be therapeutic, but it was wonderful being caressed again, consoling to be touched, even through sludge.

Jenn leaned into her husband's caress, closed her eyes and moaned out loud. Nik smiled. "It's almost as good as coming," she told him. "Under the circumstances."

Nik rubbed the warm ooze over his wife's fading breasts. Even in their sorry state, her nipples responded, standing out like poised pinkie tips during afternoon tea. "Do you remember what it feels like?" Nik asked wistfully.

"What?" she asked.

"Making love," he said.

"Sure. Don't you?"

"I remember how it felt in here," Nik told her, touching his hand to his heart and leaving a trail of grime. "But not in here," he added, gesturing downward.

"You're giving me an orgasm in my heart right now," Jenn whispered. This made Nik smile again. His smiles were so rare and fleeting that Jenn treasured them, even partially toothless as he was.

As she shifted from her knees to her bottom, the mire snuck into her butt crack. Nik rubbed the wet dirt into Jenn's pubic hair, which was lush. Covered with mud, her pubes looked like the chocolate frosting that topped the Betty Crocker cakes Jenn used to bake for his birthday. She casually tried to cover her protruding hipbones with her elbows. "Do you think people still do it?" Nik asked, dribbling mud into his wife's navel.

"Not if they feel as bad as we do," Jenn said.

"What if someone were to get pregnant?" Nik mused. "What would the baby be like?"

"Remember *Threads?*" Jenn recalled. "That girl gave birth to a monster." She forced herself to stop wallowing in negativity. "No more sadness," she pronounced, spackling her palms into the brown paste. Only happy things, only happy movie references. Like *Singin' in the Rain...The Wizard of Oz."*

Nik coated Jenn's rubber-band thighs with filth. "Don't forget *The Opening of Misty Beethoven* and *Talk Dirty to Me."*

"It amazes me how you could bring up porn at a time like this," Jenn chided. Upon seeing Nik deflate, she conceded. "Okay, I admit, they were pretty good films. But seriously, how can you think of sex with my washboard chest staring you in the face?"

Nik walked his fingers up each rung of Jenn's washboard. "Seeing your bare skin helps me remember."

"Remember what?"

"How beautiful you were."

Jenn made a face. "I was never beautiful."

Nik shook his head. "You were." With his clean hand, he dug into his pocket for his wallet. "I still have that picture of you on the beach in Bermuda."

Jenn couldn't bear to see herself before all of this happened. "Please, no..." By accident, she splashed a speck of sludge onto Nik's hand-tooled wallet, the one he'd bought on that trip to Ensenada. Without meaning to, Jenn started crying.

Nik thumbed away her tears, streaking mud beneath each eye. Jenn looked like a mournful football player, face marked with charcoal. "You never thought you were beautiful," he said. "I never could convince you."

He swirled globs of molten muck onto Jenn's cheeks then slid it down to her collar bones, her chest. Nik refused to take off his clothes and join her, though Jenn did try to coax him. "My skin feels fine," he told her. It was true. After the initial ick, Nik's addled skin had healed on its own. (Although there were occasional eruptions.) Yet his teeth were falling out and so was his hair. The burn he'd gotten on the side of his face from the Flagstaff blast was fading. And the rest of him was fading as well.

Ω

After Jenn's gritty massage, Nik led her into the spa's tiled shower room. The warm water eased the dried mud from her skin. Nik rubbed Jenn softly with an exfoliating glove. Her flesh tingled. In a good way. Then Nik dug his fingertips into her scalp until the water rinsed clear. He coated her wounded knee with aloe vera gel and dressed it. Then he applied more of the colorless balm over her skin lesions. Jenn felt good for the moment. Like a pink, happy baby fresh from the tub.

"I saw a theater a few blocks back," Nik told Jenn. "Want to see what's playing?"

"The end of the world as we know it?" she suggested.

Nik ignored her. "I think I can figure out the projector."

"Sure," she told him, ducking into a new set of sweats from the Carlsbad's swanky spa's shop.

Ω

The Mound of Venus Cinema was a short ramble away, in a strip mall not far from the motel. The movie posters showed slit mouths, spread legs and bouncing bottoms. It didn't seem to gel—a clean, friendly, little neighborhood erotic theater smack dab in the middle of a polite, little suburban strip mall. But stranger things have happened.

"I don't think they played Disney movies here," Jenn told Nik.

"Maybe *Pornocchio* but definitely not *Pinocchio,*" he agreed. "You still want to go in?"

"Why not? It's not like I never saw one before." (Truth be told, Jenn and Nik were amateur porn afficionados.)

Nik nodded. "Besides, it will be good to hear other people's voices. To have some company."

Thankfully, the theater's front door was unlocked and the seats were empty. There were no decomposing bodies to spoil Nik and Jenn's wicked adventure. This meant that the Mound of Venus was probably closed when the blasts happened.

Nik flipped on the lights. The porn palace looked odd in total brightness. An adult cinema is one of those places never meant to be well-lit. Like a cave or a Day's Inn. With the bulbs on full blast, the theater looked shabby, its maroon seats worn, some torn. The pleated curtains on either side of the screen were red; they didn't come close to matching the seats. But no one knew this in the semi dark.

The artistic nude plaster of Paris statues flanking the side aisles were chipped. Rodin's Thinker had something to think about, for someone had drawn a penis on his neighbor the Venus de Milo's thigh with a Sharpie. And Michelangelo's David had a Band-Aid over the tip of his uncircumcised member. Although no one probably noticed these additions in the Mound's usual dimness, it gave Jenn and Nik a good chuckle.

On the way to the snack bar, their feet stuck to the floor. "Some things never change," Nik said.

Behind the glass counter, the popcorn was starting to sprout mold but the cellophane-sealed candies seemed fine. One box reminded Jenn of a joke. "What do you call a flat-chested girl?" she asked Nik.

He shrugged. "Arlene Canfield?"

Jenn shook her head then shook a box of Milk Duds. "Get it?"

He got it. "I'll take Junior Mints instead."

By trial and error (mostly error), Nik finally got the projector to work at a limping, chug-chug pace. However, the sound and picture weren't in sync; they alternately became faster and slower independently of each other. But luckily, the movie was still watchable. The plot was wafer thin, but it was nice to see attractive, preatomic people having a good time with each other.

Backdoor to Tracy's Hot, Wet Family Jewels employed every adult movie cliché possible under one roof—anal sex, incest, squirting females, large-donged detectives, teen scream queens, the works. It was a harmless, interchangeable ditty about a nubile young thing who had to remain a virgin until she was 18/21/25 or she would lose her inheritance/estate/trust fund. But of course, Tracy was a nymphomaniac who seduced the gardener/parish priest/farmer/milkmaid. Or all of the above at various points in the Ariel Hart script. Tracy tried to keep her lack of a hymen a secret from her sordid uncle/attorney/governess, or the money would be lost. And in the end (usually, the rear end), something silly/crazy/unbelievable usually happened to make it turn out all right.

In this particular flesh flick, there was a profusion of pipe jobs, hand jobs, and every type of job imaginable. There was also spooning, muff diving, cowgirling and a sprinkling of bukkake thrown in for good measure.

Nik and Jenn laughed through the slender storyline, but they didn't laugh during the love scenes because they were tender/passionate/intense. Sometimes, all three at once. It was all nicely filmed by Larry Revene with the focus on the faces rather than on the gonads. In their current dilapidated state, Nik and Jenn had forgotten what an amazing thing the human body could be. As imperfect as bodies were—with their hairline scars, paunches, cellulite—they were also very beautiful. It was truly a wonder how everything worked, how opposite parts fit together so seamlessly.

Seeing those fresh, familiar faces and fannies on film made Nik and Jenn feel that they were with old friends. Pre-Armageddon, the couple had enjoyed watching pornos together. They had seen many of the performers grow up and old on celluloid, transforming from curly-haired, smooth-cheeked teenagers (Tom Byron) to pudgy dudes with porn "stashes" and bald spots (R. Bolla), morphing from skinny, gangly gals with teacup titties (Lonnie Sanders) to MILFs (Debbie Revenge). Video was honest; it hid nothing. Some porn people were as familiar to Nik and Jenn as their high school classmates were. Even more so.

"There's Dick!" Nik blurted when one of Jenn's old favorites literally came onscreen. It was no secret that Jenn had a thing for Dick Truehard, he who could so eloquently recite sonnets while schtumping. And often did.

Yes, it was like seeing old friends.

Jenn had hoped that a gynecological closeup of Danielle (no last name needed) would give Nik an erection but no such luck. Although his scrotum was no longer swollen to the size of a grapefruit, there was clearly no fire down below.

Nik and Jenn left the theater after the first skinflick, although he'd found at least six more packed into canisters. Even the newest Richard Pacheco sextravaganza. But Jenn had no desire to see another porno with Nik being newly impotent and her feeling so unattractive. In truth, the two of them were rather glum after seeing Tracy's carnal adventure. Silently and separately, Nik and Jenn lamented what they used to be until Nik finally spoke.

"We were really something once, weren't we?" he asked rhetorically. "On kitchen tables, on bedroom floors, in empty men's rooms. We were really something, weren't we, Jennifer?" he repeated.

"That we were, Nikolai."

Eight

Onward and Upward

T
hroughout their journey, Jenn wrote postcards to Nik and left them on the edge of his pillow while he slept. She nabbed the cards wherever she found them: in defunct gift shops, at abandoned service stations, in restaurant turntables. Kitschy, touristy postcards with pictures of pretty places on the front: beaches studded with palm trees, quilted, verdant mountains, cracked cliffs backed by golden sunrises. Clichéd scenes of California before the cataclysm, views that now became treasured memories.

Other notes to Nik were scrawled on motel postcards she'd found stashed in dresser drawers. Renderings of the establishment with no people in the pool, no wrinkles on the bedspreads. Various scenes of hotelier perfection. Jenn would jot silly little ditties on the back of these hotel postcards to make sure Nik knew that she still loved him, that she still cared. Or else, Jenn would write down stupid jokes she suddenly remembered. Anything to make Nik smile. His grins were so seldom as the couple crawled their way up the coast. Smiles seemed to get less frequent with each mile.

Always an early riser, Jenn was usually washing her face or making terrible hotel room coffee when she heard Nik laugh out loud and say, "Jenn, I love you too." Hearing this made her heart leap. Still.

Back at the Sanderling's gift shop, Jenn had picked up a cute postcard and stashed it away, saving it for when Nik seemed especially downhearted. The picture reminded her of an old joke she heard when she was a kid, the first "naughty" joke she'd ever been told. On the front of the card was a snapshot of a pretty, dark-haired lady with a 1960s-style bob. She wore only a canary yellow bikini bottom, her hands demurely draped over her breasts. Here's the joke:

> A woman is coming out of the water after a swim when a big wave knocks off her bikini top. She crosses her arms over her chest, hoping no one will notice. On the shore, a little boy says to her, "Lady, lady, before you drown those puppies, can I have the one with the little pink nose?"

A terrible joke but Nik laughed and laughed. Laughed till he cried.

Although he generally went to bed complaining of sore feet and a sour stomach, Nik liked starting the day with a guffaw. This was a good thing; no matter how bad the situation turned, he still liked to laugh.

Jenn and Nik took their pleasures wherever they could. Even at the end of the world. Especially then.

Ω

The AAA Tourbook described Camp Pendleton as a Marine Corps base near Oceanside, California that covered approximately 125,000 acres. It was one of the world's leading amphibious training camps.

Nik sneered when Jenn read this to him. His patience and optimism were slowly fading, giving way to sarcasm, despite Jenn's Joke of the Day or love letters. Jenn knew Nik's personality shift was because he felt so poorly. His snarky comment about the Marine base was, "All that training didn't do much good, huh?"

"Meaning?" Jenn asked.

"Meaning, we didn't have a chance to use it," he snapped. "Smart as you are, you can be so thick sometimes, Jennifer."

She ignored Nik's jibe and clomped ahead. "Camp Pendleton is also an ecological preserve," she pointed out, quoting from the Tourbook.

"Was," he corrected. "Was." Then he laughed even heartier than he had at the puppy joke. "There's nothing left to preserve," Nik reminded her.

But since they were so close, they decided to visit Camp Pendleton after all. There was always the possibility of good victuals, even tinned survival meals, to up their depleted larder.

No guard stood at Pendleton's front gate to check Nik and Jenn's IDs, which they still carried dutifully. First and foremost, so that someone, anyone, could identify their bodies. They didn't want to be anonymous in death, not that it would make any difference.

In a sort of sightseer trance, Jenn and Nik visited the Landing Vehicle Tracked Museum. Here, amphibious contraptions used by Marines since World War II were displayed. The self-guiding tour placards were a big help. The couple even popped into Pendleton's original eighteen-hundreds ranch house and chapel, which was once used as a winery.

All in all, it was an impressive exhibition. Even in the wake of the Aftermath. Americans had so many complicated, imaginative methods of defense, but in the end, none worked. Ah, the irony.

Ω

The nearby town of Oceanside boasted four miles of beach. This much was still true. Except when Jenn and Nik visited, thousands upon thousands of fish littered the shore. It was impossible to tell what type they were. Some were decaying and others were still flipping.

Only a few days earlier, the pair had shivered in the cool, dim breeze but then the weather turned sweltering again. As the fish baked on the sand, it smelled worse than a homeless person in Sarasota on a July day. Normally, the travelers would have been reduced into retching heaps from the stench, but Nik thought of everything.

On their last visit to Drug World stocking up on gauze and tape, he took a couple of pairs of swimmer's nose clips. They worked fine, although Jenn did have an LSD flashback of the bloated boy wearing them in HoJo's swimming pool. But like most things unpleasant, she pushed this thought out of her mind. Jenn was getting quite good at doing that. They both were. Selective memory is a handy survival technique. (But not so handy when you're writing a memoir.)

Although nose clips did help, breathing through their mouths made Nik and Jenn's throats dry. To combat this, they sucked on Sucrets, which didn't taste as good as Luden's, but Nik figured they were safer from fallout since they were packed into pocket-sized tins and individually wrapped. However, Sucrets also carried bittersweet memories of Jenn's childhood. They were her mom's preferred throat lozenge and Maria's remedy for just about everything oral. Jenn missed her mother and her sunny disposition something fierce. Both she and Nik really could have used Maria right about then.

The phenomena of sucking Sucrets while simultaneously wearing nose clips made Jenn and Nik's ears pop. Especially when they swallowed. Post-nuclear life was full of annoying, little discomforts. Nik and Jenn just dealt with them, muddled through. What choice did they have?

To pass the time as they walked, the couple played word association games with the names of the places they saw. Or they tossed ideas back and forth like volleyballs of thought. It helped keep their vacant minds active and hang onto whatever shreds of sanity remained. But the "Donald Duck on Steroids" trill of their voices through the nose clips was pretty ridiculous.

Ω

The name San Onofre Beach drew a blank from Nik but reminded Jenn of Concetta D'Onofrio, a slut-in-training at St. Rocco's Grammar School. Which reminded her of Patsy Reinholt with her neck brace and facial tics. Which reminded her of Sister Gertrude Ramilda, her flowing black robes and delicate mustache. And Robert Tarpin, who'd lost a front tooth in an unfortunate hockey puck mishap. And Miss Cullen, Jenn's saintly, virginal Catholic school lay teacher who bad-mouthed Jews every chance she got "because, after all, they killed Our Lord." How would Miss Cullen have felt if she knew that her prized pupil Jennifer Morrongiello (maiden name) had married one? All of that didn't matter now, did it?

Yes, something always reminded Jenn of something else. She was grateful her synapses were still snapping. But Nik seemed to be slowing down. He wasn't as quick on the uptake, although he still laughed at Jenn's goofy attempts at humor. And her parochial school rants. For Nik's benefit, she exaggerated her former classmates' Brooklynese accents and pulled her baggy t-shirt into peaks to simulate Larette Russo's mounds. Jenn was a *tour de force* when it came to relaying her St. Rocco's reminiscences.

By far, Nik's favorite character in Jenn's repertoire was Sister Lucinda. She was a super cool nun, unfailingly human despite her penguin attire. One day, after overhearing the newly-hatched teenagers in her class cursing in the schoolyard, Sister Lucinda wrote FUCK in three-foot-high letters on the blackboard. The idea was to show them how stupid and meaningless cursing was. That FUCK was only a word, like so many other words. And it wasn't technically a word, according to Sister Lu.

Jenn shared with Nik Sister Lucinda's revelation about the etymology of FUCK. She said that British policemen grew tired of writing out "for unlawful carnal knowledge" on a prostitute's arrest report so they abbreviated it to FUCK. This big reveal took the wind out of Jenn's classmates' curse word sails. After Sister Lucinda's story—and chalkboard theatrics—the word was rarely used on school grounds.

So, Nik and Jenn walked and talked. They walked until their feet bled and blistered. They didn't stop at San Clemente Beach because it had suffered a similar fish situation as San Onofre. But the name San Clemente reminded Nik of Roberto Clemente, the Pittsburgh Pirates' famed right-fielder. Alternately, it made Jenn think of Richard Nixon, the shamed US President, whose "Western White House" had been located there. And so on...

Ω

It was a pity that Nik and Jenn missed the annual Whale Festival at Dana Point. Well, all of humanity missed the festival that year, even the whales themselves. Especially the whales. There were no whale-watching cruises even though it was whale-watching season.

But the pair didn't have to venture very far to see the whales because they floated belly-up in the Pacific like small mountains. The sea was calm and flat like dirty cranberry sauce. But every so often, the surf churned and pounded relentlessly, rippled by an unseen, angry hand. There was no rhyme or reason to the behavior of the sea or the tides. Just like there was no rhyme or reason to anything.

Jenn and Nik bunked at a Ramada Inn on the outskirts of San Clemente. When she was feeling a little grim that night, Nik regaled her with tales of growing up in Levittown, Long Island and the goings on at Gardiners Avenue Elementary School. How Jenn loved hearing about Little Niky, though his tales were few and far between by then. He doled them out like communion wafers, and just like the Body of Christ, Jenn craved their dry weight.

Nik's stories made Jenn think of what their child might have been like. A child Jenn knew she would never have. From the starvation and the fallout, her cycle had come to a full stop and she doubted it would ever return. And who would be brave enough—or foolhardy enough—to bring a child into this world?

Nine

Nik and Jenn

The next day they were out before six and well on their way to Capistrano. Although the swallows hadn't returned, Nik and Jenn found the Capistrano Inn to be quite lovely, despite present circumstances.

Because AIDS had become such an epidemic, many hotels offered complimentary condoms along with palm-sized bars of soap. The Capistrano Inn was no different. Next to the Gideon Bible was glass bowl that held several rubbers. "Remember these?" Jenn laughed. She'd been on the pill almost as long as she'd been sexually active. And monogamous since she'd met Nik. There was no need for such things as condoms anymore. Now, especially.

Jenn tore the rainbow wrapper and blew one up like a party balloon. "Why does it taste like Dr. Segal has his fingers in my mouth?" she wondered.

Nik glanced at the condom cover. "It has one of those delay-action chemicals."

"Huh?"

"You know, to 'prolong her pleasure.'"

"Cocaine for cocks," Jenn nodded. Then she and Nik blew up all five condoms in the dish and sent them sailing through the room. Next, Jenn brushed her teeth with Aquafresh to get the taste of condom out of her mouth. Then she went on a mission. She collected all the candles she could find from the hotel's dining room. Which was awkward because there were cadavers seated around the tables. Jenn donned her nose clips to block out the pong of decay and narrowed her eyes to blur her vision. This reminded Jenn why she and Nik avoided places of assembly: churches, synagogues, health clubs and restaurants; too many corpses.

But even employing their best avoidance tactics, the pair came across the dead wherever they went: along the side of the road, in gas stations, in stores. Everywhere. After a long day's journey, all they wanted was to soak their feet, snack on a Slim Jim and tumble into a good, hard bed. Imagine unlatching a motel room door to see a man and woman, three weeks dead, their sightless sockets watching the black mirror of a TV screen. It was difficult to bear in an already difficult situation.

At the Capistrano Inn, Jenn ignored this self-imposed rule because she was a woman on a mission.

Ω

Just as he'd been instructed, Nik met his wife at the Jacuzzi at the designated hour. The water bubbled furiously when he arrived, Jenn having already pressed the button on the wall to activate its fervor. There were so many chemicals in the hot tub, nothing could deter the fizz.

Jenn had set the profusion of candles she'd collected along the Jacuzzi's rim and lit them all. She sat there in the midst of the furiously percolating water, waiting for Nik, looking almost pretty. Despite his gauntness, Nik stripped down and joined her, looking almost handsome. If Jenn's calculations were correct, it was the eve of their ninth wedding anniversary, or close to it. She'd even managed to find a bottle of a decent California Beaujolais, uncorked it and poured it into short, fat tumblers.

As they sipped Beaujolais in the bubbling froth, Nik and Jenn recalled their rough beginnings. For some reason, they ran over the same old ground. Maybe the numbness of repetition gave them comfort. Maybe they were getting ready to say goodbye to each other, which was inevitable. Or maybe their reflecting was a different kind of hello.

"Remember our first date?" Nik posed.

Of course, she remembered. "Rockefeller Center. To see the lighting of the Christmas tree," Jenn nodded. "I'm still sorry I suggested it. With a name like Nik, how was I supposed to know you were Jewish?"

"Nik stands for Nikolai, like Gogol," he reminded Jenn.

"Well, I didn't know that then," she admitted, floating toward him. The few limp strands of hair on Nik's shiny pate clung to his skull. Jenn's sumptuous bed of weeds was pinned up in a messy bun. Coated with steam, Jenn hoped she looked passable. "Do you remember the first time we made love?" Jenn posed.

"Three days after our first date," he said.

"Did you think I was easy?"

"Nothing about you is easy, Jenn," he told her.

Jenn drifted between Nik's thighs. Her back pressed against the front of his body. With effort, Nik twined his legs around her waist and rested his chin on her shoulder. Nik's joints had been throbbing intensely as of late but the water made him feel better. Jenn was glad when he told her this.

Nothing transpired between them that night. Nothing sexual. But neither of them really minded. Jenn felt content. Nik did too. Sometimes that was more important than sex—to feel loved.

The Jacuzzi gurgled and gulped. They dried off, went back to their room, had a supper of Ramen Noodles prepared in the microwave then fell asleep. Jenn dreamed that Nik was beautiful again. And that she was too, only she didn't know it at the time.

Jenn woke up laughing. She couldn't wait to tell Nik about her dream.

Ten

Nik and Jenn and God

Jenn seemed to contradict herself about heavenly matters. Perhaps this signaled that she was losing her mind, which was a worry to her. Case in point, sometimes she said that she didn't believe in God. Others, she was clearly praying out loud, either in words or deeds, or both.

Suffice to say, the Aftermath was a very confusing, desolate time, and humans often have conflicting feelings in times like these. Jenn decided to allow herself to waffle, to feel what she felt when she felt it. The good, the bad, the ugly and everything in between. To feel all the feels, as they used to say.

At the very core of her being, Jenn did believe in God. But Nik and Jenn and God…that was another matter. Nik swore he didn't believe in God. Even now. Especially now.

Ω

Not counting Morro Bay, the second-best "top" spot during Nik and Jenn's honeymoon trip was Laguna Beach. Hands down, they thought it was one of the prettiest places on the planet. Laguna Beach was magnificent before the blast with its steep, jagged hills rising from the sea. Waves crashed defiantly against rock and stone. The contrast of hardness against the water's airy foaminess was breathtaking.

The AAA Tourbook described Laguna Beach as "picturesque," only it wasn't anymore.

Almost a decade earlier, Nik and Jenn had stayed at the By-the-Sea Inn. It newly-opened and cozy, with just thirty-six rooms. The unassuming mom-and-pop motel had been ideal for them. They would wake up before the sun rose, and have blueberry muffins and containers of sweet coffee on the patio. Then they'd stroll the beach, which was just footsteps away, watching the sun ascend and paint the sky with blush.

Sometimes Jenn and Nik would nap for a few hours. Then they would swim and sun and *schtump* and have a picnic lunch on the beach when they were hungry. At night, after a seafood supper at Las Brisas, they would walk the beach again, shoes in hand.

One evening, they even made love on the sand. More specifically, on a beach towel that said, "Let's boogie!" And boogie they did. It was like that scene in *From Here to Eternity.* Except later, Nik and Jenn had to pick sand out of hidden crevices. Perhaps Deborah Kerr and Burt Lancaster had to do that too. Although Jenn and Nik's "Let's boogie!" beach towel was trashed, stiff with sand and sea and sex, it was worth it.

Ω

The pair had many pleasant memories buried along the shores of Laguna Beach. Maybe that's why Nik flew into a rage when he saw what it looked like this nuclear summer. But what had he been expecting? Jenn had learned not to expect anything anymore. Nik, not so much. He was a cockeyed optimist. Just like Ensign Nellie Forbush in *South Pacific.*

At Laguna Beach, Nik fell to his knees on the sand, as if he were about to start plumbing its depths for his tainted memories. Jenn carried hers around inside, so she always knew where to find her memories, tainted or not. Maybe Nik had forgotten where his memories were stashed.

It wasn't that Laguna Beach was so horrible, just that it was so different. Dismal and bare. The water was still, unmoving. "Let's go to By-the-Sea," Jenn suggested. She helped Nik up from his outraged genuflect after he nodded.

Jenn hoped it would make Nik feel better to visit the motel, but it didn't. They couldn't stay at their favorite little mom-and-pop because By-the-Sea had burned down. All that remained was a pile of charred wood and a half-lit neon sign that silently mocked them. Chalk up one for solar power because the sign still worked, even with the dodgy sunshine.

Ω

When they were walking along the beach again, Nik suddenly howled at the top of his lungs. Jenn had never heard him make such a horrific sound before. Even her hand caressing his back didn't soothe him. Nik kept right on howling. He cursed his mother. He cursed his father. He cursed his Aunt Sophie for introducing his mother to his father. And worst of all, Nik cursed God.

"None of this is God's fault," Jenn reminded Nik when he calmed down. "You said it yourself back in San Diego." It was a hell of a time to discuss theology but then again, no better time.

"Then who do I blame?" Nik jeered.

"Why do you have to blame anyone?"

"It might make me feel better," Nik said, plopping down into the sand. Jenn sat beside him.

"Then blame people," she told him. "Mankind. God gave us free will and we made our own choices."

"Well, then, it's His fault for giving us free will. He's supposed to know everything. He knew were going to do this."

Jenn was at a loss. "Maybe He thought we would learn from it. The ones who lived through it," she suggested. "Maybe the rest of us don't deserve to be saved. When you have free will..."

"Fuck free will! Look at where it got us," Nik snarled. "At least we'd still have a world. What choice do we have now?"

"There are only two," Jenn told him. But he already knew what they were: life or death.

Nik continued to rage. He screamed into the face of the sea. He screamed into Jenn's face. She'd just about had it by that point. Her rock, her foundation, was crumbling. "Don't yell at me!" Jenn sobbed. "I'm not the enemy. This isn't my fault!"

By this juncture, Nik was crying too. "I'd end it if I could. But you know how that turned out."

Ω

A few weeks earlier, Nik and Jenn had feebly tried suicide. It happened somewhere near San Clemente. They woke up in a nameless motel, felt miserable (as usual) and after a brief discussion, agreed that life had become unbearable. "This isn't really living," Nik said into the crook of Jenn's neck. "It's barely existing." Reluctantly, she agreed.

They dressed, grabbed their backpacks and started walking. Early on in this misadventure, they'd decided that they would know when and how to off themselves if the time came. And the time had come.

Before noon, Jenn and Nik found themselves in front of a huge mansion. Upon entering, they removed their sneakers and socks because the carpets were brassy white. This gesture was simply out of habit; stained carpets didn't matter anymore. Nothing did.

The house was intact and impressive. There weren't any dead bodies to be found, which was a bonus. Maybe the family had been vacationing in Monte Carlo or sailing to Catalina on their sixty-foot yacht when the blasts happened. Nik and Jenn knew these tidbits from the Bonham Clan's life because the couple had stopped to admire photographs depicting these cushy activities.

Meticulously displayed on the white marble mantlepiece and on the glass-topped occasional tables were armies of picture frames. Trapped inside them were photo after photo of the Bonhams' charmed lives. Of their plain, tan, smiling blonde faces racing O'Day sailboats. Of a lady in a full-length silver fox fur posing in front of "MOMSJAG," as the license plate read. Of winters in Aspen, summers in Tuscany. Etc.

Jenn and Nik plopped onto the white leather sofa. They looked at the trail of blood their bare feet left on the squishy white carpet. "White isn't a practical color in an apocalypse," Jenn sighed. "Or ever."

Nik nodded. They were both so weary. Of everything. After they'd sat down briefly to rest, they must have dozed. Or passed out. Because suddenly it was dark out and they were hungry. They were always hungry and never full.

When Nik and Jenn rifled through the refrigerator, they found an unpopped jar of beluga caviar from the Caspian Sea. In the larder, there were Triscuits and Macadamias. Nik and Jenn gorged themselves like wealthy swine. They chased the caviar and nuts with glasses of Château Latour. Then they puked. It was a very expensive puke.

"We can't enjoy anything anymore," Nik lamented. "Even caviar. What's the point?" He definitely had a point.

Ω

One entire wall of the mansion's living room was taken up by a breakfront of bleached white wood. Nik thought the house might have once belonged to Howard Hughes because there was a framed photograph of him standing in front of that very breakfront which seemed to have been taken in that very same massive room. A brass tag on the side of the cabinet said it was from India. "Maybe the Taj Mahal?" Jenn half-joked. Nik shrugged. The piece was so magnificent, it was entirely possible that it came from that palace of sorrow. Jenn remembered that an emperor had it built as a tribute to his third, but favorite wife, who'd died giving birth to their thirteenth child.

Jenn opened the cupboard's wide double doors to a display of fine crystal that hailed from all over the world: France, Italy, Romania. (She checked the tags beneath, an odd habit of hers.) With few words exchanged, Nik and Jenn knew what they had to do next, that this was the time to do what needed to be done.

From the breakfront, Nik plucked two ornately-carved champagne glasses. He left the room and came back with a big, white jug. Without ceremony, Nik poured them each a Clorox cocktail. Jenn managed to get only as far as raising it to her lips. The noxious fumes literally took her breath away. She gagged. Nik, perhaps more needy than she, took a quick swig but didn't swallow. Instead, he spat it out onto the deluxe, white pile carpeting.

But still, he wouldn't acquiesce.

Nik dragged Jenn into the kitchen by the elbow. It was a sumptuous room, with a white quartz island, gleaming stainless-steel appliances and a Viking stove that looked like it had never been used.

Jenn was amazed at the intensity of her husband's grip, especially in his scrawny state. With one hand, Nik gripped Jenn's wrist, with the other he grabbed a Wüsthof carving knife from its butcher block holder. This was for him. He let go of Jenn for a moment and shoved another knife between her fingers, a sharp de-boner. She took it. Nik forced Jenn to hold its point against the blue veins in her wrist. She knew what he wanted her to do; he was going to do the same with his own dagger. But she hesitated.

Jenn could feel the allure, the freedom of the cool, hard blade almost puncturing her skin, yet she could go no further. Like a skinny, bald, male, Anglo Madama Butterfly, Nik pressed the tip of his weapon to the tender space between his fourth and fifth ribs, just below where his heart lay. Jenn watched in horror, holding her breath. But even after several moments, Nik couldn't take the plunge either.

They looked at each other, shook their heads and started laughing. Nik and Jenn dropped their Wüsthofs then sunk onto the white granite floor tiles. "Who the hell are we kidding?" Nik asked. "I can't. I just can't."

Together, they made a pact that as long as there was breath in their bodies, they would breathe. They would try. They would hope. Because, without hope, what was there?

Ω

Nik and Jenn played house in the white mansion for a few days. They pretended to be rich. They play-acted at being rich folks in a fancy, frosty world. They wiped their butts with pillowy, triple-ply toilet paper. They soaked their creaky bones in the ivory and gold Jacuzzi. They slept in the huge, round bed that overlooked the Pacific. On one wall of the cream-colored master bedroom hung a zebra hide, offering the only slashes of non-white in this clean, blanched world. Jenn nodded off, staring at the animal skin, praying that its tormented soul wouldn't haunt her dreams like that creepy amulet did to Karen Black in *Trilogy of Terror.* Jenn's dreams were already haunted enough.

She slept like a baby: fitful, keening, and waking up every few hours in the silence of the white house. And in the morning, when the gray sun rose, Nik and Jenn had given up on giving up.

Ω

Back on Laguna Beach several weeks hence, Nik was still sulking. When he sulked, his face took on the characteristics of a belligerent mule. His chin jutted out ever so slightly and his jaw became set, solid. His eyes became glazed with a blankness. In her eleven years' experience with this human donkey, Jenn knew the only way to coax Nik out of one of his despondent moods was to make him laugh. But this was no easy task now.

Nik held onto his unhappiness like a life preserver in a rough surf. Or a beloved, raggedy blankie. Everyone did sometimes. Nik seemed more willing to cling to the uncertainty of that little ring of unhappiness than to relinquish it for the shaky stability of a dinghy. Why are people like that with their sadness? Many therapists warn their patients, "Don't fall in love with your depression." But it wasn't an easy thing to do. Depression is sure, familiar and safe; happiness is evasive and subjective.

So, after years of futile struggle, Jenn found that the only way to pry Nik out of his misery was to cajole him into chuckling. His stubborn anger drew the sides of his mouth into a smirk. But Jenn knew that if she could get just a flicker of a grin in one corner, she could make him smile all the way. Although reluctantly. Oh, Nik would fight that smile but he would inevitably lose the battle. Then he would LOL, hug Jenn and say that he loved her. Which he did. Truly, madly, deeply, even now. And she him.

This was the procession of woe that Jenn knew well, all too well. As well as she knew the faded pattern of roses on her grandmother's parlor wallpaper back in Staten Island. For some reason, elephant jokes seemed to work best when Nik's mood had sunk this low. One of Jenn's much-loved books as a kid was the slim treatise *101 Elephant Jokes*. She dug into her shaky memory banks and plucked out a few from the woeful recesses of her hippocampus.

On the firmly-packed sands of Laguna Beach, Nik took big, annoyed steps. Out of breath, Jenn followed and had to struggle to keep up. "How do you know when there's an elephant hiding under your bed?" she panted.

Nik knew the answer because she'd told him this joke dozens of times. However, he refused to respond. Instead, he began to walk even faster. "You can smell the peanuts on his breath!" Jenn shouted, a few feet behind him.

By now, Nik began to trot at a slow canter. Where he got the energy was a mystery. "Why do elephants have thumbs?" Jenn posed. Still nothing. She tripped on a piece of driftwood but managed not to fall. "To ring the bells on their bicycles!" Jenn giggled. This last one was so ridiculous that it always managed to crack him up. But not this time.

Although Jenn thought she detected a glimmer of a grin, Nik darted away too quickly for her to be sure. Now, he began to run. Run as fast as he could. Jenn tried her best but she couldn't catch up. Instead, she fell face first into the sand, but Nik didn't break his stride, didn't stop to help her.

There was only one more elephant joke in her arsenal that might work. Nik's absolute favorite. It was a wee bit racist, but still…

On her knees in the sand, Jenn screamed at the top of her lungs into the stale wind, "What's that sticky stuff between an elephant's toes?"

About twenty feet in front of her, Nik wheeled around on his heels. "Slow natives!" he shouted. Then his face cracked into a wide, toothless grin. Laughing uncontrollably, he stomped back to Jenn and helped her up.

"That one always gets you," she admitted, laughing too.

Nik put his arms around his wife. "You never give up," he said.

"Never," Jenn told him. "I don't know what keeps me going," she added. "But sometimes, I feel like a weird, supernatural force is pulling us up north."

"That's bullshit," Nik responded. "We're just too scared to lay down and die. We're running away."

"From what?"

"From the inevitable."

It was a nice night, as nice of a night as you get near the end of the world. The sun was setting all green and violet. Nik and Jenn decided to sleep on the beach because the weather was so mild.

After a quick supper of canned chili warmed over a fire, they took off their sneakers and socks and waded in the radioactive surf. It cooled their shoe bites, calluses, and whatnot. By the end of the day, their feet were always swollen and throbbing. Jenn's veins stood out like garter snakes under her skin. But after a good night's sleep, the swelling usually went down, and they felt better in the morning. Laguna Beach's waters soothed their aching toes and walking hand in hand soothed their aching hearts.

Epilogue

I'm sorry but I can't continue. I just read over what I've written so far and I think it's crap. It's stupid, sappy, corny and childish. And who really cares anyway?

Ω

Jenn pressed the backspace tab to delete what she'd written. Then after a breath, she retyped it, then typed some more.

Why am I writing about all these seemingly inconsequential people? The good and the bad. The pink El Dorado Lady. The Native American woman. The Methodists and Marvin.

I guess because no one is really inconsequential. Because it all matters. Because everyone deserves to be remembered. To have their story told. All of us. Especially when we're gone. And all of them are gone, every last one of them. I'm sure of it. I guess I'm their legacy, their inheritance, their biographer.

But it hurts too much to think back and remember. Here I am, finally in a nice place, and I am stumbling through this nightmare a second time. Often, I am short-tempered with Noah when he urges me on and Noah's been nothing but kind to me ever since we met.

All of you have been. Sometimes I wake up in my AquaHammock in the middle of the night, raving about bugs and Cheez Whiz. I wish I could forget (especially about Cheez Whiz!) but here I am, trying to remember the city where my fingernails started to fall off.

When I told Noah the only way I could possibly write my story was on a Xerox 630 Memorywriter with a proportionally-spaced Thesis printwheel, he magically produced one for me. How Noah managed to do this, I'll never know. But I purposely asked for something impossible so I wouldn't have to write this. And here I am, fingers poised above the Memorywriter's keys. I mean, the guy even managed to find a box full of five-and-a-half-inch floppy disks. Who does that?

To my amazement, first Noah presented me with the most advanced model in the Memorywriter line, a 645 complete with a screen and SpellCheck. But I refused it because it was such a pain in the ass to set margins and page length on this one.

Without even blinking an eye, Noah whisked away the 645 and gallantly gave me a 630 a few hours later. So much for buying myself some time! After making such a big stink, I had no excuse not to start my tale of woe. I felt like Rumpelstiltskin's princess or Colette, being prodded to write by her evil first husband. (Henry de Jouvenel even published her works under HIS name, the rat fink!)

But no one is forcing anyone to do anything here. There are no locks on the doors of this SpaceShifter, no threat of corporal punishment. There's only me and my painful recollections, a case of floppies and a putty-colored Xerox Memorywriter.

To make things easier, Noah suggested that I dictate the story to a literary droid. Or use a voice-to-text program. Or that he himself interview me. But I turned down these methods in favor of self-torture and wrestling the words into submission on my own. There is something so pleasing about feeling the story come out of my fingertips as I gaze through the big Plexiglas window at the Alpharian moonset. My love is out walking and I have nothing but time.

Yet no more words will come out of me, no matter how hard I squeeze. Not for the past few days. Maybe I need a laxative for my thoughts.

Or could it be that I'm unable to think these thoughts because I'm too comfortable here? Too almost-happy to remember the torment that seems light years away but, in another way, is fresh and runny like an infected wound. Maybe I'm just afraid. Of what, I don't know.

Ω

But in any case, I thought I owed you an explanation as to why I'm stopping. Why I can't go on. I'm sorry I've wasted your time with these hundred-some-odd pages. Try as I might to contribute wise observations that will save what remains of the universe, I only come up with silly ramblings. I'm only trying to give Noah what he wants. Or what Noah says you want—and need. But I don't think I'm capable.

Maybe I should stop thinking about you and start thinking about me. Of what I feel and need to say. Maybe I should stop worrying whether I've painted a clear enough picture of what Nik was like or if I've described my love for him adequately. Maybe I should stop judging my writing and just get on with the story.

Anyhow, love is a funny thing. No matter how warm and real and fuzzy it feels on the inside, it usually comes out looking pretty stupid on paper. Inadequate. That's why I think I should stop writing. Because I'm inadequate.

I told you from the start that I'm not a writer. I'm just a lowly former administrative assistant. Noah might propose, "No, you're not a writer, you're only human...and that's more than adequate to tell this story."

Noah believes coming to terms with one's emotions after living through a terrible experience, sharing it with others so that they might learn from it, is the most important thing a being could do. It's more important than thinking up catchy chapter titles, dangling participles, ignoring sentence structure, tenses and the senseless repetition of adjectives. I guess that makes sense. The most important thing is what you say and not how you say it. Right?

In my life on Earth, I sometimes pretended to be a writer. I crafted pitiful poetry as a melancholy teenager. (And I won that high-school contest, don't forget.) I belly-ached about my broken heart, as though I were the only thirteen-year-old who ever waited for a phone call on a Saturday night. A phone call that never came. But I guess these lovelorn teenage verses served the purpose of helping to keep me sane. Well, moderately sane. But at least they weren't set out for public scrutiny like a mutilated corpse. Like this story would be. My poems were written in a secret journal then ceremoniously torched after puberty. As perhaps I should have been.

Anyway, I'm sorry but I really can't continue. But thank you for listening.

Midlogue

It's been about three weeks since I've written in what's become known as my post-nuclear diary. That's the working title anyhow. Either that or "Cry of Silence," after the creepy "Outer Limits" episode. I'm sure I'll figure it out.

After much thought, many sleepless nights and several long strolls along the tarpits of Zeta—and a lot of not-so-gentle nudging from Noah—I picked up the project again. Noah playfully teased me and said that I had no choice; I had to finish writing it to earn my keep. Maybe he was only partly joking. But I knew for sure that he was only ribbing me when he said, "Or else, I'll send you back where you came from."

Which is impossible. Because there is no "back where I came from." Earth has since disintegrated. I watched it quietly self-destruct alongside the Alpharians, courtesy of wide-screen LaserVision. In horror, we saw my home planet fold up inside of itself like reverse origami. There was a puff of smoke, then nothing. It's like Earth never even existed at all. The people I treasured, the places I loved, all that I once knew...poof, gone in a quiet, anticlimactic flash.

Oddly enough, I felt very little. Just a momentary pang of grief, of loss, of regret. But on the other hand, I knew it was a long time coming. I knew that we deserved it. I knew that Earth was a silent victim to its people's multiple atrocities. And now it was over; She would suffer no more.

Ω

During my writing hiatus, several Alpharians gently encouraged me to continue writing. Every day or so, Noah would release a line or two from the work and project it on the maroon horizon for all to see. A teaser. Like a drug dealer releases a free line of coke every now and again: "Just a taste."

Like the daily Wordle, some seemed to look forward to these mini excerpts. To expect it, anticipate it. Our next-door neighbor Tran said that he and his family missed the tap-tap-tap of my fingertips on the Memorywriter's keyboard, which lulled them pleasantly to sleep each night like an electronic lullaby.

It really helped to know that the inhabitants of Alpha 49C truly cared about what happened on Earth. That they wanted to learn more about it. That they wanted to hear all the gory details. That they were afraid it could happen again. Here. To them. All I ask is that anyone reading this is patient with me, with my style of writing—or lack of it. Although I can't imagine the Alpharians being impatient or unkind about anything. They have been so welcoming to me and mine. No one can imagine how much this means.

Noah reminded me of what Camus once said: "The purpose of a writer is to keep civilization from destroying itself."

"Too late," I told him.

"Wait, I thought you weren't a writer," Noah twinkled.

Maybe that helped me turn the corner. Maybe not.

Ω

I did a great deal of soul-searching during the time I didn't write. A lot of organizing the events in my mind. Although I tried to convince myself that it no longer mattered, that I no longer mattered, that I no longer wanted to write, I still found myself jotting down notes on scraps of FleuroPaper. But I would usually fling these scraps of thought into the GarboVac, to be fragmented, vaporized then discarded into unfathomable space.

I did my best not to think of the past. But instead, the past thought of me, tugged on my jumpsuit sleeve and begged to be noticed. It was as if the faces were aching to be remembered, as if the emotions were begging to be recalled and validated.

For instance, I would be in the Meeting Chamber or at an Ice Cream Social, responding to BK or Stephen's query about the estimated height of the Laguna Beach cliffs or what shade of pink the walls of Linda's bedroom were painted. I would begin talking and the words would just tumble out of me in a waterfall. My companion would be captivated, as would others within earshot. A small crowd would gather and word would trickle throughout the room that Jenn was talking about Earth again. Soon, there would be a horseshoe of curious bodies gathered around me.

But the moment I realized that I was the center of attention, I would stop talking. I became self-conscious, no matter how much the listeners' eyes brimmed with goodwill or how much they prompted (begged) me to continue. But in that meganon before I realized I had an audience, I was lost. Lost in my own words.

"Please write this down," Jo-Ann urged me. "Please. It's important."

"To who?"

"To everyone," she said. "To the universe."

Yet, when I sat with a lilac Pilot Razor Point pen in hand or when I had my fingers curled above the keys of my beloved Memorywriter, nothing would come. (To buy myself even more time, I asked Noah to find me a box of a particular shade of purple Pilots, and to my amazement, he did. So, I had no excuse not to write since I now had an old-fangled typewriter and even older-fangled markers.) Writing about the Fall often made me feel downhearted but when I didn't write, I felt even worse. Unfinished and cramped up inside. It was a paradox. Like what Lloyd told Jack about women in The Shining: *"Can't live with them, can't live without them."*

Ω

My beloved tried to be sympathetic to my struggle but he was so busy that he sometimes seemed dismissive. On Alpha 49C, he was finally able to devote himself to one of his unrealized dreams: making music. After decades, he picked up the guitar again and now writes songs about the way he feels and that makes him feel good. He puts all his experiences to use, whether it be impotence or near-starvation. Or even recreating the sound of the sea lions, which I have tried to replicate for him. My guy's "Post-Nuclear Blues" is at the top of Alpha 49C's R&B charts. It's expected to be nominated for an Epsilon. He's currently in the studio, working on an album called "Fallout Rag."

You see, some people thrive in an apocalypse. Me, not so much.

Philip tries to be understanding. (Wait...did I explain who Philip was yet?) But he's having so much fun here that he can't quite relate to my struggles. Contrary to human beings' embarrassment at all things sexual, the Alpharians elevate sex to almost a religious adulation. Much like it was in ancient Mesopotamia, where sacred prostitution performed by women in temple spaces was revered. In that light, Philip has been commissioned to direct historic American and European sexual epics. He has taken me on as his P.A. (Shorthand for "production assistant" but more appropriately code for "pain in the ass" because of how cranky I've been).

The one about Napoleon and Josephine is tentatively titled Big Man under the Little Coat. *About Henry VIII:* Beneath the Belly. *(Rick Wakeman's blissful album* The Six Wives of Henry VIII *will be used as the score.) About John Smith and Pocahontas:* Brown Heat. *I fought like a demon against that last title. Besides it being overtly discriminatory, it's also disgusting. "Sounds like something that radiates from a Great Dane's poop," I argued.*

But Philip liked it. "Sour grapes," he smiled.

"Once a pornographer, always a pornographer," I told him.

Philip invited me to be his costar in the latter. Even though my beloved urged me to take Philip up on his offer, I refused. I think that maybe I just want to sulk. (Bringing to mind what I said in Laguna Beach about not falling in love with your own depression.) Philip called me a kvetch. *He called me a Debbie Downer. I relented somewhat, finally agreeing to a cameo in* Beneath the Belly, *in which Dick wore a prosthetic stomach. As Anne Boleyn's handmaiden, my lone line was: "Whatever you do, don't give him head!"*

Ω

For days on end, I bitched and moaned. I blamed my foul mood on PMS, which was quite impossible. Here I was, living in a virtual heaven and although I wasn't entirely unhappy, I wasn't happy either. Still, something gnawed away at me. I'm not sure what.

One day, when my man was shaving, he simply said, "Go with the flow." It was an annoying Earth cliché I'd heard many times before.

"What if the flow doesn't flow?" I asked.

He shrugged. "Go with that too."

Maybe that was the problem: I wasn't letting my thoughts flow. Instead, I was trying to force them into what I thought they should be. Into what I thought a memoir should look like. I was trying to contort them into shapes they weren't meant to take. I was constantly concerned about how others would perceive my account. I was always hyper-analyzing my words. Rereading my work. Criticizing the sentences as soon as they hit the page. Picking apart paragraphs. Am I overwriting? Underwriting? Both? Neither? 'Is this the way a journal should look,' I worried. Is it my imagination or does this first part sound clunky? Oh, the hell with it.

At first, I tried to date the passages. In doing that, I struggled to recall what day this or that might have happened. I put all sorts of restrictions on myself. Restrictions that held me back, constricted my creativity. And dating my experiences was ridiculous since time meant nothing when Nik and I were picking our way up the coast of California. Time wasn't relevant anymore. And days…well, sunrises and sunsets weren't lucidly defined.

Okay. Enough stalling. For the first time in my life, I'll try to be spontaneous. But first, just one more elephant joke to illustrate a theme:

Q: How do you make a sculpture of an elephant?
A: Just carve away what doesn't look like an elephant.

So, returning to the comfort and cloak of the third person and employing my best expository writing skills acquired from St. Rocco's Grammar School, New Utrecht High School and John Jay College, I will try my best to make an elephant.

Eleven

Starry Nights

Newport Harbor was a sight to behold. And not a good one. The AAA Tourbook noted that it had one of the biggest concentrations of pleasure craft in the nation. Nearly 9,000 boats were docked there. Nik and Jenn couldn't believe the astounding spectacle of thousands upon thousands of yachts and speedboats floating aimlessly throughout the harbor with no one to guide them. As the water ebbed, the boats thumped and scratched each other, marring paint and denting fiberglass. Millions of dollars disintegrated into the Pacific. But then again, money didn't mean anything anymore, did it?

Ω

After Newport, Nik and Jenn stopped at the Briggs Cunningham Automotive Museum on East Baker Street in Costa Mesa. It displayed more than 100 vehicles which had been in use from the early 1900s to the present. Or, more specifically, the past. Nik would have drooled if he had been able to—the fallout gave him blistery mouth sores and an incredibly dry oral cavity. For Jenn, the problem was just the opposite—she had an excess of saliva which made her spit constantly, like Patti Smith onstage.

At the Briggs Cunningham, there were many drool-able sports, classic and racing cars, including a 1927 Bugatti "Royalle," one of the largest and most expensive automobiles in the world. Nik and Jenn also saw the first sports car ever built, a Hispano-Suiza King Alfonso XIII. This was Nik's favorite vehicle at the museum. Jenn gave him all the time he needed to look around because so few things gave him pleasure in those days. And the Briggs Cunningham was Nirvana to a former auto mechanic like Nik.

Costa Mesa had been a budding cultural center before the blasts but was nipped in the bud post-kaboom. As was everyone and everything. All at once.

Ω

On the outskirts of Los Angeles, Nik and Jenn were faced with the decision of whether or not to go to Disneyland one last time. Anaheim was an easy detour inland, maybe twenty or so miles each way by their best estimation. But the forty miles there and back could seem like four hundred when you felt like crap. This would be Jenn's last chance to see the "It's a Small World" ride, her not-so-secret all-time fave. The syrupy song that accompanied the ride and played incessantly was a reason *not* to go, Nik said. One person's nostalgia is another person's annoyance, he pointed out.

However, Jenn didn't think the ride—or the earworm of a song— would be operational. And what kind of shape would those little multicultural, slightly stereotypical animatronic dolls be in? It would break Jenn's heart to see them in complete disrepair.

So, ultimately, they decided against a Disney detour because it would have been too sad. Too many dead families to deal with. It would have been the Flagstaff water wings clan to the umpteenth degree. Although Nik and Jenn had seen countless corpses during their voyage, children were still the most difficult to bear.

And who wanted to see dead cartoon characters? Mickey and Goofy and Donald lying in lifeless heaps. This would shatter all sorts of childhood illusions. Cartoon characters never died on TV or in the movies, even when they fell from cliffs or were flattened by giant anvils. Wile E. Coyote never caught the Roadrunner. Daffy Duck's beak always healed when riddled with bullet holes. Shudder to think how Disney's Baloo the Bear and *The Jungle Book* crew would react to radiation sickness. So, no, Nik and Jenn didn't go to Anaheim.

This meant that they also did not visit the Movieland Wax Museum, which was housed nearby, on Knott's Berry Farm. Plus, who could bear seeing Snoopy prone and unresponsive?

But the last time Nik and Jenn went to the wax museum, they'd had a blast, laughing, repeating lines from the cinematic scenes that were depicted there. Although people stared at them in shock/awe, the pair didn't care.

Unconcerned, Jenn and Nik reminisced about Charlie Allnut's rumbling stomach in *The African Queen* while Jenn did her best Katharine Hepburn impersonation, which was quite good. They ogled Sophia Loren's mounds, which seemed to defy gravity, and gestured at the bulge in the Duke's pants. (Nik swore it was an optical illusion created by his chaps but Jenn insisted Wayne wore a codpiece.) Yes, they'd enjoyed the Movieland admission price to its full extent, especially with the ten percent AAA discount.

But despite their good memories of the place, Nik and Jenn opted not to return to Movieland on this trip because they couldn't imagine the shape it was in now. Was Barbra Streisand a giant puddle of wax in her magnificent gold beaded *Hello, Dolly!* gown? Were Fred and Ginger a disintegrated pile of tails, spangles and taps? Nik and Jenn didn't want to know.

Ω

At Long Beach, they passed the Queen Mary, a sorrowful sight, lying on her side in the surf. It was like seeing someone you had once known in their glory days who was now in a heartbreaking state of decay. Although your memory recorded that person as being exquisite, upon your return years later, they were very much changed. Perhaps it was because they were in the throes of a disease which ate them from the inside out. Or perhaps it was from their own neglect. But whatever the reason, their face was cobwebbed with lines, and they were almost beyond recognition.

This was the sort of condition they found the Queen Mary, except she was a ship instead of a person. Her deck was rusting. Chunks were rotted away, probably the effects of radioactivity upon the metal. Her hull was covered with a thick layer of phosphorescent slime. She glowed in the dark like a specter. Nik and Jenn chose to sleep on a nearby pier that evening. The ship served as their eerie nightlight. But before they closed their eyes, they watched the sun slash the sky as it set.

That night, the fallout seemed to irritate the very skin of the sky, making the setting sun oddly beautiful. It threw out brazen reds, flaming pinks, bruised purples and a fiery pinwheel of oranges. It was quietly extraordinary. Nik and Jenn lay on their backs, holding hands, studying the colors until the shades sifted away. After the sun went down, the sky was navy and the stars were as big as streetlights.

Still staring up, Nik said, "Vincent would like this sky."

"I think he would too," Jenn agreed. She felt very content that they didn't have to move again until morning, happy to be with Nik and van Gogh and the sky that was pregnant with light. Maybe skies like this were a reward for walking miles and miles all the livelong day. Although Nik and Jenn wore brand new Reeboks, still, their feet bled.

Ω

The further Nik and Jenn moved north, the more they talked about their lives before the decimation. In a weird way, it soothed them. They repeated the story of how they met, talked of the zebra finches they had at home in Brooklyn and of their nieces and nephews, all of whom they loved dearly and knew they'd never see again.

Studying the night sky, Jenn and Nik recalled their wedding. Of course, each of them knew the details but they liked hearing the story on each other's lips. Even lips riddled with cuts and sores due to their poor post-nuclear nutritional intake. (Though oddly, Jenn's lips were unmarred, plump and bee stung as though she'd had Botox.) They were like children wanting to listen to a fairy tale over and over because they loved it so much, even the scary parts.

"Our wedding was so perfect," Jenn told Nik. "So romantic. Just the way I dreamed it would be. Not a three-ring circus but an intimate, special day."

"Remember how the sun shone?" Nik asked her.

Jenn nodded. "The sky was such a bright, sharp blue. Like my grandfather's eyes."

"A cloudless, 9/11 blue," Nik recalled. "A perfect spring day." He yawned, trying to fight the lassitude that invaded his pores. "We said our vows under that weeping willow on Amity Street."

"It was just after the sun rose," Jenn finished. "Because Celeste had to get to work by nine. I'm glad she stood up for us."

"I am too. And Judge Howard sandwiched us in before morning court. It all worked out perfectly." Nik paused, smiling with the memory. "There was no drama, no Aunt Sophie complaining that she didn't want to sit at the same table as Cousin Margie. No one whining that the band was too loud...because there was no band."

"And no bitter old lady sobbing because her son, her only son, was marrying a *shiksa...oy vey iz mir.*" Jenn clutched her heart for theatrics and emphasis.

Nik rubbed his wife's shoulder. "My mother grew to love you, Jenn."

"But not before she hurt me. Hurt us. All I did was love her son. What's so terrible about that?" Jenn pushed. Several years later, it still hurt.

"It's over now," Nik said quietly. "Let it go. Let it rest."

But Jenn couldn't, not even now. It had been resting for too long, dormant, like Mount Fuji. "The only reason I put up with it was because she was your mother," Jenn continued, beating that long-dead horse. "But there were times when I thought I would crumble from her hating me. Other times, I thought I should just leave you. I wondered if I were a rotten person to stay because she kept telling me to go. There must have been something wrong with me, I thought. That I was selfish or stupid or both not to leave."

"What changed the way you felt?" Nik wondered.

"It was Serena," Jenn sighed. "She told me that no matter what your mother did or said to me, I needed to respect her."

"Why?"

"Because your mother gave birth to the man I love," Jenn said simply. "And I should always be grateful to her for that." Nik kissed the side of Jenn's head and coiled his finger around one of her curls. "Because without you, I would be lost, Nik," Jenn tagged on.

He scratched his nose reflectively. "Once, my mom told me that she wished she could have had an abortion when she was pregnant with me. That I was a mistake. But she was a religious Jew and didn't believe in abortions."

Jenn was struck speechless but knew she had to say something. "I'm so sorry, Niky, I..."

But Nik wasn't looking for sympathy, just validation, so he continued. "And she wasn't even mad at me. We weren't even fighting.

She said it in a very matter-of-fact way. Like we were talking about the weather or something harmless like the price of bananas. She said it so calmly, just like that. Did I ever tell you this before, Jenn?"

"No," she conceded. "And I wish you hadn't."

Nik fisted his eyes, which were already red and swollen. They always were, especially the one that was practically sealed shut. "She really loved you toward the end, you know," he said, almost in a whisper.

"I know," Jenn told him. "It just bothers me that she wasted so much time hating me."

As was his fashion, Nik dealt with this issue as he usually did—by changing the subject. "Yeah, it was such a nice ceremony," he said, skipping back to their wedding day. "Celeste outdid herself. The sweet things she told Judge JP about us…"

"Well, C loves us both, you know."

"I know. And we love her right back," Nik pointed out. "Loved her, I mean," he corrected. "I think she's gone now."

Jenn ignored his last statement and plowed forward. "We had cannoli and espresso afterwards."

"At Monteleone's on Court Street."

"I miss Monteleone's," Nik said. "And cannoli. And Celeste. I miss…"

Something shot soundlessly across the heavens, leaving an arc of light in its wake. Was it a shooting star or a guided missile? Whatever it was, it was magical, fleeting, then just a shadow, a memory. "Niky?" Jenn asked.

"Mmmm," he said.

"Are you still afraid you might be dying?"

"Might be?" he countered. "We're all dying, Jennifer. Just some of us faster than others."

"You know what I mean. It's just that…you talk so much about the past."

"I didn't want to tell you," Nik began. "But I think I'm going blind."

"I thought your eye was getting better."

He shook his head. "I can't see out of it at all. And the other one…I didn't want to worry you."

Jenn sat up and looked into Nik's eyes, as if she could stare down his impending sightlessness, as though she could scare it off. It was so dark on the pier that his eyes were just black blobs. "Are you sure?" she pushed. "You used to have eyes like a hawk."

"Hawk eyes, hawk nose," Nik tried to joke. But it fell flat.

Jenn started to sniffle. "Hey, it's not that bad," Nik consoled her. "I just noticed that my vision has gotten worse over the past month."

"Since when?"

"Since San Diego, I think."

For distance, Jenn wore brown tortoiseshell glasses that made her look like a compassionate owl. Nik's eyesight had always been razor-sharp without visual aids of any kind. "I was hoping I might die from something else before I went totally blind," Nik said plainly. He was all business, without emotion.

He paused, tested the air, tasting it, almost, before he continued, carefully choosing his words because he knew they would wound his wife. "I was thinking that maybe…maybe you should go ahead without me."

Jenn gasped at the suggestion. "Don't you understand? Without you, there is no me."

"But I don't want to hold you back," Nik pushed.

"Hold me back from what?" Jenn dug her head into Nik's shoulder. "I couldn't live without you," she whispered.

"You might have to learn," he told her softly.

Jenn cried herself to sleep under a shield of stars.

Ω

Although there was a full moon at San Pedro, no grunion came ashore to spawn. The AAA Tourbook kindly explained that grunions were a small fish (genus *leuresthes tenuis*) native to the warm coastal waters of California and Mexico. During high tides and full moons, grunions had semiaquatic sex like randy, blue-gray Esther Williamses and Johnny Weissmullers.

The next day, Jenn led Nik through the Cabrillo Marine Museum and read to him from the little cards in front of each exhibit. He feigned interest; Jenn could see that his thoughts were elsewhere. Why would he want to hear about dioramas that were a big blur to him? But at least it was something to do. Something to pass the time. A distraction from reality.

Now that Jenn knew about Nik's failing vision, he permitted her to help him. For some reason, telling her that he was going blind freed him to do so. Made him feel less scared, maybe. The audio headphones at the museum didn't work so Jenn gladly played tour guide. She didn't mind; she especially liked seeing Nik smile at the sound of her voice.

Jenn wasn't sure how much he could see of the exhibits and was afraid to ask. Not that there was much to see anyway. All of the marine life in the tanks were dead; the smell was almost unbearable but they bore it.

Nik and Jenn also tried whale-watching from the shore but saw nothing when they watched. No tiny creatures stirred in the tidepools. They'd both loved Steinbeck's *Cannery Row* and looked forward to seeing the starfish that inhabited tidepools. (The main character in that book was a scientist who studied these ever-changing little bodies of water.) But there were no starfish or sea anemones. None to see and none for Nik to touch.

Ω

By the halo of a Durabeam lantern, Jenn read to Nik that night. The only reading material they had besides their trusty AAA Tourbook was a pocket-sized New Testament Jenn had taken from the Marina Inn at Dana Point. Nik asked her to share especially-chilling passages from Revelations. Although he was raised Jewish, he gave a nod of respect to the New Testament, with all its forgiveness, turning the other cheek and its shortage of smiting. But Revelations pulled no punches and took no prisoners. He liked that.

It was really quite magnificent, lying on a deserted beach in a deserted world. The sky was as colorful as a black eye as Jenn read, *"'Woe to those who give suck during those times...'"*

Nik interrupted. "I'm glad we never had kids." Jenn looked at him, not getting the connection at first. "These are the times Revelations is referring to," he explained. "I wouldn't want any child of mine to go through this."

Jenn had a lightning flash of water wings, nose clips, sticky juice boxes and fruit rollups. Then it passed.

Nik and Jenn always wanted to have a baby but somehow, in the eighteen months they actively tried, it never happened. Jenn's cycles were painfully regular and her basal body temperature charts were characteristic in their rises and dips. She'd been afraid to go to her OB-GYN, to try and figure out what was wrong. Perhaps she didn't want to be splayed open, poked and examined under a microscope.

Or injected with a water-soluble dye and then x-rayed. Or have a periscope speared into her navel while four liters of carbon dioxide was pumped into her abdomen. She'd heard about these atrocities from friends and didn't want to subject herself to them, unless as a last resort.

Jenn also didn't want her husband's sperm to be scrutinized, his tadpoles counted, analyzed and clocked for speed. She didn't want conception to take place in a laboratory's Petri dish or a test tube. Jenn did not want a lot of things. But what she did want was a baby.

Perhaps the problem was that Jenn thought about being pregnant too much. Not just the getting pregnant part but the whole shebang. She worried that she wouldn't be a good mother. She worried that her child would grow up to hate her, to be a serial killer, despite all the love and support she and Nik gave it. Jenn ached at the sight of babies and grew jealous when she saw smugly pregnant ladies with swollen ankles.

No one knew Jenn's silent sorrow. No one except Nik. Although he tried to share the burden with her, he couldn't fully grasp its full extent because it wasn't his body that refused to sprout a seedling; it was hers.

Everyone told Jenn, "Just don't think about it." But that was easier said than done. Because by consciously trying *not* to think about it, you actually were thinking about it. And how could you *not* think about it when you had to take your temperature each morning before you even got up to pee? And when you were fertile, you had to make love on cue every other day, whether you wanted to or not. You had to be constantly aware of what day it was in your cycle and test the viscosity of your fluids. It was like trying to maintain a finicky German sports car.

People had all sorts of "helpful" hints regarding conception. Everything short of using a turkey baster. For instance:

- prop a pillow under your tush before, during and after sex;
- use two pillows;
- bend your knees and put your feet flat against the wall;
- do it every day;
- do it every other day;
- wait five days;
- wait a week;
- go on a cholesterol-free diet;

- go on a keto diet;
- abstain from alcohol;
- have a pre-coital glass of wine to help you relax;
- do it on your knees;
- do it on your belly;
- drape your legs over his shoulders and stay like that
  for 30 minutes;
- stay like that for an hour;
- pray;
- meditate;
- douche with white vinegar;
- douche with baking soda;
- don't douche at all.

There were so many contradictions that Nik and Jenn didn't know what to do anymore. It got so that they didn't even want to have sex, that's how complicated the act had become. If there was no hope of having a child, Jenn just wanted the hope to end. Because that hope was destroying her.

Then there were the people who shrugged off infertility as though it were a convoluted blessing. "You're lucky you can't have kids," Aunt Lil told Jenn. "They're a pain in the ass. All they'll do is break your heart." Others would confess that they wished they'd never had children because it ruined their life, their marriage. Some actually had the nerve to tell Jenn that she was fortunate to be childless. Those were the worst comments of all.

The sight of curled, pink baby toes had the power to make Jenn teary. She tried to convince herself that she was a worthwhile human being—that she was important without being a breeder, that she made a decent salary, was a good person, made a nice home. But if she couldn't make a baby, what good was she? Jenn wasn't fulfilling her purpose, her obligation as a woman. Being a baby-maker had been drilled into Jenn's head since she was a child. Not in words but in glances, in emotions, in what was left unsaid but implied. A staunch feminist, Jenn was still guilty of letting the obsolete, middle-class mores she grew up with affect her sense of self.

Plus, not being able to have a baby just wasn't fair, Jenn bemoaned silently to herself. Stupid people, mean people, drug addicts, ax murders…they could all have babies. Why not Jenn?

Ω

When feelings like this drowned her, Jenn tried to remember what Dr. Song had told her. He told her that she would have a beautiful baby. But when?

Dr. Song was the acupuncturist who was trying to make Jenn's body more receptive to carrying a child by sticking needles into her ankles and knees. Dr. Song brewed her special teas made with brittle Chinese flowers, snail shells and ginseng that tasted like dirt. He burned *moxa* in bowl on her belly, explaining, "It warms the womb."

As the mugwort's sweet, red fragrance filled the air, Jenn felt so relaxed and safe with that lovely, little man in his cramped Elizabeth Street apartment. And this wasn't an easy task, to feel safe with smoke furling from your belly and needles in your legs.

Dr. Song was an intuitive and spiritual being. The first time Jenn stepped into his home office, he felt her pulse and looked at her tongue. Then he asked, "Why do you worry so much?" How could he know this by just looking at her fuzzy tongue? A chill pimpled Jenn's scalp. Then, with his fingertips, Dr. Song showed Jenn the size of the cyst on her right ovary. His crude measurement matched what a bladder-bursting sonogram and two internal proddings had revealed. It would be difficult to heal the cyst because she'd had it for so long, Dr. Song told Jenn, but he believed he could.

Jenn's Filipina OB-GYN said she'd give her a month to get holistic treatment, then would reexamine her. If the cyst was still there after the acupuncture and herbs, Dr. RP recommended surgically removing it, and possibly her ovary. This would lessen her chance of having a baby even more.

So, Dr. Song set to work. Jenn visited him twice a week. It was tedious. It was expensive but Nik and Jenn figured it was worth a shot. As she lay there on the acupuncturist's sofa, pierced and smoking, Dr. Song told her stories about his boyhood in China. About riding a horse through the mountains with a striking young lady clinging to his waist. "Why didn't I marry that girl?" he lamented some sixty years later.

Listening to Dr. Song, Jenn would smile and breathe in the scent of the herbs that crowded the shelves of his living room office in jars and crumpled brown paper bags. Dried plants hung from strings, suspended from the cracked white ceiling, drying in the overheated room.

Sometimes Dr. Song and Jenn would chew on strips of ginseng. The root made the body strong, he said. "I need it because I am old," Dr. Song began. "And you need it because you are weak." The good doctor confided in Jenn that their friend Justin's wife forbade Dr. Song to give Justin ginseng root because it made him horny. Jenn and Dr. Song chuckled naughtily about this.

During Chinese New Year, white people watched fireworks on the streets of Chinatown and the avenues choked with sulfur. While this madness transpired, Jenn was safely tucked away on Dr. Song's sofa, enjoying "golden eggs" with him to celebrate the holiday. Golden eggs were what he called tea leaf eggs. They were boiled in a mixture of black tea, soy sauce and star anise. Eating them on the Chinese New Year brought luck, he said. So, they ate.

Another time, Dr. Song did Jenn's I Ching reading, tossing dice, alternately sighing and smiling at the results each new throw brought. When Jenn voiced fears that she would never have a baby, Dr. Song smiled softly; it was as though he could actually *see* the child. "Oh, you will have a beautiful baby," he assured her again.

"Boy? Girl?" Jenn pushed.

But Dr. Song ignored her. This is what he did when he didn't want to answer a question, when he thought the asker couldn't bear the answer yet…he pretended that he suddenly had forgotten English.

Jenn tried to remember Dr. Song's words when her body swelled and cramped with premenstrual fluids. She tried not to cry on the toilet when her period came, as regular as the changing of the guard at Buckingham Palace. Jenn tried to remember Dr. Song's words, even now, in the Aftermath. But ultimately, in the prequel, she thought Dr. Song was wrong. About the baby, about everything.

Ω

Nik and Jenn had hoped the trip to California would be so relaxing and pleasant that she might conceive. If not, then they vowed to go to a fertility specialist when they got back home. But now, they'd never go back because there was no "back" to get home to.

Jenn thought about the oddest things at the oddest times. To remember her friendship with an elderly Chinese man at the dawn of destruction had no rhyme or reason as she read to Nik from Revelations on a war-torn West Coast beach town. But not much made sense in the end of days.

"Read to me about the angels," Nik told Jenn in San Pedro.

"For a Jew, you sure know a lot about the New Testament," she quipped, flipping through Revelations.

But Nik wasn't really Jewish. He was everything: he was all people, all religions. Nik truly was a child of God. He understood people's feelings and respected them, perhaps because he felt so deeply himself. He understood people's sadness, perhaps because he had seen so much sadness himself. He was an empath to the umpteenth degree.

Yes, Jenn loved the old Nik, but she loved the new Nik too. Maybe even more so. Maybe because both Niks were fading.

Jenn fumbled through the crackly pages. "Chapter Eight," he said.

She found it, cleared her throat, and read. *" '...and the third part of the creatures which were in the sea and had life died; and the third part of all ships were destroyed... ' "*

"What about the fourth angel?" Nik asked.

"Hold your horses," Jenn said. "I'm getting to that." She skimmed down the page to find it. *" 'And the fourth angel sounded, and the third part of the sun was smited and the third part of the moon, and the third part of the stars; so as the third part of them was darkened, and the day shone not for a third part of it, and the night was likewise. ' "*

Nik knew these verses by heart, but he had Jenn read them to him, regardless. "Then locusts and scorpions tormented them, and they did not die. They were tormented for five months," Nik recalled. "Do you think we'll last five months, Jennifer?"

He didn't give her a chance to answer. Nik grabbed the pocket-sized book from Jenn's hands. He held it an inch from his eye. *" 'And in those days, shall men seek death, and shall not find it; and shall desire to die, and death shall flee from them. ' "*

Nik stared at Jenn, out of breath, out of prospects, out of time. "What do you want me to say, Nikolai?" Jenn asked him.

"I don't know," he said. "I just don't know anymore." He closed the New Testament and threw it into the bleak, black ocean.

Twelve

Starry Days

During a marathon, many runners begin to urinate blood. When this happened to Nik and Jenn, she tried to convince him not to worry, that it was "normal" given their abnormal circumstances. Although the pair weren't running, only walking like fatigued snails, they were pushing their bodies to the limit. Proper hydration was nearly impossible with potable water being so scarce. So, Nik and Jenn's kidneys went into overdrive. So much so that they ached.

First, Jenn started seeing droplets of blood in her urine, then she began practically peeing it. Nik still hadn't noticed the addition of winged Maxi Pads to her wardrobe. (Adding to the joy of survival, Jenn had started to menstruate nonstop.) There was no need for them to see each other naked in their skin-and-bones states. On the road, when nature called, Jenn not-so-demurely ducked behind leafless bushes. Yes, everything was dying, not just them.

Ω

Jenn and Nik didn't see the sun for what could have been five days. Give or take. Days tended to mesh; they couldn't be sure when one ended and another began. After a stretch of sunlessness, it grew foggy.

125

So foggy, it was like moving through a veil of moss. This didn't help their navigational skills, especially Nik's. He was still working with one eye and fading vision in the "good" one. Although Jenn's eyesight was sharper than ever with her glasses, she still possessed her unbelievably poor sense of direction. Some things never changed.

At Rancho Palos Verdes, they stopped at the Point Vicente Interpretive Center. Jenn was proud she managed to get them there with only a few turnarounds. Except there wasn't much to interpret once they arrived. The landslide exhibit had gone and slid. A pile of cake crumble stood beneath where it used to be.

From the second-floor observation deck, Nik and Jenn studied the coastline. It was all a big blur to Nik, and Jenn didn't have the heart to describe it to him. So, when he asked how bad it was, she lied. "Not as bad as I thought." In fact, it was worse than she had imagined.

As Jenn scrutinized the coast, she heard Jimi Hendrix's version of "The Star-Spangled Banner" in her cerebrum. Not the studio cut but the live version from the Woodstock album. With a tremolo bar to stretch and loosen the strings, phase shifter and wah-wah pedals to make the notes weep, feedback from the amps plus equal helpings of compression and distortion, Hendrix made airplanes scream overhead; he made bombs drop with music.

At the time, people thought Hendrix's interpretation of America's national anthem was unpatriotic, but truly, it was just the opposite. To others, like Jenn, Jimi's masterpiece was filled with love and fear: multifaceted love for a country and dark fear that the country was headed in the wrong direction. Making war on a guitar was safer than waging a real war. Hendrix succeeded in fighting an anti-war war on his white Fender Stratocaster.

There was no beauty to be found in the Rancho Palos Verdes panorama, however. The cliffs had tumbled into the sea. Dead creatures lined the shoreline; it was impossible to determine what they once were. The scene was a tapestry of gray sadness: black/gray water, white/gray sky. Jenn's eyes burned with tears. "No, it's not that bad," she fibbed to Nik a second time.

"I can tell by the sound of your voice that it is," he said dolefully.

One good thing came from their visit, though. In Palos Verdes, Nik discovered that he could see almost perfectly through one of those viewing machines that lined Point Vicente's observation deck. This gave them the idea that binoculars might help Nik see better. They tried it out with the pair he carried in his pack. It worked like a charm. In town, they picked up an extra set of binocs when they came upon California Pro Sports.

Ω

With Jenn's misguided guidance, after many wrong turns and senseless corkscrews, they finally alighted in Lomita. It means "little hill" in Spanish. Nik insisted on visiting the train museum, which came as no surprise to Jenn. In Brooklyn, the Tavernas had an "N" scale Lionel train setup, complete with plastic houses, rubber trees and tiny people with outstretched arms to flag down the 8:10 to Pleasantville.

Nik was always picking up an extra bush or water tower at TrainWorld on Avenue M. He said that he liked creating a flawless, little world he had complete control over. It made a twisted sort of sense, especially given the sort of childhood he'd had (i.e., loveless). So, Jenn didn't protest when Nik said that he wanted to go to the train museum on Woodward Avenue.

Inside, scale models, photographs and paintings of locomotives were arranged throughout the rooms. They saw an all-wood 1910 Union Pacific caboose and a 1902 Mogul locomotive. A sign outside informed them that picnicking was permitted on the grounds, so they picnicked with something like delight, though very little gave them true delight. They ate liverwurst sandwiches and drank Dr. Brown's cream soda on the crisp, brown lawn. It was as close to pleasant as they could muster amid world annihilation.

Ω

The profusion of dead bodies became less profuse the further they traveled north. Seeing stinky carcasses became more routine, like spotting a pigeon or a homeless person had been "before." Before the fall of mankind, that is. At a certain point, you just stopped noticing them. Stepping over and around corpses in various stages of decay became one of Nik and Jenn's daily exercises. Like abs or leg work at Planet Fitness, corpse-stepping built up the hamstrings.

The couple had long given up visiting people's homes. It was one thing finding random bodies scattered along the PCH but quite another coming across an entire family linked in suicide in their Torrance living room beside a splash of shiny, happy group pics. Other times, the couple found people prone in their beds, barely alive. This was even worse than finding them dead.

One man in a simple ranch home in San Joaquin Hills begged Nik to hold a sofa cushion over his head. "I promise I won't fight," the man rasped. "I have no more fight left in me."

When Nik and Jenn turned to leave, the fellow shouted, "Dude, one man to another...I'm begging you." Jenn left and noiselessly closed the door behind her. Nik came out a few minutes later, avoiding her gaze. She never asked what had happened after she left because truly, she didn't want to know.

Ω

There were no muscles on Muscle Beach in Venice. The chinning bars were vacant. The canals had dried out and reeked like ripe trash. Besides their canals, Venice was also known for its miles of bicycle paths that coiled along the beach. Jenn and Nik tried to find two bicycles that were in working order. "It's not the same as stealing personal property," Nik began to explain again as they approached the sheds where Peddle Pusher's rentals were stored. "It's just like raiding Kmart because these bikes were owned by companies not by people," Nik stressed. "It's less personal."

Jenn still wasn't entirely convinced.

But they didn't have to face that moral dilemma because others who came before them had that very same idea. There were no operational bicycles left. Just bits and pieces, really. One might be missing a wheel. Another might be missing a chain. Another, a gear shift. But since Nik was a car mechanic, bikes were usually a snap for him to Jenga together. Except for these bikes. The parts fell apart in his hands as soon as Nik started working on them. He muttered something about the effects of radiation on the mechanisms, then gave up. The same could be said for cars. They were rendered inoperable in the Aftermath.

Some might ponder that if Nik were such a fine mechanic, why didn't he fix a car enough for them to use? The reasons for this were many, including:

1) he was almost blind;
2) the nuclear fallout wreaked havoc on the newer vehicles' electronics;
3) fuel was either nonexistent or fuel pumps ceased working.

So, foot power was the best, sometimes the only, option to get from one place to another.

Ω

When Nik and Jenn hobbled away from Pedal Pushers, she wailed like an overtired child on a never-ending hike, "But my feet hurt..."

Nik rubbed the small of Jenn's back as they walked down Venice Beach's deserted bicycle path. "I know. Mine too."

They passed the shuttered Fig Tree, where they'd once had memorable breakfasts with their friend Dolores. They passed Paloma Street, where Dolores had lived. Paloma meant "dove," which used to be a symbol for peace. They opted not to rap on Dolores's second-story door to see if she was still alive; the answer was evident, and they couldn't handle seeing proof.

Nik knew Jenn wasn't crying because her feet hurt. She was crying because she missed Dolores. She was crying because she missed everything and everyone, Dolores's daughter Viva too. Nik let his wife cry but still stroked her back as they walked.

Jenn was also crying because she missed her bike. She missed her early morning rides along Brooklyn's deserted streets. Jenn would be up and out by six-thirty, cycling through Sheepshead Bay, rumbling across the wooden slats of the Ocean Avenue Bridge and weaving through the exclusive community of Manhattan Beach. She relished rising at that ungodly hour and pedaling forty-five tranquil minutes before showering, putting on her makeup, getting dressed and taking the B train to the office. The mauve dawn was her reward.

During the winter months as Jenn rode, the sky was still dark. But the streets were all hers, uncluttered with pedestrians or cars. She'd plop on her headset to be serenaded by Nat King Cole walking his baby back home and getting face powder on his vest. Or else, Jenn blasted David Bowie complaining about a mellow Black chick who just put his spine out of place.

Besides sunrises, Jenn also witnessed other snippets of life that usually went unnoticed later in the day. Like the jade plant cuttings in Styrofoam cups trying to take root in a drycleaner's window. Or the crew from the Elsie K who stood on the sidewalk calling out for customers before their seven o'clock fishing boat launch. "Blues! Mackerel!" they would shout. When Jenn whizzed by, sometimes they proposed, "Come on, baby. Come along for the ride." She would laugh in response. Sometimes Jenn would see a musty, old man in Brighton Beach who sat on a bench and ate tuna fish from the can with his fingers. *At least it isn't cat food,* she would think to herself as she whipped past.

Once, Jenn saw an ambulance on Manhattan Beach's concrete boardwalk as she swerved past the boarded-up umbrella concession stand. At first, her heart sunk, assuming a vagrant had frozen to death on the sand or perhaps, yet another rat-bitten body had washed up on the jetty. But that morning, it turned out the EMS workers had only stopped to watch the sunrise. This made Jenn smile. In her own private spot, a few hundred feet away, she watched daybreak too.

Ω

Years later, thousands of miles away, in another time, Jenn could still remember the details of that particular morning's sky: the stripes in the blue above the glow of the Marine Park Bridge, the lights of the Elsie K as it chugged toward Rockaway Inlet. Jenn's eyes welled with tears as she looked; it was so damned lovely, and she felt so damned content at that moment. Yes, the streets of Brooklyn could often be enchanting. The streets where Jenn had come of age, where she'd skinned her knees on concrete, where she'd evolved from "Jennifer" to "Jenny" to "Jenn."

A wave of homesickness overtook her on the Venice Bicycle Path, several years hence. She pined away for a Meshuga Phil poppyseed bagel. She longed for one more glimpse of the majestic New York City skyline, both pre and post the Twin Towers. She wanted to pick up just one more pack of Trident from Pushpa's store, where the sprightly Indian woman greeted each and every customer with a cheerful, "Hello, love!"

Striding toward Santa Monica from Venice with Nik's arm looped around her shoulder, Jenn even missed the fetid, half-wrecked, dangerous subways. She missed the bands that played at the Times Square station as part of the Music Under New York program. She even missed the junkie who begged for coins on the B train and spewed the same unchanging sob story for years—he was perpetually looking for a job, his twins were always newborn and he had HVI. (Jenn never had the heart to inform him that it was HIV and gave him whatever coins she happened to have in her pocket anyway.) She admired the beggar's pluck and dedication, being on the B at seven-thirty a.m. every weekday morning, with more regularity than others go to their nine-to-five office jobs.

Jenn even missed the MTA, who bestowed occasional gifts on working stiffs like her. She loved the kaleidoscope images they planted on the Brooklyn side of the Joralemon Street tunnel before the train made its way into Manhattan. Jenn looked forward to seeing the mural on every ride, holding her breath in anticipation as the train approached.

The MTA hired an artist to create a delightful art installation between the subway's girders, a scene of striking colors and wild geometric shapes. As the train sped (or crawled) past the girders' slats, the colors and shapes appeared to move. Triangle people danced and rockets blasted into the darkness. Straphangers would watch CPWon's animated art display with bemused expressions on their faces, almost smiling.

However, none of this was there anymore. But it sure was grand. All of it, the good and the bad. Grand while it lasted.

Thirteen

Sunset

J enn and Nik ventured to Beverly Hills, wandering up and down the winding streets with a "Map of the Stars' Homes" in hand. But all the mansions looked the same: sumptuous and desolate. It seemed senseless to continue their star quest since there were no stars anymore. So, what was the sense of viewing their homes? Nik and Jenn didn't think there was any sense at all, so they stopped. These buildings just became structures of glass and brick and Spanish tile and stucco, just like any other structures.

Jenn managed to get Nik and herself back to Sunset Boulevard. On that infamous street, she turned to her husband and said, "Mr. DeMille, I'm ready for my closeup." Of course, he got the movie reference. Their life together was one long series of movie references. They both laughed at the line of dialogue from *Sunset Boulevard* because Jenn's once almost-pretty face was mottled with sores. (Yes, after a brief respite, the fallout began to wreak havoc upon Jenn's countenance again.) In truth, maybe it wasn't really funny; more tragic. Their senses of humor were getting darker and darker by the step.

Nik and Jenn deliberated about whether to go to Burbank. Nik was all for it, if for no other reason than out of respect to Johnny Carson. Who, Nik argued, had given him almost as much late-night fun as Jenn had. No disrespect to Johnny, but Jenn argued that it wasn't worth the twenty-six plus miles there and back. "What else do we have to do but walk?" Nik posed.

But they did compromise and go a bit further inland to Hollywood. To visit their many friends along Hollywood Boulevard in the form of their tarnished stars. They were still there, still somewhat intact.

Since Jenn and Nik were so near, they couldn't resist going to the Porn Star Walk of Fame outside of Hustler's Hollywood. There were Sunset Thomas's prints and Jenna Jameson's too. "Look," Jenn told Niky, gesturing to the brass-rimmed palm prints of her favorite blue movie star, Dick Truehard. Once more, Dick's comely, studly ghost graced Nik and Jenn on this pilgrimage. They were amazed at how delicate Dick's handprints looked, topped off with long, graceful piano-playing fingers. Since his eyesight was so bad, Nik put his own hands into Dick's prints to "see" them better. Nik's were much bigger, his fingers fatter. "Mechanic's hands," Jenn said, kissing the tip of her husband's callused pointer.

Ω

Mann's Chinese Theater was still standing. It looked stately and old, the way the pair remembered it from the last time they visited, although the red and green paint was now peeling. It was probably from the toxic atmosphere rather than from neglect. Some of the famous cement hand and footprints were gone and others were in the process of being gone. Nik and Jenn paused briefly to watch a man chisel Trigger's hoofprints away from Roy's footprints. The offending fellow offered no explanation, and they didn't ask.

With the help of his binoculars, Nik found Marilyn Monroe's imprints. Then he placed his Reeboked feet on top of her high heels. "They were so tiny," he remarked. For a moment, Jenn thought Nik was going to cry but he didn't, even when he said very quietly, "She had such a hard life."

Jenn was tempted to ask him what he thought *they* were having but she held back. Jenn was becoming very good at holding back. True, Marilyn was thrice married but Jenn was radioactive. Didn't that count for something? Jenn's sarcasm reigned supreme, even now. She often had to reel it in to spare Nik. It felt good to spare his feelings in small ways.

As enjoyable as this diversion was, Nik and Jenn couldn't wait
to get out of Hollywood. That's how bad the stench was. They tied
bandanas over their nose clips and mouths like banditos and hightailed
it out of there as fast as they could. Nik reasoned that LA's legendary
smog probably trapped the aroma of death and decay like a cap. A
small number of fires blazed. The couple managed to avoid them,
enjoying the brief warmth as they quickly passed. Because in true,
unpredictable, post-apocalypse fashion, the weather had grown
cool again.

Ω

On Highland, they saw a riot in progress down one of the side streets.
The road sign had been knocked down, as well as the traffic lights.
They were tipped over, lopped off and/or shattered. Perhaps there
were fifty or more people blobbing the street off Highland, screaming
at the top of their lungs, breaking windows. Their faces were covered
by masks to hide their identities. But not surgical masks as they'd
donned during the pandemics, but the theatrical kind. The Frankenstein
Monster ransacked Rite Aid, aided by Scarlett O'Hara. Nancy Reagan
set fire to a Prius. A witch hurled rocks at a steel and glass office
building. Baby Yoda strangled the Mummy. And so on.

As Ronald Reagan threw a police barricade into the blaze, he
shouted something about outlawing the Soviet Union. "Too late,"
Nik said.

"The bombing begins in five minutes," President Ronnie muttered.
Others covered their faces with t-shirts or had other articles of clothing
fastened over their noses and mouths. Whether it was to hide their
identities or to better breathe the rancid air was up for debate. Their
eyes were either sizzling with rage or else blank, lifeless. Like crazy
people's eyes. Except they probably weren't insane, just angry. Angry
at the way things had turned out. As Jenn led Nik away by the elbow,
they managed to pass the mob unnoticed.

On Wilshire, they paused to take a short rest and regroup. After
the riot, Nik and Jenn agreed that they didn't feel like sightseeing
anymore. So, they took a left onto Santa Monica and headed toward
the Pacific Coast Highway again. "Remember the municipal pier?"
Jenn asked Nik. "And the carousel?" She loved carousels.

"Sure, I remember," Nik said.

The AAA Tourbook said that Santa Monica was about fifteen miles away. They took it slow because that was the only way they could take it. Riding double on a discarded scooter made the voyage a little faster until one of its wheels clanked off. Then it was back to traveling on foot again.

Ω

The shops near the Santa Monica Pier were empty, many with their rolldown gates still locked against vandals. The arcades were quiet, Pac-Man and Donkey Kong mercifully laid to rest. Electronic boings and boops no longer sounded in the hollow rooms. Atomic dust had collected in the long Skee-Ball alleys. No one manned the electronic cranes, trying to grab cheesy mini stuffed animals from the glass tanks. It was just Jenn and Nik wandering about and a few lackadaisical wharf rats. Speculation was that rats would survive even an atomic holocaust and it turned out to be true.

Behind a wall of Plexiglas was Santa Monica's charming carousel with its colorful, hand-carved wooden horses. Jenn had always loved the merry-go-round as a child, and it carried through to adulthood. Coney Island had a gorgeous one which Nik and Jenn visited as frequently as others visited the Cyclone. They were typically the only adults not accompanied by children on B&B Carousell at Coney. Jenn and Nik always rode side by side, holding hands. Of primary importance was choosing the right horse: one with a friendly disposition who was adequately decorated. Even more important was finding two unoccupied stallions regaled in suitable finery, situated one beside the other.

In dystopian Santa Monica, Jenn chose a gray steed with a friendly face plus a mane and tail of soft ivory floss. A sky-blue plume rose from its noble head. Nik helped Jenn up into the saddle, which was in its highest position. Then he felt his way to the center of the carousel where all the gears and controls were.

Somehow, he knew the right lever to pull, perhaps because he had seen so many hairy-armed carnies rev up so many carousels in the past. With both hands, Nik put all his weight onto the lever and the calliope began its chant. Lights flashed and ribbons of rainbow bled through the hazy, foggy air. The theme to *Carousel* enveloped Jenn as she whirled.

Being on a merry-go-round had always filled Jenn with unbridled joy. Though this ride was bittersweet; she wondered if it would be her last. Jenn tried to feel happy, she really did, but these were strange days and "happy" was nowhere to be found. In her scrambled mind, *Carousel*'s theme song made her think of the musical itself and another popular song from it.

"You'll Never Walk Alone" is all about muscling your way through a storm and holding your head up high when you are scared shitless. That's when it dawned on Jenn that she and Nik had been walking through not a storm but a hurricane.

Just as Jenn grew sadder and sadder thinking of this, she felt the weight of her husband mounting the horse beside her. Between his near-blindness and the speed of the ride, Jenn didn't how Nik managed this feat. But somehow, he did. Nik always had a knack for accomplishing the impossible. He sat majestically atop an angry-looking steed who was jet black and had smoldering eyes that glared out from behind a blood-red mask. Nik looked frail yet fierce, bald and brave and resolute and determined.

He and Jenn went around and around on the merry-go-round. Wall-eyed, Nik stood in his horse's stirrups and reached for the brass ring. He missed. On each revolution, he tried, and tried again. And missed again. The clown on the wall seemed to be snickering at him but this didn't stop Nik. He made more attempts, most fruitless. Finally, he succeeded and waved the brass ring high above his head in triumph. Then he turned to Jenn and smiled.

It was the most beautiful smile Jenn had ever seen.

Nik's left eye was puffed shut. His skin was ragged. He was missing several teeth. But this was the face of the man she loved and it was a good face, even amid all its ravages. When Nik smiled at Jenn, she smiled back, a big, wide, goofy grin.

Nik slid the tarnished brass ring onto Jenn's bony wrist as they traced around on the carousel in neat circles. They spun until they grew dizzy. With Nik now on the ride, there was no way to stop the merry-go-round and they were growing weary of spinning. So, they slipped down from their horses. When Jenn cried, "Go!" they went, leaping off the wooden platform and rolling into the dirt, leaving the carousel behind, still spinning wildly.

When they were a few blocks away, there was a great crash as the carousel apparently imploded and the calliope crashed to the ground.

Fourteen

Cliffhanger

According to Jenn's AAA bible, the cliffs in Malibu were supposed to be breathtaking. But like the Queen Mary in Long Beach, they had the mark of a woman who had once been a stunner but was now almost unrecognizable.

Malibu had been a special place for special people to gather: both legit actors and people who made skinflicks. (Not that the latter weren't "legit" in their own right. In Jenn and Nik's book, porn folks were even more legit because they were more honest, more real.) Point in fact: a great number of high-budget, upscale blue movies were made in Malibu's quaint, not-so-little homes. Renting them out for adult film shoots helped pay the mortgage, you see.

The city was important because important people did important things there. Madonna and Sean Penn were married there. Bo Derek once had a home there. So did Lady Gaga. There was even a stretch of sand called Billionaire's Beach, which was comprised of 70 or so exclusive, luxury residences. A veritable Who's Who of the jet set. Except none of it meant anything "after."

Malibu used to be a peaceful place where creative types felt comfortable to create whatever they felt moved to create. But now, the noteworthy abodes had slid into the sea, which was, for some reason, roiling like a furious cup of Lipton tea. The artists and writers and actors and pornographers were no longer painting, writing, acting and pornografying. And that was a sorry thing.

Ω

Nik and Jenn spent the night in a modest multi-million-dollar home built on stilts over the sand. The California king bed was arranged upon a thoughtfully-placed platform to optimize its view of the Pacific. It was lovely. Except for the squirrels.

In Malibu, Jenn and Nik saw an alarming number of squirrels. These were not your average, run-of-the-mill squirrels, however. Because of the fallout, they were extremely tiny. You could heap at least four of them into a tablespoon. At first, Jenn thought they were some sort of insect, flightless flies, perhaps. But they turned out to be post-apocalypse rodents. Small as they were, people still ate them. A woman Nik and Jenn passed on Unname Street swore they were a delicacy. She even shared a recipe of sorts:

> For a quick, humane kill, pinch their teeny squirrel skulls between your thumb and index fingers, give a little squeeze. Then strip back their pelt, much like you would peel a grape. (With practice, you became quite adept at this and could unskin a squirrellette in less than a minute, the woman claimed.) If there's power, pop them into the microwave for ten seconds, sprinkle them with za'atar seasoning, if you can find it, and enjoy, bones and all. Micro-squirrels have a delicate crunch, like softshell crabs, Unname Woman said. Or else, you could pop a handful of them into a slice of Reynold's Wrap and cook them over an open fire. "They taste just like peanuts," the woman declared, mangled hand to heart.

But Nik and Jenn couldn't bring themselves to eat the mini squirrels, no matter how hungry they were.

Earlier, they'd run into a fellow who had a campfire going on Escondido Beach. The guy flipped the mini critters into his gullet as he talked to Nik and Jenn, who were mildly horrified. The squirrellette bones sounded like popcorn crunching against his teeth. But unlike popcorn popping, this was not a pleasant sound. Before she turned away, Jenn thought she spied bits of crimson spittle in the corners of the man's mouth.

But similar to calf's brains or squab, Nik and Jenn couldn't eat these little buggers, even with ketchup. It was an extension of what some hunters called "The Bambi Complex:" some people just couldn't eat anything cute. Except maybe each other. Once upon a time.

Ω

Kicking up sand en route to Ventura, Nik and Jenn had the following surreal conversation:

> Jenn: Niky, I think we should eat healthier. Man cannot live on thawed Swanson TV dinners and Spaghetti O's alone.
> Nik laughs.
> Jenn: I'm serious.
> Nik: Sure, coming from someone who used to heat spring water in the microwave to make herbal tea.
> Jenn: So? What was wrong with that?
> Nik: You don't see the irony? The contradiction?
> Jenn: No.
> Nik: Taking something organic and preparing it with electromagnetic radiation?
> Jenn: (sighing) All I want is for us to eat better.
> Nik: Why?
> Jenn: Because we'll feel better. Because it's healthier.
> Nik: How can you talk about health now?
> Jenn: Well, what should I do? Give up completely and eat dirt?
> Nik: Just face it, Jenn.
> Jenn: Face what?
> Nik: Look, there's no point in stopping me from using aerosol sprays because of the fluorocarbons either.
> Jenn: Why?
> Nik: It's a little too late to be worrying about the ozone layer, don't you think?
> Jenn: Oh, so we're back to the Renuzit incident again? If you ask me, you're a little too spray-happy.
> Nik: I didn't ask you, did I? Hey, if it makes me happy, let me do it. There isn't much that makes me happy anymore.

Jenn: Especially not me.
Nik: Jenn, you know what I meant…
Jenn: Newsflash for Nikoli…Shit is *supposed to* smell like shit. Go easy on the Renuzit, okay?
Nik: Dude, that was no ordinary shit. That was some doomsday shit!

By then, Nik and Jenn burst out laughing at the absurdity of their exchange. This is how most of their arguments ended: in laughter. Amid all the heat and ire, they realized how foolish they were being. And also, that they ultimately loved each other, even now, especially now. So what was the sense in fighting about air fresheners or whether canned peas were actually a valid vegetable.

But in Ventura, both Nik and Jenn were pretty fed up with life in general. With what life had become. They had constantly been at each other's sides for weeks upon end. In even the best of circumstances, this would have been difficult for anyone but now, feeling weak and sick didn't help their dispositions.

Nik and Jenn ceremoniously shook hands and were friends again. But they still weren't really talking until Jenn tried to pick another fight. Out of nowhere, she said:

Jenn: You're mean. You're meaner than Mean Joe Greene. You're meaner than Jamie Gillis, the meanest guy in porn.
Nik: I know who Jamie Gillis is. Everyone knows who Jamie Gillis is.
Jenn: You're…
Nik: Jenn, I'm dying.
Jenn: Well, so am I. But that's no reason to be mean. In the immortal words of Elvis Presley, 'Don't be cruel.'
Nik: You probably hate me.
Jenn: I could never hate you, Niky. I might not like you sometimes, but I always love you.

There was nothing much to say after that.
The not-so-dynamic duo fell silent again. They kept walking. With each tortured step, Jenn's mind formed a rich quilt of thoughts. Vivid memories flooded in and out of her head for no particular reason. She

let them come, welcomed the kaleidoscope of images as she and Nik ambled along. Here are some of them:

- A terrified, afraid-of-heights Nik at her side on the Ferris wheel at Great Adventure;
- A laughing Nik trying to teach Jenn how to swim properly, one hand on her belly, the other cupping her vulva; and
- A sexypants Nik trying to recreate the pensive pose of Michelangelo's David—and failing miserably.

Jenn laughed out loud at the last memory. "What?" Nik wondered. "Nothing," she said.

Before the blasts, she often teased Nik about how much he reminded her of that Renaissance masterpiece, but he was quite shy about it, unable to deal with the image of himself as handsome or desirable.

When Nik was an awkward teenager, the girls used to make fun of him, of his unapologetic nose, prominent ears, buck teeth (before braces). Years later, he still felt like that gawky teenager. Doesn't everyone? Even though Nik's body had filled out and his teeth were impossibly straight, he still felt like that skinny boy with rabbit teeth who grew up in a forlorn, cookie-cutter house in the gutter of Long Island.

Why couldn't people escape the ghosts of their childhoods, no matter how many years pass? Why couldn't they see how beautiful they were until they weren't beautiful anymore?

Somewhere outside of Ventura, Jenn pondered that paradox and laughed out loud again. "What?" Nik said.

"Nothing," she told him once more.

Ω

At Port Hueneme, Jenn and Nik visited the CEC/Seabee Museum. Her Uncle Frankie had been a Seabee, so Jenn insisted they go. Nik had no problem with this since he had loved her feisty Uncle Frankie too. Uncle Frankie's brother Tom had been part of the CEC, another reason to go. "The Seabees' slogan was 'Can do!'" Jenn told Nik. The significance of "Can do!" wasn't lost on these atomic-age crusaders in their current circumstances. They were "Can-doing" every day.

There was no one to give Nik and Jenn a visitors' pass at the Ventura gate so they strolled right in. On the base, they saw models of Seabees equipment, war scenes, weapons and uniforms. There were also arts and crafts by and about the Civil Engineer Corps and the Navy Seabees. The items on display were about wars. There were rooms and rooms of objects. The couple soon became bored and left the way they came in.

Ω

On Mission Hill, the Padre Serra Cross was still standing, though tilted. Had there been an earthquake they somehow missed? The original cross was erected on that spot by Father Junipero Serra on March 31, 1782, even before the mission was built. That first cross decayed and collapsed sometime in the 1860s. Many things had collapsed since then, namely civilization.

As the AAA Tourbook said, the view from Mission Hill was impressive. But on that particular day, it was the wrong kind of impressive. Instead of being inspiring, it was bleak. The earth below looked forlorn from Nik and Jenn's vantage point beside the cross, as though even Jesus Christ Himself had deserted it. Perhaps He had.

Nik and Jenn stumbled down the hill, her leading him by the elbow. They turned to look back at the Padre Serra Cross, Nik through his binocs and Jenn through her hopelessly-clear bespectacled eyes. It looked abandoned. Like a flag on an empty battlefield. Futile.

They forged north.

Fifteen

If I Were a Carpenter

"Didn't Serena live in Carpinteria when Jesse was a baby?" Jenn asked Nik when they passed the small green marker on Highway 101.

"Yeth," Nik answered. He had recently lost his other front tooth and tripped over the easiest of words like a lisping eight-year-old. When Nik's tooth popped out, instead of being upset, he left it under his pillow at the Inn on the Beach. Like a thermonuclear tooth fairy, Jenn replaced Nik's chopper with a hundred-dollar bill. In those days, money was both plentiful and useless. They could even use it to wipe their butts but didn't; Cottonelle was softer but harder to find.

Jenn struggled not to giggle when Nik talked but he sounded so funny that sometimes even he laughed at himself.

Ω

Carpinteria didn't look anything like their friend Serena would have remembered it, even if she could remember anything. Rows of houses were flattened. To Nik and Jenn's untrained eyes, it didn't appear as though the destruction was from a direct hit but from human mischief. Most likely, fire. There was charred wood and earth and the distinct

aroma of a burned-out campfire. It became stronger the more
they walked.

After going several blocks, Nik and Jenn discovered the cause
of the mischief when they stumbled upon an angry mob. But due to
the effects of the fallout, the mob didn't look like a mob at all.
Because they didn't look exactly human. They looked more like
unfinished people.

This crowd was perhaps twenty times larger than the one Nik
and Jenn had encountered in Hollywood. They so seldom saw people
that the throng's sheer size jarred them. But seeing so many people
in the midst of riotous behavior jarred them even more. Nik and Jenn
were helplessly drawn into the centrifuge, sucked into the middle of
the multitude without using their own motor power. It was like being
propelled onto a crowded subway train during rush hour. Your feet
didn't exactly move; you were pushed ahead by inertia.

Everyone was congregated around the Abbey Garden Cactus and
Succulent Nursery's huge greenhouse. The AAA Tourbook boasted that
the nursery had one of the biggest selections of cacti and succulents
under one roof. But not currently, because there *was* no roof. The
wood frame structure was aflame. All windows within reach had been
smashed by rocks, shoes and other people's heads. Panes higher up
cracked like fireworks from the heat. It was a spectacle to behold,
horrifying in one way yet fascinating in another. Nik and Jenn stood
there aghast, watching in sickened awe.

It all seemed so ridiculous. Yes, people were rioting, but against
what? And for what purpose? To what end? They screamed and
yelled and punched. But who were they fighting? Everyone was in
pain. Everyone was outraged and enraged. There was no purpose in
making yourself even more miserable than you already were by raging
against the machine. It would change nothing. Holding hands, Nik and
Jenn observed the uprising unfolding in silent horror, unable to pull
themselves away to a safe harbor.

Witnessing destruction in progress was unexplainably exciting.
It was like watching a fight at a hockey game (or in the stands) or
eavesdropping on a civilized argument at the next restaurant table.
Mentally, morally, you knew it was wrong, that you shouldn't be
partaking/listening/watching. But for some reason, you allowed
yourself to be sucked in. You enjoyed the threat of violence on some
sick, visceral level, as much as it shamed you.

Ω

The cacti and succulents burning at the Abbey smelled very similar to the micro-squirrels cooking in a campfire. Not entirely unpleasant but wrong somehow. The singular voices of each person in the crowd melded together and rose to a dull, collective roar as they threw stones and broke whatever glass remained. In small and insufficient ways, the mob rebelled against the state of the state. By yelling. By shattering things. By setting a building on fire and watching it burn.

The glass panels near the top of the greenhouse popped and splattered. The sound was pleasant; it tinkled like wind chimes. "When the heat inside gets too intense," Nik explained, "the glass suffers a thermal break."

"Kind of like with people," Jenn told him. Nik didn't get the reference at first. He screwed up his face in confusion. "People take the pressure until it becomes too much," she continued. "Then they explode. Like now."

Nik nodded. "Let's get out of here," he said. "I have a feeling this is about to get ugly."

"Uglier," Jenn corrected.

Suddenly, a body pushed between Nik and Jenn and their clasped fingers unclasped. Another body filled the space. And another. The void between Jenn and Nik grew. More bodies pushed into the gap between them. Jenn looked into Nik's eyes and then into the flames. The greenhouse was collapsing. It did so in slow motion, as if buckling at the knees. The way the World Trade Center's South Tower had collapsed. The wood between the Abbey's glass split and chucked into the air like oversized matchsticks. The entire structure fell like a house of cards. Jenn's body was heaved forward with the wave of bodies.

Then came a horrible crash. The sound of metal and lumber and glass breaking and twisting and shattering. Jenn ran to avoid getting crushed, tears streaming down her face. She had lost Nik!

Ω

An old song coursed through Jenn's head as she ran with the crowd and sobbed. The one by Fats Domino about his tears falling like rain and it being a shame. "What a shame! What a shame! What a shame!"

said the Cat in the Hat. Jenn remembered reading that book to Serena's Jesse when he was a kid. What a goddamn shame it was indeed. All of it.

Jenn managed to break away from the melee a few blocks from the collapse. She ducked into an alley. The air was thick, globbed with smoke that wedged down her throat, making it difficult to breathe. Jenn covered her mouth and nose with the neck of her t-shirt. At last, she stopped gasping for air but her chest still heaved. Jenn had no clue where she'd gotten the strength to run. But she hoped Nik had found that same strength, that he'd fled in the same direction.

Her muddled mind couldn't decide which was worse: the death screams or the taint of burning flesh. Suffice to say that it was a tie.

Jenn's knees buckled as she crept out of the alley to look for her husband. She wailed Nik's name along with the others wailing other people's names. It was impossible to see more than a few feet ahead. Jenn soon decided that her search, that her screaming, was an exercise in futility. She figured it would be best to wait for the air to clear, for the dust to settle. So, she made her way back to the alley and found a place to roost.

Jenn must have fallen asleep because the next thing she knew, the sun was glittering. And it hadn't shone for a handful of days. The sky was the color of the Gowanus Canal back in Brooklyn, a sick, pukey green. But at least the smoke had dissipated in Carpinteria.

She walked around aimlessly in search of her husband. Once, Jenn thought she heard Nik's voice coming from under the rubble, but it was nothing. Just the wind or a figment of her crumbling mind.

Jenn didn't have the courage to dig through the debris. She convinced herself not to search for Nik in the wreckage because she didn't have the fortitude—physical or mental—to find his corpse. So, Jenn wandered through Carpinteria's empty, broken streets, streets that their friends Serena and Jesse had once loved, the place where Jesse had learned to walk, then to run.

But what if Nik, like Jenn, had survived?

$$\Omega$$

Jenn discovered many things as she boomeranged through Carpinteria, but she did not find Nik. At what point should she give in? Jenn wasn't sure but she knew she hadn't reached that point yet.

Here are two things Jenn found:

- a fluorescent pink wagon with no wheels; and
- two people making love on the beach at dusk.

Jenn crouched behind a dry, wilted bush and watched the amorous pair, but not in a lascivious way. It was more out of curiosity, amazement. Jenn was fascinated that people could literally find love among the post-nuclear ruins. It was woeful and gentle and passionate. There were hoarse words and soft whispers that Jenn couldn't hear from her hiding spot. It didn't even matter that the two people making love were men. Jenn thought it was quite magnificent that anyone could manage the mechanics of sex now. Especially now.

One gentleman was partially paralyzed, and his right eye was sunken. Perhaps he'd lost it. The limbs on his left side hung there dead but he more than compensated for this deficiency with the limbs on his right. Sores covered the other man's almost-bald head. But the two were very tender with each other. You could tell they were grateful for the other's existence. They gazed into their mate's ravaged face with love. Then the bald one helped the paralyzed one onto his knees, propped him up with a pillow of sand he'd built. Jenn watched solemnly until they finished. Then she burst into silent tears.

Part of Jenn wanted to join the men but not for sex—for affection, for connection. She felt so deserted and desolate hunkered down like a wolf in the gloom. Jenn wanted to be held too. Needed to be held. To feel loved. Afterwards, the men sat side by side in the sand and watched the sunset. It was especially fetching that night. All swollen and purple and pink like sherbet.

Ω

After Jenn finished searching for Nik in Carpinteria, she waited. She waited for him for days. She waited until no one was left. Even the two men she'd watched on the beach were gone. That was when Jenn decided to leave too. In the back of her heart, she had blind faith that she would meet Nik along the road. But her mind didn't really believe her heart. Nik was almost blind and weaker than a newborn pup. No, Nik was definitely gone. In one way or another. Jenn was afraid she might never see him again.

All alone, Jenn worried as she walked. If Nik were dead, Jenn would never know. She would never find his body. And if he were still alive, was he looking for her? Or was he glad to be rid of her? Maybe he'd grown sick of Jenn's ugly face, she thought. Maybe Nik wasn't lost at all. Maybe he had run away because he was so sick of her.

Although Jenn felt lonely and alone, she still walked. She couldn't remember what it had been like to be Nik-less because she hadn't been without Nik for more than a decade. There was a hollowness inside and that hollowness said "No Nik, no Nik" with every beat of her fragmented heart.

At times, Jenn wanted to die. But instead, Jenn walked. Maybe walking was a kind of death for her. It was painful. It was senseless. Jenn didn't know where she was going, even though she still had the AAA Tourbook in her backpack.

Led by her epically poor sense of direction, Jenn headed what she imagined was north. She knew that the sun still rose in the east and set in the west. That is, when the sun made an appearance. So, in the morning, she walked with the sun over her right shoulder…that was east. *By midday, the sun should be right above my head*, she reasoned. And when the sun was setting, it would be over her left shoulder. On cloudy or rainy days, her sun-charting navigational method was much more challenging but somehow, Jenn traveled north. The highway signs helped but many had fallen. Others were decorated with shotgun holes and were otherwise destroyed.

Jenn trod more slowly without Nik by her side. He had a quick step, even half blind. He possessed what was classified as Type A habits on the cardiac risk factor calculator. Besides moving quickly, Nik often clenched his fists and ground his teeth (when he had them), asleep or awake. He moved at almost a jog, even when he had no particular place to go.

Trekking solo, Jenn sometimes sang to chase away the doldrums, but it was a different type of song she sang than when she was with Nik. Nothing cheerful or uplifting. Not even "Ol' Man River." Like Judy Garland in *A Star is Born,* Jenn was a one-man woman searching for the man who got away. And as Judy professed, there was nothing sadder than that.

Ω

It was far too quiet without another set of footsteps beside hers.
Although she still traveled the same road as she had with Nik, US 101
seemed different. It was a very desolate, solitary few weeks for Jenn.
She seemed to notice more, feel more. Jenn absorbed each interesting
rock formation, mourned each dead thing beside the road. She reveled
in each tree that was still standing and still green. Jenn wondered if this
increased height of perception was because she was glad to be alive or
afraid to be alone. To die alone.

She didn't want to be one of those half-decomposed bodies on the
side of the road that jaded travelers just stepped over. Miserable, putrid
corpses with no one to grieve for them. With Nik gone, no one knew
Jenn anymore. No one loved her anymore. And when the time came,
no one would care enough to bury her, she lamented.

Despite this minor detail, Jenn began to fantasize about the
best way to die. She ticked off each one like a shopping list item
in her mind.

She X-ed off slitting her wrists in a bathtub filled with gritty water
like Georgina Spelvin had done in *The Devil in Miss Jones*. Too stagy.

Jumping from a high place was messy and not entirely foolproof.
Jenn recalled reading an interview with a man who'd survived his leap
from the Golden Gate Bridge. The interviewer asked when the man
knew he'd made a mistake, and he responded: "The second my foot
left the railing."

Since there was obviously no good way to die, Jenn invented one
which she called "Death by Chocolate."

Imagine: a vat ten feet high and just as deep filled with bubbling
fudge. A chocolate fountain on steroids. Imagine: stripping naked,
climbing down a ladder and jumping in. Imagine: the sensation of
being surrounded by warm, liquid sugar as it exquisitely fills all your
crevices, oozes between your toes and soothes your ruined skin.

Slowly, Jenn would sink into the hot chocolate, unable to stay
afloat any longer. She would part her lips and the dark syrupiness
would ease down the back of her throat like a persistent lover. Soon,
she would be unable to breathe but she wouldn't panic. Instead, she
would open her mouth wider and allow her body to submerge to the
bottom of the tub. Her nostrils would fill, her throat would clog but she
wouldn't despair. Instead, she would drift off, engulfed by saccharinity.
And then, nothing. Sweet nothing.

That's the way she fantasized it, anyway.

Ω

When Jenn wasn't obsessing about dying, she tried singing songs to keep her going. That damned Judy Garland kept drawing her in. But Jenn's voice sounded flat and empty without Nik harmonizing off key. So most often, the cry of silence accompanied her footfall. Nothing more.

By that point, Jenn began to write down some of her thoughts. Not quite a diary or a journal, just something to fill the hollow hours. To occupy her mind when she was too awake to sleep, and her body was too tired to move. Jenn felt the need to talk to someone, even if it wasn't really talking, just words in a notebook. She had a favorite purple Pilot marker that she used to fill a blue-lined assignment pad. But soon enough, Jenn lost the Pilot somewhere on the road and never started another journal.

Although singing out loud was permissible, Jenn couldn't bring herself to talk out loud. To talk to herself would signify that she really *was* crazy. Only maybe she really was. Crazy, that is. But if she were, who but she would know?

Sixteen

New Beginning

T he way the AAA Tourbook described Santa Barbara; it sounded like a crusty library tome instead of a city. "Resting on a narrow shelf…" it began.

As Jenn limped along, the Santa Ynez Mountains peeked over her right shoulder and the Pacific Ocean was at her left. She marveled at the difference between rock and water. One was always changing and the other, seemingly changeless. *Niky would like this,* she thought. *If he could still see.*

Ω

Jenn didn't stay long in Santa Barbara. At one time, it was an appealing place but presently, it was just a swirl of cracked adobe and tumbled Spanish missions. At that crux in Jenn's unaccompanied odyssey, she was still certain that Nik was only footsteps away, but old churches were not the sort of thing that interested him, even when they were still standing. Not her Jewish boy from Brooklyn. Temples, maybe, but not churches. Jenn was anxious to get someplace else because she couldn't imagine Nik dawdling there. That's why she breezed through Santa Barbara so quickly.

One plus came of her brief visit to SB: Jenn found a skateboard on East Cabrillo. It was in the middle of nowhere, with no expired owners in sight. Nik always warned about the bad juju associated with taking dead people's things, but Jenn didn't sense any negative vibes. *And how much worse can my juju get?* she reasoned. The bottom line was that Jenn's feet hurt and she was sick of walking. So, she rolled.

And as she rolled, Jenn also thought. She often lived in the past because the present was so disagreeable. Jenn took comfort in remembering.

As she got used to the skateboard, her mind trundled back to Seagate. There, her friend Serena's oldest son had taught Jenn how to ride a board. She tried hard to remember Jesse's coaching as she pushed with one foot and glided away from Santa Barbara. Step, glide. Step, glide. Eventually, Jenn's glides became longer. She found her body's center just as Jesse had instructed and soon, didn't even wobble.

Before long, Jenn learned that she could sail along nicely on the straightaways, but the curves and hills were still tricky. Often, she walked up the slight slopes, board in hand. Before she got the hang of navigating bumps, she fell several times. Jenn's poor knees bled through her torn jeans. Her palms were pretty scraped up too. Jenn was a mess and Nik had the damned aloe vera gel.

$$\Omega$$

Nik. Nik. Nik. Jenn constantly thought of Nik. Throughout everything, she still wore her wedding band as well as the ring Nik had given her when he asked her to marry him. Since Jenn had lost so much weight, she had to wrap several Band-Aids around each ring to keep them from sliding off her skeletal fingers but still, she wore them.

Hers was not a traditional engagement ring; it wasn't a diamond. Because Nik was just starting out in his trade, he didn't have much money. He chose a stone with meaning instead of a mindless blood diamond. The stone in Jenn's ring was called a black star—it was a mahogany-toned sapphire that reminded him of Jenn's puppy-brown eyes. The rock was set in platinum, polished to a sheen with a bright six-pointed marking in its center.

Walking up the coast together, Nik and Jenn would study the odd shadows the thermonuclear atmosphere cast into the black star.

Sometimes the sky was blue. Sometimes purple. Sometimes pea green. But whatever the shade, it reflected in the face of the black star like a dazzling thought. In the aftermath of an atomic "accident," gems shone their most brilliant. It reminded Jenn of the adage about always finding something good in something bad. She tried hard to do this but mostly she failed. Especially after she lost Nik.

Maneuvering the skateboard, Jenn scooted and stared at her black star as she hummed "Body and Soul" and got the hell out of Dodge (aka Santa Barbara).

Ω

Continuing up US 101, Jenn alternated between boarding and walking. Sometimes Jenn studied her black star and thought of her lost husband, of how they were a matched pair of people who were now unmatched. On four wheels, Jenn sped toward Solvang with a burst of unheard-of energy. She was sure she would find Nik wandering among Solvang's empty streets. If he were alive. This was because Nik had a fetishlike appreciation for Danish rye and Solvang was noted for both its Danish ancestry and its bakeries. Reaching Solvang became a goal of Jenn and Nik's on their walk north. Solvang became their culinary oasis, their prayer. 'If I could have a slab of lox on a hunk of Danish rye,' Nik would say, 'then I'd die happy.'

'Please don't talk about dying,' Jenn would plead. 'Or food.'

'Please, please, please let me find some Danish rye in Solvang,' he would pray to the god of smoked fish and brown bread, ignoring her. As Jenn skateboarded, she recalled the many things she herself had ever prayed for:

- to *please* not have Mrs. Curry call on her in the fourth grade (she always did);
- to *please* let him call (the 'him' always changed depending on her latest prepubescent crush);
- to *please* not let her be pregnant at seventeen (she wasn't);
- to *please* let her get pregnant at thirty (she didn't);
- to *please* let her get that job at Apple (she didn't);
- to *please* let Nik's mom live after her stroke (she did).

In retrospect, some of these entreaties seemed foolish. If only Jenn could have saved all her past prayers and wishbones and crossed her fingers for the one, big, gigantic prayer that she would find Nik in Solvang. Then at least she wouldn't die alone.

Ω

With hope pushing Jenn forward, she reached Solvang in record time. Forty-five miles northwest of Santa Barbara, Solvang used to have a population of thirty-one hundred and still stood, although deserted, at an altitude of four hundred and ninety-five feet. So said the AAA Tourbook, which Jenn found herself consulting more and more now that she was alone.

But there were no Danes in Solvang. No rye either. No lox. The bakeries that once perfumed the streets with Nordic delicacies like cured fish and crusty delights like bread and rolls were abandoned. Not even a crumb or a cracker remained. Jenn howled Nik's name in the empty avenues until her esophagus was raw. And no one answered.

And even worse, Jenn lost one of her agate earrings somewhere in Solvang. She didn't know where, so she couldn't look. It felt as though she were losing Nik little by little, more and more.

Jenn's heart felt punctured. She had poured so much expectation into visiting that silly, little Scandinavian town. And now that there was no hope left, she felt an empty space where the hope had been.

But something goaded Jenn on. Something pulled her north. Something unnamable. Something caused her not to lose faith. A sense that her story was left unfinished. That something was waiting. Jenn had no idea what this "something" was, but it caused her not to acquiesce. Not yet.

Ω

Another source of hope for Jenn was a town perhaps fifty miles north of Solvang: Morro Bay. Jenn remembered it as being delightful. She remembered spending a deliriously happy few days there with Nik when they visited it on their honeymoon. Somehow, Jenn thought this same happiness would be waiting for her in Morro Bay again. She knew that if Nik were still alive, he would feel the same way and would somehow get there too. That he would be waiting for her there.

I will get my raggedy ass to Morro Bay, Jenn kept reassuring herself. *I will drag myself there if necessary.*

If Jenn didn't run into Nik en route to Morro Bay, she was convinced he would be waiting for her in Room 9 of the Anchor Inn. The telepathy that comes from sleeping soundly between the same sheets as someone for a decade told Jenn that this would be so. And if that supposed telepathy just turned out to be a wishful dream, so be it. Maybe Morro Bay would be where Jenn would end it all. If she had the strength.

Ω

Approximately two miles outside of Solvang, Jenn saw that gay couple she'd spied on in Carpinteria. But this time, they were not gay, as in happy. And they were not making love. Jenn wondered how the paralyzed one had managed to travel all this way, some forty-plus miles. Maybe on the other one's back. There was no wheelchair in sight. Perhaps they'd found a Ralph's shopping cart. But Jenn didn't ask how they got there. It didn't seem appropriate. And besides, it didn't really matter.

The one with the sores all over his body was still alive. He solemnly, silently dug a hole for his partner's body. Jenn stopped and helped him dig, using her hands and the scraps of fingernails she had left. She and the man didn't talk. They didn't need to. He thanked her with the look in his eyes.

Halfway through, Jenn stopped digging and held his hand for a moment. Both were crying as they resumed clawing the earth with their bare hands. As they tunneled deeper, the soil grew wet, though not with their tears. They burrowed further still into the sandy soil.

Suddenly, the man spoke. Jenn started at the sound of his words because she hadn't heard someone talk for days. His voice was nice, a rich baritone. "We have to make sure there's enough room for two bodies," he said plainly. Jenn nodded, thinking that another unseen friend had died too. Except this was not the case.

Although Jenn and the man didn't discuss his partner, she could tell that the man loved him very much. She couldn't imagine what he was feeling because at that point, Jenn was halfway sure Nik was alive. She couldn't imagine what it would be like to dig a grave for Nik. But still, Jenn didn't speak. She didn't speak because she couldn't think of anything to say that would matter.

Soon enough, the hole could hold two bodies. The man lifted his lover under the arms. Jenn helped by holding his partner's stiffened feet above the dirt. She cradled them like a swaddled newborn. Then the man spoke again. "I need to ask a favor," he said as they placed his dead friend softly into the void.

"What is it?" Jenn asked, her voice creaky from not talking.

"If I lie on top of Bruce, would you cover us with dirt?"

Jenn recoiled as though he'd struck her. "You mean, bury you alive?" Then she started sobbing again.

"Please don't cry," the man begged. "I didn't want to upset you. I just thought you might understand. You have such kind eyes."

"I can't do that," Jenn whimpered through her sniffles. "I'm sorry."

"It's all right," he told her. "Really, it is. I'll find some other way." He held Jenn awkwardly, his hands filthy with loam. "I shouldn't have asked you."

With Bruce lying in the hole, Jenn and Hank sat nearby on a stained bedsheet, sharing a cup of jasmine tea from his Aladdin thermos. Besides names, they exchanged stories. Jenn told Hank about Nik and how she'd lost him in Carpinteria. Jenn told Hank how much she loved Nik but she really didn't have to; Hank could tell. He kept nodding slowly, saying, "I know. I know" through damp eyelashes. Jenn was amazed Hank still had eyelashes. They were long and luxurious. When she complimented him, he said, "Falsies. Sephora's best. My last pair."

Jenn smiled, dipped her head. "It's not easy to be alone," she told him after a heavy silence.

"I was alone before I met Bruce," Hank said. "For many years."

"You don't have to be alone," Jenn argued, passing Hank the plaid plastic Aladdin mug. "You can come with me." Jenn hoped she didn't sound like Dorothy in *The Wizard of Oz*.

"Why?" Hank asked blankly.

"Why not?" Jenn asked back, like President Kennedy. "What else is there?"

Hank brushed his knuckles against Jenn's cheek. "Just one thing," he said. At first, she didn't know what he was talking about.

Hank stood up abruptly and screwed the top back onto the Aladdin. "We better finish the job," he said.

Jenn handed Hank the dirty sheet so he could cover Bruce's body with it. "I hope you find Nik," he told Jenn, smiling sadly. Then he went back to his lover's open grave. Jenn creakily rose to her feet to follow.

Suddenly, she heard a loud bang. A gunshot. Cringing, Jenn waited to feel pain. Had Hank shot her in desperation? Because she refused to comply with his request? Then Jenn heard the thump of Hank's body hitting the ground. *He had a gun all along*, Jenn thought to herself. *He was just too scared to use it.*

Instead of being sad, Jenn was angry. How dare Hank propose that she kill him? Jenn wanted to run but she couldn't just leave Hank like that on the side of Bruce's open grave. So, very courageously, Jenn turned around. She tried not to stare at the bullet hole in the side of Hank's skull, at the blood blossoming from it. Hank's eyes were wide, gaping at the sky. Jenn touched his eyelids closed. She'd seen this done in movies, so she imagined that's what you were supposed to do when someone died. Hank's eyelids shut surprisingly easily. They felt rubbery, like frog's skin under her fingertips.

Although Hank was almost six foot tall, he couldn't have weighed more than a hundred pounds. Jenn turned him onto his belly and dragged him toward the grave they'd dug together. As gently as she could, she rested him on top of Bruce. They were lying face to face. It looked almost as though they had just finished making love and were whispering postcoital secrets to each other. Jenn covered them both with the bedsheet then with dirt, tamping it down thoughtfully.

Ω

Midway between Solvang and Lompoc, Jenn spotted birds. Normally, this wouldn't be an unusual sight but Jenn hadn't seen birds in flight since the beginning of the end. There were so many dead fowl scattered about but live ones were rare. Like canaries in a proverbial coal mine.

In the eighteen 1800s, miners would carry canaries down into the tunnels with them. They even had special cages for this purpose. If the canary passed out, this meant dangerous gasses like carbon monoxide were present and the miners would exit the shaft immediately. These bird boxes even had tiny oxygen canisters attached that were used to revive the canaries. But sometimes the bird died, despite the miners' best efforts.

A rock band called The Police even sang a song about this phenomenon. "Canary in a Coal Mine" was a bouncy, peppy, reggae-ish tune, much like the bulk of their music. Some people misheard the lyrics and thought The Police were harmonizing "Mary in a Coma" instead of "Canary in a Coal Mine." Which would have made sense too.

Sometimes Jenn felt like a canary herself; the world was her coal mine. But these days, there was no place to escape. No mine to flee. The world was one big coal mine.

But back to the birds… Jenn gaped at those flying creatures on the road to Lompoc. Because live birds were so rare, seeing them was a gift. Seagulls like these were normally commonplace. They were so prone to eating garbage that pre-apocalypse, many said that gulls were like rats with wings.

Even though Jenn felt that their cries mocked her, these seagulls were a welcome sight. At first. But when they drew closer to her, Jenn realized that they were flying backwards and upside-down. They headed out to the Pacific then disappeared from sight. Perhaps weeks of eating radioactive garbage finally caught up with them. Jenn never saw live birds again.

Ω

Normally a feverish reader, Jenn wished she had something else to peruse besides the AAA Tourbook. In those days, real books were as rare as live birds. Whether they were burned for warmth or fell to some other terrible end is difficult to deduce. But Jenn was grateful to at least have the Tourbook to pass the time.

Words were her companion when the wordlessness that surrounded her became oppressive. She continued to sing songs out loud, just to hear something besides the deafening silence. Whenever Jenn sang, she tried to incorporate what her friend Serena had told her: to sing from your diaphragm and not from your throat, to find your key and don't rush the words. Serena had such an exquisite singing voice, smooth like a husky angel who'd just downed a shot of Patrón.

As much as Jenn would try to sound like Aretha Franklin, her voice sounded slight, lacked strength and substance. Serena used to say that

Jenn's singing was "cute." Except Jenn didn't want to sound like an adorable kiddie crooner. She wanted to wail like Billie Holiday. She wanted to purr like Dayna Kurtz. "If you can wail in your mind then you can wail in real life," Serena would tell Jenn. But this was easier said than done.

On the 101, Jenn belted torch songs from her diaphragm. She finally mastered her singing technique except there was no one else to hear her accomplishment. Finally, Jenn could sing the blues because she was living the blues. It reminded her of the Buddy Guy song "Damn Right, I've Got the Blues." She sang that too.

Jenn had met the blues face to face and had made wary friends with it. Therefore, she could sing "On the Sunny Side of the Street" just like Lady Day did in 1939. Filled with irony, just like Holiday's version. The tune was all about leaving your worries on your doorstep. (Jenn had no doorstep.) And not being afraid. But truth be told, Jenn was scared, scared shitless. But she sang nonetheless. Sometimes being frightened was the best reason to sing.

Ω

So, Jennifer Taverna moved solo along the 101. When the back wheels fell off the skateboard, she reverted to walking again. Which was a shame because she was getting pretty good at skateboarding. It was faster, easier on the feet and fun besides.

The rare car zoomed by on the coastal highway, often weaving all over the lawless road. Occasionally one would smash off the asphalt and spark down the cliffs like a fiery meteor. Poor judgement of a curve or suicide? It didn't really matter. Dead was dead.

Packs of dogs wandered about, many hairless. The sight of a naked collie never ceased to amuse Jenn. They're surprisingly slim under all that fur, especially when deprived of organic dog food. And collies looked just plain silly without their manes. How did she know a collie from a Dobermann, hairless? Something about the curve of the neck, the regalness of the stance.

For some reason, the wild dogs never attacked or even acknowledged Jenn, not with the fine assortment of carrion to choose from. Many of the canines were blind. Especially breeds like the sheepdog, whose long, plush coat was designed to protect their sensitive eyes. The miniature breeds, like chihuahuas and toy terriers, weren't hardy sorts even in the best of circumstances so most of them expired first. Seeing them was infrequent.

Rabid dogs were more common. When Jenn saw a canine with an off-kilter, sidewinder gait foaming at the mouth, she hid until they passed. They usually drove themselves off cliffs like pigs in the New Testament.

Getting biblical, Jenn carried a staff like Moses in the Old Testament. Both to help her walk and for protection. To pass the time, Jenn carved shapes into her wooden staff with a Swiss Army knife. Swirls and rosettes and what she remembered flowers to look like. The carved patterns felt good beneath her flea-bitten fingers.

Jenn tried to find pleasure wherever she could: observing the colorful, swollen sky, savoring the wrapped Dove chocolate drop she found in the gutter. Miniscule shreds of delight helped Jenn put one foot in front of the other as some unnamable thing drew her north to her fate.

Seventeen

Swing Low

In addition to singing, to pass the time as she walked, Jenn contemplated many things…like…

- What made the sky blue when it was blue.
- Or pea green when fallout gave it that sickly hue.
- Or how Linda Lovelace managed to deep-throat.
- Or why there was a street in Staten Island named Lovelace Avenue.
- Or who invented the language of postage stamps.

The last one was a peculiar practice that began with the Victorians but postage stamp lingo also had a brief resurgence during the Second World War. What is the language of stamps? Here are a few examples:

Angling a stamp at a particular location at a particular degree on an envelope or postcard conveyed a secret message. I.e., an upside-down stamp meant that you were sending a kiss to the soldier the correspondence was addressed to. Setting a stamp on its side meant: answer at once. Upside-down, it asked, "Do you remember me?" Placed on the upper left-hand corner facing straight up and down says, "Farewell."

Other times, when walking, Jenn would try to remember poetry she once loved. She couldn't recall entire poems, just bits and pieces and snippets.

> *"Loveliest of trees, the cherry now…"*
> *"Full fathom five thy father lies…"*
> *"Gather ye rosebuds…"*
> *"Breasts like two twin fawns…"*

These disjointed lines, in turn, reminded Jenn of bits and pieces and snippets of her own life. "Ariel's Song" from *The Tempest* made her mourn the daughter she would never have. Jenn always thought Ariel was a nice name for a girl. It meant "lion of God" in Hebrew. Every woman needed to be a lion now and then. Especially now.

Also, Jenn wondered, was she still considered a daughter if her parents were dead? She thought so. Hoped so. Because she surely still *felt* like a daughter. And this notion made her think of the song "Orphan Girl."

And so on.

Ω

In a town whose name Jenn couldn't recall, she discovered an old love: the joy of swinging. No, not partner-swapping, but swinging on a playground apparatus. In the middle of an abandoned coastal city, Jenn came upon a set of metal swings miraculously intact, faintly swaying in the radioactive breeze. Her heart leapt with joy because swinging on a set of swings was one of her purest pleasures as a child. When Jenn pumped her legs on a swing, she felt as though she were flying. It was her second favorite feeling in the universe but swinging lasted longer than the first.

Although Jenn hadn't been on a swing in several decades, she bounded into it with finesse. As she pumped her legs, Jenn wondered why being on a playground swing was something you had to relinquish as an adult. And this was a shame because it pure bliss for her.

So, Jenn became a swinger again in a tiny California coastal town whose name she couldn't remember. She smiled into the breeze her swishing created as she pumped higher and higher, until the metal seat rose above the top post. In her weakened state, it took at least fifteen minutes for Jenn's new Nikes to kick above the top bar. When she became parallel to it, Jenn stopped pumping and let inertia take charge.

As she slowed down, Jenn sang a hybrid of "Swing Low, Sweet Chariot" with a dash of "Amazing Grace" thrown in just for the hell of it; they seemed to go together in her blender brain.

> *"Swing low, sweet chariot*
> *Coming for to carry me home…*
> *I once was lost, but now I'm found*
> *Was blind, but now I see…"*

That last part reminded Jenn of Nik. Which she was trying not to do: think of Nik. She tried not to remember him so much because doing so only made her sad. Jenn prayed Nik wasn't stumbling around blindly like Gloucester in Act III of *King Lear*. But instead, that her husband had found some affable good Samaritan to help him. She also hoped Nik was still alive. She hoped a lot of things but mostly this.

Ω

Jenn moved slowly like an ant across concrete. To bide her time, she thought of pleasant things, cheerful memories that never failed to bring a smile to her cracked lips. This helped propel her forward. Things like:

- the chime of the Mister Softee ice cream truck;
- the agreeable, musty scent of her grandmother's skin;
- the image of Nik's sleeping face;
- the wrinkles in a baby's knuckles;
- the joyful wag of her friend Lauren's dog Zeke's tail when he saw her;
- the fresh fragrance of Yardley's English Lavender soap;
- her mother's lone dimple;
- the click of her father's Zippo lighter...

Jenn was lucky. Her parents had given Jenn and her brother Brian a loving, gentle childhood. Her folks weren't rich, but they were generous of spirit. They took family trips to Mystic Seaport and Pennsylvania Dutch Country, nothing extravagant but it was all they could afford, and it was enough. More than enough. These were small things that were very big to Jenn back then, and even bigger now.

More importantly, her parents instilled in Jenn a passion for travel, a sense that there was more, much more than Brooklyn. And even more important than that, Jenn's mom and dad made her feel special and pretty, even though she wasn't either growing up. She was an awkward, meek, gangly giraffe of a girl but they made her feel exceptional, even though she was ordinary at best.

How Jenn missed her mother and father.

Ω

More walking, more musing. Jenn was consumed with thoughts of her friends. Especially Serena and Lars and their rickety, love-infused house on Lyme Avenue in Sea Gate. The time Jenn spent with their two sons gave her a glimpse of the best part of being a parent. With Jesse and Jason, there was laughter and general silliness. Together, they made up State Jokes that only they thought were hysterical. Like:

> If I was a farmer, I'D-A-HOE. (Get it?)
> I caught a cold in MASS-ACHEW!-SETTS.

Maybe you had to be eight and ten-years-old respectively to think State Jokes were funny. Or a geography buff. Or both.

Once, Serena told Jenn, "You and Niky are the only adults who treat J and J like people and not like children. You really *talk* to them, not down at them." It meant a lot to Jenn to hear this. She was so moved that she didn't know what to say, so she just nodded.

It bothered the Farber boys that Nik and Jenn weren't related to them by blood. Maybe in their young minds, that would have made them closer, more tightly linked but they couldn't have been closer than they already were. As they grew older, they might be fortunate enough to realize that the ones you choose are often more important than the ones you don't.

"Are you Serena's sister?" Jesse would repeatedly ask Jenn.

When she told him that nothing had changed and she *still* wasn't their aunt, Jesse would say, "Then what are you?"

"A cousin?" Jason would suggest.

"I'm just your friend," Jenn would tell them. "That's a lot." But the boys weren't entirely convinced it was a lot or enough. "I picked you. We picked each other to be friends," Jenn would press further. "That's a big deal."

Although the boys reluctantly admitted that it was, Jenn could see that it was "less than" in their fuzzy little heads. They didn't really believe it.

Walking down the burned-out road on the coast of post-apocalyptic California, it seemed like eons ago when Jenn read scratch-and-sniff storybooks with the boys on the top bunk of their bunk bed, their bare feet dangling over the edge, all the best smells in their books scratched raw and ragged.

Or when they watched *Jesse James* on the Channel Five Movie Club over wagon wheel macaroni and meatballs. Or when they both argued who got to drink out of Jenn's Luke Skywalker cup from the Burger King giveaway when she babysat them. (They ended up grudgingly taking turns.) Or when they sobbed, one on each side of her chest, when Nik drove Serena to the hospital upstate with a fishhook stuck in her finger.

Yes, Jenn truly loved these little boys. She savored the good memories and prayed they didn't suffer too much in the end. Maybe they remembered one of the goofy State Jokes they'd concocted together and shared one last, brotherly laugh, and thought of her as they chuckled. *I'm good for a laugh, if anything,* Jenn told herself.

Ω

While traveling the road alone, Jenn thought about all sorts of nonsensical things, and serious things too. Anything to distract herself from the fact that she was utterly abandoned. By nature, Jenn was a yapper. She truly loved connecting with other people, exchanging ideas and trading stories. With no one to talk to, there was a void. But thinking…remembering…reliving…it took her mind off Nik. Or not having Nik. But only briefly.

The thing that struck Jenn the most was the absence of sound. No crickets at night. No trill of birds during the day. No breeze washing through the trees. There was nothing. Nothing but the cry of silence.

Nik, Nik, Nik. That's all Jenn thought about on her journey. Did every step bring her further away from him or closer? Did he perish in

167

the Carpinteria collapse or did some kind soul take pity upon him and assist Nik on his odyssey north? And if he were alive, was Nik pining away for Jenn? Or was he glad she was finally gone?

After being Nik's partner for eleven years and his wife for nine of those years, Jenn still loved him. Hell, she still *liked* him. She couldn't stop thinking about him. About how they met. Here's the short version:

Besides being a car mechanic, Nik did handyman work on the side and was renovating Jenn's friend Jessica's kitchen. The moment Jenn saw Nik, all covered in sheetrock dust and plaster, that was it. His smile made Jenn weak in the knees and fluttery in the drawers. She kept thinking of excuses to pop by Jess's place when she knew Nik would be working there—to drop off dinner since Jess couldn't cook with her kitchen being torn apart, to borrow the latest issue of *Vogue*. On one of these occasions, Nik asked Jenn out for coffee and that was that.

During her solitary pilgrimage north, maybe Jenn was being thick or stupid or both, but somehow, she could not accept the fact that Nik was probably dead. If he truly were, Jenn was convinced that she would feel it, that she would somehow *know*...

Being married was hard sometimes, Jenn thought, but the idea of being a widow was worse...

Ω

Jenn poised her fingers above the Memorywriter's keys. She sighed and started a new sentence. She wasn't sure how it would work in the finished manuscript, maybe as an aside or as an asterisk of sorts. But she wrote it anyway.

Meanwhile, back on Alpha 49C...

It's odd, but as I write this, I find myself feeling the same feelings I did when I lost Nik. I'm rambling on about him, I know. But I can't help it. I'm reliving the pain I felt at the time but it's okay. I have to go through it. I have to go through it one more time to get beyond it. So, please stick it out with me. I think/hope it will be worth the struggle.

As I look over this chapter, I must stop and digress a bit. It seems I can't create without going off on a tangent then circling back, doesn't it? I can't move forward without checking and rechecking the bridges I've left smoldering behind me.

My point is this: when Noah first encouraged (prodded?) me to write my take on Earth's post-nuclear holocaust, you know how reluctant I was to begin. Living through it once was bad enough. Why would I want to suffer through it again?

But Noah was thoroughly convinced that my reflections would do someone some good. That this memoir would be full of teaching moments. Especially since Alpharians were so familiar with Earthlore and its customs. They closely followed Earth History, even before the Fall. I was surprised to learn that there were several university degrees dedicated to various aspects of Earth study: not only its past but its climate and sociology. Noah was sure that my story would be of value, not just historically but morally. Emotionally.

In any case, you are all witness to my painful procrastinations. Writing about my home planet, I lose friends and relatives not just once but several times while ruminating over them in this tome. But instead of it being excruciating, the more I force myself to persevere and write, the easier the act becomes.

I also found that if I pretended this was fiction, if I wrote my memories as a fairytale of sorts, in neat, little (and some not so little) chapters in the third person, I could distance myself from it. The simpler the writing process—and my subsequent healing— became.

And soon, I made a complete three-hundred-and-sixty-degree turn. Instead of feeling that I was being forced to write, I now needed to write. I hungered for it. I had to get my thoughts and emotions out of my body and onto paper. Or FleuroPaper, as is the Alpharians version of paper.

Yes, I must admit, I feel much better now, sharing my story with you. And I sincerely hope it does some good.

I just thought I needed to explain how the writing process shifted seismically for me. Are you happy, Noah? I admit I was wrong. My frenemies could tell you what a rare occurrence that was: admitting I was wrong.

Onward.

Back to the road.

Eighteen

Almost There

Something dragged Jenn north. A magnet of thought. A rope length of promise. She didn't know what it was; she just went with it. Perhaps Jenn allowed herself to be led because she was so tired. Perhaps it was something else.

Ω

Good news: in Lompoc, Jenn found another scooter.
Bad news: a dead child was still attached to the handlebars.

Holding her breath, Jenn loosened the boy's grip and tossed him into a garbage bin as gently and lovingly as possible. The child was surprisingly heavy for someone so small and slight. Jenn mouthed a silent prayer as she disposed of him and apologized to the stiff-as-a-board boy under her breath. It pained her to take the child's scooter. But her feet hurt more than her conscience did.

Jenn also offered a prayer of thanks that she'd had the foresight to liberally apply Vicks to the base of her nostrils before putting the boy in the trash like a discarded Time-Out Doll. Binge-watching all of those "CSI" episodes had clearly paid off. That, and Nik's gesture way back in Pacific Heights. It seemed like a lifetime ago. And in a way, it was.

Ω

Jenn scurried up the coast, munching on her stash of Pepperidge Farm Gingerman Cookies. Although the bag certified that they had no mystical powers, only magical flavor, they always made Jenn feel better, whether she had a stomachache or a wounded spirit. By this point, Jenn had both.

Although she was weary to the bone, Jenn often had trouble sleeping. Her mind could not rest, even as she tried to calm it with deep yogic breaths and various calming techniques she'd learned from the nice people at YogaSole on Windsor Place back in Brooklyn. Though Jenn was physically spent, she still couldn't seem to free her mind enough to rest.

She'd long been an insomniac and repose often eluded her, even "before." Before this all happened. In the "Before," Nik would prescribe "two Marys and a Bob," but sometimes even this didn't work. Nik was a firm believer that watching late-night TV helped you relax. Specifically, watching two episodes of "The Mary Tyler Moore Show" and one episode of "The Bob Newhart Show." Those beloved classics were on the Nostalgia Channel back-to-back at two to three-thirty in the morning. Thus, two Marys and a Bob meant that you finally drifted off watching these shows.

On bad nights, it might take "two Marys, a Bob, an 'I Love Lucy' and an 'All in the Family.'" Granted, those were rough nights. But these nights were even rougher. Because on the road, there were no vintage sitcoms to sit by your side like old, faithful friends keeping vigil over your restlessness until you zonked out.

Ω

At this juncture, the towns Jenn passed were inconsequential, though she still stopped at each one, as if to pay homage. There was always food to forage and supplies to seek. The place names and fallen sights became a jumbled mishmash in Jenn's mind. Which town had the bone-dry riverbeds? Which town had the windmills? Halfheartedly, Jenn searched for Nik in every corner but never found him.

Occasionally, she consulted the AAA Tourbook, although it was losing its charm. Everything was. The coastline was still fascinating in a ravaged way but the cities themselves were not. Not without Nik by Jenn's side to search for brown Danish bread or explore extinct tar pits. It was no fun anymore, not that it had ever exactly been fun.

Ω

At the Zaca Mesa Winery in Los Olivos, Jenn chug-a-lugged a bottle of a blush-colored number as she paddled along her way. It was all going nicely until Jenn fell and skinned her knees. Again. So much for drinking and driving, even on a scooter.

Jenn passed Franciscan missions, artifacts and historic sites. But she didn't stop; she was losing steam. History no longer concerned her. Perhaps because she knew that there would be no more of it. On Earth, at least. For this was history's last stop. Possibly, this lack of interest was because Jenn no longer had anyone to discuss history with. No Nik = no interest.

Sometimes Jenn even grew tired of remembering things about Nik. It was too sad, too painful. And truthfully, she was running out of pleasant memories. Her memories were getting worn around the edges. Like over-fantasized fantasies. But Jenn's feet kept moving even though her spirit took a nosedive.

Ω

Also, Jenn's unrelentless flow grew worse by the day. "Women's troubles," her grandmother would have nodded knowingly, lisping the words under her breath, as though they were a curse. But Jenn's post-nuclear periods had become much more than occasional spotting. Somewhere between heavy and hemorrhage. Jenn was afraid that she was slowly bleeding to death from the vajayjay.

She tried everything to calm the incessant flow: assorted herbs and raspberry leaves which supposedly had legendary healing properties (courtesy of the helpful placards at Lassens Natural Foods in Santa Maria). Consulting *The Pill Book*, Jenn prescribed inorganic medications for herself like tranexamic acid tablets. But they didn't work. The book was too heavy to take along (1,296 pages!!), so she tore out the sheets she thought might be useful.

Traditional pharmacies were surprisingly well-stocked. Jenn helped herself to whatever she wanted. She quickly became dependent on Valium and Tylenol #3 with codeine. They took the edge off her discomfort but could only do so much. They couldn't work miracles. When the buzz wore off from the meds, the same problems were patiently waiting for her.

Did Jenn worry that she would become hooked? What difference did addiction make? How long did she have to live anyhow, she reasoned?

Ω

Jenn kept going, going, going. No matter what. Each day, the bleeding grew heavier. She graduated from Always Extra Heavy Overnight Maxi Pads with Flexi-Wings to toddler-sized Pampers. (She'd dropped so much weight that adult diapers swam on her and kept sliding down her once-generous hips.) But Pampers did the trick, no shame. They fit better than Huggies. Were more absorbent too.

Jenn was afraid to step onto a scale to find out how little she weighed. Her best guess was that she was down to about eighty pounds. Nik's brass ring from the Santa Monica Carousel kept sliding off her wrist. She had to wear it up on her wilted bicep. Jenn imagined that she resembled a sunk-eyed, anorexic, bang-less Egyptian. But she had no desire to check her look in the mirror. Again, what was the point?

The thought of visiting a hospital sometimes flitted through Jenn's mind. But was anyone manning them? She couldn't imagine what kind of shape they were in. Were medical centers even operational by now? And what could they do for her? No, it was best to steer clear of hospitals, Jenn thought. Especially because of what happened in downtown Los Angeles.

Back in LA, Nik and Jenn once visited a hospital called Dignity Health. But there was no dignity. Or surgical supplies. The stench was unimaginable. Like rotting mangoes, fish guts and feces combined. People lined the corridors, begging for help, moaning in agony. It was like walking into a nightmare. Or an M. Night Shyamalan movie.

Ω

Looking back, Jenn didn't even remember why she and Nik went to Dignity Health. His dwindling eyesight? Her intermittent spotting?

Jenn only remembered there was no help to be found, and that their pain was miniscule in comparison to everyone else's.

Their brief wait in DH's ER haunted Jenn. For a long time, she had nightmares about it. That her chest had been cracked open and she couldn't close it. Or that, for some reason, a doctor was trying to remove her face. Sometimes Jenn would wake up howling. Like in that old black-and-white *film noir* movie with Betty Grable called *I Wake Up Screaming*. Jenn woke up screaming too but it wasn't because she'd fallen for her sister's accused killer. It was because of the woman they'd met there. Julia.

In the Dignity waiting room, Nik and Jenn saw people whose skin had slid around on their faces like Silly Putty. Others sported raw stumps of limbs. Some puked blood into blue vomit bags. Others held their intestines in place with their hands. These hopeless cases congregated in Dignity as flustered triage nurses tried to help them. But there were so many who needed help that no one got much.

Nik and Jenn decided not to wait. He walked with purpose, following the pale green arrows on the stained floor. Jenn trailed him.

Racing down the corridor, her legs turned to rice pudding beneath her but she still followed Nik following the arrows. Toward the end of the confused maze, a dim glow of light marked yet another holding area. The air was colored with a grumble of voices, moans and the occasional scream. Jenn sidled up close to Nik and grabbed his hand for comfort. Or strength. Or both. She wasn't sure.

If it were even possible, this waiting room looked worse than the first had. Was it the main trauma center? Maybe. But it could have easily been a recreation of a Civil War field hospital. This second Dignity waiting room was filthy. Only a handful of doctors tended to the people who sat on the floors, leaned against the walls or milled about. There were no available chairs. The physicians looked as war-torn as their patients did, their gowns stained with every possible type of human body fluid. And then some.

Jenn found herself standing beside a woman clutching an infant to her chest. "Why are we here?" Jenn asked Nik.

He had no answer, but the woman did. "We're here for help," she said simply.

"Yes, we are," Jenn agreed.

"When something bad happens, look for the helpers," the woman continued. "That's what Mr. Rogers always said."

Jenn nodded. She remembered Mr. Rogers. He was a kind, gentle children's TV show host who had a program that ran for several decades, teaching kids and their parents how to be nice to everyone.

The woman smoothed the blanket around her child's head and tucked it tight like protective armor. "My baby's sick," she explained.

The infant was still and quiet. Jenn cooed to it but got no response. It did not stir. The woman pulled the baby closer, defensively, away from Jenn.

"Sleeping?" Jenn asked the mother.

"Sleeping," the woman mirrored. Her hands trembled as she rocked the child. "I can't sleep," she said. "I can't keep anything down. My milk dried up."

"Will the baby take water?" Jenn wondered.

"I can't find clean water," the woman answered. The corners of her mouth were caked with fever blisters. She kept chewing on them. "I used to love nursing Maeve," she went on. "And Maeve, she loved it too. We lived in Topanga Canyon. With Maeve's father. I used to love him too except I can't remember his name anymore…"

Nik gave Jenn a nudge that they should go. He mouthed, 'She's a nutter.' Jenn knew this was true but still, she couldn't leave the woman and her baby. "He died," the woman continued. "Maeve's father. I buried him all by myself. In the field across from our cabin. It was so nice there. We were surrounded by mountains. We built the cabin from scratch, just him and me. It even had a porch and a swing. I would swing and nurse Maeve, looking out at the hills. That seemed like a long time ago."

"Everything seems like a long time ago, doesn't it?" Jenn said, trying to console her.

But it was as though the woman didn't hear Jenn. "Why can't I remember his name?" the woman worried out loud. "It's not right that I can't remember his name. He was my husband, after all. Maeve's father."

Jenn knew that this woman had lost her mind, but she listened anyway. Someone had to. Nik was beginning to lose patience. "Now my milk is gone," the woman lamented. "I'm as dry as a bone. Maeve wouldn't touch Similac. My husband said I spoiled her. But how can you spoil a baby?"

"I…I don't know," Jenn told her.

"Mother's milk is the most wholesome substance on earth. It contains every nutrient a human child needs to grow. Did you know that?"

"No," Jenn told her. Actually, she did. Serena had told her. But that seemed very long ago too.

The woman fussed with the baby's blanket again. It was almost a tic, feathering down the cloth that covered Maeve's head. "She's cold. She's so cold," the woman said. "Feel." With that, the young mother threw back the blanket. A rancid tang wafted out—soiled diaper?—but Jenn touched the baby's sunken cheek anyhow. Maeve was as chilly as a granite floor in the winter.

Jenn caressed the baby's tiny, misshapen head. It felt rubbery and unreal, as though it belonged to a doll. There was no hint of life left in the child. Jenn folded the blanket back over Maeve's skull. "My mother knitted this afghan," the woman told Jenn. "It's a special seashell stitch. See? And there's satin woven into the yarn."

"It's lovely," Jenn told her, because it was.

Nik lightly tugged Jenn's arm. "There's nothing you can do for her," he whispered.

"Nothing but listen," Jenn whispered back.

She couldn't leave the side of this desolate woman who ranted like Ophelia. That's when Jenn noticed that a doctor had been watching their entire exchange. His eyes were bloodshot. His voice was weary when he said, "Are you ready to give her to me yet, Julia?" Julia shook her head and held her baby closer. "Then why did you come here?" the doctor asked gently. Julia had nothing to say. The doctor put his hand on Maeve's back. "She's dead," he said bluntly. "You know she's dead, don't you?"

"Maeve's not dead," Julia insisted. "She's only sleeping."

The doctor managed to disengage the afghan from Maeve. There was the undeniable perfume of decomposing flesh again. "She's dead," he said, more quietly now. "Holding onto her will only make you sick."

"I'm already sick," she told him.

An orderly approached Julia from behind. He held her arms behind her back just as the baby, Maeve, fell from her grasp. The doctor caught Maeve before she hit the ground. Julia howled inconsolably as they sealed her child into a miniature body bag. The grieving mother finally collapsed against Jenn, sobbing. Jenn cradled her close.

Nik and Jenn looked at each other above Julia's head. When she stopped crying, Jenn eased the woman to the ground. Julia huddled in a mass there. Jenn covered her with the baby's blanket, which had fallen to the floor in the struggle. "There's nothing they can do for us here," Nik said.

Before they left, Jenn patted Julia on the head, as though it meant something. She squeezed Jenn's hand for a moment then let go. When Nik and Jenn headed toward the ambulance bay, Julia began wailing again.

So, this is why Jenn avoided hospitals at all costs.

Ω

Jenn sensed that her days were growing short. In Morro Bay, her life would end, one way or another. Or begin. Depending on your POV. Until then, Jenn had her meds to keep her warm. And a dead boy's scooter to propel her toward the inevitable.

Ω

At Pismo Beach, Jenn laughed out loud. And not just because she was losing her mind. Her own voice startled her. Jenn hadn't heard a human sound for many days, let alone a happy one. But Pismo Beach reminded Jenn of Bugs Bunny so she had to LOL.

In the animated short "Ali Baba Bunny," Bugs went clamming at Pismo Beach. Jenn could still hear the way Bugs popped his p's and b's with his funny, bucktoothed drawl when he said "Pismo Beach." He even carried a little bunny-sized pail and shovel with him.

"Pismo Beach!" Jenn burst out, just like Bugs had, snapping her p's and b's. Then she laughed again. That Mel Blanc, he was really something. *Had been* really something. Mel had voiced Bugs and several other "Looney Tunes" characters, giving countless yuck-yucks over his sixty plus year career.

Back in college, Jenn had a very bizarre ethics professor who insisted that Bugs Bunny represented the white man and dark-feathered Daffy Duck symbolized the black man. But more specifically, a black man who was trying to be white but never succeeded.

To top it off, Professor Kingsley also swore that Bugs Bunny was gay because at every possible opportunity, he kissed Elmer J. Fudd on the lips. Then Professor K went on to profess that Elmer was a transvestite because he dressed up like a woman in one cartoon. In a strapless emerald green gown, matching mules and a red updo, sporting boobs, no less. Leave it to Earthfolk to complicate life to the point where they can't even enjoy a simple Warner's Brothers cartoon without hyper-analyzing it. Sometimes a cartoon is just a cartoon, bro.

Ω

Because of Bugs and Elmer, Jenn took a detour onto Pismo Beach's sand itself. But it was not the way it had looked in the cartoon. Or the last time Jenn had visited with Nik. Had Bugs seen it in the state Jenn did, he would have burrowed back into his rabbit hole and made a left turn at Albuquerque.

In its heyday, Pismo Beach was considered the perfect spot for clamming. The AAA Tourbook mentioned the Pismo clam species whose numbers had dwindled of late due to overfishing. But post-doomsday, Pismo Beach was a horror. It smelled even worse than the Dignity Health waiting room.

Jenn stumbled across the littered sand with a bandana clenched over her nose and mouth. (Damn Niky…he had the nose clips too and her supply of Vicks was running low.) The entire beach was covered with clams. The shells and gooey bivalves alternately crunched and squished under Jenn's feet. The sensation of the slimy clam meat oozing beneath the soles of her Nikes turned Jenn's stomach. Dragging her scooter through the shelly sand, she hurried as best she could through the crackly glop.

In the guidebook, Jenn noticed that there was a place called "The Great American Melodrama and Vaudeville" nearby on Pacific Street. Nik would have quipped, "Why do we need to go there? We're living the Great American Melodrama!" But Nik wasn't there so he didn't say it, however, Jenn thought it.

The performing arts theater featured nineteenth century melodramas with a side helping of song and dance. As there would be no song, no dance and no seltzer down your pants, Jenn passed it by. Living in the twenty-first century was melodramatic enough, thank you very much! Even without the pants seltzer. Yes, Jenn missed seltzer too.

Ω

Because Jenn liked the way the words "San Luis Obispo" felt on her tongue, she said it out loud. Several times.

At SLO, she laughed again. This time, it was at Mission San Luis Obispo de Tolosa. The mission was named for a thirteenth century French saint, the Bishop of Toulouse. It reminded Jenn of a horrible/wonderful old joke her dad liked to tell. Here's the joke:

> - What did Toulouse-Lautrec's tailor ask when fitting him
>   for a new suit?
> - What?
> - "Too tight, Toulouse?"

At Bishop Toulouse's place, there were the usual Native American relics and early settlers' artifacts on display. Not much to hold her interest. So, Jenn moved on to Mission Plaza. Somehow, the water in the urban oasis's creek had crystalized, resembling a bed of quartz. Jenn had never seen that type of reaction in water before; she doubted she would ever see it again. Which was all right with her.

Ω

Jenn forged on to nearby California Polytechnic State University, which had a solar-heated, wind-powered horticulture unit. But since the sun had disappeared that day and the air was stone still, there was nothing to power it, so Jenn paused there only briefly. Long enough to take a wee and nab a snack of Wheat Thins from the Chevron station.

Her pace slowed considerably after San Luis Obispo. As the highway approached that city, it dipped slightly inland. But just outside town, US 1 meandered back to the Pacific.

Taking it slow wasn't difficult to do because, once again, Jenn was traveling on foot. This time, the front wheels fell off her primitive limousine. But this scooter had lasted much longer than the skateboard had, and for that, she was grateful.

Despite her current situation, Jenn tried to be thankful. At least once a day. About something. No matter how small. Like the fact that she didn't vomit that morning. Or the fact that she'd found a sealed packet of Lance Toasty Peanut Butter Sandwich Crackers, even though they were crushed into a fine dust. Or for the puce sunset.

But Jenn did miss her now-defunct scooter. It was fun. It was fast. And it was easier on the knees. She figured the unfortunate wheel situation had something to do with the addled atmosphere wreaking havoc on metal and hastening rust. Nik would have had a better idea, but Nik was no more.

Ω

Although Jenn's body and spirit were depleted, she felt a flutter of excitement that carried her forward. She was half-hopeful that she would find Nik ensconced in Room 9 at the Anchor Inn, overlooking Morro Bay, not-so-patiently waiting for her. And if he wasn't there, Jenn would be faced with a difficult choice. For what was the sense of going further?

It's not that Jenn wished for death but a life alone in post-nuclear hell was no life at all. Period. End of story.

If Jenn truly wanted to cease living, she wouldn't have struggled all those hundreds of miles. As best as she could tell, it was at least three-hundred-and-fifty miles from San Diego to Morro Bay. Most of which she'd done on foot, the bulk of it with Nik, but most recently solo. And to her best estimation, it had to be at least a thousand miles from Flagstaff.

No, Jenn didn't want to die but she was very, very tired. She just wanted to take a nice long rest in Morro Bay and to be free from pain. Was that too much to ask? Yes, it was a tall order indeed. But she asked it anyway.

Along the final stretch, Jenn's emotions rose and fell like a restless tide. On the crest of the wave, she imagined her reunion with Nik. She pictured every last detail: how he would feel in her arms, skin and bones, but still her Niky. She would bury her head in his shoulder and breathe in the sweet, accustomed scent of his skin, the pheromones that spelled N-I-K to her. They would hold each other for a long time without talking. Holding Nik would be as fulfilling as having an orgasm had been back in the day. Well, almost. But it would be like that content feeling you get afterwards. Jenn smiled as she drew closer to that rock in the water, Morro Bay.

But then, after Jenn's crest of joy, the crash of the wave would come. Something, usually a stab of pain in her aching, ragged feet or the passing of a blood clot, which felt like warm Jell-O oozing from between her thighs, would snap Jenn back to reality. What if Nik wasn't waiting for her in Room 9? How could he have possibly made the trip alone, blind and defective? Jenn had a hard enough time making the trek and she wasn't in nearly as bad shape as he was. The journey from Carpinteria to Morro Bay was more than a hundred miles, nothing to sneeze at.

What if Nik's binoculars broke or if he lost them? He was always losing things. Without Jenn to help him find them, then what? And even with the binocs, Nik's line of vision was extremely limited. It was pinpointed to little circles of glass pressed against his eyes. How could he see gouges in the road and other hazards? How could he read street signs? How could he avoid getting plowed down by the occasional car? And what's more, why didn't Jenn see him on the road? Granted, Nik walked much faster than she did but still…

Jenn concocted all sorts of justifications for her doubts then second-guessed them. These questions swirled and twirled above her head like competing comic book bubbles. They formed a churning whirlpool in her brain that sucked her buoyancy into its bubbling center until only despair remained.

But still, Jenn walked. If for no other reason than she wanted to find out how her story ended.

Nineteen

On the Morro

It was dark as Jenn approached Morro Bay. The night was as thick and black as a good cup of coffee, which she hadn't had for some time. Even a bad cup of coffee. Quite a ways back, Jenn remembered a battered road sign that proclaimed Morro Bay was five miles away. She was dog-tired but she could not stop. She was so close. Yet so far. So, she kept going.

Jenn dug the military-grade Maglite out of her pack, briefly recalling her friend Frank, who'd collected flashlights. Frank would have loved this one; he literally had hundreds. Even though the Maglite was equipped with newish Duracells, its beam was still faint, refusing to project more than a few feet. Highway 1 sliced through small mountains and statuesque hills, winding toward the Pacific. Jenn followed where it led.

In the dim, almost nonexistent glow, the landscape seemed to be moving. This was not the first time Jenn had walked through the carbon-paper night but it still spooked her. She'd previously limited her traveling to daylight hours when it was safer and visibility was better. Who wanted to risk a shattered ankle when there was no one to set it? Unfortunately, Jenn knew firsthand what the hospitals were like.

Normally, she passed the evening hours trying to sleep while camouflaged in bushes or cozied up in someone's garage. Invading an actual home, especially alone, was too disturbing. And dangerous. Besides, sleep always evaded Jenn in these places, with the ghosts of their former residents invisibly bunking beside her, snoring inaudibly. This is why garages seemed safer, less personal. There were usually sleeping bags stashed among the storage shelves. God bless Californians and their love of outdoor activities. And gear. Californians clearly had a gear fetish.

Since Solvang, Jenn had broken her self-imposed "no traveling at night" rule. This is how anxious she was to reach her final destination. But every night since Solvang, Jenn swore she heard footsteps. She would hold still, hold her breath and listen. But the footfall would cease just a beat after she stopped. Jenn knew it wasn't the echo of her own footsteps she was hearing but someone else's. Was it a skeletal mountain lion? Was it Nik? A few times, she called out his name, shocked at how hollow and empty her voice sounded in the murk.

These mysterious footsteps pursued Jenn only in the evening. She thought she detected the feeble beam of a lantern which snapped off whenever she stopped to sheepishly investigate. Even in the Aftermath, Jenn was still a fraidy-cat. Nik called her that. So retro, so old-timey. The antiquated nickname annoyed her but she had to admit that Nik was right. Jenn wasted a lot of time and energy fearing things she had no business being frightened of. The truly frightening things that happened to you were things you'd never imagine. Like this.

Maybe it's a vampire or a werewolf, Jenn shivered, *or some other creature of the night. A zombie, even.* She'd read *World War Z,* twice, and it still haunted her, all these years later. Many times, as she walked at night, Jenn whipped her head around, concerned that some unearthly creature might be pursuing her. She half-expected to see Anthony Perkins lurching with a kitchen knife. But then Jenn would come to her senses. What did she have to fear anymore? Getting killed or hurt? Death would be a vacation when hurt was a way of life. *In the End of Days, you live beyond fear,* Jenn told herself. But did she truly believe this? Not really.

Ω

As Jenn trudged forward, she exercised her mind to stay awake. Otherwise, she was afraid she might fall asleep on her feet, as she had heard horses sometimes did. Jenn focused on a variety of nonsensical things to keep her sneakers moving firmly, one in front of the other.

To amuse herself, Jenn committed to memory what the AAA Tourbook said about Morro Bay. It had a population of ninety-one hundred at the time of publication and stood at an altitude of eighty feet above sea level. Morro Bay was your typical sleepy fishing town but for some reason, had always seemed very magical to Jenn. There was no place quite like it. Maybe it had something to do with the large, unexpected boulder that appeared to grow out of the ocean there.

Morro Rock itself was a huge, conical mound that rose to a height of five hundred and seventy-six feet. It was truly awesome to behold and was almost as pointy as Ruth Roman's breasts in the original version of *Invasion of the Body Snatchers,* but not quite.

Like a stone guardian, Morro Rock gave the impression of protecting the tiny town and landlocked bay that bore its name. In the 1500s, Morro Rock was christened "El Morro," which means "the hill" in Spanish. There is also the belief that Juan Cabrillo called it "El Muro" after the style of hat worn by the moors of Spain. But whichever explanation you favored, Jenn just thought it looked like a big rock, a huge, fascinating rock.

Also, a species of butterfly had been named for the town: the Morro Bay Blue. But they probably didn't exist anymore. No butterflies did, Jenn suspected. No more Butterfly Effect.

Ω

So, Jenn walked. She kept her eyes on the full moon that had suddenly popped out from the clouds like a fever blister. It penetrated the dim better than her Maglite. Jenn had never seen the moon so massive and swollen; it appeared so heavy that it might drop from the sky with a thud.

Staring it down as she went, Jenn recalled the "full moon poem" from *The Wolf Man*:

> *"Even a man who is pure in heart*
> *And says his prayers by night*
> *May become a wolf when the wolfbane blooms*
> *And the moon is full and bright."*

185

Or something like that.

In the vintage film, Maria Ouspenskaya was cast as a creepy gypsy woman named Maleva. Her son was played by Bela Lugosi, the werewolf who bit Lon Chaney, Jr. and started all the trouble, and the symphony of sequels.

Jenn thought of the craziest things as she walked, things that didn't matter anymore. Or did they? *Could women become wolf men?* Jenn wondered. Possibly. Probably.

Something Maria Ouspenskaya said in the movie jumped out at Jenn as she ambled toward Morro May. The first time, Maria/Maleva said it to her dead wolf-son, then later, to Lon. (In moviespeak, when dialog is repeated, the director really wants you to remember it because it's pivotal to the plot.) To be sure, it was an Academy Award-worthy speech recited from Maria's gnarled, little Russian lips. Twice:

"The way you walked was thorny, through no fault of your own, but as the rain enters the soil, the river enters the sea, so tears run to a predestined end. Now you will find peace for eternity."

These words resonated with Jenn, who also walked a thorny path. And sandy. And rocky. This is why Jenn thought of Maria Ouspenskaya as she trekked.

In her private life, Maria Ouspenskaya also walked a thorny path: in her youth, she had been an acclaimed Russian actress and acting teacher, but in her golden years, achieved a kind of fame in Hollywood, mostly in half-rate monster movies. At the age of sixty, Ouspenskaya had the distinction of being nominated for a Best Supporting Actress Oscar in *Dodsworth,* one of the briefest onscreen appearances to garner a nod. But she didn't win, however.

Something else, Maleva/Maria said to Lon:

"Go now, and may heaven help you…"

This also spoke loudly to Jenn. To be fair, there was much wisdom to be culled from a 1941 horror flick.

So, as Jenn walked up Highway 1 to Morro Bay, of all people, the specter of Maria Ouspenskaya kept her company.

Ω

Once in Morro Bay itself, Jenn turned left on Main Street. She knew the way by heart from there, as though she'd dreamed it. She *had* dreamed it, both before and after the Fall. Morro Bay was the place Jenn dreamed about most, her happy place.

She'd expected the town to be deserted but when she looked into the houses and motel rooms, there were flickering lights burning. She saw movement and life within their depths. Jenn even saw people on the street. They congregated in small groups on front porches and smiled wrecked smiles when they greeted her. At one street corner, Jenn even detected the fragrance of a barbecue. It flabbergasted her that people were doing normal things like having a barbecue. Against all odds, a sweet, little radioactive neighborhood had sprung out of the slime, doing its damndest to revive itself.

It reminded Jenn of the way John Steinbeck described life regenerating in the gunk of a tidepool in *Cannery Row*. This book took place a few hours north of Morro Bay, in Monterey.

On the entire journey up the coast, both with Nik and by herself, Jenn hadn't come upon a place quite like Morro Bay. Life along Highway 1 was singular, sparse and animalistic. The sprinkling of survivors were scavengers: stealing, hoarding, sometimes killing. Doing anything it took to get by. But life seemed different in Morro Bay. First, because there were so many people. Alive. And second, because it looked and felt like a real community.

Although Jenn nodded and smiled politely at the those she saw, she didn't stop to talk with anyone. She rushed down Market Street to her fate.

Ω

At the corner of Beach and Market, Jenn's heart felt glad and full when she saw the Anchor Inn. It looked exactly the way she remembered it: neat and white and pretty and clean and promising. From the parking lot, Jenn located Room 9, which was up on the second floor of the two-story, mom-and-pop motel. Her chest flittered when she saw a light shimmering from beneath the door.

Jenn took the AstroTurf-covered steps two at a time and wheeled around the railing at the top to Room 9's Federalist Blue painted door. Her fingers were curled into a fist, poised to knock. But Jenn's hand wouldn't budge; it was frozen in time. Her heart beat like a bass drum in her chicken-bone chest. She struggled to catch her breath and straightened her untamed rat's nest of hair, stalling for time. With a trembling hand, Jenn rubbed some Passionate Primrose lipstick over her cracked mouth, as if it made a difference. To anything. But Jenn was thankful she'd found a tube of it in Walgreen's nonetheless.

Mentally, Jenn tried to prepare herself for the way Nik might look: hairless, eyes sunken from blindness, covered with boils. *But underneath all that, he's still my Niky,* she reminded herself. *Nik...Nikolai...*

Finally, Jenn had the courage to knock on the door. Three times. No answer. She put her hand on the cold doorknob, but it wouldn't budge. The door was locked. Jenn knocked again, much harder this time. Like TV detective Columbo or Robyn McCall might. Her fist was much more insistent. The door had no choice but to open now, and it did.

Twenty

Prince of Irony

A man held the handle as he cracked the door several inches. Although Jenn didn't get a good look at his face, she knew at once that he wasn't Nik. Immediately, she burst into tears. So much hope, so much faith had been poured into the notion of seeing her husband again. Now that faith and hope were gone.

But the anonymous man was kind. He hooked his arm around Jenn's shoulder and led her into Room 9, which was surprisingly orderly. A gaggle of utility candles lit the space. He sat Jenn onto the neatly-made bed and rubbed her back while she cried, just like Jenn's mother used to do when she was a brokenhearted tween. This memory made Jenn cry even harder.

Somehow, she managed to choke out the story of Nik, their ill-fated vacation, their subsequent pilgrimage up the coast, their separation at the Carpinteria riot, Jenn's desperate search and now, her despair. All the while, fingering her ghost berry beads for strength. At least, they hadn't abandoned her.

The man listened silently, his arm draped around Jenn's back like a comforting cloak. He was shirtless, his waist circled by a thin, white towel stamped with the name "Anchor Inn" in royal blue. But just the "ch" and the "In" were visible. It looked as though the man had just come out of the shower; he smelled squeaky clean while Jenn just smelled. She buried her head into the soft fur of his chest and sobbed some more until nothing else would come.

"There, there," the man whispered, patting her back.

When Jenn finished crying, she looked into the man's face for the first time. In wonder, she gasped, "Dick!" Reluctantly, he nodded. "Dick Truehard!" Jenn gushed.

He smiled. Dick Truehard smiled that famous porn prince, "I'm-going-to-boink-you-in-the-ass-and-you're-gonna-like-it" smile. "Not anymore," Dick told Jenn sadly. Then he offered her his hand. "Philip," he said. "Philip Tobin. My real name."

Jenn took his hand. It was warm and strong. "Jenn," she told him. "Jennifer Taverna. My real name, too." Jenn shuddered at her stupid comment. Of course, it was her real name! Boy, she was nervous meeting Dick Truehard in the flesh.

No, she hadn't found Nik, but Jenn had managed to find an old friend. Although she and Dick/Philip had never met in real life, in a sense, they'd shared a bed for many years. She felt as though she knew him. Biblically, at least.

There Jenn was, face to face with Dick Truehard, the world-renowned erotic film performer she'd lusted after for a decade. Dick had won the Adult Video News award for Best Actor three years in a row and an X-Rated Critics Organization trophy for Best Gang Bang (for *Gang Bang at the OK Corral)* only the year earlier. Besides being addicted to swinging and chocolate, Jenn had been delightfully addicted to watching blue movies. And as blue movies went, Dick Truehard was the apex. Much like Montana Wildhack was in *Slaughterhouse-Five*. The world was full of perplexing parallels, even now. Especially now.

Ω

Believe it or not, Jenn's fascination with skinflicks wasn't entirely sexual. She was simply curious and captivated. Curious about how other people behaved in bed. Curious about how other humans looked naked. Curious to see how she stacked up in comparison. And captivated by what she saw: the way human body parts fit together so well and sometimes, in the case of John C. Holmes, not so well. (PS, he was a firehose.)

Jenn was extremely insecure about her body, despite the fact that Nik always told her that it was perfect. Fool that she was, Jenn never truly believed him. She thought he was just being nice. As if his erection weren't proof enough. But when Jenn watched erotic films, she realized that she was okay, that she was normal, that she was better than normal. That she was real and delightful and almost pretty.

More about the captivated part…Jenn was absolutely floored that these pleasant, uninhibited porn people up on the screen were ballsy enough to share their perfectly imperfect bodies with her. It seemed a very generous and courageous thing to do. Jenn respected their bawdy bravery, even though she doubted she could ever bare it all onscreen herself.

Essentially, Jenn wasn't a pervert (well, maybe just a little bit), merely inquisitive. Who would have ever thought that her carnal curiosity would have gotten her somewhere? When Jenn wrote an irate letter to X-rated film critic and historian Robert *The Harrad Experiment*" Rimmer because his adult video review guide was chock full of errors, to Jenn's surprise, Bob wrote back. Bob respected the fact that Jenn was irate, applauded it. Porn performers deserved much better than sloppy, inaccurate prose, he relented.

For instance, in Bob's tome, Annie Sprinkle's name was spelled at least three different ways. (Sprinkles, Sprinkled and Sprinkle.) A photo of George Payne was miscredited. And "cunnie" was written a variety of ways. Plus, there was no pic of Jenn's illustrious cousin Veronica Hart, whose nom de porn surname had also been heartily misspelled.

When Jenn wrote to Rimmer, she didn't think anything would come/cum of it. Even "straight" movie critic Leonard Maltin hadn't written back to her, and she'd been full of adoration for Ol' Len. Which proves that porn folks are also uber polite. Bob complimented Jenn's writing, her general spunk and her neat, error-free typing. He admitted that he needed help keeping the Sprinkles, Harts and Paynes straight, and that he could use a "cracker jack" proofreader. Though this wasn't Jenn's forte (she was a "cracker jack" exec sec), she agreed to help Bob. Jenn's editorial skills were sharper than the average bear's by virtue of being an administrative assistant all those years.

And that was the start of a beautiful professional relationship. Though Bob lived in Quincy, Massachusetts and Jenn lived in Brooklyn, he dutifully mailed her his handwritten adult movie reviews in his squirrelly script. Jenn would painstakingly type them and make corrections as she went. She took great pains to make sure people's sexual pseudonyms were spelled right and that "tittie" was spelled uniformly throughout. After all, these performers were kind enough to get naked for public consumption, the least reviewers could do was to spell their fake names correctly.

Along the way, Jenn compiled a smut style sheet so that "hard-on" was always spelled with a hyphen and Kandi Barbour's name was always with an initial "k," final "i" and an "our" at the end. The "d" in Vanessa del Rio's name was always lowercase. And that it was Lisa Cintrice, never, ever "Liza." Perish the thought.

Jenn was quietly proud that she was making money in the flesh trade without even showing her rosebud. She gave sex workers the dignity they deserved. Bob paid her a pittance but for Jenn, it wasn't about the money; it was about doing something that mattered.

All day long in her real job, Jenn played the corporate game, which could be a deceitful, underhanded business. If nothing else, at least porn was honest; people established what they would and wouldn't do for the camera, agreed upon a day rate and were paid accordingly. The "straight" business world was nowhere near as up front. Jenn respected porn for its honesty and its daring.

Ω

Back in Room 9 at the Anchor Inn, Dick complimented both Jenn's editing prowess and her thoughtful movie reviews when Bob occasionally let her critique a film. (She used the pen name "Pearl Chavez," with a nod to the steamy Jennifer Jones character in *Duel in the Sun*.) Then he requested once more of Jenn, "I really wish you wouldn't call me 'Dick.' My real name is Philip. All my friends call me 'Philip.'" After a pause, he added, "Or else, I'll be forced to call you 'Pearl' and not Jennifer."

"Fair enough," Jenn conceded, pleased he considered her a friend.

"Besides, Dick Truehard is dead," Philip tagged on. Although Jenn begged to differ, she did her best to call him by his given name.

"By the way, my friends call me 'Jenn,' not Jennifer," she told him.

"Jennifer…juniper," Philip sang softly, quoting the Donovan song, as he gazed at her warmly. Nik used to sing that song to her too so it made Jenn happy/sad to hear it. She immediately felt exposed, vulnerable, yet Philip was the one she'd seen naked. Many times.

"Please," Jenn said. "Please don't look at me like that."

"Like what?"

"Like anything. It's too bright in here and I'm too ugly." She covered her face with her raw, broken hands. (Yes, the fallout had begun to wreak havoc on her poor skin again. It was a pattern of blister, heal, blister, heal.) "Let's blow out some of the candles," Jenn suggested. "Please."

"I don't think you look awful, but all right," Philip allowed. He pursed lips, which Jenn had once seen pressed to Candida Royalle's glorious mons, larger than life on the big screen, and blew out a candle. Then another. "Morro Bay is a nice town," Philip added. "But for some reason, there's no electricity."

"Another perk of our post-nuclear pity party," Jenn said.

Philip went around the room, puckering his full, smoochable lips and left only four tapers burning. "Better?" he asked.

"Much better," Jenn told him. "Thank you." The muted candlelight was much kinder to her broken-out face. She felt more relaxed, less self-conscious.

Speaking of faces, Philip's was untouched by radiation, fallout and general mayhem. It was the prettiest thing Jenn had seen since the carousel horses in Santa Monica. He had smiling blue eyes capped by paintbrush lashes, a long, straight Roman centurion's nose and wavy, sand-brown hair. He even had all of his teeth, which Philip admitted were capped anyway. Jenn was riveted by his pleasant appearance. Yes, he was a bit thinner than she remembered but he still looked incredibly hale. "The camera puts ten pounds on you," Philip explained, when Jenn remarked on his slimness.

Philip got dressed while Jenn prepped their supper. Over cans of Chicken of the Sea (with that sexy mermaid on the label), jazzed up with a dash of jarred onion bits and ReaLemon, washed down with warm Jarritos lime soda in Anchor Inn tumblers, they shared speed-dating-style versions of their lives. For Philip's benefit, Jenn recounted her entire journey from Flagstaff to Morro Bay in greater detail than she had given in her tearjerking entrance. She and Philip compared notes. The opposite of Jenn, he'd traveled south from the north. Something drew him to Morro Bay, he said.

"I came down from San Francisco," Philip told her. "I'd just finished a Spike Spinelli flick. For some reason, I thought things might be better down south. As usual, I was wrong. Story of my life."

Like war veterans, Philip and Jenn talked about what they'd witnessed. He was no longer a porn star, and she was no longer a fan; they were just two survivors who'd seen hell and lived to tell the tale. They talked until their throats were raw. Pouring cups of instant Sanka she'd managed to dissolve in tap water and arranging Yodels on a paper plate, Jenn told Philip, "It's so weird that your body is untouched by fallout, though. You're lucky in that way, believe me. Radiation sickness sucks."

"Well, not untouched exactly," Philip said. "And not exactly lucky. But the Prince of Irony, perhaps." He grinned and proceeded to drop his drawers.

Dick Truehard had no dick! His celebrated crotch was as flat and smooth as a Ken Doll's. "It fell off around San Simeon," Philip explained. Then he pulled his pants back up and refastened them.

Jenn was dumbfounded. She gasped audibly. "I'm sorry," she stammered.

"Thanks," Philip conceded. "I am too."

The motel room filled with an awkward silence you could have cut with a butter knife. What was there to say after a man confides that he's penis-less? Albeit, in a kinder, gentler way than John Wayne Bobbitt had been. (In 1993, Mr. B's wife Lorena had cut off his penis with an eight-inch carving knife while he slept, then drove one-handed, while holding his severed member in the other, and finally threw his *shvantz* into a field near their home in Manassas, Virginia.)

Jenn shook herself out of her Bobbitt reverie. "San Simeon," she said after she regained her composure That's just north of here." Philip nodded. "No scar? It seems to have healed well," she babbled.

Reaching into the nightstand drawer, Philip produced a family-sized Crest toothpaste box. "I woke up one morning in the Sea Coast Lodge and Little Phil was lying on the bedsheets beside me," he recalled. "No blood, no nothing. It just…detached." Jenn stared at the toothpaste box in awe, knowing what would come next.

Philip untucked the cardboard flap and unwrapped a cylindrical object that was shrouded in toilet paper. It was his detached penis. He slid it into his cupped palm. There, Philip's phallus sat, nested nicely atop his flawlessly-formed testicles, as though resting, its chestnut-colored pubic hair still profuse. "I couldn't just leave it there," he explained. "I mean, I'd been very attached to it for a time."

Philip's dismembered member was extremely well preserved, much better than a mummy at the Metropolitan Museum of Art. In some bizarre fashion, Philip's *schlong* must have been pickled after being steeped in vaginal juices for so many years. But whatever the scientific explanation, Dick's dick was perfect.

Together, Philip and Jenn admired the handiwork of his *mohel.* (A *mohel* is the special rabbi who performs circumcisions on newborn babies.) Philip enticed Jenn to stroke his mickey, which she did gingerly. Terribly monogamous, she hadn't touched a penis except Nik's for at least a decade. But since this one was unattached to a human, Jenn figured it was permissible within the bounds of marriage.

The skin was loose on its underside like the scruff on a cat's neck. The head was velvety soft. That cute little mole still resided right next to the pee-hole. "It's funny," Jenn told Philip. "But I know your friend here almost as well as I know my husband's." Jenn paused and swallowed hard. "Knew Nik's, I mean. Past tense. He's gone."

Then Jenn flashed melancholy, but she fought away the sadness. At least she wasn't alone anymore. She should be grateful for that, right? Jenn switched gears and tried hard to be less sad. "Thanks for showing me," she said to Philip as he began rewrapping his phallus in Scott Tissue.

"My pleasure," he said, easing it into the Crest box and sealing the flap.

"Did it hurt?" Jenn wondered, gesturing at his crotch.

"For a few days, it was a little sore," Philip admitted. "But I slathered it with bacitracin ointment and covered it with gauze. Morning and evenings, I took whirlpool baths in rusty Jacuzzi water and Aveeno. Now, it's as soft as a virgin's knee. Feel." At Philip's insistence, Jenn jammed her hand down the front of his Levi's and felt his Ken Doll bump. He was right; it was silky.

"How do you go?" Jenn asked timidly.

"Go? Go where?" he questioned.

"To the bathroom. How do you pee?"

"The usual way," Philip told her. "My urethra didn't close up, at least," he said rather clinically. "I mean, there's still a hole. But I look like one of those baby dolls who whizzes and cries. Except I'm not anatomically correct. And I can't cry anymore. I'm all cried out, I think." Philip closed the Crest box into the nightstand with a quiet swish.

Ω

As odd as it may sound, Dick Truehard wasn't eminent for his penis. Though it was a very lovely *shvantz*, it was no kielbasa. But who needs a Polish sausage for a sexual appendage? No, it wasn't Dick's penis that had made him a popular swordsman; it was the emotion behind it. When Jenn told this to Philip, he seemed pleased. "Really?" he asked, coloring slightly like a bashful teen who was told he was cute for the first time.

"Really" Jenn assured him. "There's nothing wrong with having a big Johnson. But some men think that's enough. They think that's what makes a man a man. But what good is a big one when there's no passion behind it? Or nothing to talk about before and after sex?"

Philip considered the rhetorical question as Jenn continued her penile praises. "On film, you gave me the sense that you'd be a good cuddler," she explained. "You seemed very loving, like you really cared about your costars."

"Many of them, I did," Philip admitted. "The ones I didn't, well, let's say I dug deep into the Meisner Technique of Acting to seem convincing. I got my money's worth from those lessons. And they weren't cheap."

"You made them laugh too," Jenn said. "Your costars. And the viewers."

"I tried," he said.

"I always felt that you'd make a good friend," Jenn added. When Philip smiled upon hearing this, she sighed in relief. Jenn always wanted to tell this to Dick Truehard in a fan letter but was too timid to do so. And now, there he was sitting in front of her, his Delft-blue eyes glistening in the candlelight, his dick in a box.

Jenn had fantasized about meeting her carnal crush many times. Usually, it involved instant Jell-O Pudding (chocolate almond flavor) or a large, vibrating egg. But perched beside Dick on his bed at the Anchor Inn, things were quite different. Jenn had stroked herself to sleep on many a lonesome night when Nik was out of town, thoughts of Dick's friendly penis the impetus. But now…now Dick was dickless and Jenn was bleeding like a stuck pig, wearing Pampers, with no chance of reenacting her fantasy, no Chocolate Almond Jell-O Pudding to be had. But perhaps this was better, this gentle friendship that was blossoming like a summer rose.

Life is strange indeed. Strange and somewhat wonderful sometimes. And tinged with irony.

Ω

Philip didn't know how to respond to all Jenn had confessed. Suddenly tongue-tied, he offered a modest, "Thanks" and blushed again. He stared at Jenn's now-tattered Nikes and proceeded to play with her fingers. "Maybe you'll get a chance to see what kind of friend I'd make," he offered.

"That would be nice," Jenn said, deciding not to let him in on her plans to off herself ASAP.

Then Philip launched into a soliloquy about his carnal career. "I always tried to bring out the humanity in my performances, to make it real," he told Jenn. "It means a lot to me that you thought I did."

But Jenn didn't just say what she'd said to make Philip feel good. She meant every word. He didn't seem remorseful about not having sexual hardware anymore, just a bit wistful. Very sagely, Philip commented, "Sometimes it was more trouble than it was worth. My penis, I mean. It got me into a lot of hot water and whatnot."

But despite the downside of having a phallus, Philip did seem slightly sorrowful about not having one anymore. It seemed he missed the good, old days when a flick of his hips could bring a woman to the precipice of ecstasy. Or at least the illusion of it.

To make Philip feel better, Jenn reminded him of the adult film critics like Bill Caits and Shelly Rant who applauded his performances in print. Even Bob Rimmer, the Rex Reed of carnal critiques, shared Jenn's high opinion of Dick Truehard. Men didn't feel threatened by Dick and women fell in love with him. "You were always very gracious to me in your reviews," Philip said. "Or at least Pearl Chavez was."

"One in the same," Jenn told him. "And the praise was much deserved."

Another special thing about Dick Truehard was his voice. Jenn couldn't help imagining him quoting Shakespeare to his partners—or at least performing Shakespeare in the Park but then turning to smut because he couldn't make a living as a classical actor.

Philip's vocal cords were silky and golden. Like molten caramel wrapped in chocolate, the sound of his voice made women mushy on the inside. That special way he addressed even a Northern slapper with water balloon titties and hips so wide you could set a full dinner for four on her backside…it made her seem like the most gorgeous, flawless creature who ever set foot on Earth's lowly face. And wasn't that the main point of sex—to make the other person feel loved?

Eventually, Dick Truehard, in the guise of his true self, Philip Tobin, even made Jenn feel quite lovely. Although many times during their first night together, Jenn asked him not to look at her. "You're not seeing beyond the skin, Jennifer," Philip told her. The way he said her name, tripping lazily over the n's, secretly made Jenn's sore toes curl.

Philip continued, "I worked with women who were made to appear stunning with all sorts of paint and creative lighting. But underneath it all, they were horrible human beings. Under the fake nails, they'd bitten their real nails to the quick. Beneath the squirms and moans was depraved indifference. After a while, they forgot how to respond to love. Or at least the semblance of love. And that made them very, very ugly to me. Do you understand?"

Jenn nodded. "But if you hated it so much, then why didn't you leave the business?"

Philip shrugged. "Could you imagine me sitting behind a desk in a bank? Or being a greeter at Home Depot? I'm too recognizable. Besides, I was making a killing in porn."

"I see your point," Jenn admitted.

"And I couldn't make a living doing Ibsen. God knows, I tried."

"See, I knew it!"

Even when she laughed, Philip said that Jenn's eyes were filled with sadness. He said that he wanted to make her eyes laugh too. She'd made him happy, and he wanted to return the favor: he wanted to make her happy with his mouth. Jenn thanked him graciously, flattered, and told him about her bloodletting issue. He understood and redacted.

Since Philip still had that honey-coated voice, Jenn told him that there was another way he could make her happy with his mouth: he could tell her a story.

Curling up in a grin, Philip's plump lips asked, "A dirty story?"

She shook her head. "I was thinking more of a bedtime story."

"Ah," he cooed. "What's your favorite fairy tale?"

"'The Ugly Duckling,'" Jenn said without hesitation.

So, Philip told her Hans Christian Anderson's narrative of a scrappy, gray baby bird who turned beautiful. Jenn popped a valium and settled in, Philip's arms loosely draped around her waist. They lay there, spoon style. Or in Position # 39, as Philip called it.

It was lovely.

Jenn didn't want the story to end. But soon enough, Philip was drawling into her left ear, "…and his heart knew a great joy. A joy that is only known by those who were once upon a time, ugly ducklings."

Philip kissed the top of Jenn's head. Then she drifted off to sleep. She dreamed about being almost-pretty again. Of swimming naked in cool, clean waters among the snow-white swans.

Twenty-One

Duckling

"**N**o one goes out during the day," Philip told Jenn the morning after they met, the morning after he'd lulled her to sleep with the Ugly Duckling story.

"Why?" Jenn asked, reveling in the lukewarm hotel room coffee he'd just presented her in a pink melamine cup.

"Because of the way they look, I think," he said. "They're embarrassed."

Vanity prevailed, even post-eve of destruction. Darkness was kinder and gentler to the survivors' poor, devastated faces, Philip surmised. Like Jenn, he said, they were broken out in boils and covered with zits. All except for Philip. In his copious alone time, he had thought long and hard about why his body hadn't been damaged by Aftermath fallout like the others. But whatever the reason, Philip was at his most handsome, in peak condition, which couldn't be said for the rest of Morro Bay's current population.

"But let's go against the grain, shall we?" Philip suggested. "Let's go outside in the harsh light of day."

Through the Anchor Inn's dirty windows, the sun shone in a carrot-colored sky, so radiantly that it would camouflage no flaws. But after spending the night with Philip, Jenn no longer felt as self-conscious about her appearance. "I don't mind going out in daylight," Jenn told him. "How about you?"

He didn't.

What did Jenn have to hide? Her face was the face of the world. "Besides, it's been so dreary the past few days. The sun will feel good," she added.

And it did.

Ω

Philip was right. The daytime streets of Morro Bay were empty. Apocalypse empty. He and Jenn walked down the hill to Embarcadero. Scores of uninhabited fishing boats were moored in the small marina. "Fancy a ride?" Philip asked. Jenn did. Though many of the watercraft had motors, Philip chose a sturdy, old-school rowboat for their excursion. "I haven't been getting much exercise lately," he explained.

The oars slopped through the thick, oily waters as Philip rowed steadily, reminding Jenn of Charlton Heston in *Ben Hur.* But unlike Charlton and the other galley slaves, Philip leaned back and smiled as he sculled. "You talk in your sleep," he said.

"So, I've been told," Jenn admitted. "What did I say?"

"Something about swans."

Popping as they hit the glutinous water, the oars propelled them forward. "You kept robbing the covers," Jenn told him.

"Your feet were cold," Philip countered.

And so on. They argued like lovers who had never made love.

Ω

El Morro looked even more impressive the closer Jenn and Philip drew to it. Foreboding and gray and bumpy. As Philip paddled, Jenn regaled him with tidbits from the AAA Tourbook, which said that Morro Rock was something called a volcanic plug. Which is the result of magma hardening within a vent on an active volcano. Devil's Tower in Wyoming was perhaps the best-known one but the Canary Islands were dotted with them as well. And since a causeway connected Morro Rock to the shore, it's considered a tied island. "This rock is sometimes called the Gibraltar of the Pacific," Jenn began. "It is the last and most visible in a chain of nine peaks known as the Nine Sisters," she read.

Philip gazed up at the face of the pillar, gnarled and studded with bits of greenery. "Is this the prettiest sister?" he wondered.

Jenn ran her finger down the page. "I'm not sure. But the Tourbook goes on to say that Morro Rock was mined on and off until 1963. And it became State Landmark #801 in 1968." Jenn gazed at El Morro's skin. "I can see why they landmarked it. Wow, it's really something, isn't it?"

"'Tis," Philip agreed.

"Oh, and it used to be a bird sanctuary for the peregrine falcon and other species," Jenn continued.

"No more birds, no more sanctuary," Philip remarked.

"No more birds," Jenn echoed. He stopped rowing. They drifted. There was a stiff silence.

Although the night before, Philip and Jenn had opted to sleep in the same bed, they were still strangers. But they were lonely strangers who craved the closeness of another human being's flesh after flying solo for weeks. True, they'd curled around each other's bodies in sleep, but they were still unfamiliar. Yes, they brushed their teeth in the same sink, but they didn't know very much about each other. So, this was what they set out to do now—become acquainted.

Jenn and Philip's learning curve was sharp and sudden as they took turns gently grilling each other like overzealous but polite game show hosts. There was so much to learn. "Where did you grow up?" Jenn asked Philip, out of the blue.

"In Brooklyn," he said, fiddling with a paddle.

"No way!" she gasped. "Me too!"

"I can tell," he admitted. Then he proceeded to mimic Jenn's raised homophones and low back vowels. She laughed at Philip's exaggerated "dees, dems and dose."

"So, what happened to *your* accent?" Jenn wondered.

"I guess I lost it over the years," he admitted. "That and Sandy Meisner pounded it out of me." Jenn made a confused face until Philip explained further. "Sandy was an acting teacher. The Actors Studio? The Neighborhood Playhouse?" Jenn shook her head; it didn't ring a bell. "Well, anyhow, I think your accent is cute," Philip added.

"Accent? I don't have an accent," Jenn insisted in her Brooklyn drawl, drawing out the short-a split.

"Yes, you do," Philip said. "Let me guess...Bay Ridge, right? *Saturday Night Fever* country."

"That's amazin'," Jenn conceded, dropping the "g" on purpose. "You?"

"Sheepshead Bay."

"I live in Sheepshead Bay!" she gasped. "I mean, lived." Her mood darkened until Philip brightened it.

"Randazzo's, Joe's Clam Bar," he recounted.

Jenn smiled, retasting the delicious meals she'd enjoyed at both.

"Don't forget Lundy's," Philip said.

"That place has been closed for years. But their fried scallops were the bomb, weren't they?"

Again, came that silence but this time it wasn't uncomfortable, it was more thoughtful. It reflected that Jenn and Philip were getting used to each other's presence in their newly-altered lives. And contemplating the past, places and meals that no longer existed.

"It's odd," Philip said a few moments later. "I hardly know you but I feel like I've known you forever."

"And I know your body almost better than I know my own," Jenn admitted. "From the movies, that is. But in real life, I don't even know your favorite ice cream flavor."

"Rum raisin," he told me. "Yours?"

"Phish Food."

"My favorite food," Philip admitted, "is peanut butter."

"Really? Not steak or lobster?"

Philip shook his head. "To me, peanut butter is the perfect food."

"Crunchy or regular?"

"Crunchy, of course," he snorted.

"I'm a smooth gal myself," Jenn told him. "I'd have to say lobster tail is my favorite food. Or a muffuletta from Cochon Butcher in New Orleans. Hates?"

Philip counted off on his fingers. "Tama Janowitz, wine coolers and panty hose. You?"

"Video games, yappy little dogs, Tama and pantyhose too. Especially control top. They must have been invented by Nazis. Underwire bras too."

"How about garter belts? I never met a real woman who wore garter belts," Philip said.

"Well, you just did," Jenn told him. "Pantyhose are nasty pieces of work. Uncomfortable and a breeding ground for infection."

"Most nasty things are," Philip admitted.

The rowboat drifted and scraped bottom. They had reached the sandy beach around the base of Morro Rock. Until very recently, it had been a wildlife preserve. And now…well…

Ω

Up close, El Morro was even more breathtaking. Philip and Jenn walked the ribbon of beach that surrounded the turban of rock which rose almost six hundred feet into thin air. If they'd had the energy and the gumption, the pair might have tried to climb it. Because El Morro silently begged to be climbed. In fact, the last time Nik and Jenn had been there, two kids from Idaho were caught trying to scale Morro Rock. The fire department responded, citations were dispensed and the eleven- and thirteen-year-olds received a stern talking-to.

But instead of scaling the stone, Philip and Jenn pressed their spines against it. They caressed its skin with their palms. It felt sure and solid and safe and pleasantly raspy, like a prehistoric emery board. "It's taller than the Washington Monument," Jenn told Philip.

"That comparison means nothing now," he reminded her. "The Washington Monument doesn't exist anymore. It's toppled, like polite society as we know it."

"I hadn't thought of that," Jenn admitted. "I guess we need a whole new set of yardsticks to measure our lives now."

"What's left of them," Philip agreed. "Last I heard, our nation's capital was rewarded with not one but two blasts. Both north and south of the White House. Just to make sure the job was properly done. I assume everyone and everything was flattened."

"Nothing that used to be exists anymore," Jenn echoed. "I keep forgetting. So, how do we come up with a new frame of reference? For everything."

In her head, Jenn tried to imagine the nonexistence of Mount Rushmore, Old Faithful and the Pink Pussycat Boutique in Greenwich Village.

Philip took it a step further. "I don't know," he postulated. "But what I do know is that we can't say 'as big as the Grand Canyon' or 'as cold as Alaska' anymore. Because those things aren't."

"And we have to forget all about the songs that say, 'I'll be with you till the stars are falling.' Because they're already falling."

"No more Eric Clapton," Philip said sourly. "No more *Disraeli Gears.*"

"Maybe someone else will come along and make new music," Jenn added expectantly.

"Who?" Philip wondered.

"I don't know," she stammered. "Someone. There has to be someone."

"Please enlighten me," he challenged. "What is there to sing about?"

Ω

Jenn and Philip walked pensively along the shore and tried to ignore the dead fish that had washed up on it and the dead peregrine falcons that had dropped from the sky. They soon grew used to the bouquet of rotting wildlife. It no longer sickened them because after a while, like other any unpleasantness, they barely noticed it.

Wading up to their ankles, Philip and Jenn gazed across the bay at the peaceful-looking town. The water bubbled around their feet, staining them black. But they didn't care. They would scrub them later in the oxidized water from the town's gravity-fed system. (A plaque in town boasted that the local high school had partnered with a secondary school in Nepal to bring Morro Bay an onsite clean water system. This test model was still going strong, even today.)

The sea lapping against Jenn's skin felt nice, like tiny insistent tongues. And nice was good, for so little was nice anymore. "The first time I discovered Morro Bay was almost nine years ago," Jenn recalled, for Philip's benefit. "The second time was a few years later. Nik and I were very happy here. It was in Room 9 where I first learned that I was pregnant. We were out-of-our-minds thrilled."

Philip smiled, hijacking some of the joy Nik and Jenn felt back then, gazing upon the piss-stained First Response test. "So, you have a child," he said.

Jenn looked at him sadly. "We'd been trying for almost a year. Trying was the fun part. Failing…well, I was inconsolable every month. But when that strip turned blue, Nik and I were ecstatic." Jenn stopped for a moment, remembering how it good it felt to be knocked up. "I loved being pregnant, feeling the baby move inside of me,' she continued. "Niky and I, we'd always wanted a baby."

Philip understood. "I did too. But it never worked out that way. It was for the best, I guess." He put his hand on Jenn's arm. "What did you have?"

Jenn drew a squiggly line in the wet sand with her big toe. "It was a girl. But I miscarried in the fifth month."

Philip held her hand, pressed it. "I'm sorry," he said.

"Thank you," Jenn told him. "You don't know how difficult it was for people to tell me that. All I needed to hear was 'I'm sorry.' But they would say stupid things. Or else say nothing. Not even acknowledge my lost pregnancy. Or my lost daughter."

"What would you have named her?" he wondered.

Jenn thought for a moment. "Gina. Regina. It means 'queen.'"

"Well, you are my queen," Philip told her.

"Stop the bullshit," Jenn smirked. He did. They were reticent until they walked halfway around the rock. "How did you discover this place?" she wondered.

Philip smiled vaguely, staring out past the horizon. "We were filming *Hot, Wet, Lusty Sex* just outside of town. With a mule named Jocko."

"I remember it well," Jenn told him. "Jocko had great comedic flair."

Philip laughed. "More than my leading lady."

"The chicken?"

He laughed again. "No. Tiffany Glass."

As Philip told it, Pornoland was a bizarre place, much like Wonderland, Oz or downtown Newark. In Pornoland, people were willing to strip off their clothing but wouldn't dare show their soft, vulnerable underbellies. There was usually a calloused shell coating their hearts, Philip said. Many wouldn't reveal their real names, as if their birth name, their true identity, was the most private part of them.

"Most just wanted to do their job—which was bang their brains out— then go home," Philip explained. "There was very little friendship in the industry, true friendship, I mean. No one you could call at four in the morning when you were lonely or when you'd done too much coke and thought there were teeny-tiny policemen hiding in the trees. Most of the women saw you as work, as a job that had to be done. Like stuffing envelopes. Like a letter that needed to be typed. The sooner it was done, the sooner they could go home and watch 'Abbott Elementary.'"

"How about the men?" Jenn wondered.

"The men were very cautious," Philip began. "We were rivals because we were up for the same jobs. The producers and directors made us feel that way. They made it clear that we were all dispensable. 'Rent-a-Cocks' they called us. I guess it was true. We were."

"But you were so much more than an anonymous body part, at least to me," Jenn told him. But she didn't think it would make a difference to the way Philip felt.

He threw a stick into the bay, which landed with a resounding plop. "It was weird," he began. "In one scene, you might have five women pleasuring every millimeter of your flesh. You're the center of attention. You're at the pinnacle of bliss. But when it's over, you go home to your sad, little studio apartment in Reseda. Pathetic, really."

"It sounds very lonely," Jenn agreed.

He nodded. "That was the worst part. In people's fantasies, porn was a very glamorous business. But in reality, you're all alone."

"Aren't we all?"

"I guess we are," Philip conceded.

Jenn followed the grain of conversation. "Watching those movies, I assumed the women were all nymphos and the men were all blistering studs."

"Then that means we did our jobs well," Philip said. "There were times when nothing could be further from the truth. Some of the women didn't even like sex."

"Why not?"

Philip put his hands on his hips and stared back toward town. "Either they'd been abused as young girls or they'd had partners who took advantage of them. Either way, they thought sex was dirty and that they were bad people because of what they did onscreen."

"That's so sad," Jenn told him. "I always thought porn people were kind of noble."

"How so?" Philip wondered.

"They share their bodies with anyone who cares to look, no prejudice, no exceptions."

"I see where you're coming from," he admitted. "But it didn't feel noble to me. For men, being in porn was difficult too, but in a different way than it was for the women. Making love to a female who didn't want to be there, who cringed when you touched her, that wasn't easy. And the pressure of getting an erection on cue was also a chore."

Philip tipped his toes into the onyx surf. "But…if you pay a person five hundred or a thousand dollars a day or more, they'll do just about anything that's asked of them. Man or woman. People are funny that way. They find a way to do something, even if it's unpleasant."

"I guess you're right."

"I *know* I'm right," Philip stressed. "I've done it myself. Those movies don't show the guys struggling to get a boner. Or keep it. It also doesn't show the production grinding to a halt as the male lead wanks tragically in the corner, trying to get hard again. Or touching a woman who is repulsed by your very existence and the only reason *she's* there is because she has to pay her Visa bill that month. Or keep herself in coke so she can numb her brain enough to forget what she's doing. Or…"

"I get the picture," Jenn broke in, lightly touching Philip's arm to end his rant.

"The magic of cinema," he drifted off. Then after a beat, "I have a theory."

Jenn picked up a piece of driftwood, hurled it; she heard a splash. "Go for it," she encouraged him.

Philip shrugged, "When you make a dirty dollar, you spend it twice as fast."

"So, you think porn money was dirty money?"

He didn't even have to consider this. "Maybe I didn't, but society sure did. My parents were embarrassed; therefore, I was embarrassed. It didn't matter how many AVN awards I'd won; I was scum in society's eyes. Lower than scum. I wasn't welcome at family reunions. They made that crystal clear."

"Well, I think you guys were kick-ass," Jenn told Philip. "Bearing everything, warts and all, to entertain others. To teach others. To give solace to the lonely, the handicapped, the hopeless..."

"That's erotica at its best but unfortunately…"

Jenn broke in, "Did you know that in ancient Egypt, prostitutes were considered sacred? Their acts were thought to be divine, respectable even, and that they pleased the gods."

"No," Philip said. "No, I did not."

They didn't talk much after that. Philip seemed withdrawn, aloof. Like something more was bothering him. Jenn gave him the space to be silent with his sadness as they made their way back to the rowboat.

Ω

Midway to Morro Bay, Philip began to talk about an actress he'd met on the set of *Hot, Wet, Lusty Sex.* "We really liked each other," he said. "So, we began to see each other off set. I remember once we had dinner together in town."

"Where?" Jenn wondered, charmed at the start of the story.

"At the Great American Fish Company. We were just two regular people. No one asked for our autographs. No one asked what it was like to work with so-and-so. No one recognized us in this sleepy, little town. I felt..." Then Philip stopped abruptly, shaking his head from side to side. When Jenn asked him to continue, he wouldn't initially.

"...you felt...normal?" she tried. "Like anyone else?"

"Right," Philip grunted between rows. "I truly think you give up a piece of your soul when you have sex in front of a camera," he said.

Although Jenn begged to differ, she let him cleave to his beliefs.

Fearing that Philip was sinking into a dark mood, Jenn told silly stories in a sorry attempt to get him to smile. This usually worked for Nik but not for Philip. Jenn crammed the silent space with nervous energy, talking enough for them both. Although Philip was quiet, he was attentive. He listened closely as Jenn rattled on about her misplaced husband. Not once did he beg her to stop. He even asked pertinent questions.

"I'm jealous of you, Jennifer," he said, finally. "I was in the adult film industry for fifteen years. I had sex with one thousand one hundred and fifty-nine women on screen, not counting those in my private life or stunt cock work. And of all those women, I only loved one of them. And not nearly as much as you loved your Nik."

"Love," Jenn corrected. "I still love him, whether he's here or not, whether he's alive or not." Philip nodded; he understood. "What happened to her, this woman?" Jenn wondered.

Philip took a breath. "She put a shotgun to her head."

Although Philip didn't mention the woman's name, Jenn knew who he was referring to. Noreen. Noreen Applewood. She was a striking, strawberry-blonde nymphette from the Midwest, angelic, sweet. Too sweet for a business that ate her up and spat her out. To the video companies, Noreen was a commodity, someone they could sell on glossy box covers. Someone whose innocent beauty would make them a lot of money. And it did. Noreen's parents, her friends back in

Michigan shunned her, shamed her, all because she bared her perfect body and had sex on the silver screen.

Now it was Philip's turn to cry. It was pitiful to see. Jenn slid the oars from his hands and took over rowing, pausing first to take a Valium. *When we reach the shore, I will hold him,* Jenn told herself. *If he lets me.* But in the meantime, Philip cried alone. It was an intense boo-hoo, the way someone sobs when they haven't permitted themselves to cry for months, years. So, Jenn rowed and let Philip cry. There was nothing else she could do.

When the rowboat bumped into the pier's pilings, Jenn scrambled up onto the dock, moored it with rope, then coaxed Philip up the ladder. They sat side by side on the wharf, dangling their feet above the waterline. Jenn curled her arm around Philip's shoulders and kissed his hair. It was very nice hair.

"There was nothing I could do for her," Philip lamented. "I knew she was sad, but I couldn't help her. I knew she was depressed, but I couldn't reach her. And she refused to get professional help." Philip sighed. "After she killed herself, I kept thinking there must have been something, something I could have said or done."

"But there wasn't," Jenn told Philip knowingly; she had lost several friends to suicide. "It wasn't about you. It was about her."

"I suppose," Philip sniffled. "But my God, Noreen was only twenty!" He lay his head on Jenn's lap and bawled into her Sergios.

Say her name, Jenn thought, *Say her name and she isn't really gone. Say their names and you start to heal. Say it. Say it. Noreen. Nik. Noreen. Nik.*

"Noreen…" he sobbed. "Noreen…"

Let the healing begin.

Twenty-Two

Dick of Life

Back in Room 9 at the Anchor Inn, Philip lay on the bed and stared at the ceiling's peaked, swirled popcorn surface. Jenn lay beside him, doing the same. The ceiling reminded her of the top of a home-baked birthday cake but she didn't share this tidbit with Philip. He probably wouldn't have appreciated it, not now.

Jenn thought she saw him brush away a tear once or twice. It bothered her that Philip was silently crying but she left him to his private tears. At least his crying was more in control, more in check this time. "What are you thinking about?" she finally asked.

"Nothing," he said..

The toothpaste box containing Philip's penis was at his side. He must have been looking wistfully at his detached member, reminiscing while Jenn was Pampering herself in the bathroom. Philip tended to break out Little Phil when he was feeling blue. Mental masturbation, he called it. "Do you miss it?" Jenn wondered. "Your penis, I mean."

"Not really," he admitted. "Honestly, it was pretty tired after all that in and out."

Jenn flopped onto her belly next to Philip and began flipping through the AAA Tourbook. "Why don't you ever share that?" he snapped.

"It's all yours," Jenn told Philip, holding the paperback out toward him in surrender. Philip took the worn tome from Jenn's hands, fingering the pages hungrily. His mood lightened considerably. "I haven't touched a book in months," he said. "You don't mind, do you?"

"What's mine is yours," she insisted.

Philip turned to the street map of Los Angeles. Eyes vivid with recollection, he pointed out the places he'd lived, ate and worked. He managed to locate the exact spot on Van Nuys Boulevard where Bill North's office had been, plus the warehouse where hundreds of porn movies had been churned out "…like babies from Mormon mommies," as he so eloquently phrased it.

After finding the pages dedicated to San Francisco, one of Philip's long fingertips traced the route to Alioto's on Fisherman's Wharf, went down and made a left on Lombard Street. Not the crooked part, but the part where he'd owned an apartment in an old, restored townhouse. "If the paint on those walls could talk," Jenn laughed.

But instead of laughing, Philip brooded. He closed the tattered book. "What's the sense of reminiscing?" he said. "Nothing's there anymore."

"It's good to remember, though, isn't it?" Jenn asked. "It's comforting."

"Comforting? When it doesn't hurt, sure, it's comforting," Philip barked. He was in a rare foul mood, seething beneath the surface. It was the treacherous kind of mood where people seek to hurt someone else, to wound their spirit. Jenn forced herself not to respond but Philip was primed for a fight. He pressed his face closer to hers. "Tell me, is that why you pop so much Valium? Because it's comforting? Or to forget?"

Jenn sat up straight and fast, as though he'd slapped her. "That's not fair," she said.

"Is it?"

"I'm in pain," she stammered. "I'm bleeding…"

"We're all in pain," Philip told her plainly.

Jenn bit her lower lip, struggling not to cry. "That was a cheap shot," she frowned, wrapping her arms around herself. She suddenly felt chilled. "You know why I take the Valium. Because I hurt. I ache. And not just in my heart." Jenn snatched the book from Philip.

"I'm sorry," he offered. "I have no right to judge you. Do whatever you want. Whatever it takes to survive. Whatever makes you happy."

"Nothing makes me happy," she told him.

"Thanks, Jennifer."

"I didn't mean you, Philip," she tried to explain. "I'm glad we met. I really am. I was so tired of being alone. But I don't think I could ever be happy again, truly happy, that is. However, you do make me less sad."

"I suppose, considering everything, that means a lot."

"It does," Jenn said.

The hush in the room bathed them like a patchwork quilt.

The sun had just set, making it comfortably dim. In those final days, the yellow dwarf known as the Sun had the habit of receding abruptly, like a sledgehammer. And of rising like a two-alarm fire. Sneaky bastard.

Despite their tiff, Jenn rested her head on Philip's chest, the diffused light a cushion. "Philip?" she asked into the inkiness.

His eyes fluttered. "Mmmm," he answered.

"I just wanted to let you know that…that before I came here, I had already made up my mind."

"To do what?"

Jenn exhaled audibly and began. "I decided that if Nik wasn't here in Morro Bay, waiting for me, then I would commit suicide." Her words seemed to suspend lifelessly in the air. There was no response from Philip. No words to accompany hers. However, Jenn noticed that Philip had stopped breathing for a moment. Then he let out a steady stream of carbon dioxide. "Philip?" she asked.

"I couldn't take another one," he murmured. "Another suicide." His chest concaved as he breathed out. Jenn could count his ribs pressing against the side of her face. Five, six, seven… "It's not fair," Philip said softly. "Everyone I care about leaves me." He lifted a hand to rub the tears from his eyes. "You can't do that to me, Jenny."

"Why?"

"Because I love you."

"I love you too," she admitted. "But…"

Philip rocked Jenn in his arms. They were ropey with muscles and covered with a fine, honey-colored fuzz. *How does he manage to stay so fit in the middle of the end of the world?* Jenn wondered. "But…" Philip echoed.

"But does love really matter? Here and now?" she continued.

Philip got up from beneath Jenn. She heard the scratch of a match then saw a sputter of light. He touched the paper stick to two candles, then was moving toward the third. Jenn blew out the flaming scrap before he could light Candle # 3. Philip looked at her in a curious way. "Three on a match," she explained. "It's bad luck."

At the same moment, they both realized how ludicrous Jenn's statement was—how bad could their luck get, post-apocalypse? Philip swatted at his tears then rubbed his snotty nose on his arm and started laughing. "Does luck really matter? Here and now?" he posed, mirroring what Jenn had told him about love.

"I guess nothing matters if you look at it that way," Jenn admitted and started laughing too.

For a brief flicker of a moment, Jenn saw the old Dick Truehard when she looked at Philip Tobin. There was that familiar, impish spark in his eyes. The same one Dick had gotten when the nymphette he was delivering a pizza to claimed she didn't have the money to pay for it. Wink, wink, nod, nod. That magnetic quality which made him such a fine actor, even beyond flesh flicks.

At the Anchor Inn, Dick/Philip jumped back onto the bed and bounced on his knees, much like Jenn and her brother Brian used to do at HoJo's as children. "And therein lies the whole secret of life," Philip said.

"What?" Jenn asked him.

"Hope!" he shouted.

Jenn rolled her eyes. "A second ago, you were hopeless."

"I know, but that's the beauty of life; things change. All the time." Jenn was unconvinced but Philip plowed ahead, regardless. "Hope. The belief that something wonderful could happen at any given moment, even when everything looks like utter shit. You never know."

"Oh, I know," Jenn insisted. "And what I know is that it isn't good. Just look at me."

"Yes, just look at yourself," Philip told her. "You're still alive, despite everything. It's a miracle. You're still breathing."

"Just barely," she quipped.

Jenn looked at Philip and again and saw the Dick Truehard who could convince a pious nun to copulate with an electric razor and a live chicken. (But only if the chicken were willing.) "You aren't going to break into a verse of 'I Believe,' are you?" Jenn asked. "Please don't," she added before he could.

But Philip ignored her cynicism. "If there isn't hope, Jennifer, then what's left?" he posed.

The current situation was so wretched that she decided to laugh instead of cry. "What a pair we are," Jenn said between giggles. "An administrative assistant who's hemorrhaging and a former porn star with no penis. I mean, together we make no sense. We can't repopulate this dying planet or do anything noble. Why are we here?"

Philip squished Jenn's face in his hands like her Aunt Henny used to do. It kind of hurt but in a good way. "When are you going to stop thinking of other people?" he admonished. "You don't owe anyone anything, especially now. Gather ye rosebuds, toots."

"Huh?"

"Robert Herrick? 'To the Virgins, to Make Much of Time'?"

"Still nothing," Jenn told him.

Philip released her face to explain, "Basically in his poem, Herrick is telling this chick he digs to *carpe diem*...to seize the day. Because time is fleeting."

This was something Jenn didn't want to deal with: the fleet footedness of time. So, she took a sharp left turn and changed the convo. "I was wondering about something, Philip," she said.

"Shoot," he encouraged.

"A while back, you said that you loved me. Do you remember that?"

"Of course."

"Well, did you mean that you loved me loved me? Truly, madly, deeply? Or in the California sense of the word, like someone loves avocados?"

Philip wrinkled his face in concentration, as though he were trying to figure it out himself. "I know we only just met," he began. "But I love you love you. I *really* love you." Then, like an insecure teenager, Philip asked, "Why? Don't you love me?"

"Like the brother I never had. Like the lover you'll never be," Jenn said, gesturing toward the extra-large Crest box.

"That's why God gave men mouths," Philip said. Jenn snapped the waistband of her Pampers in response. "Oh, right," he corrected himself. Then he backtracked. "I love you, Spartacus, like the father I never had..." Philip lisped just like Tony Curtis did as "Antoninus" in *Spartacus.* Philip was a film buff just like Jenn, so he got all her obscure references. Just like Nik had.

Nik…It's not that Jenn didn't miss Nik anymore; it was just that it didn't ache in the same way now that there was another human being to fill in the blank spaces. However, there were some spaces that only Nik could fill.

Jenn and Philip laughed in quiet appreciation of their *Spartacus* repartee. "You're something special, Philip," she told him. Then she kissed him long and hard on the mouth. Sometimes a kiss could be a weighty thing.

"I feel like I have an erection," Philip said after they pulled apart.

"I've heard it happens to people who have lost a limb," Jenn conceded. They get itches in fingers and toes that aren't there anymore."

"This feels more like a boner in my heart," Philip tried to explain, "which is almost as good. And a lot less complicated."

Twenty-Three

Dinner and a Show

T hat evening, Jenn and Philip dressed for dinner. She wore a billowy rose silk chemise he had scavenged for her in a fancy shop on Harbor Avenue. The frock was soft and floaty, and the outline of her diaper barely showed. The dress begged for kitten heels instead of sneakers, but Philip couldn't procure any pumps that properly fit Jenn's skinny arches and swollen toes. To jazz up the ensemble, Jenn wore Bonnie Doon anklets with fake pearls sewn into the cuffs.

Topping off the snazzy ensemble, Jenn twisted her hair into a French braid and tied it with a satin ribbon. At the last minute, Philip plopped a faux leopard-skin pillbox hat onto her head. He had great fashion sense for a straight man and chose the most wonderful things for Jenn to wear whenever he went on one of his shopping jaunts. Things you wouldn't think went together ended up working like magic. Jenn's friend Yoko, a professor at the Fashion Institute of Technology, had that gift too. God, how Jenn missed Yoko.

Philip fussed with the hat's veil. It formed a kind curtain over Jenn's face, masking her cystic skin. "Very Jackie O," he approved, handing her a light wrap. A "frug," he called it, just like Jenn's friend Roger used to.

Philip himself looked dashing, reminiscent of the horny, one-legged yacht captain he played in *Lust on the Rocks*. Decked out in a double-breasted navy-blue jacket complete with brass buttons, carefully-creased white slacks, a powder blue shirt, matching socks and Bass walking shoes, Philip cut an impressive figure. Yes, he was quite the fashion forager.

"Can I say it now?" Philip begged as they stepped onto Radcliffe Avenue.

"If you must," Jenn conceded. Philip had been nagging her to let him recite a poem he'd written in her honor.

Philip cleared his throat theatrically and began:

> *Iris, truly a flower,*
> *Yet bottomlessly brown,*
> *Instead of purple hued.*
> *So sensitive, so delicate in soul*
> *That you are God-protected*
> *With sword-shaped leaves.*
> *Some call you 'eye of heaven'*
> *Or 'rainbow,'*
> *But I know that you are*
> *Woman...*

Jenn was speechless, a rare occurrence. No one had ever written a poem for her before, not even her husband. She didn't know what to say. Philip explained the significance of the verses, "You once told me that your favorite color was purple and that your middle name was 'Iris,' didn't you?"

Jenn nodded. "I did…Your poem. It's, uh, it's beautiful."

Philip smiled. "It's not finished. A work in progress, like most poetry is. I call it 'By the Sea's Gate.' Your friend Serena lived in Sea Gate, right? I tried to work it all in there."

"Yes, I see that," Jenn stammered, still *verklempt*. "It's lovely. I'm flattered. And kind of embarrassed."

"Don't be," he said. "I'm starving. Let's sup."

"Don't get all Shakespearean on me," Jenn complained, taking his arm.

"Don't get all street on me," Philip countered.

They headed down to the Harbor Hut, their favorite place to rummage. There wasn't much left in the way of the gourmet delights the shop advertised but Jenn and Philip managed. They fixed tasty crunchy peanut butter munchies topped with apricot jam on Carr's Table Water Crackers. Jenn was about to down a Valium with her can of Goya Coconut Milk, but Philip stopped her. He twined his hand gently through hers. "No more of those," he said. "Okay?"

"Okay," Jenn told him reluctantly, though she'd been popping them like Tic Tacs for weeks. Even though she worried about withdrawal symptoms, Jenn still assured Philip, "I'll do my best."

"That's all anyone can do," he said. "Their best."

Ω

Philip and Jenn shared a pleasant meal at the Harbor Hut. The sea was calm behind the big picture windows and the sun managed to set its usual time instead of haphazardly. Jenn did miss watching the otters floating on their backs while they ate their dinner. Because the sea otters, well…

Besides its big rock, Morro Bay was also famous for its playful otters. Nik and Jenn had enjoyed watching them frolic their last time in town. Philip fondly remembered the *enhydra lutris* as well. He recalled how their antics had made Noreen laugh. Oh, how he'd loved her laugh. So free, joyous and unguarded. But now there were no more sea otters. No more Niky. No more Noreen.

"A group of otters is called a romp, by the way," Jenn said, totally out of context.

Philip nodded, other things clearly on his mind. Munching thoughtfully on a cracker, Philip told her, "Did I ever tell you that I tested positive for HIV?"

"When?" Jenn gasped.

"About a month before the blast."

"And you were still working?" she said, in shock.

"How else could I make a living?" he snapped. Jenn had no words for what Philip had done, for the people's lives he'd endangered. But he displayed not a shred of guilt. "Don't look so indignant," Philip told her. "How do you think I got it in the first place?"

"But it still wasn't right, what you did."

"A lot of things weren't right," Philip said stoically. "But none of them matter now." He licked a smear of apricot from his finger. "Anyway, I'd been feeling under the weather. Then I noticed that I'd lost weight. I went and got tested at Mitch's clinic. My diagnosis was just starting to sink in when…" His voice drifted off. "But the funny thing is, now I feel fine. That is, except for losing my prick. I feel strong, healthy, better than I've felt in years."

"And your point is?" Jenn prodded.

"My point is that I think they finally found a cure for AIDS."

"Oh, please!" Jenn snorted. "Nuclear war isn't a cure!"

"Granted, it's a bit drastic," Philip admitted. "But how else do you explain my newfound vigor. Here I am, the picture of health." Jenn gave him a doubtful look but he continued, undaunted. "Consider it—I might have been dead by now. Untreated, AIDS can kill quickly. I've seen it happen."

"I have too," Jenn agreed sadly, thinking of her cousin Jack. She nibbled the chocolate off the top of her Hostess Cupcake, saving the white swirl for last. "Maybe that's why the radiation doesn't make you sick," Jenn conceded in wonder. "The AIDS virus protects you. Like a vaccine."

"Live and learn…" Philip nodded.

"With my friend Irma," Jenn added for a bit of jocularity. Philip smiled. It was good to be with someone else who understood the old movie reference, no matter how little-known the film *My Friend Irma* was.

"That Marie Wilson was a hottie," Philip confessed.

"You're such a scoundrel," Jenn told him, laughing.

Ω

After supper, Jenn and Philip enjoyed a brief *passeggiata* then interrupted their walk to visit with the neighbors. Since Philip was already acquainted with them, he introduced Jenn all around. There were frail handshakes, ruined smiles and kindly pleasantries shared. Everyone was glad to meet yet another person who had survived the same ordeal they had.

The calling-after-dinner gesture had a pleasing, old timey feel, which Jenn loved. It reminded her of summer nights during her Bay Ridge childhood, hanging out on a stoop, waiting for the Good

Humor Man, collecting friends to play a feisty game of stoop ball. Only in Morro Bay, there were no Spaldeens, no ice cream trucks. But gathering on a wide wooden porch suited Jenn just fine.

For some unknown reason, people from all over North America had been drawn to this quaint, little corner of California. They didn't know why; they just had the urge to stop traveling when they arrived in Morro Bay.

In attendance were the Redman clan from Vancouver, originally five but their numbers had dwindled to three. They'd begun their descent south, passing without papers through the Peace Arch before the seventh (or was it the eighth?) bomb had been deployed.

There were also two sisters who'd been turning tricks in Tijuana before they were compelled to travel north. Business had perked up after in the Aftermath. People were keen to fuck one last fuck, they noted. No one stopped them at the border either; there *were* no borders anymore.

A weathered cowboy named Bob from Skull Valley, Arizona was also present. He'd ridden his faithful steed, Lightning, west until the poor thing died beneath him. Kevin, a farmer and his wife Sylett hailed from Wisconsin. Plus, there was a woman originally from Trinidad who was waitressing in Lake Tahoe before the blasts. And so on.

Although they had different backgrounds and different shades of skin beneath their wounds, in Morro Bay, people came together as fellow human beings searching for a shred of tranquility. In Morro Bay, they were equals. It was homey and sweet and good.

The post-dinner gathering was something Jenn would grow to look forward to every evening. This loving assembly, the playful banter, refueled her soul, especially after she'd seen the worst of humanity—gluttony, starvation, cruelty, murder. The inhabitants of this serene enclave recalled what young Anne Frank had written before the Nazis killed her:

In spite of everything, I still believe that people are really good at heart.

Slowly but surely, Jenn was starting to believe this again herself. Some of the survivors wore gauze to cover their damaged visages. Others wore ski masks with eyes, nose and mouth holes punched out. Some covered their toothless mouths when they spoke or laughed. But others, wizened children of the Sixties, let it all hang out. Jenn fell somewhere between both camps, alternately covering up and revealing. But that first night, she was grateful for the protective coating of her Jackie O pillbox hat's netting.

Recognized by many, Dick Truehard was something of a celebrity. But not just for his former erotic prowess. He was a fine specimen of humanity when most of them were rotting away. Dick/Philip was admired much like a painting in the Louvre had been admired, the way Michelangelo's David had been venerated. The man was just *that* handsome.

Collectively, everyone marveled at the fact that they all seemed to have been mysteriously drawn to the same place—Morro Bay. Whether they hailed from the Midwest, the Southwest, Canada or Mexico, something pulled them there. Some unknown force that was stronger than their weakness, stronger than their will, stronger than anything. They didn't know what it was but still, they acknowledged it, bowed to it, respected it, feared it, even.

The desire, the invisible tug to reach this particular picayune peninsula that jutted so absurdly into the Pacific, was different for everyone. For those in the middle of the country, the draw might have been the overwhelming urge to see the ocean before they died. Those from the north sought warmth. Those from the south sought cooler climes. And here they all were, at the end of their journeys, in Morro Bay.

"Now what?" Kevin, from America's Dairyland, asked. Now what, indeed.

As it turned out, no one found what they were looking for in Morro Bay. But they waited anyhow. They waited for something unnamable to happen. But at least they'd discovered a safe haven while they could cool their heels, catch their breath, and try to figure out what to do next.

In other places, everything was topsy-turvy. There were no morals, no sense of right or wrong. For most, anything was acceptable in the unacceptable circumstances of the Aftermath. The roadside atrocities the lot of them had witnessed were similar, no matter where they'd come from, no matter what route they'd taken. There was no need to discuss the details of their private strife, for they were all much the same.

But despite who they were or where they'd come from, one constant that remained: once they arrived in Morro Bay, they felt the desire to stop. It was as though they were all anticipating something. Only they didn't know what it was.

It reminded Sylett, Dairy Kevin's wife, of what Justice Potter Stewart had said about obscenity in that oft-quoted 1964 trial: "I know it when I see it."

So, when everyone reached this pretty place perched on the Pacific, they knew it was "the" place. And they stopped. They laid stakes there. And waited.

Ω

"I walked and walked," Cowboy Bob drawled. "I thought I'd be walking forever. Or till I dropped like poor old Lightning did. But when I got here and saw that big, old thang in the water," he gestured to Morro Rock, "I don't know what happened. The wanderlust in me settled down and I settled in."

Dairy Kevin from Freedom, WI described it this way: "Suddenly, we felt the need to stop moving. For me and Sylett, it was like we couldn't go another step. Turned out it was the right decision."

"But it wasn't so much that *we* decided," Sylett tried to explain. "It was like the place made the decision for us. If that makes any sense. It doesn't, I know, but…"

Kevin finished for her. "We immediately liked it here. It felt right. The journey felt finished. But in a good way, in a positive way. Yes?"

Sylett nodded. "But deep inside, it's like we're expecting something. I'm not sure what. But when the time comes, I think we'll know what it is."

All the stories were much the same.

"But why do we stay?" Kathleen from Trinidad, posed. "There's no electricity. Other places I've passed through have power, but we don't. Why are we here?"

They all shook their heads. "Damned if I know," Cowboy Bob said.

"This town is different," Philip remarked. "It's beautiful. Or as close to beautiful as you can get now."

"*Che linda,*" one of the Mexican whores agreed.

"*Hai,*" assented the man who had run a restaurant in San Francisco's Japan Center.

225

The night sky was pewter and crammed with clouds. They watched it in silence, all eyes inexplicably drawn there. The clouds began to tumble like towels in a clothes dryer. A uniform gasp rose from the people congregated on the porch. "Storm rising?" Cowboy Bob suggested. "Twister?"

"Nah," said Pat, who hailed from Hampton, Iowa and had seen his share of tornados. "Something else. Something bigger."

"What's bigger than a tornado?" Kevin asked.

Then the sky flashed with silent, internal fireworks. First blue, then red, then green. "It's better than a Grucci show," Jenn said. As a lifelong New Yorker, Jenn knew that the Grucci Family staged the fireworks for Macy's Fourth of July extravaganzas and the like. Some of the others knew this too, from watching the pyrotechnics on TV.

Jenn was mesmerized but terrified. She clutched Philip's arm. "But seriously, what the hell is that?" she whispered.

Philip shrugged. "It could be anything. The Northern Lights?"

"Can't be *aurora borealis*," the dairy farmer's wife explained. Sylett was something of an amateur astronomer as well as a budding herbalist. "The Northern Lights happen in higher latitudes. Norway… Sweden. Alaska. We're too far south."

"North is south now," Philip reminded her. "There's no rhyme or reason to anything."

"I suppose," Sylett conceded. "But it's still not the Northern Lights."

"Che linda," the other Mexican whore said.

"Hai," agreed the Japanese man.

Streamers and arches of colored illuminations continued to blink through the heavens. "I bet it's an electrical reaction of some sort," Philip told Jenn. "Remember that scene in *Northern Lights, Southern Exposure?"* She did; who could forget it? "I imagine it's something like that."

"But whatever it is," the island girl lilted. "It's lovely."

"Yes," Jenn agreed. "But it still scares me. And the way the clouds swirl around…it looks like something's trying to burst through."

"Pshaw," Cowboy Bob said. "It's like Dick Truehard said, it's the Northern Lights that lost their way."

"A gift from God to give us a bit of joy in these sorry times," said Lisa, the defrocked televangelist.

Everyone nodded in agreement whether or not they believed in a higher power. Then the conversation drifted off into different paths, as conversations often do. To the baseball standings at the time the season was called and predictions as to who might have won the World Series if none of this had happened. To what path the long-running soap opera "All My Children" might have taken. To if Michael Jackson had really been such a kook and if so, what caused it. Etc.

Jenn's mind was lulled by the contented bumble bee buzz of talk which zipped through her body. She listened halfway to all the words at once and to the thoughts in her own head. This is when she realized that she no longer craved the warm, fluffy cocoon of suicide. Something unnamed, something much more than finding Philip, than finding Morro Bay, than finding community in an apocalypse made Jenn want to stay alive. If she had to give it a name, Jenn would call it "hope." Perhaps it was the sensation of love that warmed her hollow chest once again. But ever since Philip and she had "that talk," Jenn felt there was something…a promise…a possibility…lurking just around the bend.

Ω

Maybe twenty in all were clustered together on that broad, smiling Main Street porch. They downed pitchers of Tang and jugs of Gatorade, taking turns to tell abbreviated versions of their life stories in two minutes or less. (Iowa Pat timed them.) Some passed around photos they'd managed to save before they fled: wide, smiling faces from better days. But all days were better days compared to this. Even the worst day imaginable was better than facing nuclear annihilation. Of course, there were tears but there was no shame in crying. Everyone understood.

Philip, or "Dick Truehard," stood out as a local luminary. Most in the group confessed that they partook in observing the amorous art of pornography, either obsessively or casually. The ladies mourned the loss of Dick's notorious phallus. Like Jenn had done previously, some admitted that they had known Dick's privates more intimately than they had known their own husband's. (Later, Philip told Jenn that before her, no woman had been willing to cohabit with him when they discovered that his member had been dismembered. And that was a shame.)

The gentlemen had a slightly different reaction to Dick: they revered him like an erotic god. They were anxious to learn about his costars and were sad to discover the truth—that these women weren't so different than their girlfriends and wives. Porn princesses had the same insecurities, the same fears. The only difference was that they were a bit braver than most. Why? Because they bared it all for the camera and shared their bodies with strangers. That took a lot of guts.

Philip didn't want to lie but he didn't want to sugarcoat the flesh trade either. One man wept when he learned that Tiffany Glass was lax in the personal hygiene department. Another was horrified to hear that Taffy Pull was toothless and that her uppers often dislodged during oral sex. Or that Patti Pink had chronic vaginitis. "Going down on her was like eating a dish of cottage cheese," Philip opined, "without the fruit." Cowboy Bob gagged audibly upon hearing this. Philip burst many balloons that night, as gently as possible. But balloons were meant to be broken; that's the way balloons were designed.

Ω

While the men spoke of matters of the flesh, the women spoke of their tormented flesh. Sylett Lighthouse, Dairy Kevin's wife, was very gifted in her knowledge of natural remedies. In fact, she'd grown up with Doris Joyce Kloss, granddaughter of Jethro Kloss, author of *Back to Eden,* the holistic health tome. It was Sylett's second bible.

Grandpa Kloss used to give her and Doris slippery elm as chewing gum and they never had a cavity. He also fed them soybean milk and whole wheat raisin bread, all of which he made himself, created from soy and wheat and grapes he grew himself.

Both Sylett and Doris grew up straight and strong. Being a pastor's kid, Sylett never swore but she swore by Pop Jethro's treatments. The only thing that made her uneasy was his fondness for high colonic enemas. He suggested them for practically every ailment, including nightmares. Luckily, Kloss never gave the girls an enema, which everyone except for Dick Truehard, agreed would have been too weird. But then again, Dick had starred in the remake of *Water Power,* reprising the Jamie Gillis role.

Sylett and Kevin had laid claim to the handsome clapboard house on Main Street whose wraparound porch everyone had gathered upon. Inside, bookshelves lined the walls and on those shelves sat bags and vials and jars of herbs that Sylett and Kevin had collected from health food stores along their journey. They'd managed to get their hands on a sturdy shopping cart from Ralph's which made the ferrying easier.

For scalding urine, Sylett prescribed glycerin capsules filled with equal parts of fennel, burdock and milkweed. For gangrene, she recommended powdered charcoal, smartweed and whole wheat applied in a poultice. For eczema, herbs like yarrow and yellow dock usually did the job.

Sylett said that Jethro Kloss also prescribed "plenty of fresh air" for good health but there was none of that to be found. So, she suggested, "Just remember to breathe. And breathe fully and completely. The exhale is as important as the inhale." Sage-like advice because many admitted that life was so stressful, they often found themselves holding their breath without realizing it. Sylett led them all in a few rounds of deep breathing called *murcha pranayama,* which roughly translated to "breath of joy." It felt good to breathe together collectively, in one unit, they all agreed.

If Morro Bay survivors hadn't been falling apart in various capacities, Sylett said that she would have held yoga classes. But many could barely manage walking, let alone pigeon pose.

While the men chatted outdoors, Sylett skittered around her spotless kitchen. On the stove was a six-quart pot filled with her special skin liniment. (Kevin had rigged up something so that the stove worked.) She gave all parties present empty margarine containers filled with a magical concoction. Sylett swore it would help heal everyone's inflamed epidermises. Jenn was skeptical but took the poultice anyway.

When Jenn told Sylett privately about her female troubles, she gave Jenn a bottle of raspberry leaf capsules, to be taken twice daily. Next, Sylett deftly dredged out scoops of herbs then mixed the small piles together and put the mixture in a Ziploc bag. This was to be prepared as a tea and taken thrice daily. Jenn had a brief flash of Dr. Song and smiled.

Jenn would have to heat a kettle on a pile of burning trash on the beach like an old hobo in order to get the water boiling but that was all right. It would be nice to sit under a blanket with Philip and watch the flames until the water sizzled. The herbs smelled sweet as Jenn sealed the Ziploc. Those days, she craved sweetness in all forms, and sweetness was so difficult to find.

Twenty-Four

Photographs and Memories

T he following day, when she was dusting the flaking, white, French provincial furniture in their motel room and Philip was changing the sheets, he asked, "Why didn't you show any pictures of yourself last night, Jenn? Everyone else was showing theirs. Why didn't you? You must have some."

"I do," she told him. "But I didn't think anyone would care."

"I care."

"I know you do. But anyone else, I mean."

"Show me," Philip slurped in the same caramel-coated voice Dick Truehard often used to coerce a nubile nymphette out of her thong.

Jenn fumbled with her backpack's zipper. "I have a few," she admitted, reddening. "But I haven't looked at them in a while."

"I want to see what you looked like," Philip told her. "Before."

Jenn considered the great abyss of her pack and rifled through it to comply with her friend's request. She knew the snapshots she was seeking by heart: her "wedding picture," which had been taken by Judge Howard under the weeping willow on Amity Street; Jenn holding up the first bass she ever caught like a prize, though miniscule it was; Serena, Lars and their boys at Swann Lake; Nik covered in grease, blissfully working on their friend Nancy's cherry red '57 Chevy; her parents and grandparents at her cousin Michael and Jane's wedding; Jenn in Bermuda, posing in a strapless turquoise bathing suit; Jenn and her brother Brian one Halloween when they were little, dressed like a princess and Spiderman, respectively, wearing so many sweaters beneath their costumes that they looked pregnant.

Jenn routinely took a handful of pics with her when she traveled, to feel close to the people she loved. Now she was happy for that ritual because those snaps were all that was left of them. She handed the whole lot of pics to Philip. He unfastened the rubber band and shuffled through them slowly, pausing and asking thoughtful questions about the people in each.

"You were lovely," Philip told her when he got to the bathing suit shot.

"Really?" she responded. "I never thought so. Though Nik told me many times, I never believed him."

"I would have tapped that," Philip said, gesturing to Jenn's pronounced camel toe, visible in the crease of her one-piece.

"Thank you…sort of," she winced. "But you would have tapped… almost anything."

Philip ignored her. "There's something about you," he continued, staring intently at the Bermuda swimsuit pic. "Something vulnerable. Like a kitten who needs to be rescued."

Jenn took back the picture. "Now, I'm a scrawny alley cat," she sighed.

"Purrrrr," Philip said.

Jenn considered her reflection in the white, wood-trimmed vanity. Her mind drifted to the time several years earlier when she and Nik had made love standing up in front of that very same mirror. Jenn had assumed a tippy-toed position, bent over, clinching the sides of the sink. Nik had cupped his hand between her parted thighs, bringing her off swiftly and deftly.

"Jenn, where are you?" Philip asked.

"Here," she said, snapping out of her memories. "But many years away."

Philip sat Jenn on the half-made bed and plunked down beside her. He hooked one hand around her waist, and with his other hand, flipped through her remaining photographs. She told him who everyone was and where the photos had been taken. He listened carefully and made caring comments like "You have your father's smile" or "Your grandmother looks very kind." Philip's remarks were usually spot on; he was a very intuitive soul.

It made Jenn sad to see these photographs, which is why she hadn't looked at them since the flight from JFK to Phoenix. It was easier not to look, not to remember.

"You really were lovely," Philip repeated.

"How can you bear to look at me now?" she asked him, as she had asked many times before.

"All I see is beauty," he said.

Ω

Later that evening, Jenn sat in the bathtub and Philip knelt on the tiles in front of her, scrubbing her back with a washcloth. She wasn't ashamed or self-conscious; it felt very natural. When Philip was done bathing her, she would bathe him. The subject, as it often was for people who couldn't copulate, was sex. "Who was the first woman you ever saw naked?" Jenn wondered.

Philip laughed. "My father took me to see a stripper perform at the Nevele Grand Hotel in the Catskills. It was soon after my Bar Mitzvah. My dad said now that I was a man…" Philip's voice drifted off.

"What do you remember most about her?" Jenn asked.

Philip made a face. "That her pubic hair was shaved into a thin stripe. It just covered her labia. For some reason, this upset me very much. Maybe because when she lay on one hip and spread her legs, it reminded me of Adolph Hitler."

"Do you remember her name?" Jenn wondered.

He thought for a moment. "I think she called herself Audrey Cha Cha Boom Boom. Or something ridiculous like that." They both laughed. "And your first penis?" Philip asked Jenn, in turn.

"Peter Lupus," she chirped, without hesitation.

"From 'Mission Impossible' on TV?" Philip gasped.

"The very same. He posed in *Playgirl*. I caught my Aunt Chubby and my mom giggling over his centerfold and managed to take a peek."

"And what did you think?"

Jenn took a breath. "I was shocked. It wasn't what I expected. It was…so unfriendly looking. And he was so hairy."

"Whose was the first you saw in real life?"

"Niky's," Jenn told him. "But yours was the first one I ever saw in a box."

Philip switched to washing Jenn's feet. It was the most pleasure she'd had in a long time. He slid the cloth between each toe on her right foot then went to town on the left. She leaned into him. "What an odd couple we make," Jenn sighed. "Do you know that you've had more lovers in one movie than I've had in my entire life?"

"Depends on the movie."

"Take your pick."

"Do I count as one of your lovers?" Philip wondered, moving the cloth up Jenn's calf.

"I don't know," she admitted. "Technically, no. Spiritually, yes."

Philip worked the amber oval of Pear's soap up to Jenn's knees. "Hold on a sec. I thought you said that Nik was your first lover."

"He was."

"Then how do you explain the others? Did you cheat on him?"

Jenn elbowed Philip in the chest. "Don't get all Judgy McJudge on me."

"*Moi,*" he squinted in mock hurt. "But do tell."

"Nik and I had a rocky first few years," she confessed. "At one point, he said he thought we should see other people. I think he was afraid to commit, as many men are. Reluctantly, I agreed to date others. Even though I knew he was 'the one.' I just prayed he would realize that I was 'the one' too."

"Obviously he did."

"Eventually. Nik said that if we really loved each other, dating other people wouldn't make a difference."

"Ah, from the Richard Bach school of thought: 'If you love something, set it free. If it comes back, it's yours. If it doesn't, it never was.'"

"Something like that."

"And did it? Come back, I mean." Jenn hesitated; Philip persisted. "Clearly, it did, but what happened? Give me all the deets."

"What happened was that I went to bed with other men and Nik had a tough time getting a date."

Philip snickered. "Served him right for not realizing what he had. So, when did he agree not to see others?"

"Not until he slept with another woman," Jenn frowned. "Then he finally realized how empty it was, how silly the whole thing was.

I told him that if he wasn't ready to commit, then I would leave him. I couldn't bear the thought of another woman kissing him, let alone making love to him."

"Let me guess, you were never good at sharing," Philip injected, helping Jenn onto her knees.

"Even as a kid," Jenn admitted.

"Who is?" Philip said. He pressed his head into her belly button. "You're almost wonderful, did you know that?" he whispered into it.

"So, I've been told," Jenn blushed.

Next, Philip scrubbed her neck. Jenn's hair fell to her shoulders in wet wisps. He took her Native American beads lightly in his fingers. "What are these?" he asked. "I notice you never take them off."

"Ghost berry beads," she told him. "They're supposed to be good luck."

"And how's that working out for you?" he wondered.

"Not so good," Jenn conceded.

Philip rinsed her down with murky, lukewarm water. Reverently, he cupped each of her sunken breasts then kissed a wet line down her belly to her untended black forest. Jenn was finally out of diapers and had graduated to tampons. Sylett's concoction of golden seal root, red raspberry leaves and ginger root had worked its mystical might overnight. A ridiculous, baby blue tampon string hung out of Jenn's body like the cord at the neck of a talking doll. But Philip didn't seem to notice or care. He caressed her thighs, unconcerned by her string. "Please don't," Jenn begged. "Please…I'm so ugly. And you've been with so many gorgeous women."

"But they weren't half as beautiful as you," Philip explained. "Most of them were flesh mannequins with false fingernails, mountains of hairspray and tons of makeup. But you…you're real. I like to count your ribs. I like to trace the tiny veins on the back of your thighs. I like the scalloped curve of your belly. Jennifer, you're the most real woman I've ever been with."

Philip turned on the faucet. He splashed almost-hot water onto Jenn's vulva. He swirled the soap's lather into peaks. He feathered the inside of her thighs. "Your skin is all clear now thanks to Sylett's magic liniment. So smooth," he whispered into Jenn's pelvis.

Then Philip found the part of Jenn's anatomy that used to be her favorite but most recently, had been ignored. He got it to come out and play. And Jenn let him. She shifted her body from beneath the water to the edge of the bathtub and wrapped her legs around his chest. Pressing against Philip's fuzzy belly, Jenn climaxed, burrowing her head into his shoulder. She hadn't orgasmed in many months, so it was incredibly powerful, gut-wrenching, almost. She alternately didn't want it to end and couldn't wait for it to be over.

As Jenn's body convulsed, she closed her eyes and saw herself lying on her back with the soft grass cushioning her, the lacy pattern of green all around. She felt herself floating up into the air then gently touching down, swaying to and fro like a feather in the wind.

When it was over, Jenn felt Philip smile against her neck. "That was big enough for the both of us," he said.

"I love you, Niky," Jenn sighed dreamily, eyes still closed. And when she realized what she'd called Philip, she started to cry.

"I've been called worse," Philip joked. Then, when Jenn cried harder, he admitted, "It's all right. I love Nik too."

Twenty-Five

Yeorpi Skies and Sea Lions

The next morning, the sky was a strange mixture of yellow, pink and orange. Since the color didn't have a name, Philip and Jenn made one up. They decided to call it "yeorpi."

Neither had ever seen anything like the yeorpi firmament before. "It's like a tequila sunrise cocktail, but not," Philip offered. Since the sun beamed and it was pleasantly warm, they decided to take a walk. Philip had his penis tucked into his back pocket in a purple drawstring Royal Crown sack— "for that emasculated ex-porn star on the go," he liked to quip. Since he hated to leave it behind, Dick took his dick wherever he went. "Just like I used to," he explained.

Jenn and Philip let themselves into Kelli's Candies, their favorite sweets shop in Morro Bay. This was a rare treat. But why? Did they worry about cavities in Armageddon? Were they concerned about packing on the pounds or the evils of sugar? No. It was just that eating too many sweets bothered their already-tender tummies.

By now, pickings at Kelli's were slim. All the good stuff was gone. No more Milky Ways, no more Kit Kats. There was a profusion of black licorice, which the pair both liked but most of the general population didn't. However, Wiley Wallaby Black Liquorice Candy made Philip and Jenn's hearts happy.

On this particular visit, Philip lusted for some chewing gum to work off his sexual frustrations. It was rough having amatory feelings with no way to release them. Philip still had the desire even though his equipment was gone, he explained. So, Philip tossed aside Juicy Fruit and Chiclets. He sought a specific type of gum, a rarity in a sea of peppermint and wintergreen. He rejected a mini-tower of vintage Freshen Up Gum, the kind that squirts a blast of goo into your mouth. "Too much like Fallon," he lamented. "And I really liked Fallon," he added sadly as he tossed the Freshen Up aside.

But then he found the object of his desire. "Would you like a piece?" Philip asked Jenn, hiding his treasure in his fist.

"Sure," she told him, still not knowing what chewing gum prize he'd found. Jenn hoped it wasn't Sour Patch Kids-flavored and trusted Philip's judgement. "Anything to wipe the stench of death from my mouth," she added.

"Close your eyes," Philip commanded, similar to the way Dick Truehard spoke to Christy Lynn in *Eyes Wide Slut*. Jenn did as Philip asked, just as Christy had in that erotic opus. Jenn heard Philip first unwrap the gum package, then the paper, then the foil from the stick as he slipped it into her mouth. "Chew," he said, just like he'd said to Mickey Canyon in *I Plugged Lucy*. Jenn chewed and was surrounded by licorice bliss.

"Black Jack Gum," Jenn sighed between chews. "My favorite."

Jenn could tell that Philip was missing his penis again. He tended to get wistful and nostalgic whenever he did. A sad look veiled his eyes as he reminisced, and he sometimes talked dirty, pining away for the bad, old days when his penis was still attached. It was as if his words accomplished what his body could not, and this gave him an erotic charge. Vigorously chewing gum became a substitute for sex. So, Jenn asked Philip for another stick of Black Jack and licked her lips just like Annie Vera did in *Sprinkle Street*.

Ω

Besides sweets, Kelli's Candies also boasted a bona fide, old-school soda fountain. To cheer up Philip, Jenn made him a Brooklyn-style egg cream with Parmalat boxed milk, seltzer and Fox's U-Bet chocolate-flavored syrup. She used a slightly-stale pretzel rod as a swizzle stick.

"Just like I used to get at Shirley and Abe's Luncheonette," Philip told her. "Except no dirty glass."

Philip told Jenn about the duo's filthy candy store on Avenue Z. His mother strictly forbade him to buy anything unwrapped from Shirley and Abe's. No Candy Buttons. No Circus Peanuts. "How I loved those wax lips," Philip told Jenn, launching into a confectionary litany. "I would sneak them even though they were *verboten.*"

"Me too," Jenn confessed.

"You were such an oral child," he said.

"Still am," Jenn admitted.

"Abe was a sloppy drunk," Philip continued reminiscing. "Shirley always wore a dirty housedress, sweat socks and open-toed sandals from Woolworth's no matter the season. She also wore thick-lensed, cat's eye glasses. Blind as a bat, they didn't seem to help her vision. Boy, did Shirley and Abe hate each other. So much so that Abe tried to get kill her."

"How?" Jenn wondered, fascinated. She was drawn into the tale by Philip's storytelling prowess. Those Sandy Meisner classes really paid off.

"By rearranging the furniture when Shirley was working down at the candy store. Multiple times."

"Did it work?" Jenn asked.

Philip shrugged. "Once she fractured her big toe."

He laughed so hard telling his Shirley and Abe story that the egg cream went through his nose. Philip blew the mess into a napkin. "Better than cocaine," he snorted.

Ω

Back outside, the sky's yeorpi tint painted Philip's handsome face with a warm glow while it made Jenn's look sallow. They walked and talked as they so often did. To pass the time, to get to know each other better. It was working.

"When I heard about the blast in San Diego—I believe it was the third after New York City and Washington, DC—I was making a movie in Mill Valley, north of San Francisco," Philip reflected.

"What was it called?" Jenn wondered.

"Working title: *Bible Lust.*"

"Is nothing sacred?" she sighed.

"No," Philip said without pause. "Not in porn, anyway. But this was high-quality work. The stories were taken directly from the Bible, which happens to be a very naughty book: brimming with incest, buggery, adultery. You name it, the Good Book had it. Scripted by Ariel Hart."

"In my opinion, the best screenwriter in the industry," Jenn thew in.

"Mine too," he said. "Next to Raven Touchstone, of course." Philip continued, "They were shooting the film on 35mm, not video, and it was directed by Christian Christian."

"So nice, they named him twice. Damon Christian's son?"

"The very same. Anyway, I played 'David' and Nellie Nips was my Bathsheba."

"Who was Abishag the Shunamite?" Jenn asked.

"Judy Juggs."

"Uggh. Killer boobs but she couldn't act her way out of a paper bag. Well, only if she happened to have someone inside her."

Philip agreed. "You might recall that Judy became a Born-Again Christian and left the business abruptly."

"I do," Jenn said.

"She lasted only a year before she made her comeback or 'cumback.'" For emphasis, he made air quotes on the last word.

"Change of heart?" Jenn wondered.

"Hardly," Philip said. "Judy was three months behind on her rent so she returned for a 'special appearance.' But this was only because of a revelation from the Holy Spirit, Judy claimed. But *I* thought it was the five thousand smackers Smegma Productions offered her for an interracial double-cuntal. I can't be sure, though."

"I'll go with the latter."

Philip smirked. "Ya think? Anyhow, after the first blast, Judy proclaimed that the world was ending because we were making a Biblical skinflick. And when the gaffer told us of the San Diego hit, the set flew into an uproar. Too close to home. People were thinking that maybe Judy was right. But Christian insisted we finish the scene regardless. He wanted his film in the can. Judy swallowed the salami— my salami—like it was the last one on earth."

"For her, it probably was."

Philip laughed. "It was a magnificent scene. But *Herr Director* was pissed off because there was no money shot. He wanted a retake, which was out of the question. We were done. Literally and figuratively."

"Did you guys get paid?"

He nodded. "In cash. I still have it. There's nothing to spend it on." Philip continued his reverie as they walked toward The Shell Shop, a place that sold seashells from seashores around the world. At Jenn's urging, they stopped inside. She fished out a pink-bellied conch from Mozambique and held it to her cheek. The ocean whispered promises in one ear as Philip rambled in the other about *Bible Lust.* "It was a star-studded cast…"

"…of studs," Jenn finished.

"You could say that," Philip conceded. "It had a little bit of everything. Outdoor sex with Adam and Eve. A massive orgy with a thirty-person daisy chain in Sodom and Gomorrah. Rape with Tamar and Amnon. There was even some drunken homosexual incest."

"Where?" Jenn challenged.

"Noah and Ham. Genesis 9, Verse 22. It says that Ham saw his father's nakedness."

"I've seen lots of nakedness, but it didn't always mean sex," Jenn admitted.

"Biblical scholars have taken the phrase to mean that Ham took advantage of Noah when he was drunk and unconscious. Although most Christians don't agree with that speculation."

"Who played Noah," Jenn wondered.

"Ron Jeremy." Jenn gagged aloud. "I know, ugh," Philip added.

"The movie sounded very promising," Jenn admitted. "A guaranteed Collector's Choice rating from Bob Rimmer. Despite Ron Jeremy."

"I still can't believe you worked with Bob. He was very kind to me in his reviews."

"Bob was a great guy," Jenn agreed, "but his appreciation of you had nothing to do with kindness. You're a fine actor."

He shrugged awkwardly in response. Jenn shielded the citrine sun from her eyes and told him, "Bob kept trying to get me to take over the film reviews. But I knew I couldn't be an impartial critic."

"How so?" Philip pushed.

"Well, I couldn't stand perfectly good performers because I didn't like the way their boobs or their penises looked. I mean, if they had a bad circumcision, forget it."

"What the hell's a bad circumcision?" Philip wondered.

"You know, when the foreskin's too tight and the glans is pointy like an arrowhead."

"Like Blake Palmer?"

"Exactly. Jerry Butler used to say it looked like Stevie Wonder did the circumcision."

Philip laughed. "Butler was too much. So are you."

"I've been told that before," Jenn conceded. "I guess I am. But back to your movie. I don't think God was mad at you. People put a lot of words into God's mouth. I truly think He wants us to be happy, to enjoy our bodies with love and respect for them and for each other. If God thought sex was dirty, He would have thought up another way for us to procreate. You know, like earthworms do or something involving earwax. He wouldn't have made our bodies so much fun. But go on, Philip. I love the idea of *Bible Lust.*"

"I think Oral Roberts would have approved too."

"The televangelist?"

Philip nodded. "The very same. Though his name was much more suited for a porn star." He paused, "Yes, I really believed in this one. So much so that I coproduced it."

"Meaning?"

"I put my own money into it."

It was Jenn's turn to nod. "Were you really that rich?"

Philip thought for a moment. "I suppose I was," he admitted. "In terms of money. But I was poor in other ways. Dirt poor."

Jenn handed Philip a conch shell from St. Thomas so he could take a listen. He held it to his ear and smiled. "You mean you never had a woman who loved you," Jenn said, amazed.

"Oh, I've had many of those," Philip admitted. "But they didn't love me the right way. Not truly, madly, deeply." Jenn didn't know what to say. The very notion of never being truly loved was so sad.

Philip tried to explain it further. "Not the way you love your Nik. Oh, these women claimed they loved me. But what they really meant was that they loved my house, my pool, my cocaine, my cock, my fame. But I couldn't cry with any of them. Except for one." Philip's face became cast with clouds.

"Noreen," Jenn said, because he couldn't at first.

"Noreen," he repeated, like a prayer. He was finally able to say her name without crying and it felt sweet, like honey in his mouth. "The others, they just wanted the good stuff, the fun stuff. But they didn't

want to hold me when I felt lonesome. Well, only if my dick
was hard."

"Tell me more about Noreen," Jenn nudged.

"There's nothing to tell," he insisted. But Jenn knew there was a lot
more to Noreen's story. *Frontline* had done an episode about her called
"Death of a Porn Princess." Instead of condemning her, PBS captured
the profound tragedy of a lost little girl who committed suicide.
Jenn recalled seeing "Dick Truehard" providing heartfelt onscreen
commentary in his cluttered bedroom with Monopoly game boards
decorating the almost-bare walls and dirty laundry spilling out of the
basket onto the floor. He spoke angrily about how the industry had
used and abused Miss Applewood.

"You sure you don't want to talk about Noreen?" Jenn
prodded gently.

"She shouldn't have been in the business," Philip told his friend
sharply. "She was too fragile. It ate her up alive. No matter how much
I loved her, it couldn't make up for the way people used her. For the
way her parents reacted when they found out what she'd done."

"They disowned her," Jenn sighed.

"Not only that, but they publicly denounced her. So did her friends
back home. But I'll tell you something, they wouldn't have reacted that
way if she had been a murderer but porn… Noreen was shamed and
because of that, she was ashamed. So much so that she couldn't live
with herself anymore. End of story."

Philip's normally-lovely eyes were glassy, but like a stubborn
child, he wouldn't allow himself to cry, not this time. "She should have
never left Michigan," he said. "Noreen should have married her high
school sweetheart, had babies and grown plump. No, she never should
have left home. It's as simple as that. Less than two years after she
came to Hollywood, she was dead."

Philip threw the conch shell. It shattered on the ground. Seeing his
mood degenerate from euphoria to despair was like watching a sunset
fast-forward; it went from light to dark in a matter of seconds. "Hard
times," Jenn said, rubbing his back.

"Literally and figuratively," he croaked. "People glamorize the life
of a porn actor. Sure, I was with lots of women. They were paid to be
with me, though. It was work. And outside of work, women expected
sex from me too. What if I didn't like them? What if I wasn't attracted
to them? It didn't matter. I had an image to uphold."

"So, you never got to stop being Dick Truehard," Jenn offered.

"When I met people off set, boyfriends and husbands were offended if I didn't make a pass at their women. One time at a party, a guy started a fistfight with me because I told his wife I really liked her, but only as a friend. Three people had to hold him back and all the while, he was shouting, 'What's the matter, you fucking bastard, she's not good enough for you?'"

Philip picked up another seashell to hurl. It was all right, though. Especially if it made him feel better. There were plenty more where that came from. When he was through smashing and destroying, he and Jenn left and continued their walk.

Ω

Passing the Morro Bay Aquarium, they heard the most horrible grunting noises. "Reminds me of Trixi Lord on the brink of a fake orgasm," Philip said, his sense of humor returning.

He and Jenn entered through the gift shop where nothing was amiss. The T-shirts were in neat piles. The nautical ashtrays, postcards and assorted souvenirs were all in place. But still, the terrible clamor continued. The sounds were even louder inside the shop than they were out on the street.

Philip noticed a door just behind the cash register. A handwritten sign Scotch-taped to it read "Aquarium." In a picture frame next to the door was a yellowed article that described how wounded sea lion pups were rescued from local waters and nursed back to health by the community. These orphaned pups were on display in the aquarium and any donations to help with their upkeep were greatly appreciated.

"I remember coming here with Nik," Jenn recalled hopefully, trying to ignore the infernal sounds from within. "The pups were so cute, swimming around and clapping their flippers. They even sold little Baggies of raw fish to feed them. And boy, were those little guys smart! They would clap and bark to get Nik to throw them some fish."

With great expectations, Philip and Jenn pushed into the aquarium's swinging door. But it would only open partway. They could hardly believe what they saw when they peeked inside.

The exact opposite of the teaspoon-sized squirrels, the formerly-cuddly sea lions had expanded to the size of full-grown blue whales. They had burst from their ten-foot concrete pit. The entire room was wall-to-wall sea lion. Their normally sleek, oily skin was dry and cracked. Of the six creatures in the rancid concrete pit, four were dead. The other two cried out in anguish. They were starving. So much so, that chunks were bitten out of their flesh from where they'd tried to eat each other.

There was nothing Jenn and Philip could do for the poor sea lions except leave. They closed the door, retreated into the gift shop and never walked through that part of town again.

Twenty-Six

New Dawn

The following day, Jenn woke from a bizarre dream. She dreamed that one of the huge, bloated sea lions had Nik's face. It called her name as she shrunk away from it, horrified. Meanwhile, Philip had grown another penis, only it was ten feet long. Much too big to be of use. Jenn slid down its length like a banister.

She woke up laughing. And climaxing. What did it all mean?

Still chuckling from her crazy dream, Jenn turned to share it with Philip. Only he wasn't in bed beside her. Instead, he was standing on the balcony staring up at the sky. It reminded Jenn of the way she'd found Nik after the blast.

She threw on her tattered Raider's t-shirt and joined Philip on the balcony. Without looking at her, he said, "Something's going on up there."

Jenn looked up. Indeed, something seemed to be.

Thick clouds layered the sky. They rolled and tumbled in the heavens even wilder than they did most nights. This time, they resembled ashen cotton balls in a Cuisinart. Thundercracks exploded but there was no show of lightning. The sun was bright, and except for that odd patch of clouds, the sky was an antifreeze blue.

But it was clear that some strange meteorological phenomenon was manifesting itself in the firmament above El Morro. Rain? No. It hadn't rained since the Aftermath began and the Earth was parched, hungry. What else could it be but an enormous storm brewing?

Jenn went back inside, slipped on a pair of jeans and her new turquoise Keds. (Her faithful Nikes had since bitten the dust.) Philip grabbed his toothpaste box. He didn't even take the time to switch its contents into the Royal Crown travel pouch, perhaps sensing this might be longer than a quick stroll. He and Jenn headed to Embarcadero for a better vantage point to study that wayward patch of clouds.

Several others were also walking down Beach Street toward the ocean. Philip and Jenn nodded to Kevin and Sylett, the displaced dairy farmers, and said hi to the Alfonso sisters. More people migrated from the south of town and from houses perched in the hills. Everyone seemed to be drawn out of their hiding places, like cockroaches from cracks in the walls. "Like the rats in the Pied Piper," Philip remarked. "Without the flute."

They blinked their eyes in the bright light of a new dawn, silent. A crowd of a hundred or so had already pooled in front of The Great American Fish Company. And even more arriving were from all over town. Jenn and Philip tried to count how many were present but failed.

Expectantly, Jenn scanned the new faces. Hoping. But there was no Niky among them. Not as far as she could tell.

It was the oddest thing…all these people were gravitating toward the same spot. All eyes, whether clear, cloudy or almost sightless, focused on the same patch of turbulent sky that hovered directly above Morro Rock. Suddenly, a hole tore through that brilliant Hollywood soundstage firmament. A giant meteor-like object crashed through the clouds. *This is the end,* Jenn thought. *The real end.*

Ω

One great, mountainous cry rose from the crowd. Some began to run. Some dropped on the spot, passing out from fear. Others dragged these prone bodies off to the side so they wouldn't be trampled. But most, including Jenn and Philip, were stuck to where they stood, gazing straight up. It was as though their feet were glued to the ground. Philip touched Jenn's elbow. "Do you think we should run?" he asked, just to make sure, though he didn't feel like running anymore. Philip was tired of running, he said.

Jenn shook her head. Like her companion, she felt no need to flee. It was like being caught up in a bad movie; she wanted, she *needed,* to see how the story ended. Even if it ended badly.

Those who remained gawked at the object that had just crash-landed on the beach at the base of El Morro. The thing stood about four stories high, a block wide and resembled the rock itself. Which resembled a generous helping of Rocky Road ice cream, melting. But instead of being chocolate-toned, the object was covered in tarnished silver. Like a spaceship in a B-movie Jenn's friend Mark Monzingo had so loved, but bigger. Lots bigger. It didn't appear to be damaged.

In super slo-mo, a hatch opened near the base of the craft. This time, even the curious began to run. A wide wave of bodies swept up Beach Street. Many were so fragile and slow that they fell underfoot. No one stopped to help them this time. Philip and Jenn broke away from the rest of the crowd and joined the few stragglers who cut down Market Avenue.

As she ran, Jenn glanced over her shoulder to see a thick ray of light tracing toward them. She marveled at the way she and Philip glowed briefly in the fluorescence. Then the light moved past them to the others ahead. Although the beam didn't cause pain, they were paralyzed in its wake. But instead of feeling panicked, Jenn was washed with a sense of calm. Somehow, she knew she wouldn't be hurt. Somehow, she knew that everything would be all right. In some sense of the word, at least.

Philip asked her, "Are you okay?"

"I can't move," Jenn told him. "But I don't care."

"Same here," he said.

No one cried out; they just stood, waiting.

After a few moments, Jenn was able to wiggle her fingers, then her toes. She took a furtive baby step. So did Philip. The rest of them did too, like toddlers hesitantly testing out toddling. But no one fled. Instead, they fell into a neat line and walked. They walked down to what appeared to be a spacecraft of some sort. After all, it had fallen from the sky, so what else could it be?

Like soldiers with internal orders, they marched along Beach Street then Market in an orderly fashion. They congregated at the Great American Fish Company where a tall man and a tall woman waited to greet them.

Were they human? Were they extraterrestrials? No one could be sure. But they certainly resembled *homo sapiens.* In fact, they looked more human than post-blast humans did. They weren't broken or battered, inflamed or sick. These two were fine specimens of humanity. They represented the best of what humanoids could be.

There were slight smiles on both beings' faces. Not big, fake, toothy grins, but pleasant expressions that set the crowd at ease. Those gathered seemed to emit a silent, unanimous cry of relief, for this was either the end or the beginning. Jenn hoped and prayed for the latter. She grabbed Philip's hand and squeezed. He squeezed back, looked at her and nodded. "It's going to be all right," he whispered. For some reason, Jenn believed him.

Ω

The waters of Morro Bay were angry and swollen behind the visitors. Again, Jenn tried to count the people. Again, she gave up. Again, no Nik.

Once more, Jenn surrendered to the realization that there would be no Nik. Ever. And for the first time, it was all right. Something in that blinding ray of light had given her a sense of peace. It had given her the gift of acceptance. And it felt good.

The sea of bodies was arranged in an uneven crescent around the alien beings but no one stood closer than ten feet. It was as though an invisible force held them back. The male creature was of average build and had nondescript but agreeable features. The female was nice-looking enough. She had a shapely body and her breasts were neither too large nor too small. Her hips were neither too wide nor too slender. Her buttocks were neither too prominent nor too flat. "I'd tap that," Philip said.

"You'd tap anything," Jenn reminded him.

The pair of visitors wore plain, one-piece jumpsuits of a medium, unremarkable blue with a long zipper up the front. Their outfits seemed to be made of some sort of cotton. Or the equivalent of cotton from wherever the two hailed. The female's hair was nut brown, cut bluntly to her chin. The male's was short, pushed back from his forehead and graying attractively.

There was nothing outstanding about either of these creatures. They could have easily slipped into a crowd unnoticed. They would blend into any surroundings well, like movie extras or CIA agents. There was a kindness in their eyes and a slight upward curve to their mouths which signified that they were friendly, that they wouldn't hurt anyone. But what could these two possibly do to the survivors that hadn't already been done to them by the perversity of human nature? What could be worse than the horrors they'd already endured? Than the awfulness they'd already witnessed? In many ways, to many of them, death would be a reprieve.

The couple smiled amicably until the crowd stopped shuffling their feet and settled. Jenn thought she saw the man's shoulders tremble slightly just before he spoke. His voice was even-toned and relaxing. Similar to a radio announcer's, someone like Jim Kerr or Rick Schneider on WKZE, who always signed off with, "Help people, don't hurt people."

The first thing the man said was, "My name is Noah. And this is Naamah."

The second thing he said was, "Don't be alarmed."

For some inexplicable reason, they weren't.

Even Jenn, who was, by her own admission, a scaredy cat afraid of everything, from zombies to wurdalaks and dybbuks, wasn't afraid of Noah and Naamah. Oddly, she wanted to get to know them better. And the other onlookers seemed just as intrigued and curious. The effects of that tranquilizing light had the mellow vibe of indica THC, only better.

$$\Omega$$

In her workspace, at the Memorywriter, Jenn rested her chin in the cup of her palm.

As I write this, she typed, *it seems almost silly to go on with the story, because most, if not all of you, know what happened next. With the press releases and the hype connected to Noah's visit, no stone has been left unturned and you are aware of how it all panned out. Or I wouldn't be here to write this book.*

But for the sake of the few who don't know, I'll continue. And to fulfill my pledge to Noah, I will finish what I started. A promise is a promise.

Besides, the words are flowing and I'm actually enjoying this. So, I'll keep going.

Ω

In front of the Great American Fish Company, Noah explained that he and Naamah hailed from Planet Alpha 49C which was located deep in the Andromeda Galaxy. Or, as he aptly illustrated it, Planet Alpha 49C would be on the fingertip of the index finger on the left hand of the Andromeda Galaxy, if the Andromeda Galaxy had hands.

The assembly learned that Alpharians possessed a much more sophisticated system of technology than Earth ever had, even at its finest hour. Which, in retrospect, was never all that sophisticated. Apparently, the Alpharians had been watching the antics on Earth for decades. Live feeds from the Big Planet were like favorite sitcoms where the beloved characters constantly made bad choices. Think "Insecure" or "This is Us."

Planet Alpha 49C was second only to the Plaxians in their obsession with all things Earth. Intergalactic hotspots broadcast Terra happenings as beings throughout the galaxy hungrily watched, metaphysical cosmic popcorn in hand. Imagine their exasperation at earthlings' stupidity and hubris, Satulians yelling at their LaserVision screens, Uluvians shaking their fists in annoyance at Earth's repeated idiocy. Like diehard fans of the Mets. And now this, Sol 3's impending annihilation.

From 1936 until just recently, Alpharian anthropologists had lived on Earth in various locations around the globe. They peacefully observed behavior, studied shenanigans, mastered the lingo and took copious notes. Much like Jane Goodall did with her adored chimpanzees. But humans proved to be a lot less lovable—and a lot more destructive—than chimps.

Hascends and hascends have been written about anthropoids and what has become known as the "Earth Personality." Alpharians were quite smitten with "modern" hominoids and explored every aspect of what it was to be human, figuratively and literally. For instance, the average Alpharian knew more about American History than the average American. Plus, Alpharians were uniformly brilliant. They could run rings around Earthlings in areas such as geometry, geology and just about anything else.

In addition, Alpharians were well-versed in Earth trivia. For example, there was a popular parlor game (not that Alpharians have parlors) called "Earth Mirth," which is based on Trivial Pursuit. Alpharians knew all sorts of arcane minutia like who won the Oscar for Best Actress in 1941 (Ginger Rogers, of all people, for *Kitty Foyle*!). And they could do the Hucklebuck right alongside Ralph Kramden when they watched reruns of "The Honeymooners."

Noah continued his quick, concise rundown of the Alpharian/ Earth connection. As simply as he could, he went on to explain that through a complex apparatus which resembled a high-tech three-foot-high screen attached to a keyboard, it was possible to zoom into people's homes, from famous folks' luxurious Beverly Hills estates to Appalachian shacks. "The goings-on in the hovels were usually much more interesting," Noah admitted.

This sophisticated spying network was made possible through coordinates supplied by such diverse sources as telephone directories, tax returns and *Village Voice* Personals ads. It enabled Alpharian anthropologists to infiltrate intended study subjects and cull information which was then fed into mainframe computers.

Noah patiently described the intricate process. Although members of the crowd nodded, it was likely that most didn't fully understand the complex technological aspects. Even those with IT backgrounds. But suffice to say that Alpharians were able to study Earth and learn a great deal about its inhabitants.

So intrigued were Alpharians with Earthfolk that they were devastated to watch the planet's slow, painful, purposeful destruction. At the same time, they were surprised it had taken so long. While Earth people had Lotto and the third race at Belmont, Alpharians had an interplanetary network of wager parlors that established odds as to when the third rock from the sun in the Milky Way galaxy would self-destruct. There were also smaller, weekly pools and wagers related to minor pop-culture phenomena like:

- if Tammy Faye Bakker would become the spokesperson for Maybelline;
- the identity of the Son of Sam;
- if Donald Trump's hair was real; and
- if Melania Trump was humanoid.

But the "End of the World as We Know It" pool was by far the most popular on Planet Alpha 49C. Some might think this a morbid pastime, but similar "death pools" were a common phenomenon all over the galaxy, even on Earth. Throughout offices in America (including Jenn's), come January, a new death pool was formulated where the participants wagered on the youngest famous person who would die that year. Officemates would throw in ten or twenty dollars and pick some foolish old soul or young soul destined to join the 27 Club in the coming twelve months. Britney Spears, Kanye, and so on. If no one on the list died, the money would carry on to the next year.

Similarly, the size of the Alpharian pot continued to swell through the Cuban Missile Crisis, through the Iranian Hostage Crisis, 9/11, the January 6th Insurrection and the Great British Baking Show debacle. Time rattled on. Earth's destruction didn't happen during the reign of the President who had his legs cut off in *Kings Row* ("Where's the rest of me?") or the one who played "Urkel" on "Family Matters." (Bonus points if he said "Did I do that?" just before Earth went kaput.) But none of the above happened.

And when the end finally came, it was as though the Alpharians' favorite team had lost the Super Bowl. Noah reluctantly admitted that he won a bundle correctly predicting that the United States' fearless leader would fearfully commit suicide. But Noah said it felt like dirty money, so he donated it to NUDES (Nuclear Universal Disarmament Educational Society).

Ω

Standing beside the silent Naamah, Noah seemed sturdy and sincere. His words appeared to be heartfelt. His voice was soothing and caring, just the balm the tattered survivors needed. He and Naamah stood like pillars amid the desolate, desperate people. Even though they were crushed and all but destroyed, Noah managed to make them laugh with his good-humored chatter. Then came his proposition: to come away with the Alpharians.

"We feel as though you are our brothers and sisters," he admitted, trying to explain the Alpharians' feeling of allegiance with the inhabitants of Earth. "Like we are brothers and sisters of the cosmos. As though your planet is our twin of sorts. And we want to save you."

A woman cried out in a toothless voice, "Why? Why do you care?"

"How could we not?" Noah said plainly. "Besides, we all came from the same place. Way back in the beginning."

"How can you be so sure?" a ragged man challenged.

"It has been proven many times over by our scientists and statisticians," Noah smiled calmly. "We share the same DNA." Groans rose from the nonbelievers among them, from those who thought science was a sham. The same ones who thought Covid-19 was a hoax. "I'll be happy to provide you with the data. If you come with us, I'll show you all the proof you need."

"Sounds like a scam if you ask me," an old woman crowed.

"He didn't ask you!" Jenn yelled. The words flew out of her mouth, a kneejerk reaction to the cynicism. "Please, let's all be quiet and just let him speak." Noah smiled in Jenn's direction. Then he stared at her, studying her face, as though filing it for future reference.

"Thank you," Noah nodded and paused, waiting for Jenn to present him with her name. So, she offered it to him like a gift.

"Jenn," she told him. "Jennifer Taverna."

"Thank you, Jennifer Taverna," Noah said with a small bow. Then he turned to the crowd and away from Jenn. "It pains us to see your great civilization destroyed. What happened to you could very easily happen to us. And we need you to help us make sure this doesn't happen."

"So, you're using us," someone behind Jenn and Philip shouted.

"Not exactly using," Naamah conceded, speaking for the first time. Her voice was friendly, deep for a woman's, with a timbre reminiscent of a viola. "We're hoping you'll agree to teach us. Some of you, at least."

Small handfuls of people began drifting away. Audible were mumblings like "Screw this" and "Fat chance."

Noah chewed his lip then continued. "Unfortunately, we can't take all of you with us. But clearly, not all of you want to come."

Those in the process of leaving left, grumbling as they went. Noah continued, unruffled, "We have the resources for fifty, perhaps sixty on our spacecraft." Anticipating the next question, Noah added, "And if we returned to pick up the rest, it would be too late."

Jenn knew he meant that they would already be dead, but Noah was too polite to say this. Still, someone persisted, asking, "Too late for what?"

Noah ignored the heckler and finished his thought. "This causes quite a dilemma for us."

Naamah picked up, "How could we possibly choose who will live and who will..."

"...stay," Noah burst in. "It is quite impossible."

"So, we will not make the choice," Naamah said.

"Who will, then?" a lady screeched.

"You will," Naamah told them. "You will judge for yourselves."

Noah explained further, "Before we came here, we recruited a number of your people from different corners of the planet."

"Where are they?" Philip asked.

"Rest assured, they are safely aboard the craft," Naamah told him.

"Let us see them," a man with a croaking voice demanded.

"It's too dangerous," Noah began. "Exposure, contamination..."

"You'll have to trust us on that one," Naamah trilled.

"Why? Why should we trust you?" another man yelled.

"Why should you not?" Noah said. "Why not trust instead of doubt? What have you got to lose?" He let those present digest this statement for a few moments, let them chew on it, ruminate on it. "A few weeks before we began the rescue process, we hovered above your atmosphere. Observing. We studied the cluster of survivors we drew into communities through the subliminal magnetic signals our spacecraft emitted."

Philip whispered to Jenn triumphantly. "So, *that's* why we were all drawn to Morro Bay. I *knew* it was something. It was them all along."

Noah plowed on, "Most of these communities were peaceful like yours. But some destroyed themselves by violence or fire."

"Or mass suicide," Naamah injected. "But we've been watching you for several days. You are exemplary. You have built friendships from nothing, fellowships from rubble. Close bonds from anonymity."

"Those lights in the sky," a young girl wondered aloud. "The clouds tumbling...was that you?"

Noah conceded, "It was. A minor electrical reaction from the radioactivity in your atmosphere meeting the protective alurion that coats our spacecraft," he assured her, then went on. "In addition to saving people, we've also been salvaging great works of art. Treasures from the Louvre, the Vatican and the National Gallery. Sadly, the Metropolitan and the Museum of Modern Art in New York City were flattened, and all was lost."

Jenn bowed her head at the thought of never seeing "Young Woman with a Water Pitcher" and "The Starry Night" again.

"Perhaps even 'Guernica'?" a man with a Castilian lisp asked hesitantly.

"Yes. We managed to save several masterpieces from the Reina Sofia," Naamah said with a touch of pride. "*'Las Meninas'* from the Prado too."

"*Gracias a Dios*," the Castilian sighed. "Thank God."

"Thank Noah," Naamah said. "This rescue is his brainchild."

"It's a joint effort, a labor of love," Noah corrected. "I truly love this place and its people." Maybe it was Jenn's imagination, but Noah appeared to tear up, to get all *verklempt*, as Nik would have put it. Maybe Noah really *did* care.

To lighten the mood, Naamah added, "On Planet Alpha 49C, we already have a modest collection of your movies but managed to rescue several classics from the National Film Archives. *Gunga Din, The 400 Blows* and *A Clockwork Orange,* to name a few. Luckily, most of Caballero's catalogue was salvaged..." Dick Truehard's eyes lit upon hearing about the library of the porn giant which had engaged his service often; so did Philip's. "...as was much of the Marx Brothers, Laurel and Hardy, and Abbott and Costello."

"Colorized?" a film nerd asked.

"Heavens no," Noah responded. "We even have *March of the Wooden Soldiers* in its original black and white glory."

"Good," a few voices assented.

Those assembled were told that there was also a profusion of vinyl records and CDs on board—Coltrane, Miles, Richard Cheese and Weird Al Yankovic, included. No tapes, however. The Alpharian atmosphere was unkind to the magnetic coating, you see.

Jenn could hardly wait to hear Gloria Lynne singing about the folks who lived on the hill again. She wondered if Darby and Joan still lived there.

But would Jenn be among the chosen ones? *Probably not,* she thought.

Twenty-Seven

Tough Choice

"**B**efore we go into detail about the selection process," Noah continued, "we will tell you about life on Planet Alpha 49C." Again, he paused for emphasis and looked around, taking in the mottled faces surrounding him, as if memorizing them.

"Understandably, some of you might not choose to come," Naamah conceded. "For many reasons. We understand that it is a very personal decision."

Noah took the figurative baton from Namaah and began, "In many ways, our planet is like Earth. But in others, it is very different. The sky and ground are reversed, for one thing. There are no flowers as you know them but rocks and boulders sprout trees and blossoms."

"Physically, we are very compatible with Earth people," Naamah picked up. "Externally we are very similar and so are our internal organs. Only we have two hearts, two stomachs (though they're smaller than yours) and no useless parts like gall bladders, appendixes and tonsils." She paused. "Luckily, our genitalia are wonderfully harmonious," said Naamah, her eyes twinkling with naughtiness.

"Did she just wink at you?" Jenn whispered to Philip.

"Everyone's a fan," Philip conceded.

"And we've watched enough episodes of 'Marcus Welby, MD' and 'ER' to know how to care for human bodies."

Noah cleared his throat and scuffed his rubber sole into the wooden decking surrounding the fish restaurant. "There are many personality and emotional differences," he began. "For example, we exalt, even praise the wonders of our bodies. The climate is very pleasant year-round, so we wear very little in the way of clothing."

Naamah qualified, "And what clothing we do wear is for sexual adornment, to accentuate our corporal attributes. To us, the physical touch is sacred. We make love quite freely, young and old, although only with consent and after the age of consent. And there is none of what you call 'body shaming' on Planet Alpha 49C. Alpharians believe all bodies are attractive, no matter how unique they might be."

Noah interrupted to clarify. "Now, you may think this peculiar but we never consider lovemaking to be 'taking' or 'getting' something from someone else. To us, it's an even exchange of bodies, of emotions."

"It's almost a Beatles philosophy," Naamah said.

"I hate the Beatles," Jenn sighed to Philip, who shushed her.

"From 'The End' on 'Abbey Road...'" the female alien continued.

Philip broke in, locking eyes with Naamah. "The love you take being equal to the love you make, you mean," he said.

"Precisely, Mr. Truehard," Naamah told him. "In fact, we call the sex act 'sharing.'" Then she turned to the rest of them, unlocking her gaze from the azure wonders that are Philip's eyes. When next Naamah spoke, her voice trembled. It was as though Philip had ravaged her with his eyes. "Also," she sighed, "There is no such institution as marriage. There is no such ownership or claim. In a sense, we are all married to each other."

As an aside, Naamah added that each home had electronic copies of the entire works of Robert Rimmer. Even Jenn was impressed that the man she'd collaborated with later in his life—and earlier in hers—was so revered. Before becoming the King of Porn Reviews, Rimmer's claim to fame had been *The Harrad Experiment,* a social investigation which encouraged fluid premarital living arrangements. "Ah, free love and all that," Philip commented.

There seemed to be an undeniable connection between him and Naamah which amused Noah and confused Jenn. "What the..." Jenn began and elbowed Philip in the side.

Naamah assented, "There is nothing free about free love, Mr. Truehard."

"Don't I know it," he sighed. "And please, call me 'Philip.' It's my real…"

Naamah smirked sexily. "Oh, I know your real name. And a great deal more about you."

Ω

By now, the survivors were sitting on the dock's wood planking in an arc around Noah and Naamah. Gradually, they became more comfortable, with each other and with themselves. Their new selves. Or the promise of their new selves.

Noah took the verbal torch from his partner and picked up where Naamah left off. "Also, Alpharians know nothing of murder, hatred or war. Except what we've seen in your movies. Perhaps that's one of the reasons we've watched your antics on Earth with such curiosity."

"And understandably," Naamah interjected, "the citizens of our planet do our best to ensure that these evils never make their way into our society. Thus far, we've been successful."

Noah said, "To be honest, a small faction of Alpharians were against importing Earth people for this very reason."

"They didn't want you to infect us with violence or hate," Naamah added. "This is why, as a safety measure, the self-selection process was agreed upon. Those of you who wish to leave and not be considered for immigration may do so now."

Jenn shifted slightly to get up. Perhaps it was more a shift of attitude, of thought, than an actual movement, yet Philip perceived it. He gently touched her hand. "What have we got to lose?"

She laid her hand over his. "A life without Niky…" Jenn began.

Philip cupped his other hand over hers. "But how do you know? Even without him, there could be…indescribable joy. There could be…" Jenn touched her fingertips to Philip's perfectly-pouty mouth. He nibbled on her index finger, slipped it out of his mouth, then continued. "There could be…something. Anything. Aren't you the least bit curious?"

Jenn was. Only she wouldn't admit this to Philip. Not right then. She was also scared, though. But she stayed. For some reason, she stayed.

During Philip and Jenn's *tête-á-tête*, she was aware of people getting up around them. Of those people thanking Noah and Naamah and leaving. Jenn was also aware of the rescuers' eyes upon them, watching, gauging their response. And of the tiny smiles on the aliens' pleasing lips, in the corners of their intelligent eyes. "Thanks," an elderly gentleman muttered to Naamah with a bow, "but I don't care to live anymore. I've seen enough." Then he hobbled off.

For a split second, Jenn contemplated breaking away from Philip and going with the man but she stayed put. *What if?* Jenn thought. *Just what if?*

Plus, it would be nice to see Abbott and Costello do "Who's on First?" again. And again.

After those who chose to leave left, Noah explained how the judgment would proceed. But after only a couple of sentences, someone interrupted him. "Wait, I thought you said the selections would be made by us," the man clarified.

"I did," Noah agreed. "But please, let me finish. All will be revealed." Everyone settled down and silence bathed them once more. "In a few moments, you will be asked to enter the large building on my left," he said, gesturing to a warehousy structure that could have been a cannery in its former life. "It is filled with objects of varying worth. All you must do is choose one. Choose one and leave. Then show it to Naamah and me. The selections will be made based upon the thing you choose."

"That's it?" a young woman with a young child beside her asked.

"That's it," Naamah echoed.

It seemed easy enough. But infinitely difficult.

Ω

When Noah gave the word, the crowd pressed toward the factorylike building. It reminded Philip of the orgy scene in *Gangbang at the OK Corral.* It reminded Jenn of last-minute Christmas shopping at Macy's and the D train at rush hour all rolled into one. Like the mob in Carpinteria, you didn't even have to move your feet; you were swept along in a human tidal wave.

"I can't make such an important decision in the middle of mild hysteria," Jenn shouted to Philip over the rush of bodies and voices.

He agreed. "Let's wait until the crowd thins. Even if there'll be less to choose from, I'd like to think we'd still make the right decision."

Jenn nodded. Silently, she thought that maybe Nik, wherever he was, would make the right choice if given the chance too. She didn't tell this to Philip, though, because she didn't want to risk getting another lecture about sinking hope into the hopeless. Not now.

Together, Philip and Jenn made their way against the surge, fighting against the rip current. They tried to move off to the side. Eventually, arms linked, they succeeded. As difficult as it was, they would wait until the crowd dissipated. Then they would make their selections, if it wasn't too late.

As Philip and Jenn waited, they watched Naamah walk calmly toward the factory, trailing behind the slightly-unruly crowd. When the last of them disappeared inside, Naamah did as well.

Noah remained on the marina beside the restaurant, closer to Jenn and Philip. The visitor stared out to sea with such a desolate expression on his face that Jenn pitied him. "I hate this part," Noah said to no one in particular. Maybe to himself.

"How did a spaceman get a name like Noah?" Jenn called out.

Philip whispered to her, "You're pretty ballsy, talking to him like that. Our fate is in his hands."

Jenn shrugged. "What have we got to lose?"

Noah turned to Jenn and smiled. "It's a very long story," he said.

"We have time," Philip told him.

"Not as much time as you might think," Noah admitted, gesturing toward the once-abandoned factory. "Most of them will plow through quickly, taking the most expensive thing they can find. Most will not be chosen."

"Wait a minute, isn't that cheating, telling us this?" Jenn wondered.

Noah looked at her. "The die has already been cast."

"Meaning?"

Noah didn't respond but instead, considered the sky. It was pea green, as though ill. But in truth, the sky *was* sick. "This is not the first time I've been here," Noah told Jenn and Philip. "I came as part of an expedition in late 1945. We looked at various locations after the war. Since I spoke Californian, I was assigned to the West Coast."

"So, you got to see the internment camps," Philip said knowingly.

"Yes," Noah responded. "It was an ugly piece of your history." He paused, then continued, "But as I wandered the streets of Los Angeles, a woman handed me a book. A lady from the Gideon Society. I flipped the Bible to a page near the beginning and a name stuck out."

"Noah," Jenn said.

He nodded. "Now, I'd read many of your books but somehow, I'd missed this one. I was fascinated. In the days that followed, I read the Bible from cover to cover. Twice. I loved the stories. Especially the one about the ark."

The sky slowly morphed from green to yellow, the same yellow urine turns when you've eaten asparagus. It wasn't a good color. Noah studied the chartreuse clouds and continued, "It was a special expedition for me. The first I ever led. I felt very much like Noah myself. So, I took his name."

"It fits," Jenn told him. "And Naamah?"

Philip broke in. "In the Old Testament, Naamah was the name of Noah's wife. It means 'pleasant.'"

"Very good," Noah admitted.

"I was bar mitzvahed," Philip said shyly. "I still remember some Hebrew."

"I'm impressed," Noah told him. "We thought Naamah was a fitting name, even though we don't have marriage as you know it. On Alpha 49C, relationships are much more…flexible."

They fell into silence, their eyes drifting from the sky to the factory then back to each other. "I'm glad this isn't your first time here," Jenn tacked on. "I'm glad you're not seeing us at our worst. This used to be a beautiful place."

"Hell, *we* used to be beautiful," Philip quipped, trying to make a joke. But it fell flat on its face, perhaps because of all the razed faces.

"Some of us still are beautiful," Jenn told him.

"Oh, I remember what Earth was like," Noah said. "Some think the canals of Mars are the most impressive sight in the Milky Way. Others favored the rings of Saturn. But I fell in love with the coast of California." Jenn thought there might be more to it so she gave Noah time to finish. He took a breath and did. "The next afternoon I ran into the Gideon lady again. Loura drove me up here, to Morro Bay. It was a long drive and by the time we arrived, the sun was setting. It was magnificent. Loura and I shared on the beach, slept in each other's arms then woke to the rising sun."

Noah's story was like a good book that left you hanging off the precipice in anticipation. Jenn wanted to hear all the deets but didn't want to pry. After a pause, Noah said plainly, "She loved me."

"Did you love her back?" Philip wondered.

"I suppose I did," Noah nodded. "Alpharians don't really call it that but yes, I loved her in the Earth sense of the word."

"What happened?" Jenn pushed.

"Nothing," Noah said with a finality. "I couldn't compromise the mission so I couldn't tell Loura the truth about why I was here or where I was from. As it was, I broke the rules by sharing bodies with her. When the expedition was completed, my team and I left. Taking Loura with us wasn't an option. Besides, I don't think she would have come."

"Why not let her decide?" Jenn asked.

Noah frowned and shook his head.

"So, you broke her heart, then," Philip sighed.

"I did," Noah said with true regret. "But not on purpose. And certainly not with malice."

"Did you ever see your Loura again?" Jenn asked.

"Not in the flesh, but I observed her whenever I could."

"And? What did you see?"

Noah pursed his lips in thought. "Well, she was very sad for a time. She would drive up here to cry on the beach. But after a year or so, Loura seemed to recover. She got married, had a few children. She seemed…happy."

"That's good," Jenn told him, trying to make him feel better.

"It is," Noah confessed. "She would even come up here with her family on holiday sometimes. Her husband seemed like a good sort. I would watch them build sandcastles with their offspring. They had three together. All boys. She named the eldest Noah."

"Of course, she did," Philip told him.

Ω

As if to break the stream of conversation, an enormous, bloated, dead sea lion floated by on the gray current like a stiff two-by-four. The breeze brought with it an interesting and not entirely unpleasant odor. "Like White Castle hamburgers," Philip noted. "Remember them?" They did; the aroma was unmistakable.

Jenn told Noah about Nik and gave him the CliffsNotes version of their separation story. Philip listened politely, though he had heard it many times. Jenn was proud of herself because this time, she didn't cry or even sniffle. Although she did get misty. But misty was all right. Misty meant she was healing, accepting.

Noah reached out and clasped Jenn's shoulder as she spoke. It was the first time the alien had touched her. Or anyone. An odd, healing sensation radiated down Jenn's arm and drifted throughout her body. Maybe it was her imagination, but at that precise moment, Jenn thought she felt her bleeding stop.

It looked as though Noah wanted to hug Jenn, wrap his arms around her and circle her with his benevolence. But he yanked back his hand quickly and apologized. "I'm sorry. I shouldn't have done that," Noah said. "It was…inappropriate."

"It's all right," Jenn assured him.

"But still, I broke protocol," Noah sighed. "I should have known better. We're not supposed to have any physical contact. I…"

Ignoring what he'd just told her, Jenn reached out and touched Noah's offending arm. "Really, it's okay. This must be very hard for you."

He nodded. "You know…" Noah began, eyes full as he gazed beyond the two who stood before him. "You are the first people who have spoken to me privately at any of these events," he confessed. "Well, not counting the women who tried to seduce me to get onboard ship. I think everyone is terrified of me. Like I'm an interplanetary Gestapo."

Noah sighed like Atlas might have sighed, as though the weight of the world were on his shoulders. In a sense, it was. "There have been many of these selections, but few have been selected," Noah offered. "Do you know what I mean?"

They did.

Looking out to sea again, Noah seemed mesmerized by its sluggish ripple. Like a doughy baby's tummy when it laughed. "Some Noah I am," he lamented. "The purpose of this mission was to take a sampling of different creatures. Two by two, like my namesake. But the problem is, there isn't much left to choose from. Vermin. Mad dogs…"

"And us," Philip said.

People were starting to gather outside the factory where Naamah now stood, waiting. She caught Noah's eye and cocked her head to bid him closer. "I must go," Noah said. "Choose wisely," he warned Jenn and Philip. Then he left to join his partner.

Twenty-Eight

Slim Pickings

I nside, the warehouse looked like your friendly neighborhood Sam's Club or Costco. Trussed roof, corrugated steel ceiling, a vast, cavernous space. A handful of people still scurried about, some muttering unintelligibly to themselves with the heft of their decisions. But this time, the hustle and bustle didn't remind Jenn of the Christmas rush. It was more like the day after Christmas. Slightly more civilized but still harried.

The choices were limitless. Almost too many. Yet, in other aspects, the pickings were slim. There was much to choose from but these items seemed to be the wrong sizes, last season's colors, "off" in some way.

Dozens of departments were delineated throughout the building. Signs suspended from the ceiling guided the choosers toward whatever they sought, from clothing to housewares to linens and toiletries. There were toys, lingerie, jewelry, sporting goods, even furniture. Jenn had no inkling how Alpharian explorers had managed to procure these items, but they'd done an excellent job encapsulating American society. At least, what used to be American society.

Some survivors tried to sneak out more than one item. For instance, a woman who clutched a zebrawood pen in her fist stashed a large, sparkling emerald-cut diamond ring between her cheek and teeth. How low must you sink to wedge a Weeble up your ass, your Mack Weldon sweatpants bagged around your ankles? And why? Their bizarre Charlie Chaplin walks always gave away these butt bandits, and believe it or not, there were several.

But no matter where the contraband was hidden, Noah and Naamah always discovered the smugglers' secrets at the other end of the judging line. Although the pair were perceptive, as in any box store, there must have been cameras capturing the action. Alpharians were no doubt watching the selection process on their home planet like Earth people used to watch "Survivor."

Other people fought over objects, their voices hitting decibels that would shard glass if recorded on Memorex. Didn't they realize this would immediately disqualify them? These were not the sort of people Alpharians wanted mingling with their kind.

Still others lay in crumpled heaps on the speckled linoleum, either trampled underfoot or overcome by the gravity of their choice. Quite a few babbled incoherently, weighing their options out loud, either to themselves or to invisible companions. It wasn't clear which. People who had gotten on so politely as neighbors just days earlier were now at each other's throats. Because this was different. This wasn't a friendly glass of Tang on a front porch. This was life or death. Literally.

Yes, Jenn and Philip witnessed many odd things…emaciated arms layered with solid gold bangle bracelets ("But he said *one*, Grace. Not one of every kind!"); an almost hairless lady toting a cosmetics kit; a young man carrying a pea coat many sizes too large for him; an old woman hugging a teddy bear; a little boy clutching a Royal Doulton cup with John Barleycorn's face on it; a teenage girl with a tape recorder tucked under her arm. Then there was the man (unsuccessfully) trying to drag away a white pedestal bathtub—he eventually settled upon lugging a more manageable set of Oneida silverware.

Ω

Jenn didn't know what she wanted or needed. She needed so much and wanted so little. So, she just stood there watching everyone else while Philip confidently strode toward Giftwares. Halfheartedly, Jenn browsed through Stationery and Books. But there were no whole books left, just loose pages scattered about.

The El saw everything but said nothing...
She was like a fire...
Church bells, school bells, doorbells, the bells on the knife
man's cart...
There are thousands of different kinds of roses...

It occurred to Jenn that it might be a good idea to have something to read other than the AAA Tourbook, which was in tatters by this point. Perhaps something weighty like *War and Peace* or something light like *Without Feathers*. Something, anything. What if Philip was chosen and she wasn't? Jenn would definitely need something to read then.

She crawled along the floor and picked up a random page.
It began:
Love brought tears, and so much more.
Another said:
What the hell am I doing climbing an active volcano in Guatemala?
Still on her knees, Jenn read:
Don't you have a friend like that? A forever friend, no matter what?
The last page she looked at said:
That's what the passage of time can bring. It can bring peace. It can bring closure.

Ω

Jenn realized that she was stalling. Brushing off her knees, she spotted a book that had been pushed under a rack. Its spine had been trampled and squashed. When she picked it up, some of the pages fluttered out. But most of them seemed to be intact. The title was stamped onto the front of its soft, brown leatherette cover. It read *The Holy Bible*.

She brushed the dust off the front, read a few lines about Noah and smiled. Then Jenn remembered what Nik had once told her—that when a religious Jew dropped a sacred object like the Talmud or a yarmulke on the ground, they kissed it, as if to purify it. She raised the Bible to her lips then nestled it onto a pile of Crane's Crest ecru-shaded stationery. To choose the Good Book would be to kowtow to what

Noah had told her earlier. It would be cheating. And although Jenn was many things, she wasn't a cheater.

Jenn wandered up and down the aisles of the makeshift big-box store like a lost child searching for her parents in Walmart. She fingered resplendent silk scarves. She toyed with amethyst pendants. She briefly considered an ivory carving of two copulating deer.

Waiting patiently for Philip in the agreed-upon spot near a rack of crotchless panties, Jenn held a frilly mint green negligee to her withered chest. "It's not your color," Philip said from behind. "I'd go with something bolder. Red, maybe."

He was smiling that blue movie star smile of bright white teeth. Jenn immediately noticed that Philip's Crest box was gone. Instead, he held a finely-crafted black lacquer case. Opaline flowers and jade tree branches adorned its cover. "Look," Philip said as he unfastened the brass latch and lifted the top.

Laid to rest on a bed of indigo satin was Dick Truehard's famed member. It looked happy there. "I'm not sure what they're expecting from our choices," Philip began. "Something selfless? Something necessary? But I figured this guy deserved a decent final resting place. Especially after giving me and so many others so much pleasure."

Jenn nodded. "I think you chose well."

"What did you pick?" Philip wondered when he saw that Jenn's hands were empty. "Is it too big to carry? Do you need help?"
Jenn shook her head. "I couldn't find anything I wanted. Or needed."

"You sure?" Philip asked. "One more quick go-around?"
Jenn told him that she was sure.

Ω

Outside, many choices had been made. But as Noah had told them earlier, few were chosen. Jenn and Philip took their places at the end of the long, crooked queue. Noah and Naamah stood at the front, listening earnestly to each person explaining why they picked what they picked in one simple sentence, as per the Alpharians' instructions.

There didn't seem to be any rhyme or reason to the selection process, though Philip and Jenn attempted to figure it out as they waited. The monetary value of an object didn't seem to matter. The more something was worth, the less difference it made.

For example, a woman who chose a plush coyote coat was cast aside but a man who chose a sequined turban for his wife's bald head was not. His beloved, who had picked a box of Cella's cherry cordials (milk chocolate with liquid centers), was chosen. She explained that they were her husband's favorite thing in the world besides her. A young woman who presented a bottle of Kaopectate was chosen. A tween who fingered a Luger was not. (It was promptly taken from him and dismantled.)

As previously noted, Noah and Naamah always knew when someone had taken more than one item and had hidden it somewhere on their person. These individuals were immediately disqualified when the second item was revealed. "But I just *have* to get on that ship..." one man began in his defense. In his next breath, he silenced himself, realizing that cheating his way onboard reflected a deep character flaw and was the very reason he *shouldn't* be chosen.

Others looked strangely relieved when they weren't picked. As though it would have been too much pressure to start anew. A few collapsed into tears. A handful were angry and began to yell and curse. Noah and Naamah's quiet acceptance of their rudeness spoke volumes; it wordlessly told the ragers that they weren't worthy of being selected.

When the Unchosen were asked to move aside, besides yelling and ranting, a few swung their fists at the judges. (Perhaps these individuals were immune to the bright rays' calming properties like some were immune to anesthetics.) But no blows ever connected. Noah and Namaah seemed shielded by an imperceptible Plexiglas. It was as though an invisible force field protected the alien couple. One or two of the disqualified pounded the air around them, resembling crazed mimes trying to get into a box instead of out of one.

These hysterics never carried on for long, however. It was as though their unsuitable behavior reminded the offender of Noah's words describing the peaceful Alpharians and how his planet-mates were concerned about keeping violence from their world. These aggressive Earth people would then walk away in silence, their heads downcast, knowing the consequences of their actions.

Throughout it all, Noah and Naamah looked as though they wanted to comfort those gathered before them, both the ones who were chosen and the ones who were not. But they never touched anyone. Except for that one instance when Noah had briefly touched Jenn's shoulder as they spoke outside the fish restaurant, the aliens had no physical contact with any of the Earth folk.

Ω

The line progressed relatively quickly. Before long, Philip and Jenn were next. Frightened to learn her fate, Jenn made Philip go first. When he handed his box to Naamah, she noted its craftsmanship with appreciation. "Open it," Philip urged her. She glanced at Noah who nodded that it was all right for her to do so. When Naamah lifted the lid, she murmured fondly, "Dick Truehard, you scoundrel," and actually blushed then fell mute.

"Naamah here is quite a fan," Noah said to smooth over his partner's speechlessness.

"So, I gather," Philip conceded.

"I'd know you anywhere," Naamah cooed. "Even in the dark."

On Planet Alpha 49C, Noah explained, Dick Truehard, was a sexual luminary and revered to a godlike status. Quality pornographic movies were highly regarded on Alpha 49C and shown on high-rez LaserVision for all adults to enjoy. There were shrines devoted to gifted directors like Henri Pachard, Candida Royalle and Cecil Howard. And film appreciation courses led by respected historians like K.C. Scott and Bill Holliday. Adult films like *She's So Fine, Three Daughters* and *Snake Eyes* were considered classics on Planet 49C planet like *Citizen Kane* and *Casablanca* were on the Big Blue Marble.

Just as he had been among his Earth peers, on Planet Alpha 49C, Philip/Dick was noted for his passionate yet caring sex. He always communicated sweetly with his partners, putting their pleasure before his own. There was an abundance of eye contact, caressing and loving conversation. It was obvious that many of Dick's costars didn't know how to deal with this kind of onscreen treatment. Probably because it was too close to actual love offscreen, which they may not have been able to deal with either.

Philip later learned that Alpharians were unimpressed with a garden-hose endowed performer like John C. Holmes or the sadistic antics of Jamie Gillis, even though the latter was a very good actor. Besides hate and war, Alpharians had no tolerance for rough sex.

Passionate sex, yes, but mean copulation, no. For their AlphaBucks, Dick Truehard was the uncontested King of Smut.

So, it came as no surprise that Dick was chosen. Even minus his peaceful sword. Both Naamah and Noah agreed that Dick's member had been the source of joy for many, not just for himself. They also thought he had much more to give to Alpharians in the way of erotic education through filmmaking. Like the punchline of the old joke about the nun in heaven that porn queen Gloria Leonard liked to tell, Dick/Philip demurred, "I always wanted to direct."

Ω

During the Choosing, other exceptions were made on the sheer virtue of future (and past) contributions. Ben Cohen and Jerry Greenfield, of Ben & Jerry's ice cream fame, were included in the final selection. (At the time of the Fall, the Vermonters had been in San Francisco on business.) They were picked even though their chosen items had been a Fire Island beach towel and a melon baller, respectively. The Alpharians apparently appreciated sweet things of many sorts, not just love.

A man who'd manufactured dribble glasses and whoopie cushions made the cut because the inhabitants of Planet Alpha 49C also had an unanimously keen sense of humor and had an admiration for all things funny, even practical jokes and gags.

There were several vacancies in Planet Alpha 49C Jazz Ensemble so musicians were being recruited. But understandably, no heavy-metal maniacs or mascaraed men who bit the heads off live bats were picked. No satanic worshipers who drank their fans' blood from collection plates were included. But exceptions were made for Dee Snider of "Twisted Sister" fame, Luther Campbell of "Two Live Crew" and Vinnie Spit who founded the punk band which shared his surname. (And of course, Vinnie's wife, a caring therapist who specialized in sexual trauma.) They were all good eggs, despite the hype.

Ω

After Philip passed with flying colors, Jenn was next in line. Her right knee shook uncontrollably just as it had when she'd taken the road test for her driver's license on crowded Jamaica Avenue out in East New

York. Remarkably, Jenn aced the road test but wasn't all that confident she'd ace this test.

Philip waited with Jenn instead of congregating with the others who'd been chosen. He hung close to Jenn's side and encouraged, "I know you'll make it" into Jenn's ear, just like he'd said to Sue Nero in *Red Heat.*

But Jenn knew the real reason Philip wouldn't leave her—it was because he wanted to give her a proper goodbye if she wasn't picked. Earlier, in the factory, he'd promised that he wouldn't go to Alpha 49C without Jenn but she'd protested. She couldn't do that to him. It was a wonderful opportunity, a second chance at life, and Philip had to take it, with or without her.

Alternatively, Jenn had promised she wouldn't go without Philip either, but she knew he would have convinced her to go just the same.

All these thoughts vaulted back and forth in Jenn's head in the space of a split second. Philip patted her hand for good luck then took one step to the side. "Yes?" Noah said to Jenn as she stood before him. He glanced into her empty palms which stood plaintively at the ends of her arms.

Jenn said nothing.

"Let's see what you picked," he requested in a kind voice.

That's when Jenn started to cry. "I couldn't find anything I wanted," she babbled. "I want my Niky. That's all I want."

Even more than before, it looked as though Noah wanted to hold Jenn, to comfort her. His brow was lined with thought and his chin wrinkled in emotion. "This is highly unusual," Noah said to Naamah.

She agreed. "It's never happened before."

"Are you absolutely sure there's nothing?" Noah asked Jenn. "Nothing at all?"

"Nothing," Jenn repeated, chewing on her lower lip.

Noah and Naamah stared at each other, then whispered back and forth unintelligibly. After a moment, he looked at Jenn and said, "Welcome aboard."

Philip hugged Jenn tightly. They broke apart and took in each other's faces, eyes aglow with happy tears. Then they stepped across the imaginary line that would bring them to a new life.

Jenn realized that if she went to Planet Alpha 49C, she had to abandon all promise of ever finding Nik. Boarding the spacecraft would signify that she was finally, emphatically, declaring her husband dead. But Jenn supposed that it was about time to bury Nik.

Ω

A trail of perhaps ten people still awaited the Choosing. Out of those, Naamah and Noah harvested only one. The rest sifted away silently.

The Chosen assembled on the pier where the Tiger's Folly II used to dock. There were about two dozen people in all. They were told that the previously-picked survivors and the rest of the crew waited for them on the boulder-shaped spacecraft, which was called the Omega.

With Noah leading the way, one by one, they climbed down a ladder from the pier and into Morro Bay. Jenn thought there would be a boat waiting to take them to the Omega but there was nothing. Only the jelly-rolling sea.

Twenty-Nine

Walk Across the Water

T he Chosen walked across the water to the Omega, which waited patiently for them on Morro Rock's beach. The ragtag group's bodies drifted above the bay. "It's a little parlor trick I learned from the New Testament," Noah admitted proudly, looking down at his dry boots. And indeed, it was a nifty stunt at that, one to be proud of; their feet didn't even get wet.

Behind them, the force field that had surrounded Noah, Naamah and the Chosen was deactivated. As it was, Jenn thought she detected an almost imperceivable hum that ceased, a slight displacement of matter. Maybe others did too because a handful of the Unselected tried to follow them out to the bay. Instead of heading to the spit of earth that connected Morro Rock to the mainland, they dropped into the water from the wharf, just as the Rescued had. But the Unchosen sunk into the thick sea like rusted anchors, screaming in anguish, pounding their fists into the surf in frustration. They paddled desperately to stay afloat in the gooey water while the non-swimmers among them immediately disappeared beneath the sludge like stones.

No one turned back at the tortured cries or responded to the frenzied thrashing. Jenn grasped Philip's hand, then her heart but spoke not a word. Noah and Naamah stared straight ahead as they led the group. One big, fat tear sat in the corner of Noah's left eye. It reminded Jenn of Ingrid Bergman's stubborn tear in the airport scene of *Casablanca*. Finally, Noah's tear slid down his cheek. He didn't even brush it aside. It hung there in suspended animation for a few moments, clinging to his upper lip. Then he licked it away.

The sun had begun its descent and the sky was Jenn's favorite shade of purple. "I asked Naamah about Nik," Philip whispered.

"And?" Jenn gasped hopefully.

"She said there were no blind, bald car mechanics on board."

"Not helpful," Jenn said.

"I'm sorry," Philip told her.

"I am too."

They fell silent until they reached the Omega.

Ω

A handful of people tried to reach Morro Rock by land. But before they could, they were cast back by an unseeable dynamism. They never got closer to the ship than fifty paces. The Omega's open hatch lay high above the Chosen. After the intruders were safely repelled, a ramp descended. From inside the Omega, a warm, blanched light shone. Like the light you supposedly see when you are about to die.

Single-file, Namaah, the followers, then lastly, Noah, stepped onto the ramp. It angled up a hundred feet or more to the ship's hatch. The ramp's moving walkway drew them inside the Omega to a large reception area. There, the Chosen waited in wonder, waited for their new lives to be revealed, waited for their next move.

Noah was the first to step through a hazy, cellophane-like screen which separated the inside of the Omega from the Earth's atmosphere. The screen closed behind him, appearing to seal tight. Naamah stood with the Chosen, sending them through the translucent screen one by one. Finally, Philip entered, then it was Jenn's turn.

She took a step.

Pushing through the curtain's veiled slit was like a birth of sorts. A rebirth, if you will. The sheer barrier parted like a plastic cervix, and woosh, Jenn was on the other side. Noah stood waiting for her, wide-armed, with the ever-faithful Philip flanking him. People stood around them, talking excitedly. Although their faces were unfamiliar to Jenn, their voices seemed oddly recognizable. *Was that Kevin, the...,* she pondered.

But Jenn didn't have a chance to consider her surroundings for longer than a breath, because the next moment Noah swooped her up into a snug embrace. It caught Jenn off-guard and put her off-balance.

A tingling sensation spread throughout her entire body. It was so much more intense than the feeling that enveloped Jenn when Noah had touched her shoulder earlier that day. A sense of peace pulsed through her entire being.

Jenn closed her eyes, savoring the warmth and emotion flowing into her from the press of Noah's body. When she opened her eyes again, Jenn noticed a mirrored wall behind them. That's when she saw someone else in Noah's arms, not her. Jenn gasped. This was the exact opposite of all those horror movies she'd seen as a child—when a vampire looked into a mirror and saw no reflection. But instead of no reflection at all, Jenn saw the image of another woman. This woman was pretty, slightly spectacular even. Jenn couldn't stop looking at her, no matter how hard she tried.

Noah's likeness in the glass burst into a wide grin as he pulled away from the woman. Immediately, Jenn understood that the woman wasn't a random stranger at all; it was her. It was Jenn at her very best. It was twenty-seven-year-old Jenn on Horseshoe Bay Beach in Bermuda in the turquoise bathing suit.

Before Jenn could ask Noah to explain her metamorphosis, he stepped forward to hug the man who'd stood just behind Jenn in line. "I told you, all will be revealed," Noah said to Jenn just before he engulfed the man.

She approached the mirror. Jenn fingered the outline of her face, the impeccable curl of her hair. "It's a magic mirror, right?" she said to Philip.

"Oh, it's magic, all right," he told Jenn. "But it's not the mirror that's magic; it's you. The new you. Or the old you."

Jenn carefully examined her face in the glass then touched herself. Her skin was smooth and lightly tanned to a healthy glow. No more rashes, breakouts or lesions. Jenn ran her tongue around the inside of her mouth. There were no abscesses. Her fingernails weren't ragged. Her cuticles weren't bloodied from biting.

Looking around, Jenn now recognized the people surrounding her. They were the same crew who'd walked across the water with her. The Chosen. Sylett and Kevin and Abby and George and all the rest. Some were tinged with gray now. Some were teenagers again. Some were prom queens or basketball stars. But all perfect and whole and in their prime.

Ω

After the last of the Chosen passed through the cosmic Saran Wrap, Noah attempted to unboggle the mystery. Although it did take several moments for him to quiet the excited babble enveloping him. Everyone was present except for Naamah and Philip. Jenn couldn't seem to find her friend among the handsome faces. He'd always stitched himself so close to Jenn's side. And Namaah… perhaps she'd gone off to finalize the onboarding process. Or maybe she and Philip had…

Noah interrupted the Habitrail swirl of possibilities in Jenn's brain. "Well, now you know our secret," Noah beamed. "We couldn't reveal it to you earlier because the knowledge would have devastated the others. And it might have affected your choices."

"But why couldn't you fix everyone down there?" Sylett asked sadly.

Noah shook his head. "It would have served no purpose to transform the Unchosen on Earth because the radiation would have reversed the healing process in a few weeks. And unfortunately, we don't have the space or the means to accommodate everyone, so…" Noah's voice drifted off.

He considered each of them, impressed with his handiwork. Noah's beatific expression perfectly illustrated the Yiddish word *kvell*, which means to swell with pride. Noah was surely *kvelling*. "As you can see, all of you are restored," he continued. "Healed. Some of you are younger than you were at the time of the blasts, some older. But you are at your own personal best. The heathiest you have ever been or ever would be. And the happiest."

"What do you want from us?" asked Kevin, the former dairyman from the former State of Wisconsin.

"Nothing, really," Noah said. "Only that you live among us. That you educate us by example, that you school us with the wisdom you've attained. And that you reproduce…"

"Will we be on display, like in a museum?" a teenage boy asked. Jenn noticed that the child clutched a worn copy of *Slaughterhouse-Five*. She recalled that its hero Billy Pilgrim, slipped back and forth through time, and once ended up on the planet Tralfamadore, where he copulated with blue movie star Montana Wildhack in a zoo-like setting made to resemble Earth. This was most probably the root of the boy's question.

"No, you will not be on display," Noah assured the boy. "You will live with us. You will, in a sense, become us. All we ask is that each of you, in your own way, contribute to our society. Teach us about your experiences. Share what you've learned on Earth."

There was thick silence among the almost two dozen assembled. They were trying to digest what they'd just learned, to take it all in. Many seemed confused so Noah tried a different tack to clarify what was expected of them. He began, "There was a saying among the survivors of your Holocaust…"

"Which Holocaust?" a voice rang out.

"The biggest one. The one during World War Two," Noah explained patiently. "Holocaust survivors had a saying. It was, 'Never to forget.' And we on Planet Alpha 49C don't want you to forget. We will help you heal but we want you to remember. We must learn from what you remember so that this, all of this, was not in vain."

Noah paused. "Do each of you think you can do this?" he posed. "Because if you're not able, then you're free to go. No strings attached." He gestured toward the ramp beyond the cellophane. No one budged. It was as though the Chosen all held their breath in unison, then exhaled.

"All right, then," Noah smiled. "Let's begin again."

Thirty

Take Off

As Jenn listened to Noah, her eyes kept drifting to her own face in the mirror. She'd always thought that twenty-seven was her prettiest year. And her most joyful. Back then, she was two years married and insanely content. This was exactly what had been reflected in that Bermuda bathing suit snapshot Nik had taken. Except now there was no Nik behind the camera.

Someone tapped Jenn's shoulder. She whirled around in anxious expectation. *Could it be?* But it was only Philip. At least Jenn had Philip, no matter what. It was a good feeling to have someone. Even if it wasn't the right someone. "My, you are lovely," Philip told her.

With a theatrical flourish, he unlatched the black lacquer case which had recently replaced his Crest box. When Philip opened it, Jenn saw that the small, polished chest was empty. No more penis upon regal blue satin. They both smiled. Then Philip held Jenn close. She felt his member's elated outline carving into her thigh. It strained against the cloth of his slacks, as though it were glad to be back home. Yes, Philip was whole again too; they all were.

Jenn had to admit that Philip looked wonderful and happy as well. Just the way he did in *No Ifs, ands or Butts*. In Jenn's opinion, this was, hands down, his best performance ever. *NIAOB* had earned him his fourth Erotica Award. "Where were you before?" Jenn asked him.

"Breaking it in," Philip admitted. "And I'm very pleased to report that it still works." Just like John Wayne Bobbitt's had after his reattachment —JWB'd even made a porn film called *Frankenpenis* to prove it.

As if on cue, Naamah entered the mirrored room, beaming and humming "Fine and Mellow." "Ah," said Jenn.

"Ah, indeed," Philip echoed. "That's what *she* said."

Ω

Next, Noah and Naamah led the Rescued out of the mirrored reception area down a maze of narrow corridors and ramps illuminated with ruby-red neon tubes. Through speakers recessed into the ceilings came the sound of "The Four Seasons." Not "Frankie Valli and the..." but Vivaldi's exquisite concerto. More specifically, "Spring" with its cheerful, optimistic violins.

Along the way, they passed numerous crew members who were dressed in the same one-piece suits Noah and Namaah wore, in that same unceremonious yet agreeable shade of blue. Everyone they saw was pleasant looking and well-formed. Not strikingly gorgeous but easy on the eyes. The Alpharians were super friendly and they all knew who this motley crew were, some of them literally dressed in rags. The spacefolk nodded greetings or spouted pleasantries as Noah and Naamah briskly led the newcomers past. "Hello" or "Welcome" echoed in their wake. The immigrants from Earth returned the Alpharian nods and thanked them but kept moving.

Ω

Jenn didn't know where they were being taken but she could tell that they were going slightly upward, toward the Omega's coned top. After a short while, the yawningly-wide space seemed to level out. The procession entered a large, circular common area that was dimly lit. Alpharians were scattered about on the chunky pillows and curved sofas. Some were partially clothed, quietly murmuring in groups of two or more. Perhaps they were sharing sex but the lighting was too dim to tell. But whatever they were up to, it seemed very natural, genial and right. They were so immersed in their activities that they didn't acknowledge the group or seem aware of their presence.

A curved screen covered roughly one third of the vast wall.
Upon it, Bud Abbott bellowed, "Who's on first?" while Lou Costello
sputtered and coughed and rubbed his head in frustration. The room's
ceiling was constructed of domed glass. It was dark by now and Jenn
could see pinpricks of stars through it. There were so many stars. Lou
Costello remarked, "Today, and tomorrow's pitching."

"Now you've got it," Bud Abbott said.

Jenn briefly recalled an unfortunate waitress at a Ranch House
Restaurant in Sarasota who resembled Lou Costello. She chuckled
to herself about this, remembering how she and Niky had to choke
back their laughter as "Louise Costello" served them key lime pie and
coffee. "What?" Philip asked.

"Nothing," she told him.

Ω

The Chosen continued to follow Noah and Naamah through the
labyrinth. They were led out to the other end of the common room
where several uncommon acts were transpiring.

Back in the light, Namaah said, "You must be tired from your
ordeal." There were nods and sighs. "We'll show you to your sleeping
chambers," she continued. "But first, I'm sure you'd like nice,
hot showers."

"Oh, yes. And fresh clothes, please," Sylett, formerly of Freedom,
Wisconsin, said. "I've been wearing this *schmata* for months."

"Of course," Naamah smiled.

They were efficiently split into two groups, male and female, each
moving separately into two long, tiled rooms. There, they were told to
disrobe then toss their clothes and shoes into a great pile. Anything of
worth like jewelry or of sentimental value should be retained, handed
over to be purified, then would be returned to its owner. The rest of it
would be incinerated.

For a flash, Jenn's mind tripped to the gas chambers of the
Holocaust. There, Jews and gypsies were told to strip off their
garments before being murdered in communal bathhouses where
Zyklon B was pumped through shower heads instead of water.

But Jenn willed herself not to think of cyanide-based pesticides.
Instead of poisonous gas, Jenn and her compatriots were rewarded with
a scalding, steaming, glorious spray of H_2O as the row of showerheads

switched on simultaneously. Twelve women sighed a unanimous sigh of pleasure as they watched their filth wash down the floor drains. Although they'd bathed (albeit in tainted water) and laundered their clothing regularly on infected Earth, they never felt especially clean.

For Jenn, it was absolute bliss to scrub her scalp, her skin. The grime ran down her body, between her breasts, her legs, and her unruly thatch of pubic hair. The ghost berry beads, still strung defiantly around her neck like flimsy armor, seemed to drip red, like old blood. Was this actual dirt or from the soul of the beads themselves? Were their protective qualities leaching out now that Jenn no longer needed protection? These unanswered questions were rinsed from her mind and swirled down the drain just like the dust that coated Jenn's skin from her recent odyssey.

The liquid soap was silky soft as the steamy room filled with the scent of lavender. Jenn loved lavender. Beside her was Robin, a former marijuana farmer from the Salinas Valley, who luxuriated in the bubbly foam her soap created. "Lemon is my favorite scent," she said.

"Lemon?" Sylett, of Freedom, remarked. "All I smell is roses."

"Evergreen," said Jane.

Jenn said nothing, realizing that the Alpharians were giving them the gift of their best-loved aromas. The same cream-colored foam smelled different to each bather. But whatever scent the women detected, it was their personal favorite. What other surprises did the Alpharians hold in store for them?

Jenn hummed "I'm Gonna Wash That Man Right Outa My Hair" as she lathered and scrubbed. *South Pacific* had been her mom's favorite musical. Sylett, Jane and Robin joined in too, just like the other nurses had in the staged number; perhaps it had been their moms' favorite musical as well.

When the women were done bathing, two female Alpharians were waiting for them at the other end of the shower room with mounds of warm, fluffy, white towels heaped in their arms.

After the new arrivals dried off, these same attendants handed them piles of neatly-folded articles of clothing: azure jumpsuits, underthings, socks and short, faux suede pull-on boots. The immigrants donned them in the adjoining dressing room. The clothes fit each one as though they were bespoke garments. If at first, they were baggy or tight, the apparel instantly shrunk or stretched to fit their frames. "This is wild," an editor named Carla said. "How is it even possible?"

No one knew. But they didn't question it any further. They just reveled in the softness of the material, in the fineness of the stitching. They simply reveled in being truly clean, in being freshly clothed.

Noah and Naamah were waiting at the other end of the shower room. The second group soon joined them, Philip looking as sparkly and shiny as the rest. While they were led along another corridor, Noah explained, "On Planet Alpha 49C, everyone has a job, a purpose."

"Forced labor?" a frightened voice asked, echoing back to the raw scar of concentration camps, to the motto displayed above Auschwitz's gate: *Arbeit Macht Frei. "*Work sets you free."

"I knew this was too good to be true," someone groaned.

Naamah ensured them, "It's not forced, and I promise you, it won't feel like work."

"Jobs here are based on everyone's individual gifts," Noah continued. "We believe that everyone has a special talent, and we make the most of these skills sets on Planet Alpha 49C."

"We'll talk more about your roles tomorrow," Naamah tagged on. "Today, you rest."

Ω

Jenn's living cube was compact but comfortable. It reminded her of a Roomette on Amtrak's Auto Train. There was a place for everything she could possibly need except one—Nik. Drawers were cut into walls, carved out beneath the bed. The walls themselves were painted a soothing shade of ocean. A full-length mirror was tacked to the back of the pocket door's stationary side. A handful of prints depicting swirls of stars in faraway galaxies were projected onto the wall space. Circles of supernovas, rectangular splashes of red dwarfs and hot ceruleans shifted into calming neutrons and peaceful black holes.

Though the mattress beckoned, the last thing Jenn wanted to do was rest. But she compelled herself to sit on the bed, which was three-quarter size, firm and welcoming. Beneath it were compartments filled with more clothing and linens. In an alcove, two shelves were mounted beside a mirrored cabinet that was outfitted with any sort of toiletry Jenn might need: toothpaste, a toothbrush, antiperspirant, antibacterial cream, ear swabs and more. There was a petite personal sink beneath the mirror. A small, private restroom lay beyond another door with a shower and a toilet/bidet combo.

In the main cube, a wafer-thin tablet sat charging on a ledge. Instructions on the home screen explained its use. A few swipes gave Jenn access to all the books, images and videos in the Alpharian library as well as entrance to their version of the internet. Jenn marveled at all that could be reached with a few fingertip taps. After having no information except the AAA Tourbook for months, here was the entire galaxy at Jenn's disposal.

Ω

Just as Naamah had promised, supper was announced by a winking light. Famished, Jenn and the others followed a series of glowing moss-green arrows which brought them to a large dining hall. Dinner was served cafeteria-style, probably the most efficient way to fill the bellies of the sixty or more present. But instead of evoking the horrors of a high school lunchroom or a prison mess hall, the lighting was warm and inviting, the tables small and intimate, seating no more than six, and the food smelled wonderful instead of evoking *au de* Purina.

Jenn scanned the faces but didn't see Philip. She grabbed a tray and slipped into line. Others chattered around her, but Jenn didn't feel like joining in. Not yet. Despite the allure of the food, her appetite had suddenly vanished. She wasn't sure why. Her frame of mind would be best described as untethered. Adrift. She didn't know where she belonged or where she was going. Yet oddly enough, the feeling was tolerable. At least for the time being.

As she moved toward the steaming tins of food, Jenn felt a slight rumble beneath her feet. Out the windows, she saw the night sky swirl. The Omega had taken off! It was unbelievably smooth and fluid. Like a flawless dive into a swimming pool, the atmosphere barely shifted. A pang of excited loneliness filled Jenn's chest as she surged toward her new home, to parts unknown.

Where was Philip to soothe her with his good humor, positive vibes and wicked smile of perfect teeth? Where was her new friend Sylett, the displaced dairy queen? Where was Robin? Where was Jenn, the old Jenn? And would she still be Jenn in this new place, living among the kindhearted Alpharians?

Jenn wanted to watch the Earth fall away like a bad dream. Or a dream with occasionally good bits and pieces amid the shit. *There are always good bits and pieces,* Jenn reminded herself. *You just have to find them.*

"Jenn!! Jenn!!" someone cried. It was a man's voice, deep and tender and delighted.

It wasn't Philip, Noah, Dairy Kevin or Poet Darryl. Who else knew her on the Omega? Jenn turned and searched the supper hall. The tray clattered from her hands as she found a familiar face.

It was Nik!

They held each other for a very long time. Jenn could feel a hundred eyes on her back, poking at her skin but she didn't care. She breathed in Nik's warmth, his familiar scent which had lately become unfamiliar. She buried her head in the space between his chin and shoulder—*her space*—and sobbed and laughed there. "I thought you were dead," she told him.

"I thought *you* were dead," he told her.

"I looked and looked for you in Carpinteria," she said. "I can't believe you slipped from my hands."

"All these bodies came between us," he sighed. "And then..."

"And then you were gone," she finished. "I cried and called out your name on every street corner."

"I know," he croaked. "I heard you. I tried to find you, but I could barely see. I tried to call out but my voice..."

Nik started to cry. "It's okay," Jenn consoled him. "It's okay. You're here now. We're here now. Together. That's all that matters."

Ω

Nik's path had paralleled Jenn's. They kept missing each other on Carpinteria's smoke-filled streets. He stumbled about, almost sightless, discerning nothing in the big, blobby shadows. Except when he used the binoculars. But something, something unnamable, led him north.

Somehow, Nik managed to locate a stale piece of Danish rye in Solvang as he combed through it on his Jenn quest. He took the same route she did, but the only difference was that he traveled at night. Nik discovered that he could see better in the dark. Because of this, he and Jenn just kept bypassing each other, moving beyond each other unseen, like blindfolded snails in a race. Or something like that.

Noah's spaceship had harvested Nik on Pismo Beach. When the Omega crew spotted him, Nik was wearing not one but both pairs of nose clips he'd stashed in his backpack. That's how bad the tang of rotting clams was. "I'm surprised they even stopped for me," Nik remarked. "I must have looked like a total maniac."

"The Alpharians seem to be very intuitive," Jenn told him. "Somehow they knew you weren't a nutter." Then after a breath, she said, "I'm glad they picked you up, Nikolai."

"I am too," he said.

Nik explained that Noah and his crew had detected him via some sort of complex radar system. The Alpharians aboard watched Jenn's husband's quiet desperation from afar. They watched as Nik consoled a frightened, seriously-ill child. Watched as he sang to this child, offkey, watched as this child died in his arms, not so frightened anymore and not alone. "What did you sing?" Jenn interrupted in a whisper.

"'The Wayward Wind,'" he whispered back.

"Gogi Grant," she said, biting her lip. "Good choice."

"I thought you'd approve," Nik told her.

He described how Noah and his comrades observed solemnly as Nik dug a grave for the child in the sand with cupped hands because there was no shovel. They observed as he gently cradled the dead child then placed it within the hole as if putting it down for a nap. "I never knew if it was a boy or a girl," Nik said. "It was hard to tell."

"It didn't really matter, did it?" Jenn offered.

"No, it didn't."

Nik said he covered the child's final resting place with wet sand, marking it with a piece of glacial blue sea glass. Then he sat on a rock and sobbed.

"The next part is a blur," Nik recalled. "I felt a comforting warmth, then was bathed in a bright white light. The next thing I knew, I was on the Omega."

Jenn nodded. She and Nik looked into each other's eyes and clasped hands. "I can understand why they took you," she said.

Nik shrugged. "I did what anyone would do."

"Not anyone," Jenn said. "You're not like anyone."

"You either," Nik admitted, squeezing her hand.

"Let's go somewhere so we can talk," she said. "Talk more. Talk different, I mean."

"I know exactly what you mean," he told her.

Ω

As they hurried down the corridor, Jenn was pleased to discover that Nik was whole once more. His formerly-broken body worked fine. His eyesight was sharp as a red-tailed hawk's again and his teeth were strong and straight, just as they'd been when his braces were first removed at age fifteen.

Nik and Jenn sequestered themselves in Jenn's room, which was soon to become their room. They talked. And talked. And kissed because they realized they hadn't kissed in eons. Then they kissed some more. And talked again because their lips were getting sore from kissing. Nik and Jenn were happy to learn that their pieces still fit. Her cabin's firm, three-quarter bed was the lucky recipient of their renewed exploration. Though not quite as luxurious as a California king, or even a full, it would suffice until they reached Planet Alpha 49C and were given permanent lodgings as a couple.

Jenn and Nik ran their fingers across each other's skin, reacquainting themselves with their various parts. He was elated to reconnoiter with Jenn's twenty-seven-year-old self but swore that he had been very content with her thirty-five-year-old-before-the-apocalypse self. In their recent Alpharian restoration, Nik was now several years her junior. "Can you handle being with a younger man?" he asked.

"I think I can," Jenn told him, dipping in for Round Two.

Ω

They alternated between talking, making love, laughing and fucking.

When they came up for air, Nik and Jen realized that they were starving because they'd both forsaken supper—Steak Diane, Potatoes Anna and what appeared to be Dom DeLuise's East-West Asparagus. It was rumored that dessert was to be banana pudding.

At one point during a lull in the talking part of their reunion, Nik and Jenn heard a soft tap at the door. When she went to answer it, no one was there. But a tray waited patiently on the floor in the hallway like something a steward on a Holland America cruise ship might leave. On the tray, beneath a silver dome were their favorite sandwiches: a Cuban *medianoche* for Jenn and a Reuben for Nik, cut into quarters so they could mix and match. Plus, a tub of rice pudding, liberally sprinkled with a snow of cinnamon.

"How did they know?" Jenn wondered, her mouth full of pork, ham, cheese, pickle and lightly toasted *pan dulce*. "I mean, it's both freaky and thoughtful. Is it the Alpharian version of the Vulcan mind meld or…"

"Shush," Nik told her, pushing an itinerant shred of juicy corned beef into his mouth. "Don't question it, just enjoy it."

After they wolfed down the sandwiches and polished off the rice pudding, Nik turned serious. "Jenn," he began. "I have to tell you something. When they harvested me, I thought you were dead, so…"

Jenn finished the difficult sentence for him. "So, you've been with someone else." She sucked in a breath, trying to digest the news and the sandwich. "It's all right," Jenn decided to say. Even though she wasn't sure whether or not it was okay. "How could you have known?" she tagged on for good measure, trying to convince herself that it was true.

Nik faltered. "I was so sad, and she was…"

"You don't have to say anything more," Jenn told him. The truth was, she didn't want to hear anything more. Jenn didn't know if she could handle it. Could she ever embrace the Alpharian concept of open relationships and non-ownership? Jenn wasn't sure she even wanted to. Especially so soon after having her lost property (Nik) returned to her.

It was a good opportunity for Jenn to let Nik know about Philip. Her husband was glad she'd found someone who could make her feel less lonely, who could make her happy, even penis-less. "I'm glad you found a friend," Nik told Jenn. "And it's all right with me if you want to…"

"…take Dick for a test drive?" Jenn finished. "Thanks, but no thanks."

"It would only be fair," Nik said.

Jenn considered her husband's proposition for a breath, maybe two, then decided, "I have a feeling Philip might make a better friend than he would a lover. Besides, I think I'd have to stand in line. Dick Truehard is more popular on Planet Alpha 49C than he was on Earth, if you can believe it."

Nik believed it. "He's even more handsome in person," Nik admitted reluctantly.

"Some people are just as beautiful on the inside as they are on the outside," Jenn whispered, digging her head into her own private nook on Nik's shoulder. "If you know what I mean."

He did.

Ω

During Jenn and Nik's reunion in the dining hall, the Alpharians had taken the liberty of moving his few changes of clothing into one of the drawers beneath Jenn's bed. There were now two sets of towels, the couple noticed, hanging in the condensed but perfectly-appointed bathroom. "Want the fifty-cent tour?" Nik asked her.

Jenn nodded and was soon winding through the ship's intricate corridors and passageways with Nik. He took her on a more in-depth exploration than the cursory walkaround Noah and Naamah had given the new arrivals. Jenn tried to locate Dick/Philip to properly introduce him to Nik but her friend was nowhere in sight. Neither was Naamah. Jenn had the feeling Philip Tobin would be even busier when they reached Planet Alpha 49C. And that Naamah would be very sore. It was a good thing Alpharians possessed those nifty healing powers; they would come in handy for a nymphomaniac. (Not to be judgy.)

There was a slight rumbling under the metal floor. Jenn started slightly. "It's nothing," Nik assured her, "we're just gearing up for warp speed."

"Like in 'Star Trek'?" Jenn asked.

"Only better," he said. "On Alpha 49C, they consider 'Star Trek' an old-time comedy show. Kind of like we think of 'I Love Lucy.'" Jenn nodded as Nik went on to explain more about space travel, "This ship can travel even faster than the speed of light. But don't worry, you won't feel a thing."

Jenn clutched Nik's hand and dug her fingernails into his wrist, just as she used to do during takeoff and landing on an airplane. Just like she did when the jet had touched down in Phoenix in what seemed like a hundred years ago. Warp speed qualified for nail digging, too. "Some things never change," Nik smiled.

"And sometimes everything does," she said.

"It's much smoother than a 747," he promised. And it was.

Nik peeled Jenn's hand from his wrist. "Come on, I want to show you something," he said and led her to a large window. The universe lay spread out before them like a succulent meal on an impeccably-set table.

Nik and Jenn held hands tightly as they watched the veil of black sky swirled with stars zoom past. The stars themselves seemed to rush away and grow tails as Jenn and Nik and the others crashed through the Earth's poison atmosphere and sped toward the left fingertip in the Andromeda Galaxy on Noah's spaceship.

And you know the rest.

Fine

Jenn pressed the Memorywriter's return key again and again so that the FleuroPaper advanced through the roller and fed into her hand. She added the page to the others in the heap and fanned through them. However, Jenn didn't feel the satisfaction of completion. It was the same feeling she had when an orgasm vanished in mid-shudder, like the proverbial rug had been pulled out from beneath her.

She sighed, pressed another sheet into the machine and twisted the roller. Maybe what she was typing was just for herself, for her eyes only. And then again, maybe it wasn't.

But am I truly finished? I'm sure there are more things you'd like to know. But would I like to tell them? No doubt, you have many questions. But can they be answered?

I'm going to let this manuscript sit, ferment, for a time. Then I want to give it a quick edit. And maybe another. Then perhaps it will be ready to show Noah, who, I suppose is my editor. (Though he swears he won't change a word. Even my profuse asides, italics and parentheticals.) Also, I swear the tone shifts when Philip comes into the picture. I'll have to examine that too. Or not. Maybe raw is better. Maybe raw is more real.)

Or...is Noah more than my editor? Is he my publisher. My mentor? Is he all three? Or neither. Regardless of what Noah is, I think I'll edit this again. And maybe one last time after that.

Writing is a long, painful process. Getting it down on FleuroPaper is half the battle, as well as the most important thing. Writing's the easiest part, though it sometimes feels like pulling teeth with pliers and no Novocaine. Then comes the most complicated part: the editing. Noah says editing often takes longer than the actual writing. But then editing is also writing, isn't it? Of course, it is. I think...

It is my job, my task, to write this story. So, I will. I must sing for my supper, Noah jokes. I guess I...

Oh, shit, the baby is crying. It's just me here right now since Nik is in the studio, putting the finishing touches on "Post-Nuclear Blues." It's a great name for an album, don't you think? I might even steal it for the book.

Speaking of books, Noah says that after mine is published, he will make a book of the suicide notes Nik collected along our travels. Would you believe that Nik kept them all, shoved them into his battered Hello Kitty backpack for safekeeping? Nik clung to his pack, to the letters, even as the Alpharians rescued him on Pismo Beach. Noah agrees that someone must remember these people we lost. And intergalactic folks must remember the reasons we lost them. So, there will be a book which assures this.

Ω

Okay. The baby is in my lap. I'm trying to nurse her, cradled in my left arm while I type with my right hand. She palms the strand of ghost berry beads around my throat as she suckles, as is her custom. I wonder whatever became of the old Navajo woman who sold these beads to me. Is she still alive? And if so, does she ever wonder what became of me?

But anyway...

I never got the hang of voice-to-text and it's never any good anyway. *Crap* becomes *wrap* and VTT doesn't type out the curses. So, I am Old Skool through and through and type everything out with my fingertips.

For what it's worth, I don't hear the cry of silence anymore. But for some reason, Lou Reed's "Satellite of Love" keeps going through my head.

More about the baby. Yes, I finally had a child. It only took a nuclear event to jumpstart my ovaries. Her name is Alpha because she is the first. The first Earth baby to be born on Planet Alpha 49C. But certainly not the last. And she is beautiful beyond description, so I won't even try. All these years later, Dr. Song was right. I did have a beautiful baby.

I am here to tell you that there's always hope. Even when all seems hopeless. Especially then.

Ω Ω Ω

Acknowledgements

This novel began as a nightmare I had back in the 1980s. The bad dream morphed into a short story, which I showed to my friend Joe Piegari, who is a fine writer. Joe liked it a lot, but said he thought my short story was trying to be a book. After ruminating this, I tried my hand at first-time novel-writing. Finishing it took several years since I was working full-time as an administrative assistant back then.

When my book was done, I sent "My Post-Nuclear Diary, or, Noah's Spaceship" to publishers and, surprise-surprise, no one bit. But instead of destroying the manuscript as I probably should have done, I hung onto it, shoved it into a corner of my crumbling basement (into a series of crumbling basements, actually) and mostly forgot about it.

But something about the story haunted me. I kept thinking about "Noah's" post-apocalyptic narrative, kept coming back to it. And finally, in late 2021, as the Covid-19 pandemic waned, I pulled the withered manilla envelope that held the manuscript out of the cobwebs and took a fresh look. As abysmal as that first draft was, I thought something might still be there. A spark. A message. About resilience and hope and different kinds of love. I thought it might be important, especially post-pandemic and amid the melting polar ice caps.

So, I resurrected "Noah," and over the next two years, I worked with it, wrestled it, and cajoled it into submission.

Luckily, my publisher and friend Vinnie Corbo thought something was there too. I'd like to thank Vinnie for his never-ending faith in me and my words. I'm grateful to my friend Jackie for being my first—and such an enthusiastic—reader. Some forty years hence, I'd like to thank Joe for his premonition that "Noah" could be a novel. I'd also like to thank my husband Peter for his steadfast love, especially when I am at my most unlovable.

The "Dick Truehard" character was inspired by aspects of several porn princes I have been fortunate to know—Rick Savage, Richard Pacheco, Jose Duval, Eric Monte, Paul Thomas, and especially the late Jerry Butler, to whom this book is dedicated (under his real name). I applaud them for their raw courage and for their friendship.

My hope is that moving forward, we learn not to judge each other by what we choose to do for a living—or anything else—but instead, accept each other for the people we are underneath it all. Car mechanics, office workers and adult performers alike.

And also, that we stop destroying the planet…and each other.

About the Author

Catherine Gigante-Brown is a Brooklyn-born writer of fiction, nonfiction, poetry and plays. Her articles and essays have appeared in publications like *Time Out New York, Essence, Ravishly* and *Industry*. Her poetry and fiction are included in several anthologies. A handful of her films and theatrical works have been produced. Gigante-Brown's novels *The El, The Bells of Brooklyn* and *Brooklyn Roses* (aka "The El Trilogy"), *Different Drummer, Better than Sisters* and *Paul and Carol Go to Guatemala* are all published by Volossal. Gigante-Brown and her husband split their time between their hometown, Florida and upstate New York in Rosendale. Together, they have one son.